*Dear Elizabeth —
Let's go hunt
monsters some time!
All the best —
JD Blackrose*

# THE DEVIL'S BEEN BUSY

# THE DEVIL'S BEEN BUSY

Monster Hunter Mom Season One

J.D. BLACKROSE

Tweety & The Monkey Man Copyright © 2017 by J.D. Blackrose

Runaway Copyright © 2017 by J.D. Blackrose

Handle with Care Copyright © 2018 by J.D. Blackrose

End of the Line Copyright © 2018 by J.D. Blackrose

Cover Design by Melissa McArthur

All rights reserved.

No part of this book may be reproduced in any form or by any electronic or mechanical means, including information storage and retrieval systems, without written permission from the author, except for the use of brief quotations in a book review.

This book is a work of fiction. Any resemblance to any person, living or dead, is coincidental. Except that bit about that guy. That's totally a thing.

*The book is dedicated to my family.*

# TWEETY & THE MONKEY MAN

# CHAPTER ONE

I stepped back with my right foot, arm cocked and ready for the creep to show. I made sure to distribute my weight equally on both legs and look straight ahead, knowing where the vampire was most likely to appear. My night vision was good. It had to be. Monsters liked to come out at night.

My enemy was stealthy and at one with the dark, which caressed him, cherished him, and held him as if part of itself, a lover who could never leave. His thin frame disappeared into the night.

I caught a flit of movement to the left, and I realized he was moving fast, getting away. I couldn't let that happen. Not now. Not ever.

My sneakers were slick from the wet grass, and when I took a step, my right shoe squeaked. I kicked off the trainers, pulled off the socks, and took up the chase barefoot. My feet slipped and slid, but I strained for balance and quiet. Stalking a vampire was a matter of silence, concentration, and timing. You had to be perfect, or you were dead. There were three ways this could go: I kill him, he kills me, or the third option and the worst thing a vampire could do to a monster hunter, he turns me. I intended to go home tonight in one piece, with my mind and ability to sunbathe intact.

I never underestimate a foe. This vampire was clever and studied my techniques. He knew my favorite weapons and my most-used tactics. He even knew my kids' names and where I lived.

I don't wear perfume or use smelly soaps because monsters of all types have good noses, but I knew my prey could smell me. He had my scent like a bloodhound. I might have trouble following him, but he had no trouble finding me, a huge disadvantage when hunting a vampire. As his shadow slipped out from behind a tree, I calculated his speed and direction in a split second. I didn't hesitate; there was no time. I launched the projectile directly at the vampire's head. It landed on target, bursting open, covering him in water.

My assistant, Liam, emerged shaking his head. "Goddammit! Jess! Vampires don't like to get wet. We're like cats that way."

I couldn't help it; I grinned. "Just be glad it wasn't holy water, my friend. Any other challenges you want to try?"

Liam drew closer, soaking wet, with tiny bits of blue balloon in his hair. "No. I admit it. You're the best pitcher I've ever met. With that arm, you could have been in the majors."

I handed him a towel. "Women can't play professional baseball, Liam. We play softball, which men don't consider a real sport. It would have been me and a bunch of well-muscled women, all with mind-altering foot odor, on a bus earning a nickel ninety-eight and a steady diet of French fries. Besides, I met Nathaniel and well, you know . . ."

"I do." The vampire did a shimmy glamour thing, and five seconds later, he was wearing completely new jeans, sneakers, and a green and gray Ohio University sweatshirt. Go Bobcats.

"I wish I could do that. I'd do it a dozen times a day, every time someone spilled milk on me, or rubbed my leg with paint-covered hands..."

"Hey, remember that time David painted the wall with spaghetti sauce? That was awesome."

"I wonder who gave him the idea, Uncle Liam."

"Well, he's eight now, so no more of that. I've got plans for him though. Such a smart boy." Liam whistled an innocent tune and slid in the driver's seat of his BMW convertible. "Call me tomorrow?"

"Absolutely, but first I have to bring in a snack to Devi's kindergarten class. It's my week. The other moms bring in fruit and veggies. I'm considering Cheetos. What do you think?"

"I think kids like when their hands turn orange, and preservatives are like vitamins." He paused. "I'll let you know if I have any emails from the diocese. I'm a little concerned because it has been so quiet lately. It's like something big is coming and we're in the calm before the storm."

"You worry too much. Maybe everyone knows not to mess with Ohio. Things don't work out well for monsters in this state." I rubbed my hands together with glee. I loved my job.

"Oh, no doubt your reputation keeps some of the baddies away, but you know monsters. Most of them aren't what we would call forward thinkers. They bite, maim, suck, tear, and generally cause mayhem, and that's about it."

"They don't even call first," I said, hunting around the grass to retrieve my shoes.

"Ungrateful wretches." Liam winked. "Talk to you tomorrow. I'm all for the Cheetos."

I got into my mini-van and reached down to the cup holder for my water, which I carried everywhere. It's important to hydrate. I closed my eyes and brought the drink to my mouth.

"Ugh!" I studied the half-empty bottle of apple juice and realized it must be two days old since Daniel, my three-year-old, had gotten it with his McDonald's Happy Meal. It was sour, warm, and disgusting, but I shrugged and downed it in three gulps.

I was about to leave the school playground area, the place Liam and I liked to train, when there was a flicker in the corner of my eye, just a hint of something out of sorts, though I didn't know why. I almost turned away, but my gut told me to stay. I've learned to trust my instincts, and if there was a chance, any chance at all, that a monster was on a school playground, I couldn't leave.

I exited my car, grabbing a baseball bat from the back seat. I also slapped a batting helmet on my head. Better safe than sorry. I'm a switch hitter and equally comfortable with the bat in my left or right hand. Now, I carried it in my left.

I listened, concentrating on blocking everything out that was natural, normal, harmless. I stepped forward, and something snapped under my feet. I squatted so I could pick it up and hold it in my hands. Was it a feather? It had the right shape, but it was stiff and unusually long. I ran my hands up the sides and winced when I touched the apex, so sharp it nicked my thumb. I could feel the cut swell as my blood dripped on the grass, a dangerous circumstance as most monsters loved the taste of blood, or worse, could find a witch who could use it against me. Whatever this was, I had to find it.

It could have been a bird's feather. Maybe a large owl, or even one of those turkey vultures on the side of the highway picking at the latest road kill, but to be honest, I'd never felt a feather like this one, and I couldn't imagine a bird large enough to have such a feather. It most certainly could not fly.

A *scratch, scratch* caught my attention, coming from about twenty feet in front of me. I thought I could hear it breathing, a soft whistle in the stillness. Even the night critters crawled or slithered inside their homes, sensing that something was off. My mouth was dry again, but as my belly tightened, I thought of my children, and the other children who played here, and held strong. I jumped when a light flared in the distance, as bright and sudden as a struck match. The flame lifted high in the air, its smoke trailing in the breeze.

Not good. Glad I had put my tennis shoes back on, I moved toward the not goodness, pulling my light black sweater tighter so I'd be as invisible as possible. I rounded the swirly slide, my back to the ladder, and bent into the shadows, gaping at what I saw.

A six-foot tall bird stood before me, flapping his gold and azure wings, which were soaking wet. The body was covered in bronze and silver, scalloped, overlapping feathers, like armor out of ancient Rome. It was shaped like an emu, with a long neck, an ovular body, and long, skinny legs with three-toed feet, slightly webbed.

I considered my next move, my gut telling me to kill the thing and kill it fast, my head saying, hey, maybe you can talk to it.

"Helloooo, Big Bird," I said, raising my voice so that the creature could hear me, hoping I'd achieved a soothing tone, which wasn't normally in my wheelhouse, truth be told. "You're a long way from Sesame Street. Want me to tell how to get there? Sunny days and all . . ."

I trailed off because the thing, which looked like it sprang out of a dinosaur diorama at the Natural History Museum, backed up like a bull, shuffling its Tweety Bird feet into the grass and dirt. It attacked in one swift, bounding leap. Not quite flight, but its feet were not on the ground. More like an astronaut on the moon. Its beak was open wide revealing— what the hell?—shark teeth dripping gelatinous fluid. The creature shot toward me like its butt was on fire.

It flicked its tail up like a peacock, a beautiful display of colors including blues and greens, touched by an outline of yellow and white. I didn't have time to study it, however, as I was beating a path to higher ground.

"You're not anything like Big Bird!" I yelled over my shoulder, as I hoofed it in the opposite direction. "He's six years old and learning his

ABCs. He has friends and knows how to share. You should be more like him! Calm down. I mean you no harm! Parley! Parley!"

Negotiation was not in this creature's lexicon. I scrambled up the slide ladder and balanced on the bars of the swing set. A gymnast as a child, I'd maintained my strength and worked out every day to keep it, because it was necessary for occasions like this one. At five feet tall and a hundred and fifteen pounds, I wasn't the biggest monster hunter on the block, not nearly, but I managed to get the job done. While others liked to go full steam ahead and Hulk-smash things, that wasn't my way. I had to be clever, deceitful, and prepared to down-right cheat when required. I was okay with that.

My subconscious put two and two together. Gigantic bird, gorgeous plumage, and fire. Only one bird fit all three. I hadn't known about the rows of shark teeth and reminded myself to pass that information on to the other hunters. It was necessary to swap intel, and I assumed it went into a central repository somewhere.

"Hey. I figured out what you are! You're a phoenix. I thought phoenixes were nice birds. Or, is it phoenixi?"

In response, the newly reborn phoenix, still leaking a viscid amniotic fluid, screamed, its neck stretching to reach me. I was glad I'd gotten up high.

The phoenix screamed again, snapping its beak and jumping just enough to gouge my ankle. Those pointed teeth rent my stretch pants and clipped my ankle something good. The teeth were so sharp that I didn't feel them cut me and only knew a second later when the pain hit and I felt the slick blood pooling in my shoe. The bird squawked and hissed, licking its beak as it tasted the blood, its eyes rolling in anticipation of fresh meat.

"Fine. Fuck you."

I waved my bleeding ankle at the bird, who couldn't wait to get another bite. I lifted my free arm above my head and held onto a branch from the maple that overhung the swing set. This allowed me to swing my injured ankle at him again and again, riling him up. The phoenix squawked, louder this time, crazy with need for a filling main course. I let go of the tree branch, planted my feet as best I could on the metal crossbars, and showed him why I batted fourth in the line-up.

As the phoenix hopped up, I swung the bat down, bashing it on the head. The phoenix fell like a stone. I slid down the slide, leaving a red blood trail that would certainly be noticed in the morning, raised the bat, and slammed it on the phoenix's skull and beak, repeating as necessary. I gave it a swing to the middle of its body as well and was stunned when my bat rebounded from the attempt, a frisson of pain running up my left arm.

"Those body feathers don't just look like bronze—they *are* bronze. Glad I caught you before you matured. You look like something out of a steampunk novel. Yeesh." I stood over the remains, tapping my foot, thinking about what to do. "Look what you made me do, you overgrown ostrich. You made me use a bad word. That's ten push-ups. But first...."

The newly hatched and now dead phoenix, having lived what was possibly its shortest life yet, kindled in a burst of flame. All that was left was ashes. Good thing I have baggies in my car. Never know when you'll need them.

I walked to my car, stored my bat, and returned with three Ziploc bags and a gardening trowel. Working fast, I scooped up a third of the ashes and put them in one bag and then did the same with the other two, hoping that by keeping them apart, I'd slow down the regeneration process. I popped those babies in the car seat, strapped them in, and drove straight to 90 and the lake. I flicked on the radio and wasn't even surprised when the song was "Fly Like an Eagle." Someone up there has a funny sense of humor.

I stopped at three different outlets, spilling the content of each bag into Lake Erie approximately one mile from each other. I wasn't sure if a phoenix could be killed, but swirling the ashes in the cold water of a Great Lake seemed like a terrific way to slow it down.

Must tell Liam about that one; no one warned us about a phoenix. I wonder if anyone knew. Fingering my Star of David, the one my grandmother had given me, I considered the meaning of phoenix's appearance as I drove to my comfortable, suburban home on the East Side.

# CHAPTER TWO

Liam and I met when we were students at Cleveland State University, me on scholarship, him working his way. I didn't know him well. To me, he was the Irish-looking guy who took my order at Starbucks.

I was studying late at night, at the Starbucks, when he was working a late shift. I ignored him, and he ignored me until it was closing time and he needed me to skedaddle.

"Hey, miss. You've got to go. Closing up," he said.

I was smack in the middle of the *Iliad*, which I loved, reading it in English with commentaries and notes about the subtleties of the original Greek on the opposite page. Greek, Roman, and Norse mythology intrigued me, but being a Classics major was frowned upon in my family, where earning money was the only goal. In fact, I'd just had an argument with my father that morning.

"Jess, have you figured out a major?" my father had said. He still read the *Plain Dealer* in print and spread it on the table next to his breakfast, a fried egg and toast, *always* a fried egg and toast, and looked at me over his reading glasses.

I played with my cereal spoon and mumbled. "Classics."

"What? Speak up."

"Classics, Dad. I'm fascinated by Classic, and I'm thinking of becoming a professor. At CSU, it is a multi-disciplinary major along with Medieval

Studies. The major prepares you for a lot of things, you know, giving you such a breadth of knowledge…"

I trailed off because my father had set down his fork and taken off his glasses.

"Can you make money with this major? Support yourself? Support a family?"

"I would get a Ph.D. and teach, do research."

"And live a pauper's life! What about law? You have a propensity for argument. You seem suited for it."

The thought of going to law school made my stomach shoot acid up my throat. I choked and coughed at the vile taste and replied, "I'd rather die than go to law school."

My dad slammed his hand on the table so that my cereal bowl jumped.

"Don't get smart with me, young lady." He took a deep breath and offered the next statement, in the belief that he was being magnanimous.

"You can major in law and minor in Classics. How about that?"

My hands shook in anger, but he'd always been the king in our house, and his word was gospel, so I held myself in check. "Dad, I promise I will find a way to support myself."

He leaned back in his chair so only the back legs stayed on the ground, arms up, hands behind his head. "You'd better because your scholarship runs out at the end of next year, and I'm not giving you a penny after you graduate. Your great-grandparents came here with nothing and worked their way to success. You need to do the same."

So, there I was sitting in Starbucks late to avoid going home to face my father, and this ginger-haired, freckled-face, lanky kid interrupts me and has the nerve, *the nerve*, to tap me on the shoulder. A student of martial arts from three years-old, I grabbed his left hand with my left, pushed his elbow up and outward with my right, and pushed him on the floor in a hot second. Without thinking, I placed my right foot on his back and pressed down hard.

Ginger swiveled his neck to look at me from the floor. "What the hell are you doing? It's time to close, that's all I'm saying. I've got homework too, you know, but I don't get to sit here and do it because some of us *work* to pay for college. Don't hurt me!"

I released him and stepped back, surprised at myself. "I'm sorry," I said, but it sounded lame to even my ears.

"I apologize," I said again, my mood still foul, but now I was embarrassed too. "Let me help you up."

"I don't need help," he grunted, pulling away from me, his ears red. "Just get out of here."

"I'm really sorry."

"Just leave." He was rubbing his elbow.

I gathered my books and shuffled out, hesitating for a moment, wanting to apologize again for my overreaction, but he turned his back. I walked to my car, a beat-up thing that my brother also used, and pondered how to make things right. The guilt ate at me all the next day.

I went back the next night but didn't see him, so I went every night until I caught him on his late shift.

"Hey," I said when I walked up to the counter. There was a line behind me, so I couldn't start a discussion there.

"What can I get you?" His face was stony, and he drummed his fingers on the counter.

"Small mocha, please?"

"Name?"

"Jess."

"Wait at the end of the counter."

I took a seat after I snagged my drink and sat studying, waiting for closing time. Time passed in loud, ticking seconds as I anticipated how my apology would be received.

"Why are you still here?" His name tag said Liam, and he stood five feet back, keeping his distance.

"I wanted to apologize again. I'd had a bad day, and I was in nasty mood, so when you tapped me on the shoulder, I overreacted."

"No need to apologize," he said, to my surprise. "I thought about it later. I shouldn't have tapped you. Touching a woman without being asked is stupid. I'm lucky you did a karate move and didn't pepper spray me."

"I don't carry pepper spray. It can blow back in your eyes and blind you instead your attacker."

"How do you know that? And where did you learn those moves?" He propped himself up on his mop and quirked his head. He was genuinely curious.

"Martial arts and gymnastics, both since I was three. My parents thought it would be best to keep me busy since, left to my own devices, I climbed trees too high or rode my bike down a big hill without brakes. I did a back flip off the high dive board the first time I went up there."

"Troublemaker, I see. Adrenaline junkie. Interesting. So, you know how to take care of yourself?" He scraped the toe of his sneaker on the ground and studied it, avoiding my eyes.

"Yeah, I guess. I don't go searching for trouble, but I'm not afraid, either."

He cleared his throat but didn't anything. He cleared it again.

"Do you want to ask something?" I said, watching him struggle.

"Maybe you could walk me to the bus stop? There are some guys hassling me when I leave, and I think if I am with another person, they might lay off. It's embarrassing asking a girl to protect me from bullies, but..."

"Stop right there before you dig yourself into a hole you can't get out of," I said, although I was grinning ear-to-ear. "No one should walk alone."

"Well, how are we going to handle this then? If you wait with me at the bus stop, who will walk you to your car?"

"No worries at all. We'll get my car together, and then I'll drive you to the bus stop."

He gave it some consideration. "Genius."

## CHAPTER THREE

Post bird slaughter, I dragged myself up the stairs from my basement, where I had entered from the garage, to the main floor. I was almost at the top when an ear-splitting voice announced, "My mama!" I bent to pick up the squishy thing under my foot, my daughter's Love Doll. The things were a little too Chucky for me, but I hunt monsters for a living, so maybe I'm not the right person to judge. All I know is that it makes me cringe, but she likes it. I think it's a $150 nightmare engineered by marketing hit men, and I would have gladly thrown the thing into the garbage disposal, but Devi, my beloved Devorah, cherished the doll.

On the main floor now, I turned to the left to check on the kids in their bedrooms. Devi slept fitfully, if she slept at all, a trait she'd inherited from me. Blankets stood no chance next to her flailing legs, so as usual, her linens were on the floor, and the five-year old's arms were askew. She breathed in and out, thankfully in a deep sleep. I smiled at her innocent beauty and placed the doll on the bed next to Devi's pillow.

Next, I checked on my oldest son, David, who was curled into a little ball, burbling spit between his lips. I gave him a gentle kiss, saying a prayer of thanks for having him and my other kids in my life, and moved one room over to check on the baby.

My three-year old, Daniel, still used a crib even though he had a big-boy bed in his room. The child simply couldn't stay on a mattress and fell on the floor every time he tried to sleep without a guardrail. Sure enough, he lay squished up against the railings, held back by thin pieces of Italian crib plywood, which was better than other plywood because it came with directions in Italian. Or, so my mother-in-law had said. It made no difference to me. I couldn't care less where the crib came from, but I did enjoy the English translation of the Italian directions. The bed, she is made!

I tiptoed into the master bedroom, careful not to wake Nathanial, and washed up at the sink, throwing my brain-coated clothes into the hamper. I know, it's gross. Shouldn't I have thrown them in the washing machine right away? Yes. I should. But my clothes were regularly disgusting, so Nathaniel and I used separate hampers. No need to get bodily fluids on his work clothes. I flicked a sharp piece of beak out of my hair, slid into bed, wrapped my arms around my husband, and sniffed him in, loving his smell. "How was training?" Nathaniel murmured.

"Good. I hit Liam with a water balloon."

"That must have been hilarious. Sorry I missed it. Why do you smell like chicken?"

"Shh…go to sleep."

"Love you."

"Love you, too." I was asleep in two minutes.

I was awake in two hours. My phone buzzed at dawn with a text from Liam. *Warning: A phoenix may be in the area. Keep an eye out. They tend to hang out near schools. Resting now.*

*Thanks for nothing, Liam.* I hauled myself out of bed and headed to the kitchen. I made a cup of coffee in the Keurig feeling guilty about hurting the environment, but I liked dark roast and Nathanial liked a morning blend. It didn't pay to make a whole pot of one kind.

Time to pack lunches. David's class was a no peanut class, so I gave him a microwaved hot dog, which he didn't mind eating cold. Devi would never eat a hot dog cold, so she got the peanut butter.

The shower was running, and I knew that Nathaniel was up, the stomping telling me he'd also woken the two oldest kids. The crying told me the stomping also woke the baby, and I cursed under my breath because the baby could use more sleep.

I padded upstairs and retrieved the crying child, holding him to my chest, and he calmed down right away. He clapped his hands together and said, "down," pointing to the floor. "After a diaper change, kiddo," I said, and set about the task. Daniel squirmed, anxious to get to breakfast.

All gathered in the kitchen where normal morning mayhem ensued—

oatmeal flying, bananas squishing, and several blobs of jelly landing on the floor. "Mom, I started an experiment in my room," yelled David as he ran to the bus. "Don't worry about it."

"What?" Nathaniel yelled after him, then turned to me, mouth agape. Nathaniel held Devi's hand, ready to take her to kindergarten. "What do you think that means?" he whispered, dabbing at a spot of jelly on his tie. I shook my head.

I was too afraid to guess. "I'm sure it isn't alive," I said, trying to be helpful.

Nathaniel shook his head and said, "You never know. Hopefully nothing crawls out of his room, nothing explodes, and whatever it is, the smell isn't too bad. Taking Devi to school now. Don't forget the snack this afternoon."

"Cheetos!" yelled Devi, bouncing up and down, her gnarled hair bouncing with her.

"At least let me brush your hair," I said.

Devi stuck out her lip and stomped a foot. "No! I like my hair messy. It hurts when you brush it, and it gets messy again anyway, so why do it?"

Nathaniel smiled. "She has a point."

"It's my hair," said the burgeoning feminist. "I control my body."

I realized there was no good argument to that statement, so I waved them off and blew them kisses.

"Don't forget the snack!" Nathaniel said one more time.

I waved again and returned to the kitchen to find Daniel on the floor, happily shoving the last of a banana into his mouth.

"Did you eat the whole banana?"

Daniel smiled, banana seeping between his teeth, and stuck his tongue out so I could see the rest of the banana in pre-chewed form.

"That is a lot of banana for a tiny tummy." I grabbed a wet paper towel and wiped his hands. Daniel was not a great conversationalist; in fact, he was somewhat *delayed* in the speech department, a word I despised, but he understood everything and was the sweetest child on the face of the earth. I gave him a kiss on the head, then another one. God, I loved this kid.

"Okay, hot stuff, let's get changed and head to the gym."

A few minutes later, I stuffed Daniel in his car seat and headed to the local Jewish Community Center for a workout with my trainer, the Thing of Evil. The mini-van, or as I called it, the Urban Assault Vehicle, rattled the whole three miles, but I paid it no mind. It was a 2003 Toyota Sienna in silver, one of the most popular vehicles of its year, and no matter what I did to it, it wouldn't die. Sometimes I secretly prayed for it to break down so I could get another vehicle, but the damn thing was an obstinate old friend.

The butterflies set in as we parked. I sat in the car a moment, twisting my wedding ring and bouncing my knee before I told myself I was being ridiculous and I could do this. The scary, bad monster hunter was afraid of babysitters. In my case, one specific babysitter, who was a prude and had a stick up her ass.

Regina. My heart rate sped up to the red zone at the thought of her. Regina was the babysitter who judged you, your actions, and your every word. She'd cross her arms, sniff, look down her nose, and say things like, "I never allowed my children to do that," or "If that is how *you* want it," while curling her lip. You came out short no matter what you did, and for some reason, it affected me.

My chest loosened when Faith appeared at the door, not Regina. Faith was a lovely young woman, kind and great with kids. She was Daniel's favorite.

"Daniel! There you are, baby. I was wondering if you would come in today." Faith held out her arms, and he ran into them, smacking into her knees in his enthusiasm. She must have braced because she didn't budge an inch. I breathed a sigh of relief at having dodged the Regina bullet. Dani made happy cooing noises and hugged Faith's knees as I handed her a new set of backup clothes.

Faith bent and sniffed. "Did you have a banana, big guy?"

Deciding silence was the better course of valor, I ignored that subject. "I'll be an hour, Faith. Ten dollars, right? Plus tip?"

Faith let Daniel run to the blocks. "It's always ten dollars, Jess. You know that, and you don't have to give me a tip."

"You deserve it. See you soon."

My trainer, Ovid Sitler, the Thing of Evil, was tapping his foot and staring at his watch by the time I walked in. He raised an eyebrow at me. I wished I could do that.

"Two minutes late, Jess. That's ten extra pushups."

"Make it twenty. I used a bad word yesterday."

"Monster hunter mom can't use a swear word?"

"I don't want the kids to swear, so I shouldn't either. I need to be a good role model."

"You be nuts, girl." Ovid pointed to a mat indicating I should start pushups immediately.

"No stretching?"

"Get going, cupcake."

I banged out a quick five. "I'm nuts? You are the one who chose to change his name to that of an ancient Roman poet."

"I've explained this. My parents named me Adolf. I had to change it."

"Sure. To Mike or Larry or Sam, not to Ovid."

"Twenty more pushups for you."

Pushups, crunches, and a myriad of other core exercises later, Ovid ushered me into a basketball court and locked the door. My stomach plunged, knowing pain was on the way. I said a quick prayer and pushed myself into the right headspace.

"Now, we train." Ovid pointed to the far end of the gym, and it was then that I noticed the rope course.

"What are we doing?"

"Upper body strength. Do the rope course from one end to the other and then back."

"That doesn't seem so hard." I stalked to the first rope, ready to take this course on. I grabbed the rope with my right arm and pulled, placing my left above the right. I wrapped my legs around the rope…

"No legs! You have a broken leg," yelled Ovid.

"Now you're pissing me off," I grumbled, but I let my legs dangle and pulled myself with only arm and core strength. By the time I reached the top, twenty-feet up, my arms were fading, and I faced nine more obstacles. Like I said, Thing of Evil. Master of Torture.

"This is hard!" I yelled, prepared to complain about his training protocol. Instead, I hedged to the left as a rubber bullet flew at my head.

"You've got a broken leg and the monster is shooting at you. Go! Go, for God's sake."

Newly motivated but grumpy, I rappelled down the rope, swinging it left and right to avoid the rain of bullets Ovid shot at my body. I hit the floor and ran to the next rope, a ladder course.

"Go back! What about having a broken leg don't you understand? You can't run."

"You're going to have a broken leg when I'm done!"

"No whining. Just do it."

I backtracked to the first rope and hopped to the second obstacle, grunting as a bullet whizzed by my back, missing me by a millimeter.

"Move! Move! Move!"

Using only one leg, I propelled my body to the top so I could grab the long rope and Tarzan across. As the bullets zipped by my head, I forced myself to move faster. Dropping to the ground at the end of the ladder, I rolled to the next obstacle and scrambled up the spider net, holding one leg stiff, and at the sound of a pop, shifted right to avoid getting shot.

"Stay light on your feet and turn sideways. You're too big of a target."

"You mean stay light on my foot," I said, shooting him a withering glance.

"Don't waste time making faces. Hop to, hop to!"

I panted to the next target in a crawl, dreaming of all the nasty things I could do to Ovid later. Mindful of my "broken leg," I lay on my back and got my hands on the rope in a prone position.

*Ping*! A rubber bullet bounced of the metal girders on the ceiling.

"Whatcha gonna do, pussycat?" yelled Ovid.

"Don't call me that!"

Holding my "bad" leg still, which was a terror on the hamstrings and hip, I dragged myself up the first-quarter of the rope, grasped the end with both hands, and pushed off with my one good leg. I dropped into the foam pit at the other end, quickly swimming to another position so Ovid couldn't get me. Feeling superior, I rolled toward the edge and was ticked when a bullet flipped a blue foam square only a few inches from my body.

*Fuck this.*

The truth was that my arms couldn't hold me anymore. I tried to climb out of the pit using only upper body strength, and I realized that in a real-life situation, I'd be dead. A basketball cart stood near the rope course, and that's when I saw my chance. I used my last bit of arm strength to crawl out of the foam pit, lay on my stomach, and roll to the cart. Time to change the game.

"What are you doing?" yelled Ovid. "Get to the next obstacle."

I didn't respond, and Ovid shot off two bullets, but the angle was all wrong, and the bullets hit the floor several feet to my right. I snickered and rolled behind the cart, keeping to the rules somewhat by only using one leg. I hopped up and propelled the cart directly toward Ovid like a gimpy racecar at Daytona. I managed the curve around the final rope obstacle and pounded toward my trainer.

"What the hell? You're cheating," Ovid grunted as he zig-zagged to his left.

"There is no cheating. Just winning," I replied, as I smashed into him with the cart, basketballs bouncing all over the place. "So, take that, you demon." I pushed the cart on its side so that it landed on Ovid's prone form, picked up a basketball, and slammed into the ground next to his head.

Ovid flinched, threw up his hands, and said, "Uncle."

"Damn straight, uncle." I put my hands on my knees to catch my breath.

"I'm not really a demon, you know."

"I know, silly. You are a Thing of Evil. Thanks though. It was a challenge. My upper body strength needs work. If that situation were real, I don't think I'd make it." I pulled Ovid to his feet and gave him a quick, smelly hug. He gave me one right back and said, "That's why we train."

"Shit! I'm late for daycare pick-up."

"Ten more pushups," Ovid yelled as I ran out the gym doors.

I rushed through the showering, deodorizing part of my routine and walked to the daycare with a nonchalant sway, hoping no one would notice my tardiness. As soon as I noticed Regina in the doorway, I knew I was toast.

"Hi, Regina. Here to pick up my little guy. How is he?" I did a little sing-song thing in one last stab at not getting the stink-eye.

"He's not well at all." Regina stood ramrod straight, her sensible shoes at perfect parade rest.

"Why? What's wrong?" I peeked around Regina's head looking for Daniel.

"Exactly how much banana did you allow him to eat this morning?"

I hate it, but my face flushes when I'm embarrassed. "It's not how much I let him eat, it's how much he stuffed in before I saw what he was doing…"

"Why weren't you watching?"

"I was, but David said something about an experiment, and Devi wouldn't let me brush her hair because she's in control of her body, and before I knew it, Daniel had shoved a whole banana in his mouth."

Regina stared at me with a disapproving air until I was rocking back and forth on my feet with discomfort. "Let me just get him."

"You're past your hour."

I sighed. "I know. And I'll bring in a new change of clothes for next time."

Regina sniffed and stood aside for me to gather my child, who was zooming a truck across a play mat, howling with laughter, yelling, "Die, vampire, die!"

"What did he say?" asked Regina with alarm, one hand on her hip, the other reaching for a phone as if to call Social Services.

"Oh, ha…ha. He's saying, 'Mine, mine.'"

"That's not what it sounds like."

"Really, that's what it is. Gotta do better at teaching him how to share. Three-year-olds, you know." I dumped the original ten dollars on the registration table plus an extra fifteen for being late, grabbed Daniel and his dirty clothes, and backed out the door.

I gave Daniel a look. "Now you decide to talk?"

Daniel snuggled to my shoulder and let out a gigantic banana burp. He fell asleep in the car seat on the way to the synagogue.

## CHAPTER FOUR

"Rabbi Stein, how are you?" I gave the wizened old man a hug, once again wincing at how thin he was. "How's your back?"

"It is what it is."

"No, seriously, how is it?"

"It hurts, Jess, but they give me drugs, and I don't take them because they make my head fuzzy. What do the doctors know anyway?"

"The doctors know you have severe spinal stenosis, Rabbi, and a bulging disc."

"Shush." Rabbi Stein looked at me over his glasses. "Let's chat." He gave the snoozing Daniel a pat on the head and sat behind his desk, gesturing to a chair. "Tell me what is going on in your monster hunting world."

"I killed a phoenix last night."

The rabbi startled. "You *killed* one? I mean, it's a miracle you got to see one. Are you sure?"

"Big, colorful chicken? Bronze armor scales? Sharp, pointy teeth?"

"Sounds correct."

"Then, yes. I thought they were supposed to be nice creatures. Not this guy, or was it a girl? I'm not sure. I didn't get to look up its skirt."

"Let me see." The rabbi did what came most naturally to learned scholars and searched for a book. "Can you get this one, Jessie dear? I can't reach it."

I jumped up and grabbed the sliding library ladder, rolling it to where he was.

"This one?"

"The leather one."

"They're almost all leather, Rabbi."

"The small one. No, an inch to the right. Yes, that one."

"How do you remember what's here? There's no system." I climbed down from the ladder and handed the book to the rabbi.

"Ach. It's my system. I know. Sit."

The rabbi opened the book right to left, so I knew the book was in Hebrew. Or maybe Aramaic. The rabbi read a lot of languages. His body was frail, but his mind was sharp. He opened to a table of contents, ran his index finger down the page, and then flipped to a chapter. He read several paragraphs, rocking a little in his chair, his right hand pulling at his earlobe.

"Rabbi?"

He held up one finger. "Patience, please."

I bobbed my knees up and down and double checked my diaper bag to make sure I had snacks, which was completely unnecessary because I always packed snacks. They were a critical component of my arsenal. Daniel was going to be hungry when he woke up, especially since he'd lost most of his breakfast, and I wanted to head off a crying fit at the pass.

The rabbi kept reading. I took a deep inhale and let it out with a whoosh.

The rabbi ignored me, except for a single judgmental sniff.

I counted to ten, then twenty. Then one hundred.

"Rabbi?"

The rabbi held up his finger again. "We do not rush such things."

"We do if…"

The rabbi waved a hand, and I shut up. "Here it is. Shem, son of Noah, reported that the phoenix waited patiently on the Ark and didn't bother Noah or his family about being fed, because the pair saw that the family struggled taking care of the other animals all day and night. For his patience, Noah blessed him to never die."

"I didn't know that story, but I did have the general impression that they were good creatures, yet this one was insane."

"Tell me."

I related the story to Rabbi Stein, keeping an eye on Daniel, who was still asleep in the stroller next to me.

The rabbi closed his eyes and listened. It was one of the things I loved about him. He listened with his whole body. If you were there in front of him, you had his complete attention, and he wanted nothing more than to know you and understand you.

When I finished, he opened his eyes, a distant look on his face.

"Rabbi?"

"Let me get another book."

Rabbi Stein stood, and I pretended not to notice his wince of pain. I closed my eyes and listened to him talk to himself.

"Where is it? Here? No."

He shifted to another section. "Maybe with the Rashi? Where is it? Commentaries? Mishnah? Ah! Here it is."

He tottered back to his desk and sat with a sigh, opening the book. This one was folio-sized, and he placed it on his desk.

"There's another story. The commentary says that after Eve ate from the apple, she gave all the other animals fruit from the Tree. The phoenix was the only animal to not eat the forbidden fruit and was blessed to never die."

"So, what does it mean?"

"It means the phoenix is the pinnacle of the animal world and every other animal descends below it, more or less self-aware, more or less sophisticated in behavior. For example, chimpanzees use tools, but the praying mantis gets his head lopped off after procreation."

"Taxonomy."

"Yes, but bigger than that. What we might call the natural order of things."

"So, what does it mean when a phoenix goes rogue?"

The rabbi rubbed his beard and gazed out the window. "I think it means the natural order has been disturbed."

"That can't be good."

"No, my dear. I don't think it is. My advice is to scrub through the news and find anything that refers to animals gone wild."

"Is that like 'Girls Gone Wild'?" I said with a wink.

The rabbi gave me a baleful look. "Seriously? To me? Your rabbi?"

It made me sad, but I noticed that although he joked, he touched the framed photo of his late wife. I pretended not to see by readying myself to go, making sure the diaper bag was on the shelf beneath the stroller seat. I walked around the desk and gave the old man a kiss on his bald head.

"You were once a young man. Come on, you've never seen a naked girl before?"

Rabbi Stein's eyes twinkled. "I have, my dear, but I prefer my women in my bed, not on my television."

"Rabbi!"

Now, he winked. "I'm seventy. Not dead."

I stopped before leaving to ask one more question. "Rabbi, do you mind that I work for the Catholic Church?"

The rabbi shook his head. "We're all on one team. We bat for the same God, whatever we choose to call Him."

"Or Her."

"And Her, I think is a better way to say it."

"Do you mind that my best friend is a vampire?"

Rabbi Stein was quiet. "He doesn't kill?"

"No, but he must drink to live. He's learned to sip so he always leaves them alive, and he consumes bagged blood whenever possible."

"Honestly, Jess, I don't understand why vampires exist, but I suppose humanity needs an apex predator, too. I don't know. I'm still working on accepting that part of your life."

"I understand." I did. Even I fretted about it sometimes, but then I remembered that it wasn't Liam's choice.

## CHAPTER FIVE

That night, it really wasn't his choice. We became friends after our initial encounter, and I agreed with Liam's idea, which we put into effect the next day.

Liam closed the coffee shop, we walked to my car, and I drove to the bus stop to let him off. He lived in Euclid and could take a bus home, but he didn't live in the greatest neighborhood, and being a skinny white guy didn't always play well in Cleveland's tougher neighborhoods.

He was right, too. I could feel someone watching us. My car was parked in the garage just across the street, and for safety, I carried a whistle and a pocket knife, which I'd made a point of learning how to use by feel alone. I'd been hassled a few times, but nothing serious. The guy in my biology class who did everything possible to look down my shirt was more troublesome. Looking up my skirt wasn't possible because I didn't wear them. I was a jeans girl.

But no one bothered us that night, and from then on, I drove him to the bus stop on nights he closed. Each time, although no one showed up, I sensed that someone was always watching. I carried a large backpack and decided the whistle and pocketknife weren't enough, so I upgraded.

We'd been doing this for three weeks when two men approached us, one African-American with a goatee and some serious muscles, and the other a middle-sized white dude wearing a bandana and a prominent belly, who copied everything his friend did.

"Liam, I see you brought protection with you," Goatee said, laughing. Bandana laughed as well.

"Go away, guys. There's nothing for you here," I said, standing my ground. "We're just waiting for the bus, no need to be assholes."

Liam mumbled something beside me, but I couldn't make out what it was. I placed my bag on a bench and opened the back pocket, keeping my right hand on the top strap.

Goatee nudged Bandana, and Bandana took that to mean he should say something rude. "You're a tiny thing, aren'tcha? Maybe you'd like to see my big thing right here?" He humped the air as if I needed a visual.

"I'm sure you'd show me a great time, but with great regret, I have to decline." Once again, Liam mumbled something, but I was staring at Bandana and paid no attention.

Goatee folded his arms and studied at me. "You disrespecting my guy?"

"No, not at all."

"Sounds like you are."

"I'm not. I'm sure his dick is huge."

Liam stepped forward and stood in front of me, which took a lot of guts, and said, "Look, we don't want any trouble. Leave us alone, okay? Big tough guys like you don't need to bother with the likes of us. We're not a challenge."

"Just lookin' for a little money, man. We're stuck out here in the freezing cold, no place to go. Doncha want to help a brother out? Doncha want to help yourselves out by giving us what we want?"

Liam snickered. "It's sixty degrees, and you don't need money. You get off harassing people is all. You're nothing more than a playground bully."

"I don't bully, Ginger. I take." Goatee jumped forward, swiping his right hand at his left wrist, drawing a knife that looked major cool, and I wanted to get a closer look, but I couldn't focus on that because it was at Liam's throat. First things first.

This time, Liam spoke a little louder. "Jess, he has a knife."

"So do I," I replied, pulling out my Fiskars X7 Nyglass/Fiberglass composite backpacker's hatchet. Lightweight and unbreakable, I'd fallen in the love the second I saw it.

"Shit, girl! Who goes around carrying an axe? You crazy. Mental." Bandana was green around the gills because I swiped my pretty weapon in a clean arc down around the groin area. It made a fine swishing noise.

"It's a hatchet, not an axe, and this one has a great power-to-weight ratio, so if I chop with it, things are coming off. I like that knife you've got there. What is it?"

Goatee stepped back, shaking his head as if to clear water in his ear. "Never mind, you guys aren't worth our time." They turned to go.

Once again, the filter from my brain to my mouth shorted out, and I spoke at the worst possible moment.

"Hey, you didn't answer my knife question."

Goatee flipped around, charged at me, and put his knife to my throat. Finally, I could get a good look at it. "Is it one of the demon skull throwing knives? I saw them when I bought the hatchet. I might have to get me some."

He bore his weight onto me, and it dawned on me that I should act before he hurt me. My hatchet was still in my hand, but I'd lost rotating room, so I did the only thing I could. I jerked my wrist back and snapped it at whatever body part I could. The hatchet landed squarely in Goatee's ass, and since it was so sharp, it went through his pants and into his derriere like *buttah*.

Goatee howled, and Bandana jumped in, pulling his friend away from me. Goatee was holding his butt as blood gushed down his pants, screaming at me.

"You bitch! Get her, Curt!"

Curt came in for the kill, but I was hyped now. I drew back the hatchet over my right shoulder, jumped up on the bench, and grabbed Curt's throat with my left hand. I don't care how big you are, if someone has enough leverage to cut off your air, you're going to notice. I brought the hatchet to his throat. "The Euclid corridor takes you very close to the Cleveland Clinic's emergency room," I said. "Take your friend and get him help. You can tell them I was six feet tall and looked like I played the front line for the Browns, if that makes you feel better. Maybe skip the Browns and say the Steelers; otherwise they'll wonder why you're such a wimp."

After a few tense, uncertain moments, Curt jerked his head in a nod. I released his throat, and he backed up to put his arm under Goatee. They limped off with Goatee screaming, "This isn't over."

He was right.

## CHAPTER SIX

I was still thinking through the obstacle course Ovid put me through, going over every detail in mind, trying to figure out how I could have handled it better when Daniel and I got home. It was running on replay in my mind, and I couldn't think of a single thing.

I scooped Daniel up from the kitchen floor and wiped his hands with a diaper wipe. The crunch of Cheerios grinding into the wood floor was loud under my boots, but I ignored it. If I cleaned up all the smashed Cheerios, the house might fall. I was pretty sure half-chewed Cheerios were the glue keeping the walls together.

"Want to watch Elmo?" I asked my smiling son, after changing his diaper, which led to changing his entire outfit, his third for the morning. Daniel cooed happily and shimmied his backside into a bean bag chair while the red monster counted to ten.

"What news involving animals is out there?" I asked him, smart enough to know he wouldn't answer, but I was full-on into the stay-at-home mom habit of talking to small children and inanimate objects. Don't judge until you've stayed home a month with only a baby for companionship, and in my case, the occasional the vampire, troll, or ogre. Sadly, the monsters were confused when you tried to talk to them about current events or the latest must-see TV. Better just to kill them.

I studied Cleveland.com for local animal news. "Cute cat videos from around Cleveland. No, that's normal. Dog ordinance calls for all dogs, regardless of size, to be leashed. Nope. Coyotes found in Lakeland. That's nothing new."

Instead of animal news, I typed in odd news. "Visitors swear they saw a long-necked monster with gills in Lake Erie."

The monsters in the lake were a peaceful family of plesiosauria who needed to come up for air once every twenty-four hours. Damn. I'm going to have to talk with them again. We'd had *discussions* about this.

"A Boy Scout troop camping in the South Chagrin Reservation discovered footprints they say looked like they belonged to an African lion. The troop leader said he'd been camping in that spot for years and had never seen tracks like these. Wildlife enforcement is investigating whether cougars have moved in the area, although they say that is unlikely."

I added a mental note to talk with the sphinx.

"The historic Miller house, after a year of legal debate, is set to be demolished this week to make way for the new Angel Crossing shopping center. The contractors inspected the site this week, marking off the rest of the power and sewer lines. Miller descendants warned that the ghosts that haunt the house will take residence in the new buildings."

I didn't know anything about ghosts on that property, but I made another mental note to check into it later.

A large man in the southeastern United States emerged from a swamp this week, banged up and covered in sludge. When asked what happened, he muttered, "A chupalupa. Bertha fixed it." Despite concern from a doctor on the scene, a local priest vouched for him and took him home, saying he just needed rest.

I snorted.

I kept reading, and although there was a lot of odd news, nothing pinged my hindbrain. I scrolled to "Openings and Closings."

"Playhouse Theatre received a generous grant to open a small 'black box' theatre for experimental playwrights who might otherwise not get to see their work produced. Per the endowment rules, each play will use local actors and run for one month."

That sounded awesome.

"The Cleveland Metroparks Zoo closed the Primate Exhibit, including Monkey Island, for extensive cleaning. Though the cleaning was unscheduled, Zoo Communications Director, Elisabeth Borhring, said that this is simply routine and will be concluded in a few days. The zoo issued free re-entry passes to those who paid full price and encouraged zoo visitors to explore the other parts of the zoo, including the Rainforest, which houses marmosets and tamarin monkeys."

I picked up the phone. "Angie, want to take the little kids to the zoo?"

We met Angie at the zoo entrance. I don't have many female friends, so I treasured Angie and her kids, all four of them. She hauled the twin girls along in a trendy double stroller, an expensive side-by-side contraption so that Rose and April wouldn't fight over who was in front. We were dressed for the weather, which was sunny but on the cool side with a pleasant breeze. I wore black stretch pants, a gray long-tailed T-shirt, and a light zippered sweatshirt with a hood. My friend eyed me.

"You're wearing stretch pants with boots?"

"They're ankle boots. Very fashionable."

She nodded, her mouth serious, but her eyes twinkled. "If you say so."

I considered her stretch pants and high-top Chucks and raised an eyebrow.

"Chucks are tried and true!"

"If you say so." Shooting me a look, she pulled ahead, pushing her stroller a little faster. Angie's deadbeat husband killed himself in a drinking and driving accident in which he was the drinker, the drunk, and the driver. Luckily, the other party was a guardrail on Chagrin River Road, a treacherous path of blind switchbacks popular with bicyclists, so no innocents were killed. I didn't say no innocents were hurt, since Angie was left with four small kids and what cash she could rally up by babysitting other people's children. She received a monthly payment from a trust originally set up for her husband by his late parents, which she hadn't known about while they'd been married. That's what allowed her to get by.

Angie didn't need to know where that money really came from. I'd cleared a chic new condo of some ornery minor demons who'd been invited in by one of the residents, a greedy investment broker who worked downtown. We made a deal that involved him not going to jail in exchange for spending some of his ill-gotten wealth to pay for the damage the demons had caused and the establishment of Angie's trust.

I caught up with her and bumped her with my hip. She smiled and bumped me back. We were fine. The kids squirmed in their seats, so we walked even faster.

"This is so nice to do with the little ones," she said. "The twins are in trouble with their fourth-grade teachers again. Did I tell you how they switched clothes last week and pretended to be each other?"

"Identical twin boys are going to do that, don't you think? It seems natural. I'd do it if I were an identical eight-year-old twin," I said.

Angie waved off my comment. "They're going to drive me bonkers. James came in the house crying the other day because his brother was teasing him. It took several hours and a Netflix movie to calm him down."

"What was that about?"

"James said he saw a jackalope, but Jack said there was no such thing, and the two got into a fight about it. James pushed his brother into a puddle, which made Jack push James, and by the time they both got inside, they were soaked, bruised, and James was crying, saying he didn't lie."

"What did Jack say?"

"Jack wouldn't back down either and said James was lying."

I asked the next part with care. "Did James say what the jackalope looked like?"

Angie made a wry smile. "A rabbit about the size of a medium-sized dog, but with antlers. Of course, Jack is right, there is no such thing, but I do love James's imagination."

I was quiet, wondering what was happening in the southern and southwestern territories. Jackalopes didn't usually come this far north. If James had really seen the damn thing, I might have to educate him in the way of monsters right quick, since many of them cast a glamour to go unseen. If James could see through that, he was in for a tough time if I didn't get to him first. My kids could already see through any glamour since they were raised with monster lore from the very beginning.

"Hey, did you see that they closed the gorilla exhibit?" Angie asked this as we got to Elephant Crossing, which was near the entrance and always our first stop. The goal was to get past the stuffed animal gift shop as quickly as possible.

"I did, and I was disappointed because I was hoping to get up there today," I said, keeping my voice nonchalant. I kept Angie in the dark about my monster hunting to protect her and the children. The only thing Angie knew about my work is that I handled "crisis communications."

"Well, we'll walk past and see if they have opened anything. Did you hear about…"

I got a nose full of something and stopped, sniffing this way and that.

"What is it?" Angie asked.

"Something smells strange."

"We're at the elephants. Of course, something smells strange."

"No, like something is burning. Aw, crap." I closed my eyes to hide my alarm while wondering how quickly a phoenix could regenerate. I was also a little curious about why the phoenix was here and why it burned again.

"Jess, what's wrong?" Angie inhaled too, walking up the hill toward the burning smell. "Chicken?" she asked. "Is there a stand selling fried chicken? That would be new."

"I'm not sure it's chicken," I replied as we rounded the hill, getting closer to Waterfowl Lake. That's when we heard the screaming, high-pitched screams only children make, and sprinted toward the chaos.

"I saw a big turkey on fire!" cried a girl who looked about eight years old, pointing to a pillar of ashes close to the lake. The boy next to her, a younger brother most likely, was sobbing. Their mother was snatching tissues out of her handbag to wipe their tears and offering granola bars. Other people ran as fast as their legs, strollers, and crutches would carry them.

Angie managed to gasp, "Who would come to the zoo with crutches? The paths are miles long. Stupid."

An entire field trip of first graders was in hysterics, teachers struggling to corral them into a safe area. One of the teachers stood on tip-toe counting heads, but the herd shifted, and she started again. She mumbled, "Please be twenty-three. Please be twenty-three."

"What do you think happened?" Angie yelled, attempting to be heard over the squawking geese, swans, and children. "Ahhhh! Duck!"

I ducked, lifting my hands over my head. "What? What is it?"

"A duck pooped on my shoe." Angie stomped her foot. "I like these shoes. Damn. You can't get duck poop out no matter how much Spray n' Wash you use."

I swallowed a laugh. "I guess this chaos scared the crap out of him."

My friend rolled my eyes, mouthing, "Very funny."

"Everybody calm down!" A woman wearing the blue blazer uniform of a zoo employee spoke through a megaphone. "I'm afraid a gentleman didn't observe our no-smoking policy and set a topiary on fire when he discarded his cigarette."

The teacher coughed into her hand. "Bullshit."

"We are calling in the fire department in an abundance of caution. Security guards are at every egress. Please take your children and exit in a calm manner. Everything is okay."

A man holding an infant on his shoulder, rocking a stroller with his right foot, couldn't take it. "Birds set themselves on fire every day? I mean, a massive goose or a swan or some other large bird combusted and you stand there and say, 'Everything is okay?' Are you insane?"

The woman smoothed her hair. "As I said, it was a topiary, not a real bird, and it was caused by a lit cigarette butt, which is strictly against our policy. We will investigate this incident, but for now, no one is injured, and we need to regain order. Everyone please make your way to the…"

"Gorilla! Gorilla!"

"A gorilla is loose!"

"Run for your lives!"

A frazzled man wearing a "zoo blue" blazer rocketed down the hill, waving hands over his head to point to the exits. "Evacuate! Evacuate!"

"Archie! What's happening?" yelled blue-blazer lady, stopping him mid-run.

He whispered to her, gesticulating with his hands to indicate something tall and big. Then he whispered something else that made the lady blanch.

"Ladies and gentlemen!" announced blue-blazer lady. "I'm sure there is nothing to worry about, but if you would please make your way to the exits."

Dozens of people ran full-tilt from the monkey house down the path, running over other people, dropping lunch bags, bottles, diapers, snack bags, and juice boxes as they went. One woman exited from the lavatory struggling to run and pull her pants up.

Sirens rang out, and a recorded message played over the zoo-wide loudspeaker.

"Ladies and gentlemen, please find your closest exit and leave the zoo immediately. Again, find your closest exit and leave the zoo immediately. We have an emergency and need you to evacuate in an orderly fashion. If anyone needs assistance, please ask any zoo employee."

Blue-blazer lady dropped her megaphone, placed her hands to her temples, and started a controlled breathing exercise. I suspected this was Elisabeth Bohring, the Communications Director, who had been quoted in the news. I turned to Angie. "Could you take Daniel with you? I think this woman may need some help managing this crisis, and you know, that's what I do."

Angie placed her left hand on her stroller and her right hand on Daniel's. "I'll find a way out of the ruckus. Don't worry, the kids are safe with me. And, no, Rose, you cannot get out to find the gorilla. Be careful, Jess. I know you are an expert in crisis management, but rampaging gorillas? They're monsters, those silverbacks."

I hugged Angie. "I'll stay out of the line of fire, promise. Speaking of which, how come you're so calm? I'm used to crises, but you're remarkably serene compared to this mob." I jigged out of the way of a flapping flock of geese, jump-hopping out of the lake toward the giraffe enclosure, then juked the other way to avoid being hit by a runaway cooler on wheels.

"I have two sets of twins, Jess. Pandemonium is my normal."

"That's very zen of you."

"Plus, I have a prescription for medical marijuana."

"You do? Hey, wait. How'd you get that?"

Angie wiggled her fingers. "Toodle-loo."

"We're going to talk about how I can get one!" I yelled at Angie's departing back. "Or maybe you'll share?" She kept walking. "Aw, fuck."

I smacked my forehead. "Now I have to do more pushups."

Like a salmon swimming upstream, I fought my way through the crowds to get to the zoo employee, who I could now see wore a lanyard with a name tag. "Elisabeth?"

Elisabeth squinted at me. "Yes? Sorta busy here staying conscious. Passing out is bad for the zoo's reputation."

"I think we're past that, don't you? My name's Jess, and I would like to help. I have some particular experience with crises, particularly monstrous ones?" I raised my eyebrows, drawing out the last words so she would get the hint.

Elisabeth stared for a moment and then said, "Oh, thank God. I thought no one would believe us. Do you know what that bird was? What it really was?" Her voice rose to such an ear-splitting pitch that the neighboring wild dingoes howled in their enclosure.

"It was a phoenix."

"It was a phoenix. Hey, how did you know?"

"I killed one the other day."

"Same one?"

I shrugged. "Don't know. Possibly. Probably. I have no idea how many of them exist."

"It was set on fire by a cigarette, you know. That part was true."

"They're flammable. It's part of the gig."

I'd no sooner said that then I realized something horrible. I'd given away my diaper bag. All my weapons were gone, and I doubted that any of the forgotten diaper bags laying on the ground contained a hatchet.

## CHAPTER SEVEN

E lisabeth grabbed my hand and pulled hard. "Come on, let's go. If you can help, then you need to be at the gorilla house."
I shook my hand free but followed. "What's with the gorillas?"

"Were-gorilla."

I stopped running. "What?"

She turned to me, circling her hands to tell me to hurry up. "Don't dawdle!"

"I'm sorry, but I thought you said were-gorilla?"

"That's exactly what I said. Catch up." She tugged my hand again, and we ran faster. I was impressed with her fitness. I told her so.

"Pilates and the elliptical. But I think you're losing focus here. We have a were-gorilla loose. A visiting professor from Uganda, Dr. Alupo, turned into a gorilla the other night and ransacked the place."

"What did you do?"

"We called a cryptozoologist, who told us to contain him and wait for sunrise."

"Decent advice. What's the problem?" I asked.

"Dr. Alupo didn't change back."

We arrived at the primate exhibit, and Elisabeth gestured for me to go in. "Wait," I said, holding up a finger. "You're saying the professor didn't turn back to a human once morning came?"

"That's correct."

"What happened to the cryptozoologist?"

"He drove out here and visited us personally. Dr. Alupo ate him this morning."

"What! Gorillas don't eat humans."

"Well, tell that to Dr. Alupo."

"Why did you keep the zoo open today after all of this happened?" I asked, grabbing her shoulder and making her look at me.

"It's bad for business. We never close the zoo. It's a point of pride."

"Screw your pride! You close the zoo when there's a were-gorilla on the loose!"

"I think 'on the loose' is a bit of an exaggeration."

"I don't. When people are at risk of getting eaten, I think it is only responsible to keep them away from danger."

"We closed the gorilla exhibit," she said, not looking in my eyes.

"Yip-e-o-ki-yay! Too little, way too little. Who made this decision?"

"The executive board."

"Are any of the executive board here?" I asked this through clenched teeth.

Elisabeth shook her head no. "They don't get involved in the day-to-day operations of the zoo."

I switched gears before I killed her. "What happened to the containment area?" I asked. My hands were on my hips now, to hide that they were clenched into fists. I have no problem with monsters. They were born or made that way and were living to their nature. I have a lot of problem with stupid humans.

She pulled out a talking point for that one. "It held for a bit, but it seems to have experienced a structural failure."

I huffed. "You mean, he broke it."

She toggled her hand in the air. "Does it really matter what the mechanics were?"

I believe in karma, which is the only reason I didn't punch her in the face. Plus, I also *knew* there was a Higher Power, given my job and all, and I figured I could trust whomever was up there to be making a list.

I pressed my lips together and then asked my next question through gritted teeth as well, keeping my anger in check. I was very proud of myself. "Who's back there now?"

"Not sure, but we got all the people out, and the animals, so you should be fine." She turned to go.

"Wait. I must ask one more question. Has he bitten anybody?"

"No," Elisabeth said, staring at the painted green gorilla paw prints on the ground. "But he bit a gorilla."

I was afraid to ask, but it had to be done. "What happened to the gorilla?"

"Oh, you'll see. Interested in your take on it." She patted me on the shoulder, already moving away. "Thanks for helping. Good luck. Let me know how it all turns out so I can write a fictional press release. Rocko is right inside."

"Who's Rocko?" I called to her as she took off down the hill.

I studied the double doorway, knowing I had to go in, but certain I didn't want to. I didn't even have my baseball bat or hairspray with me. Hairspray hurts when it gets in your eye. Don't try it at home. Combine it with a cigarette lighter, and you'll get their attention.

I pulled the door handle and entered the facility, anticipating the weird and scary, but nothing jumped out at me. The only thing out of order was the little podium where the greeter usually stood. It lay on its side, official zoo pad and pen on the floor next to it. A fish tank decorating the front entrance was cracked, but the fish swam along, unaware that their world might collapse at any moment and they'd be sent gasping onto the cold floor.

Whatever it was I expected, I sure didn't expect what I got. I came face-to-chest with a hirsute six-foot naked human male waiting in the main viewing area. This guy's pecs ballooned from his chest and his legs looked like they belonged on a sumo wrestler. "Uh, hello?" I ventured this with trepidation, not certain this caveman throwback could speak.

The man beat his chest, his impressive junk jiggling with the movement. It must have felt nice, because he did it again, leaning over his beer-belly to watch his genitals wave in the air.

"You can stop that now. Tell me what happened. Why are you naked?"

The man bared his teeth, turned, and showed me his hairy butt.

"That's disgusting and totally unnecessary. Do you speak English?"

The man turned around, his face long and sad. He rubbed his face with his hands and swayed back and forth on his feet, not speaking. He ran his hands over his body and held out his arms.

He was trying to communicate with me, but either he didn't or couldn't speak. "Rocko?" I asked.

His face lit up with joy, and he bounced up and down with pleasure that I'd guessed his name. "Okay, big guy, let's go inside and see what we can see." I passed Rocko, who let out a grunt-grunt sound and grabbed my ass.

"No! That is *not* okay. Bad touch."

The entire primate enclosure was trashed. The glass fronts of the cages were either destroyed or cracked. The other inhabitants—the chimps, the macaques, and the baboons—must have been evacuated through the back doors, which were all open. Or, at least I hoped so, because otherwise we needed to wrassle up a barrel of monkeys.

The viewing area was no better. Tables turned upside down, chairs broken, even the snack bar was ransacked. The largest cage was decimated, and I toed through the remains until I found a metal plate. I picked it up by a corner.

*Rocko, Mountain Gorilla, Care and feeding provide by Friends of the Zoo.*

"So, you were bitten by a were-gorilla and turned into a human? That's one for the books. I had no idea that could happen." Rocko moved closer to me, letting out a quiet hoo-hoo'ing sound.

"Hey! Personal space. Back up."

Instead, Rocko moved closer and pawed at my hair. "I don't need grooming. Wait! What was that you just ate? I don't have bugs. Oh no, do I have lice? Oh, God, no lice, please. I can't take it again. The nit combs, the shampoos, the multiple rounds of treatment, and taking off work because they aren't allowed back to school when everyone knows the Smiths send their kids anyway, even when they're scratching." My voice escalated in pitch as I screeched the last, the tendons on my neck taught and visible.

No, I wasn't bitter.

He combed through my hair again, gentle and methodical. I stood still and let him search, sighing in relief when he didn't eat anything else. Go gorilla! Most thorough lice check *ever*. The zoo could rent him out to every elementary school in the state.

My gorilla-man friend stayed within arm's reach of me whichever way I went. I was looking for a weapon of some kind. That's when I discovered that gorillas love rubber tubing. The black tubing was about two or three feet long and an inch thick, and it was everywhere. Rocko hooted in happiness as he saw a piece twisted into a knot. He picked it up and banged it against an upturned table, watching it hit and spring back with a huge smile on his face.

I grabbed a nice long section that wove through some slats in one of the cages, untwisted it, and flicked it like a whip, grinning from ear-to-ear when it made a sharp cracking sound in the air.

Rocko held his rubber tubing toy in one hand while he used the other to retrieve an orange from the floor. The fruit basket from whence it came was upside down, and the fruit, slightly more bruised than normal, lay on the floor. He snagged the orange, opened his mouth to take a big bite, peel and all, when a tiny monkey arm snatched it out of his hands. He and I both looked up and saw a collection of skinny little black-masked monkeys sitting on the girders above. One was eating his purloined orange with glee, and, on seeing Rocko's shock, turned to show the gorilla-man his butt, farting a stream of air that nearly blinded me.

Even blind, I couldn't miss the most remarkable thing. The monkey's balls were bright blue. The entire monkey was tan with black and a little white except for the gonads, which were as blue as the sky. I stared open-mouthed, wondering if the monkey was hard up or if this was normal. He was certainly acting perky, and the troupe chittered at us in the most condescending manner.

*Crash! Boom!* The blue-balled monkeys sped off. Rocko and I jumped at the noise, which came from the animal keepers' and veterinarians' supply area. I pulled my sleeve over my hand to give it some protection and grabbed a sharp piece of glass from the wreckage on the floor. Rocko copied me. I shoved mine into my sweatshirt pocket. Naked Rocko was stumped by that one.

"No, no, big guy. No glass for you." I leaned in to take the glass from him but stopped when he stood his full height and stomped on the ground, screeching and hooting.

"Alright. Rocko wants sharp glass, Rocko gets sharp glass. Don't apes use tools, anyway? Or is that chimpanzees? Whatever, just don't hurt yourself."

Rocko grabbed me by the shoulder and pushed me behind him, the silverback in him taking charge. Although he looked like a big hairy construction worker, he was a gorilla in a man suit. I considered my options and decided that if the silverback wanted to go first, I'd let him. Probably couldn't stop him anyway, but I was worried. He was a victim in all of this, and that made me mad.

The two of us moved forward "hunting wabbits" style and peered through a broken doorframe to see what had caused the racket.

I imagined that a were-gorilla would be big. I mean, gorillas are size-able animals. I didn't expect this, however. Rocko curled his lower lip under and let out a low, menacing growl that made me glad he was on my side. I patted his arm in what I hoped was a reassuring manner.

The were-gorilla was approximately twelve feet tall, maybe more. Hard to say. I gave it a good estimate and finally decided that if he stood in a pool's diving area, his head would be well above water. His chest was proportionately broad, and his hands were the size of serving platters. He was eating, and had been eating for a while, if the mass of slimy detritus around him was any signal.

I pulled back. Rocko pulled back, too. I hesitated. Rocko hesitated right along with me.

I exhaled and said, "I'm going in." Rocko exhaled, too, which let loose a waft of noxiousness. I shifted my eyes to his face. "What the hell do you eat?" Rocko wrinkled his nose for a moment, and then pointed to the corner to a pile of fruit, leaves, and bamboo shoots.

"You pushed all of the bananas to the side. Don't like bananas?" Rocko stuck his tongue out. "Hum. Good to know. Animal Planet got it wrong."

I peeked around the corner and suddenly experienced an epiphany. He's a were-gorilla. I could talk to him. Were-animals were usually sentient.

I slipped out from behind the doorframe and stood under the metal overhang that protected the food and supplies. Rocko lumbered out after me and put his body between mine and what had been, and hopefully still was, Dr. Alupo, primatologist.

I shoved my way around Rocko, to which he grunted his displeasure but I ignored him. "Dr. Alupo! My name is Jess Friedman, and I'd like to talk with you."

Alupo turned, training his eyes on me like one would an annoying gnat.

"A girl? They sent a girl to stop me?" His voice was guttural, but understandable. And, as much I hated to admit it, his point was valid. He outweighed me by at least a thousand pounds.

"Not to stop you." I paused. "Okay, yes, to stop you. But not by force. I'm here to talk. We seem to have some miscommunication here. You've turned a gorilla into a man, sort of, and ruined the entire enclosure…"

Alupo opened his mouth, revealing gigantic pointy teeth and screamed the scream of the damned. My hair blew back, and I stumbled from the force of it. Rocko wrapped his arm around my waist and held onto the doorframe.

"Thanks for the assist, big guy," I whispered. I was so shocked that I didn't even mind that Rocko held me to his naked body and seemed to like it, by all available evidence.

I pushed my way out of the embrace and yelled as loud as possible. "So, I guess you're saying you don't want to talk?"

"I like who I am now, tiny, weak, putrid human girl. I'm strong now. Invincible!"

"I'm not putrid. I smell fine." I sniffed my underarm to be sure. All good. "You know that the longer you stay in that form, the more likely you are to lose your humanity, right? Soon, you'll just be a hormonally overactive gorilla. Large for your size, but unintelligent."

Rocko smacked my arm.

I bowed my head in shame. "I'm sorry. Sincerely, Rocko."

"Let me amend," I yelled to Alupo. "You won't be able to read, write, do math, all of the academic-y things that get you tenure. Hard to use a computer with fingers like the ones you're sporting. And, no doubt about it, your nude modeling days are over."

Alupo's nostrils flared as he bent his head to be equal height with mine, reminding me of a pissed-off guard dog deciding if you were friend or foe. I stumbled, but managed to strike out with the rubber tubing, smacking the bad boy on the nose. He yelped and backed up. I attacked, whipping his toes with the tubing, chortling with each smack of the rubber on his feet.

"Take that, you overgrown ape! Bet that stings! Turn back to human and let's settle this. No one else has to get hurt."

Alupo swung an arm, batting me about fifty feet. I survived because I made a soft landing in a pile of crap. Literally.

"Ugh! That hurt." I slid further into the muck so that my pants and the back of my shirt were covered in monkey manure. The goo sucked me down like quicksand, and I couldn't extricate my right foot at all. My body was bruised head-to-toe, and while I felt okay now, I was going to pay for it big time later.

"What is it you want?" I shouted, leaving my boot where it was but pulling so that at least my foot came with me.

"A little acknowledgment, that's all, maybe a Nobel Prize in biology. I trekked through mountains, climbed trees, lived through multiple episodes of Montezuma's revenge, and even survived a bout of Dengue fever to make this discovery. And what happened when I wrote it up? Ridicule!"

"That's terrible. I'm very sorry for you, but the human mind is trained to ignore things it can't explain. It's amazing what our brains will do to explain away something bizarre."

I was worried about Rocko, who was beating his chest and roaring. Before I could stop him, he charged Alupo, throwing his considerable body weight, coupled with good momentum, at Alupo's leg.

Alupo shook him off without a second's thought and kept eating, talking with his mouth full, spitting food in the air, and letting it dribble down his body. He sneered, more food squishing out between his incisors to plop on the ground.

"I had evidence and witnesses, although the other scientists with me on that day denied that it happened. We saw him. We saw a man change into a gorilla right in front of us!" Alupo growled. "After being rejected by the entire science community, I went back into the jungle and hunted for that man for six months."

I ran toward Rocko and executed a second base slide through the discarded and half-eaten food. Pretty sure the orange stuff was cantaloupe. Hoped the orange stuff was cantaloupe. Poor Rocko's head was weaving back and forth and his eyes were glassy. I practically saw birdies flying round his cranium. I grabbed Rocko's massive arm and pulled with all my strength. We slid a few feet, but no matter how hard I tried, I couldn't move Rocko by myself.

I talked at Alupo to buy time. "How did you convince him to bite you?"

"Ah! Good question. Hold on a moment." Alupo opened a jar of peanut butter, shoved two fingers in, and scooped out a mouthful. "Mmslsmmmm garf."

"Chew, then swallow, please. Talking with your mouth full is rude, and I can't understand you anyway."

He swallowed and burped. "Sorry. As I was saying, and as you guessed, he wouldn't voluntarily bite me, but I tricked him. I followed him until the next full moon, watched him change, and then shot him with my rifle. In his pain and rage, he didn't have control. I placed my bicep in his mouth, shoved my finger into the gunshot wound for added incentive, and *voila*!"

"He bit you."

"Umhummm. Wasn't sure I'd live through it, but here I am, making a scene, getting TV time." He gestured at the sky where helicopters circled above. "I'm living my true self."

"Oh, don't use that line. There are real people out there doing the hard work of living their true selves, and you took a dangerous shortcut. You're living a lie, and it will be a short lie because you need to change back."

"I'll title my lecture 'Gorilla from the Inside Out,'" he said, shoving a dozen apples down his gullet. "I'll be famous. The most famous primatologist in the world and no one will laugh at me."

While the good doctor was glorying in his imaginary fame, I was trying to rouse Rocko. "Rocko, get up," I begged. "I can't move you. Come on. Can you sit up, not even stand, just sit?" Rocko stirred and made a groggy attempt to sit up.

I continued talking to Alupo. "I get it. You feel rejected, and that's made you want to hurt those that hurt you. What made you become a primatologist in the first place?"

"My dad was one, and my mom was a primate veterinarian. I wanted to be a circus clown, but that wasn't acceptable in my family. No! It had to be science or nothing. Do you know that I was accepted to Clown College and everything?"

"I don't think that made it on your CV."

"Anyway," Alupo said, shoving heads of lettuce in his yapper, "I was on safari with them half the year anyway, so eventually I let gravitational pull take over and did what was easiest. I followed in their footsteps."

"I'm sure they were proud of you." I placed my hands under Rocko's shoulders and heaved. We got another few feet.

"No, they weren't proud," Alupo responded, and I could have sworn there were tears in his eyes. "I made the mistake of staring a troupe leader, a silverback, directly in the eyes, and it was all the team could do to get out of there in time without any of us losing our heads. We lost all our equipment and our records. Plus, the troupe never let us near them again. Five years of patient habituation, and I blew it with a look."

"I can see why you'd be resentful of something like that." I checked Rocko's eyes to see if the pupils were dilated.

"What I want to know, and this is a purely scientific question, primatologist to monster hunter, how are you avoiding the change? It's daytime. You should be changing back."

Alupo's grin was the most gruesome thing I'd seen in a long time. "Well," he said, munching a pint of strawberries, "I realized that the change takes energy." He waited for me to put the rest together.

I smacked my forehead. "I got it. That's why you're constantly eating. You need fuel to maintain the change."

"Got it in one. Luckily, I have a big appetite. Hey! Thieves!"

The blue-balled monkeys formed a chain, tail to arm, and dropped down to steal a bunch of grapes from the were-gorilla, who had been about to drop them in his maw. They showed no fear of the monstrosity and, in fact, twittered and chirped like they thought this game was a lot of fun. They dropped to his back, head, and front, crawling all over him like ants at a picnic. The larger ones distracted the were-gorilla while the sneakier, smaller ones, went after the food.

"Damn vervets!" Alupo yelled. He smacked at them with his Frisbee hands, but the monkeys were dexterous speed demons, and he couldn't catch a single one. I, for my part, thanked them for the distraction.

"Rocko, come on. I know what to do now." Rocko blinked at me a few times but finally he struggled to his feet, shaky and unstable. I let him stand there a moment to get his bearings, but one moment was all we had.

Alupo kicked at his tiny vervet tormentors and missed me by inches. "Run, run, Rocko," I urged.

"Scat!" Alupo waived his arms in the air, trying to catch the trickster vervets. I shoved Rocko away, then ran in the opposite direction, toward Alupo, and sliced at the were-gorilla's Achilles tendon with my pointy glass shard. The first cut was shallow, just a graze along the skin, but it must have hurt. Alupo roared, and seeing the opening, I snuck in a second time and sawed away in the same location, dancing and skipping out of the way of his hands and feet, working at it until blood sprayed into the air and fountained to the ground.

Losing an Achilles tendon would slow him down—heck, it would slow anyone down—but I needed even more time. That's when I saw them.

A hose and fire sprinklers. A little-known fact about gorillas is that they hate the rain. They can't swim and in real-life just sit there, letting the rain sluice down their bodies while they pout in total misery. I slid to a stop, dropped my rubber tubing, and unwound the hose. "Grab this, Rocko." Rocko stayed close, despite my earlier requests for him to run. He snagged the hose and hauled it in front of him, swallowing at the sight of the oncoming one-legged, hemorrhaging were-gorilla, but the courageous gorilla-man didn't budge an inch. I turned on the water full blast. "Hold on tight, Rocko!"

The hose was industrial size and had the power to go with it. I guess if you're using it to clean out gorilla cages, you needed some force behind the flow. Rocko recoiled at the blast but braced himself, kept his body behind it, and aimed the water straight at Alupo.

"Good job, Rocko," I yelled. I pointed at the dung. "Spray the crap pile!" Rocko screwed his face up, not understanding. I was several feet away, hauling a box over so I could reach the fire alarm, so I did the only thing I could think of. I squatted, squeezing my face in concentration in an imitation of pooping. Say what you will, it worked. Light dawned in the gorilla man's eyes, and he chuffed-chuffed, baring his teeth. He sprayed the poopy mountain and hooted as the pile dissolved into a swirling swamp of excretory discharge. Yeah, it looked, and smelled, as bad as it sounds.

The were-gorilla wrinkled his nose and fled-hopped in the other direction, growling in a way that sounded more gorilla-like than before. He couldn't escape the water, though, as I flicked on the fire alarm and the sprinklers, high-grade and huge, and created a rainstorm on a sunny day. The were-gorilla stopped and gave into instinct. He sat, miserable and motionless, as gorillas in the wild do, the water droplets falling on his shoulders while the whorl of fecal feculence pooled around his body and got into his bleeding cut. I could only hope for a virulent infection.

I pulled Rocko back and looked for a way to get past the were-gorilla into the forest part of the exhibit, which lay beyond.

"We've got to get to the trees, Rocko. How do you get to the trees if you don't walk?"

Rocko pointed up to the network of swinging ropes and rope ladders installed to give the gorillas an opportunity to swing and climb.

"Let's go, big guy." Rocko led me a few feet back into the cage area, both of us keeping a close eye on the were-gorilla. His gorilla face was scrunched up in a human look of confusion as the man part of him tried to figure out why he was just sitting there. Alupo scratched his head and wiggled in the water, shifting back and forth but not getting up.

Rocko led the way, climbing the first vertical rope with ease. I followed, not using my left, still-booted foot because the sole of the boot was slick, and I couldn't get purchase on the rope. I flashed back to my training with Ovid and wondered if he had a touch of soothsayer to him.

"We have to keep him away from food," I explained as I hauled my body up, arm over arm to the top, where we met a series of looping ropes. Rocko swung one to the other, but I knew my short arms wouldn't be able to do that, so I turned backward, grabbed the horizontal rope with my hands, and lifted my feet to pull myself backward to the next rope. By the time I finished all three, Rocko was all but looking at his watch. He patted my head when I finished.

There were a few more ropes to go when Alupo figured out he didn't have to sit there. He gave a roar that shook the ropes, making them swing so that my stomach flipped, and I thought I was going to throw up.

"Scoot, Rocko. Go!"

The ropes thrashed and swayed from Alupo's roaring and Rocko's climb. I shimmied to the next obstacle, which was a cargo net, narrowly avoiding Alupo's hand as it sliced through the mesh webbing, tearing it from its moorings, so it hung from one corner only, and I couldn't reach the last rope to the trees. I dropped down and attempted to scoot between Alupo's feet, but he caught me by the hair.

My skull was on fire as he pulled a chunk full of hair out by the roots, and I shrieked with pain. I still had my shard of glass, which I had shoved back in my sweatshirt pocket. I grasped it, giving myself a shallow cut on my hand in the process, and slashed at my hair and his hand until I hacked myself free. I wiped my eyes with the back of my hands and flicked away blood from my forehead, where I'd also carved a deep gash.

The vervets called to Rocko from the top of the trees, and he followed their call, while the were-gorilla behind us finally collapsed to the ground, unable to support himself on one ankle any longer.

We ran through the trees as fast as possible, the vervets shrieking up ahead like kids at a birthday party. Unlike everyone else, they seemed to be having a blast. I stopped a few trees in and put my hands on my knees to catch my breath. "If he stops eating long enough, he'll change back, especially now that he's wounded." I waited until my pulse was down to a normal rate, and then I looked around for Rocko. I couldn't find him, until I looked up.

Rocko was up a tree, his face a picture of bliss.

"Good. You stay up there. Just don't get any splinters."

I took off again. Never having seen the back of the habitat, I was dismayed to find that the "forest" was ten trees deep, so calling it a forest was a stretch. I hit a back door running and burst through. A dozen or so policeman stared at me.

A cop with a name plate announcing he was Captain Morgan, stepped forward and asked, "Ma'am, why you were in there with that thing? Didn't you get the order to evacuate? When we learned of your presence in the enclosure from the news broadcasts, my people were obligated to go in there to rescue you. Your presence is putting them and everyone else at risk." The poor captain's face was red, and his eyes bulged with fury.

I got distracted when several firefighters arrived wearing T-shirts, overalls, and fire-retardant turn-out pants with orange stripes. I stared in open admiration, and the only thing I could think was that they'd make a great calendar. The guy with the beard would have to be the cover model. His cheekbones were amazing.

The captain didn't like that I was ignoring him and barked, "Bob, I thought we evacuated everybody?"

"We did, sir. No one was supposed to be in there."

Morgan squinched his entire face up and let the muscles relax one at a time, letting out a huge breath. "Ma'am, you come with me now, and we'll take care of you. Officer, arrest this woman for trespassing and get her some medical help."

I waved my hands in the air, flinging God-knows-what at the poor cops. "Sorry, gentlemen, and ladies," I said, nodding to the female police officers. "But, what we have hereah is a failure to commmmunnnicate."

Not a flash of recognition. "Oh, come on, no one's seen *Cool Hand Luke?*"

Not a twitch.

"Ma'am, I'm losing my patience. This is a crime scene, possibly terrorism, and given the transformation of that gorilla, there may be biochemical agents involved. At this point, we are cordoning off the area and calling in the DEA and FBI. You need to let the experts deal with this."

"No, siree can do, sir, 'cause that there is not a regular gorilla. He's a were-gorilla, which means he falls under my jurisdiction, as bestowed upon me by the Pope himself. Or at least the Catholic Church. And my rabbi."

Captain Morgan gave me a pained look and, showing bravery above and beyond the call of duty, placed his hand on my arm. "I think you need some rest, and maybe a doctor. Let me help you..."

I chopped my hand down on his elbow, twisted, and flipped his arm behind his back, and found myself facing a dozen or so guns with rounds in their chambers.

I let him go and held my hands up in a gesture of peace, giving them what I hoped was a friendly smile, but was probably more of a scowl. "Captain Morgan, love the name, by the way, I'm telling the truth."

"That's it! Officers," he said, gesturing to a man and woman in uniform behind him, "grab this woman and cuff her." The male officer's tag just said Bob, which must have meant it was his last name, or perhaps he only used his first? I couldn't tell.

Morgan turned to me. "I'm arresting you for assaulting a police officer and trespassing, and anything else I can find to charge you with."

"Sir, please don't do this. I apologize for my smart mouth and my belligerence, but I get annoyed when I'm touched without permission. Besides, you have to believe me."

"No, lady. I don't." He cringed when the vervets screamed overhead and then scampered off.

"What the hell are those things?" Captain Morgan demanded.

"Vervets, sir. They're devious devils, and we should thank them because they're giving Alupo a hard time, which is slowing him down." Alupo bellowed from within the enclosure.

"What the hell is an Alupo?"

"A primatologist named Dr. Alupo. He tried to publish about were-gorillas, and the academic community ridiculed him. The rest is textbook. 'They'll believe me now; I'm all powerful,' kinda thing. Yada, yada." I moved my hand in a yapping motion.

Morgan turned to the male officer. "Bob, get Dr. Barlow."

"Who's he?" I asked.

"The primatologist that consults for the zoo. He teaches at Ohio University. I want to hear if this story makes any sense to him. In the meantime, don't move or I'll throw you in Bob's cruiser."

Bob blanched. "Mine, sir? We just got it cleaned."

The captain, a former Army man if ever there was one with his shorn hair and big neck, castigated his junior officer. "Now, Officer! Or, we'll send you back to police academy." Bob skadoodled.

"Captain." Another cop, an older guy who looked like he been around a while, pulled the captain aside. "Robert, one of the witnesses said that thing can talk. I don't know of any gorilla that can talk. Let's hear what she has to say. You can throw her in Bob's car later."

"Were-animals don't exist…" Captain Morgan trailed off.

"Robert," said the other cop, in what was supposed to be whisper. "Remember those things from last October?"

Morgan gave an involuntary shiver.

I perked up. "The scarecrows? I burned them. A little Pam cooking spray and a match. Works wonders. They won't come back."

Captain Morgan gave me a wide berth, wiped his hand on his pants, and called his people together. They huddled while I tapped my feet and let out conspicuous, aggravated breaths.

I couldn't wait anymore. "Sir? With all due respect, we need to get that thing before the moon comes out. He's going to gain power then. He's eating now to fuel the change, but when night comes, he won't need to do that, and he'll be on the rampage."

A young man came forward wearing wire-rimmed glasses and a squint, escorted by Officer Bob. He didn't give my appearance a second look and wasn't bothered by the smell. I figured he was Dr. Barlow and used to gorilla stink. I told him the story.

"That's Dr. Alupo?" Dr. Barlow exclaimed, reaching out with his hand for a shake. I held up my hands, and he pulled back fast. "I remember this story. He tried to publish in multiple journals, but no one believed him. He had no proof. His photos were grainy at best, and the other scientists with him denied his claim. Besides, there is no scientific evidence supporting lycanthropy."

I shook my head at the ignorance of people and plopped on the ground to take a quick rest. I rubbed my hands over my eyes, a terrible idea given the grime I'd collected, and said, "Yeah? Well, he's sorta holding a grudge and means to take it out on Cleveland, which I can't allow."

"What are you?"

"Monster Hunter Mom, at your service. Some of the baddies call me the Buckeye Bitch, but that's a little harsh, wouldn't you say?" We needed to move, and I was done with the chatting. "We need to tranquilize that great ape and put him out in the sun while it's still shining. Baking him should turn him back into a man."

"I still don't know," Captain Morgan continued, but I hauled my ass up and got in his face. He was short; it worked out.

"Sir, with all due respect, this is not your call. Like I said, I'm on a mission from God, with apologies to the Blues Brothers, and that is exactly what we have to do." I dragged a ragged, filthy card from my back pocket. "Call this number." Morgan screwed his eyes up but walked off to do as I suggested.

Dr. Barlow hopped up and down as the scientific discovery dawned on him, and he peppered me with questions. "How does were-ism work? Is it a virus? It is a whole new species? Or class even? Maybe a new phylum. The taxonomy for this is going to be complicated." He rubbed his hands together. "This is amazing."

"Look, Mr. Attenborough, I get that you're amazed, but what you should be is scared. That were-gorilla *ate* the cryptobiologist that zoo personnel brought in, and he will be unstoppable by this evening, and the longer he stays gorilla, the less man he's gonna be. So, get your head out of your ass and help me."

Captain Morgan double-timed back, eyes glassy. He took a large inhale and gestured to me. "She's legit. Do what she says." He whispered to me, "Did I just really talk to the Holy See?"

"I don't know. I've never called the number," I replied. I turned to Dr. Barlow. "Barlow, we need tranquilizers, a lot of them. All of them. Let's get that together first."

## CHAPTER EIGHT

Zoo staff fanned out to grab all the tranquilizer darts they could. Some wouldn't be much use on a gorilla since they were meant for reptiles, and the avian drugs came in tiny doses, so they weren't going to be effective. The only ones that could do what we needed were the large mammal ones, and it turns out, not as much of that stuff is kept on hand as you would think.

"Can we get some human tranquilizers from the local hospitals?" I asked. "We've got University Hospitals, the Cleveland Clinic, Metro…they all have anesthesia. Is there anything we can put in a dart?" Captain Morgan gave a sharp nod and dispatched a deputy to call the hospitals.

While we waited, I scoped out the park, looking with a new eye. High ground, hiding spots, vantage points, places where sharp shooters who could fire off tranquilizer darts without risking themselves? I wandered down the deck walk, examining every nook and cranny, every climbable tree, and searched for the best angles and line of sight. I focused on this task, absorbed by the plan I was sketching in my mind, when a screech made my skin crawl. I knew that sound, and if there was one thing for sure, I didn't have time for this.

I spied a broken bench, probably cracked apart during the melee earlier. I picked up a strong piece of the seat, approximately bat length, swung it over my shoulder, and followed the sound, relying on Alupo's injury and the mischievous vervets to slow him down.

I found the phoenix considering the lorikeet cage, blowing huge snorts of air as it got increasingly frustrated by not being able to reach the pretty birds who pressed their beaks to the glass to stare at him.

"Hey, phoenix. Are you a bad phoenix or a good one? Are you the same one I met in the playground?" I held the "bat" in front of me so he could see it. "I can't keep bashing your head in, so maybe we could come to an agree…"

I bolted down the path encircling the Australian Adventure section of the zoo as the giant bird came running at me, emu style, shrieking a battle cry. I now had no doubt this was the same one. This bird had murder in his eyes. His tail feathers were still a brilliant display, and now his wings were out, making him look like a Boeing airliner. The bronze armor clinked as he ran.

I was tired, covered in thick, toxic gunk, and worried about the were-gorilla. My legs were heavy, and filth got up my nose, making it difficult to breathe. I blew hard and hacked gray-black chunks that fell to the ground with a worrisome clunk.

I couldn't care about black lung disease now, I told myself and took a shortcut through the Australian Adventure exhibit, which wasn't heavily gated, and bolted through the marsupials.

"Sorry! Sorry! Didn't mean to disturb you." Kangaroos bounded in every direction. The phoenix hopped the fence, rudely ignoring the door, and chased me again. I scrambled up a tree in the kangaroo enclosure, using only one hand because I still held the piece of wood. Once I was up high enough, I mustered the wherewithal to look down. The phoenix was pacing a circle around the tree, snapping its beak.

The dingoes on the other side of the fence howled, pawing at the ground. The roos boxed among themselves, and even the normally friendly koalas, hid high up in their eucalyptus trees. The rabbi's words came back to me. *"The natural order has been disturbed."* I needed to deal with the were-gorilla fast, but first I had to deal with the damn chicken-hawk.

I went for broke. I sat on a mostly horizontal branch, just outside of the phoenix's reach, held the purloined lumber from the broken bench, swung down penny-drop fashion, and brought my feeble weapon up with as much force and acceleration as I could muster, hitting him right in the underside of his beak. A crack rang out as the tip of the beak snapped off.

The phoenix stared at me, looked left and right, then down and up, and blinked a few times. I turned, ran out of the enclosure, and beat it back up the hill, only to hear the slap-slap of giant chicken feet following, although not as steady as before, a fact that I found only mildly reassuring. I rounded the corner and leapt for the lorikeet feeding exhibit, pushing through the self-locking door. As my legs slipped from under me and I fell hard on butt, I recalled an important tidbit about the lorikeets. These colorful birds drank a sweet nectary syrup all day long out of these tiny paper cups, but today those cups lay discarded in a heap, dropped during the brouhaha, and were now congealed on the ground in a sticky glissade, forming a death trap for Monster Hunters. I caught myself with my hands, felt something in my wrist go, ignored it, popped up, ran my sticky fingers through my shaggy hair, and kept going. No time for pain, but boy, if I thought about it at all, I was *sore*.

The phoenix didn't hesitate and followed me into the small lorikeet space while I ran out the exit. I shot a look over my shoulder. The phoenix couldn't figure out how to work the electronic door and was stuck, hanging his head as the lorikeets flew about him, but instead of attacking him, they hovered around him like he was a rock star. I guess in the war of plumage, he won, wings down.

My feet hurt something awful, particularly the bare one, but I shoved that out of my mind because new voices and strangled gurgles caught my attention. Now, I may occasionally hear voices in my head, but these voices were the ones of policemen and firefighters being chased by a were-gorilla with a mangled ankle. It is a distinctive sound.

Captain Morgan, still red-faced but calm and in-charge, issued directions to his officers in a clipped, measured tone, which was remarkable considering a police officer's head lay at his feet, the body flung yards away. Police were stationed at every bend on the paths that led from the gorilla exhibit to any other place in the park, all armed with shotguns with rounds big enough to bring down deer. The problem was that the were-gorilla was a gazillion times the weight of the lowly white-tailed deer that ate my hostas.

"What happened?" I asked the captain, who was belting orders as fast as he could.

"Shut up," he replied. "I'm busy."

I scuttled to the side to let him do his thing, but even with disciplined, trained troops, the landscape was a nightmare.

Alupo twirled in the middle of a path in front of the gorilla enclosure, spinning like an off-balance tornado, whooping, "Wheeeeee!" as he turned like a lawnmower blade chawing weeds. He'd stopped eating long enough to have both hands free, and as he whirled, he ladled a cop up in his hands, pretended the man was a hard-to-open jar, and twisted the officer's head, tearing it right off. Then he hurled the head and the body in opposite directions. He repeated this action one more time while the officers fired their rifles. A few bullets hit him since he was such a large target, but Alupo's swirling, manic dervish made a lot of the bullets miss. One cop was caught in the shoulder by friendly fire and fell to the ground moaning in pain. His partner army-crawled in and pulled the fallen officer to safety.

The cops regrouped, and the firefighters begged to charge in with their axes. Captain Morgan nixed this without a second thought, saying that there was no way anyone was getting that close to that thing, but it gave me an idea.

"Captain!"

He did that face squeezing thing again. "Yes, ma'am?"

"I used water in the enclosure to slow him down. I don't think he'll fall for the same trick twice, but if we make the ground nice and slippery, it could help, especially since he's essentially one-footed at this moment."

"Pull back! Pull back!" commanded Morgan, who had somehow gotten access to the loudspeaker system in the park. The cops pulled back, and once they were far enough away from Alupo, the were-gorilla stopped caring about them and went back to eating. His ankle had stopped bleeding, and he didn't seem to care about the pain, but I could see the yawning laceration and knew it would get to him at some point.

Morgan gave the firefighters the "go" nod, and within three minutes, all the hoses were spraying ice cold water on the were-gorilla. Alupo dragged his body farther and farther away from the hoses until he was almost within the enclosure's visitor's center.

"Keep that up! He's contained!" I yelled, forgetting that there was no way they could hear me, but Morgan and others relayed the message to the brave men and women on top of the ladders.

The officers around me were still and pale, shaking from what happened to their comrades. I re-approached Morgan. "How did this happen?"

Morgan wiped sweat from his brow, but that was the only sign of his fury and sadness. I grew to admire him in that moment. He was a staunch leader, but I knew his kind. The guilt about the lives lost would eat at him.

"We gathered our guns and nailed that son-of-a-bitch with every round we had. I thought that if we surrounded him and shot from all sides, we could injure him enough to take him down. It didn't work. He did that pirouette routine, we kept missing, and then...then...he killed them."

The last was a tough admission. This man was mentally adding demerits to his ledger and counting on paying for them somewhere along the line. I had to make him okay with his role and his loss. Monsters are *monsters*. They don't play by any rules, and the Almighty, or something or someone close, had established a squad of hitmen, and women, exactly for this reason.

"Morgan," I snapped. Then, more gently, "Morgan?"

He looked at me, and I was glad to see his eyes flashed and his hands were clenched into fists. This was good. He needed to be angry, furious, laying the blame where it ought to go, at a jacked-up primatologist with a chip on his shoulder who'd stepped beyond saving and now needed to be put down.

"This is not your fault. This is the fault of one beastie who has found a way to cheat the system and stay in were form for much longer than he should. We will mourn the dead later, but you do not hold the blame for their deaths. Remember who you talked to earlier when you called the number on my card?"

Morgan nodded.

"Then you know there are more mysteries between Heaven and Earth than in all of your imaginings."

"I think it is philosophy."

"It is, but give me a freakin' break. I'm not at my best right now, and I'm trying to help you by making a point. Nothing red is on your ledger, understand? Absolutely nothing. If anything, you deserve credit for standing your ground and making the hard decisions. Now, look at me."

He did.

"Where are the tranquilizers?"

"They are supposed to be on the way. We didn't hit him with many bullets, but the ones that hit home didn't seem to bother him. If bullets won't stop him, how will the tranqs?"

"They don't have to stop him. They need to slow him down, get him to stop eating. We may need a tractor or something once he's down to make sure all of him is in the sun. We've got to broil the gorilla right out of that man, if there is any man left." I frowned, and I knew my eyes were hard. "I'll stop him, don't you worry."

## CHAPTER NINE

Alupo relocated to the grassy area that stood between the big cat and Waterfowl Lake, near the playground equipment, and stood there like King Kong. Clouds roiled the sky, keeping Alupo protected from the sun, and the air smelled like rain, or snow, or hail. With Cleveland, you never know.

Law officers and fire fighters moved to the were-gorilla's new position and stared at the creature like they were watching a bad movie, seeing but not really believing.

"What's that he's holding?" said one red-faced policeman, who looked like he wanted a cannon right about them. It was a good idea, but I didn't know of any available, and I was certain that if Morgan did, he'd have it on site by now.

"I think it's a giant bunch of bananas," said another. "He's shoving them into his mouth one after the other, peel on. What's in his other hand?"

Barlow limped toward me.

"What happened to you?"

He was so out of breath he couldn't speak, and instead pointed to Alupo's other hand. "Lulu."

Alupo dangled a gorilla in his left hand. All she needed was a spaghetti strap dress and the bad movie analogy would be complete.

Barlow caught his breath enough to say, "That's Lulu. I tried to get to her, but we must not have locked her transport cage well, and she burst through and headed back. I twisted my ankle while chasing her."

"How'd she get caught?" I asked.

"She charged him! She was hooting and hollering. Her vocalizations were the ones gorillas make when they are apart from their group. She was looking for someone."

"I know who," I said and pointed my chin toward the ruined habitat door, where a naked, hairy man made it plain that he was displeased with the current situation.

Rocko stormed out onto the grass on all fours, gorilla-style, and on all fours, he resembled the three-hundred-pound silverback he was. He rushed Alupo's feet like an Ohio University linebacker slamming a quarterback on the blind side. Alupo stumbled when Rocko hit him, hampered by the lack of a properly function ankle tendon, and because both of his hands were full of either bananas or Lulu. He dropped the bananas to use his hand to stop his fall but still struck the ground with a heavy thunk. Rocko barked a challenge, and Alupo, now on all fours, pushed Lulu aside and faced him.

"This is fascinating," whispered Barlow. "We are witnessing a silverback challenge, albeit an unusual one. It's a classic dominance fight over an available female."

Classic, my ass. My heart was in my throat watching Rocko face off with the were-gorilla. He was mismatched at every level, but like a brave soldier, he held in there, charging and retreating, using his smaller size to his advantage by moving fast.

I was out of patience and spoke a bit sharper than I had intended, but I gripped my hands together so they couldn't fly of their own accord. Instead, I said, "Hey, Dian Fossey, that 'man' out there is one of your gorillas engaging in human cosplay against his will. He's a victim of this maniac, just like those cops. Put the *National Geographic* documentary on the back burner and get those tranquilizers."

Barlow blushed from the neck up and backed away toward the waiting police. I left him and ran into the fray to help Rocko.

A dropped diaper bag with a long shoulder strap caught my eye, and I snatched it on the run. Neither of the combatants saw me coming as I held on to the bag with both hands and scampered into the fracas. Rocko must have sensed me though because he shifted his body with a slight turn to the right, giving me space to dive in.

Unfortunately, that small distraction gave Alupo time to give Rocko a kick to the stomach with enough force that the big guy flew several yards and went down hard.

"Rocko!" I yelled, but he didn't answer and lay still. With a knot in my stomach, I pivoted mid-step to go to his side. I didn't reach him because suddenly Lulu was *on* my back, growling in my ear. She pushed me to the ground and rolled me like a rag doll.

"I'm not his girlfriend! I'm not the competition. He's all yours. Stop, Lulu!" I fell on my back so she hit the ground first, allowing me to struggle out of her embrace.

Lulu responded by baring her teeth and making a sharp, staccato series of grunts. I log-rolled away, but love is a possessive thing, and Lulu was staking a claim. She charged me, getting right up in my face, her mouth wide so that I couldn't miss those incisors. I scrambled to my feet only to be knocked over again by her sheer bulk. She didn't even put any muscle into it. I crumpled like a can.

When she sat on me, I had a real moment of terror, knowing that if I didn't get her off, she'd squash me like a bug and my poor husband would have to scrape up a Jess-sized pancake to bury me. I struggled for breath, gagging as my ribs almost gave way and my throat tightened. I held on another moment and whispered, "Rocko."

He heard me, and he lifted his head an inch from the ground and made a gentle grunting noise. Lulu grunted back and ran to him, sighing relieved little whimpers as she went to his side, letting me breathe at last.

This left me with Kong. My initial plan to lasso his foot and send him crashing to the ground was dead on arrival, so I emptied the diaper bag, keeping only one item in it.

The good news was that Alupo had run out of food. The bad news is that he ran away, his feet chewing up real estate so that he got farther and farther away with every step. I heaved myself up, taking in huge gulps of air, and waved down a policeman who was holding a Diet Coke with both hands as if it were a magic lamp.

"Hey. Anyone there got a motorcycle? I need a ride." My voice so was cracked and weak from almost being macerated by a possessive primate that he had to lean close to understand what I was saying. I repeated my question.

"Yeah, I got one. I'll grab it, I guess. What are we doing with my motorcycle?" His face was pale and pinched as he hoped against hope that I didn't say chase the were-gorilla.

"Chase the were-gorilla," I rasped as I pointed to Alupo's disappearing figure. When he wasn't looking, I grabbed his Diet Coke and downed it in one draw.

I'm pretty sure he muttered, "You bitch," but I could be wrong.

"You don't have a helmet, ma'am," he said, holding his body stiff and not meeting my eyes.

"Officer, a were-gorilla is storming the castle, during the *day*, and murdered several of your friends. I locked a phoenix in the lorikeet cage, the closest thing I have to a friend around here is a semi-conscious, naked gorilla in a man-suit, and I was almost flattened by his jealous lady-friend. I think we can forgo the helmet, just this once."

I said the last words one at a time, slow and drawn out, so he knew that the crazy lady with the crazy hair and the crazy stench was a woman on the edge who was pissed she didn't have a baseball bat.

I vocalized that last part, much to my chagrin. I thought I was talking to myself, but the cop heard me.

"Baseball bat? Burt's got one in the car. He helps with Little League on the weekends. Hey Burt! Got your bat?"

"And a ball?" I said, an excited uptick in my voice that made me sound like I was a prepubescent boy. A tall, gangly officer unlocked his patrol car, which was parked on the grass, and handed me a bat and a ball, silent the entire time. I offered my hand in a fist bump, which he ignored. I stuffed the items in the diaper bag, the bat's handle positioned for an easy draw, threw it over my shoulder, and hopped on the bike.

"Thataway!" I screamed, or at least I tried. My abraded throat made it sound more like a banshee with strep, which scared the poor cop so much that we jolted forward and stuttered to a stall. He straightened his shoulders, said something about Mary and Joseph, and hit the gas. We took an educated guess on his location based on the howling of the…

"Wolves?" I said out loud, slapping my hand against my forehead. "Aw, crap. Wolves are dangerous."

Officer Motorcycle said, "They like cheese."

"Whaaaat?" My throat was as dry as sandpaper.

"I come here with my grandson all the time. The wolves like cheese. That's how they train them. I guess it makes sense. My dog loves cheese, but of course, he eats anything, so he's not a good metric to go by."

"Stop here."

The were-gorilla was foraging for grass, hay, anything he could find. The camels, next to the wolves, had piles of vegetation in their enclosure. Once he found those, he shoveled handfuls in his mouth. Some of it dropped out and got caught in his pelt, and he must have chewed something he didn't like because he spit it out like some two-year-old eating mashed peas. The camels didn't seem to be bothered by this, the fluttering of their long eyelashes the only outward sign of pique.

"Go back and get those tranquilizers and shooters in place. That is the top priority," I said to Officer Motorcycle. "And thanks for the tip about the cheese. Do you know if it is any particular kind of cheese?"

The officer gave me a *look*.

"I guess whatever's in there. I've never asked." Officer Motorcycle made the sign of the cross and drove off without a backward glance.

I grumbled to myself. "It matters. I hate pimento. Why does everyone want to put pimento in cheese?"

The random thoughts brought me up short. Afraid for my sanity, I stopped, shook my body like a dog in a bath and said, "Get it together, Jess. You can do this. Use your wits and stay calm."

My pep talk helped, so I gathered my courage and clomped to the waiting were-gorilla, who moved to the leaves and branches of the trees in and around the exhibit. He sniffed as if he could tell something was near, but I smelled so much like him, minus the lorikeet nectar, that he brushed it off.

What he didn't brush off was the direct hit to the head from the baseball. I'd thrown it up in the air, took a championship swing, and home run! I knocked his noggin hard. He let out an earth-shattering roar of pain that riled the wolves and hurtled toward me.

"You need to die," he snarled as he coiled a fist and swung toward my face. Now, I was exhausted and hurting, but when a wrecking ball is getting ready to wallop you, somewhere, somehow, you find the energy to run. In my case, it was more of a slow jog, but I got out of the way, and I did what Alupo least expected.

I ran toward the wolves.

## CHAPTER TEN

Running toward the wolves wasn't a brilliant idea, but I needed some allies, and I figured the wolves would realize the gorilla was the bigger threat. Besides, I planned to bribe them.

First, I had to get inside the enclosure, which I did by scooting around the "Learning Cabin," finding a back entrance. I rammed it with my shoulder, the door flew off one hinge, and I staggered through, hands up in fists, snarling as I challenged whatever was behind that door.

Turned out that ramming wasn't necessary because the door was unlocked and no one was there, but it looked good, in case anyone was watching. Moving on.

I spied a refrigerator in the zoo keepers' private area and flung the door open. Sure enough, it was stocked with cubes of cheddar in gallon-sized plastic bags. I grabbed two bags, plus the key hanging on a nail next to the enclosure door, and unlocked the door. At the last minute, I picked up a Jack Hanna safari hat someone had left and smashed it on my head. I could smell rain and was hoping it would arrive soon. Rain in Cleveland tends to come with dark, roiling clouds, and while the darkness might work to his advantage, being out in lake effect rain was an experience of biblical proportions. Whomever had written the Noah story hailed from Cleveland.

Before I could lose my nerve, I lurched into the enclosure, holding my cheese in front of me like a shield. "Cheese! Cheese!" I announced, my voice a crackling caw. Every wolf turned its eyes on me with a disconcerting intensity, and the entire pack was slavering at the mouth. They paced toward me in a semi-circle formation, the alpha wolf at the head, in the middle, his gold eyes on me. I backed up against the wall and closed my eyes. Maybe this was a really, really, bad idea.

Nothing happened, and when I opened my eyes, the wolves were sitting in a polite semi-circle, waiting for their treats. I opened the bag and tossed a handful of cheese to each wolf. Some of the ones in the front must have been lower in the pack because they waited to eat until the others started. They gulped down their cheese just as Kong's foot smashed their fence.

They may have been trained to sit for cheese, but no one messes with a wolf pack's territory. The alpha dropped his cheese and turned, snarling at the intruder. In an amazing display of unspoken coordination, the omega wolves pulled the three pups to a hiding place, and the rest of the pack kept their eye on the intruder.

Kong brought his other foot down on the fence, and the rest flattened, the electric part at the top, designed to keep stupid people out of the enclosure, fizzled to nothing. The wolves could now run free, but before they could realize this, Alupo, who'd run out of foliage to eat, grabbed a wolf by the scruff of the neck and held him up like a goldfish going down an eight-year-old's throat.

Or, that's what he thought he was going to do. The alpha wolf led the charge, with me following. The wolves fanned out, each taking their place, and the lead wolves, the alpha male and alpha female, sped in to bite his feet and claw his legs, ripping chunks away. I don't know how much it hurt the were-gorilla, seeing as how he shook off bullets an hour ago, but wolves are smart, and they harried his injured ankle.

He hopped around, trying to get out of the wolf pack's range, but they weren't going to let him. He dropped the wolf he'd been holding, who landed on three legs, the fourth off the ground, obviously injured. He tried to fight anyway, until the alpha barked a command, and he limped out and let another one take his place.

As the wolves harried the gorilla, I saw my chance. Following the wolves' lead, I swung my bat as hard as possible into Alupo's feet, then ran back out, only to repeat the exercise from another angle. I soon followed the wolves' rhythm of moving in, out, and around.

Alupo's body flashed like a supernova, forcing me to close my eyes. When I opened them, all I could see were spots. It took a full minute to see clearly, and by that time, he'd reformed as an unnaturally tall human. He flashed again and was back to were-gorilla form. The wolves stood back, on guard but not attacking as they watched.

Alupo flickered in and out of human form, each time forming and reforming so that his sliced Achilles tendon bled anew. He roared to the sky and got down on all fours to fight, continuing the out-of-control shape change every few minutes. "Why do you care about these animals, woman?" he bellowed, his voice a grinding, discordant mixture of human and animal. "Why do you care about those police officers? Why do you care about my revenge?"

I didn't stop fighting, knowing I couldn't stop until he was finished permanently. "Well," I said, taking a hard swing toward his knee. "That's what separates humans from monsters. We care about people and animals and the planet. We know when the natural order of things is misaligned, and we realign it." I took another thwack at his knee in the same place.

His voice was slower, more guttural, and he missed some words.

"Walk...walk away and let me eat my fill. When moon...come...I'll have power. I don't kill in Cleveland now. I kill in New York, London, Boston, big cities. Cleveland nothing. Nothing I want here."

"Them's fighting words, and there's one thing you need to know about Cleveland..." I bashed the same knee two good hits in a row and looked up at the darkening sky. "If you don't like the weather, just wait a minute."

The rain came down in buckets. It sluiced down the were-gorilla's body, dripped in his eyes, and pooled in his ears. With the wolves harrying his feet, me bashing at his knees, and the rain pouring on his head, this were-gorilla didn't know where to focus. One last, hard hit to the knee and the joint broke, giving way so that Alupo crashed to the ground in were-gorilla form.

The wolves didn't stop. Now that Alupo's head was where they could reach it, they ran in and out, tearing chunks out of his face, where the skin was delicate. Blood spattered everywhere, and the increasingly animalistic primatologist could do no more than roll back and forth, thrashing his arms and legs. He rolled over onto his stomach, almost flattening a few wolves, and reached for the alpha, who stood his ground. I had to stop this now.

Knowing one thing that would work, I ducked and weaved between Alupo's flailing legs until I was in position, then I took my bat to his king *and* his kongs. A geyser of blood shot up in the air, and the gorilla's screams echoed through the park, setting the zoo animals on edge.

The dingoes barked, the elephants trumpeted, and the lions roared. The wolves howled the news of the battle to the rest, letting the inhabitants know that they'd defended the zoo pack. The were-gorilla's screams became whimpers and then silence as he collapsed to the ground.

I didn't celebrate. The wolves thought the deed was done, but I knew better. There was only one way to be sure this were-animal never killed again, and I was sick to my stomach at the thought of it.

Like a vampire, I needed to cut off his head or remove his heart, and no amount of rationalization would hide the fact that I was killing a person.

## CHAPTER ELEVEN

I waited, watching the still form of the were-gorilla, baseball bat at the ready in case he twitched.

Barlow and Morgan came to my side with quiet steps, staring at the gigantic figure on the ground, an animal that never should have been, and I knew there was at least one more in Rwanda. I wasn't sure who to call about that, so I figured I wouldn't call at all. Whoever is there, if anyone, is surely aware of such a thing in their territory, and maybe that were-gorilla possessed more control.

"Is he dead?" Barlow asked.

"I think so, given the amount of blood he lost," I said, gesturing to the lake of blood and rain where the were-gorilla rested and beyond. It looked as if it was draining right into the "Bear" parking lot.

Morgan squatted and touched the were-gorilla's hand and wrist. "No pulse. Why isn't he turning back?"

I shook my head in a slow back and forth. "I honestly don't know, ah… here he goes. He'd been in that shape a long time, and it took longer to wear off."

"Were off?" Barlow offered the pun with a grin. I lifted the corner of my mouth. It wasn't a good enough pun for a whole smile.

"Oh," Barlow said, clearing his throat. "I'm supposed to tell you the tranquilizers are here."

I gave him a hard look and stayed silent.

The change was a slow process, and if Alupo been alive while it happened, it would have been excruciating. The feet shrunk to human size, and the change worked up toward his head. I gritted my teeth at the snap, crackle, pop of bones breaking and tendons tearing. The head shrunk, as did the tongue, but the incisors stayed, poking over Alupo's mouth and chin like a walrus's tusks. The gorilla's fur stayed as well, covering his whole body except for the hands, feet, and face. I swallowed hard at the sight and noticed Barlow and Morgan looking away.

The combination of ape and man was horrifying, but it gave me a sense of relief. This man's humanity was gone. He'd been taken by the animal and couldn't have been saved. It made my job easier.

"Hey, look, the rain's letting up," said Barlow, wringing out his shirttails and his hair. Looking at his shirttails dragging reminded me of something. But first, I took a moment to take stock of my injuries. I had an alarming popping thing in my right wrist, a healing phoenix bite on my ankle, and I was bruised from head to toe. Oh, and the gash across my forehead, which would probably leave a scar.

"Ooooops, I better check on someone. Watch the body, and if anything happens, an eye blink, a muscle spasm, take my bat and smash his head in, okay?"

Morgan furrowed his eyebrows. "Do you expect him to? I thought you said he's dead."

"He is. I'm just being cautious. Super freaks can do odd things."

Morgan nodded. "If he moves, I'll shoot him."

"Multiple times." He grimaced but nodded again.

The fatigue was catching up with me, but there was someone I wanted to see, so I retraced my steps, walked around what was left of the gorilla habitat, and made my way to the location where I'd last seen him. I bit my bottom lip and crossed my fingers.

His eyes were sad, and his tail feathers drooped. The lorikeets still tittered around him, but he'd stopped caring. His colors were just as beautiful, and his armor just as impressive, but he was aware of where he was and how he'd gotten there.

I grabbed a stick before I approached the door. The sight of the stick made him hang his head lower, and he peeked up at me from beneath his eyelashes.

"We're good, right?" I said.

Images floated in my head, flashes that expressed shame and sadness. I saw him fight the change to the Hyde version of himself and his attempt to force a burning to avoid it. I saw him eating fresh meat and his revulsion at the manic pleasure he took from the violent kill. I saw him chasing me and his true-self's relief that he was locked in the lorikeet cage.

I entered the correct door to get in, walked the path to where he stood, and by holding my hand out, asked if it was okay to pet him. He moved in closer, and I stroked his neck.

"It's not your fault. The natural order got screwed up and rebounded to you. If it hadn't, it would have infected dozens, maybe hundreds of other animals. You were the pain eater for the entire animal kingdom."

*Remorse. Regret.*

"Let's get out of here, and we'll start over again. I'm honored to meet an actual phoenix."

*Pride. Self-satisfaction.* He turned his head so I could admire his profile.

"Don't be so smug." He tweeted something that sounded like a laugh. I hit the electronic button to open the door, and the phoenix studied my motions. He wasn't going to be trapped by that trick again.

We got outside, and I tapped my foot, anxious to get back to the body. "I hope to see you again," I said to the phoenix. He gave me a hard look, and I flinched, my ankle still hurting from where'd he bitten it. "I'm sorry about bashing your head in. It wasn't personal."

The phoenix rolled his eyes. You haven't seen strange until you've seen a phoenix roll his eyes. They're grapefruit size with pupils the size of quarters, and they move like a chameleon's eyes, in almost total circles, so a phoenix eye roll puts any human teenager's to shame. The phoenix leaned his neck and head forward and, in the most calm, gentle manner, pressed his cheek to mine. I thought I felt a tingle in that cheek, but it happened so fast, I didn't have time to ask about it, because as soon as he did that, he disappeared. *Poof.*

"Nice knowing ya," I said, and then walked back up the hill, again, and shuffled my tired, aching body to the gorilla enclosure, picked my way through the broken concrete, wood, and glass, and found what I needed. I made my way out of the shambles and jumped when shots reverberated through the air.

I took off like a bat out of hell and ran as fast as I could to Morgan and Barlow. When I got there, I pressed my hand to my mouth. I was too late.

## CHAPTER TWELVE

Morgan lay on the ground ten feet away from Barlow, who knelt while what was left of Alupo tried to pull his head off like a cork out of a wine bottle. Barlow held his hands over Alupo's, which were on each side of Barlow's head, and pulled back, screaming in pain.

Alupo's body looked like a piece of swiss cheese. I could literally see through the holes in his torso and legs to the other side. Whatever caused him to regenerate didn't care about bullets, and he didn't seem to bleed anymore. Zombie were-gorilla.

Morgan *was* bleeding though, and from my angle, it appeared to be from his head, which meant he needed medical help fast, but first I had to save Barlow. I ran straight at the zombie were-gorilla, my anger giving me new energy.

"Stop!" I yelled. Alupo, or whatever this zombie version was, released Barlow's head to twist his body in my direction, but I had a head of steam and wasn't going to pussyfoot around. I lifted the steel-headed shovel I'd retrieved from the gorilla enclosure and, coming in on my left, clobbered the reanimated monstrosity with one-hundred percent good old American craftsmanship.

I also had a good bat speed, averaging seventy-miles-per hour in my prime, and I knew how to create torque.

This meant that the zombie were-gorilla's head popped clean off. It flew in the air like a fly ball heading for right field.

What was left of the body collapsed to the ground in a heap. Not one to take any more chances, I brought the square-headed cutting edge of the shovel to the body's mid-section, put my left food on the top of the blade, and pressed down like I was digging into clay.

Two more stomps later and the body was in three parts, spliced by a shit scooper-picker-upper shovel. It felt good, but the standing ovation by the cops and fire fighters, who'd come at the sound of gunfire, made me feel even better. I took a small bow.

"Hey, Jess?"

I turned to Barlow. "Yes?"

"Thanks. I thought I was going to be severed in two, Marie-Antoinette style."

I gestured to Morgan, who was already being tended to by paramedics. "What happened to him?"

Barlow massaged his neck and rolled his shoulders. "We watched the body, like you said, but neither of us believed he'd come back, so we let our guard down. We both thought this nightmare was finished, but we were wrong." He held onto the wall of the Learning Cabin and pulled himself up inch-by-inch to a standing position.

"I'm going to need a chiropractor," he commented, and then continued. "I pulled out my phone to text my wife that I was okay. Next thing I know, Morgan's in a shooting stance putting bullets into a standing and moving were-gorilla, man…whatever it was."

"I think we can call it a zombie now. It was a reanimated dead body. That's pretty classic zombie stuff, right there."

"Yeah, well, Morgan must have seen him get up and managed to get to his gun in time, but even with bullets in and through him, the zombie got to the captain and pushed him to the ground with one arm. Morgan banged his head hard and didn't get up. I was too shocked to do much but run."

"Wise. Very wise. I recommend running in situations like that," I said.

He scowled and shook his head. "I should have been smarter, faster, and helped him. As it was, all I was good for was getting caught and almost decapitated."

I gave him a bump on the shoulder. "Listen to me. Do I have your attention?"

He looked directly into my eyes. "Yes."

"You have no experience with this stuff. Today you encountered things beyond your imagination, and no one trains for this kind of thing. Except me. I train for exactly these types of things, and I couldn't have beaten him without the wolves. Don't be so hard on yourself. You did quite well for a first supernatural monster situation. I gave the same speech to Captain Morgan, by the way."

"Thanks for sharing that, but I'm not convinced. I need to better prepare now that I know what is out there."

"Can't argue with preparation, but don't let it eat at you."

We heard them before seeing them. One gorilla's hooting was matched by another's as they came up the ridge to where the remains lay. The larger, silverback gorilla spied the pieces and charged, barking and grunting a challenge before realizing that it was a dead body trifecta. He sniffed the parts, making sure the were-gorilla was truly dead.

"Rocko may be different now, Barlow," I said, studying the gorilla back in his natural form. "You won't be able to treat him as you would other gorillas. He's different now, and I don't know whether that is a good thing or a bad one."

"What do you mean?"

Before I could answer, Rocko sniffed Alupo, got a good nose full and then, nose to the ground like coondog, headed out toward the edge of the green. He sniffed around out there for a while until he found what he wanted. He returned with the zombie's head in his hands, made sure everyone was watching, placed the head on the ground, and with one powerful stomp and a roar that echoed over the whole zoo, mashed it into paste. I lowered my head as the dominant gorilla regarded Barlow, Morgan, and me.

Eyes averted, I said, "That's why. That was retribution, revenge, a human trait. Rocko made a *decision*, don't you see? That wasn't instinct. That was vengeance."

"Look at Lulu," I continued. The female gorilla hid behind Rocko giving me the stink-eye. "She couldn't care less about Alupo anymore because it is in the past for her, but Rocko remembers and understands. He wanted us to watch, to show us that he's not going to forget or forgive. He made a statement."

"I don't know how to handle this," Barlow said.

"Think about it. You get to study the first gorilla that ever became human. The fame, the fortune, the publishing opportunities! You've got a gold mine here. You'll start a new field of research."

Instead of agreeing, Barlow shook his head and winced at the pain. "No, I won't do that to him. He's a person to me now, stuck in between gorilla and man. I want to earn his trust and be his friend."

Rocko heard Barlow and chuffed at him, as if saying, "Maybe, if you stop giving me bananas."

Out of nowhere, another guest arrived at the party.

"Thank you for help us with this, ahem, unusual, situation," said Elisabeth, already tapping notes on her phone. "We at the zoo, and our funders, the Friends of the Zoo, thank you for your assistance." She stared in my eyes. "I know we can rely on your discretion, as well, correct?"

"Sure. I won't tell anyone what really happened here, but you have to do a few things for me."

"Yes," said Barlow. "We'll see," said Elisabeth.

Barlow threw her a disgusted look and said, "Name it."

"I want free, lifetime membership to the zoo for my family and my friend Angie and her family."

"Done," said Elisabeth. "That's an easy one. Just email me Angie's contact information." She noted my request in her phone.

"Barlow."

"Yes?"

"Rocko and Lulu are an item. Please put them together so they can keep each other company."

Barlow cocked his head. "That seems fair. Maybe we'll get a baby gorilla out of it."

Elisabeth poked her head up. "A baby gorilla? That would be a great news hook. We could hold a contest to name it. Wonderful, wonderful." She continued murmuring to herself about all the fabulous publicity ideas.

Barlow and I exchanged glances. I pinched the bridge of my nose and let out a breath.

"Also, stop giving him bananas. He hates them."

"Oooooookay…? I had no idea."

"If you watched his feeding habits more closely, you would have seen it. He pushed all of the bananas to the side, but he seems to enjoy apples and grapes."

"I never knew. The zoo employees make the food baskets. I will pay more attention from now on."

"Good. And last, when you rebuild this exhibit, add more trees and high climbing spaces. Mountain gorillas live on *mountains*, lest you forget. They need high spaces and opportunities for solitude."

"Anything else?"

"Yes, I want to visit him privately from time-to-time."

"Call me first and it'll happen," Barlow promised.

"Lastly, the wolves will receive regular treats from me, cheese, bones, jerky, whatever floats their boat. I'll set this up later with you, but they get them until the alpha dies, or I do, whichever comes first."

"That's very nice of you. We'll set up a plaque in your honor."

I waved that away. "Not needed. They earned it, and they were so cute when they lined up for cheese. They reminded me of kindergartners lining up for..."

I smacked my hand on my thigh. "Dammit!"

## CHAPTER THIRTEEN

I checked my watch. *Oh no. Fuck. Fuck. Fuck.* I was so screwed. Forgetting about the wreckage behind me, I humped it down the trail, skimming the wooden walkway, and dashed to my car.

Something felt off. Right. I'd lost a boot. I loved the boots, but too late now. I grabbed a flip-flop from the back of the mini-van, revved the engine, and flew down 480, praying a cop didn't stop me.

I rounded my exit and squealed to a stop at the grocery store, vaulting out of the car to rush into the entrance. My hair stood on end on the left and was squashed flat on the right. My clothes were covered in mud, manure, cantaloupe, nectar, and blood, and the unholy mess dried into a dust that migrated from my torso and legs to the floor, in a sifting, floating Pig-Pen like cloud. My boot tracked in an astounding amount of smelly, reeking brown muck, my flip-flop a jarring pink accent. Focused on my task as I was, I didn't notice all of this until later and missed the employee picking up the phone to call the police.

Skidding to a stop in the correct aisle, I locked onto my target and filled my arms, clomp-sliding toward the self-checkout.

Two newly arrived cops stopped me before I could reach the checkout aisle.

"Ma'am, you are creating a disturbance, not to mention a health hazard, and I've been asked to…" said one.

He got no further. I shook my head and snarled, sending a cloud of wet gorilla stink toward the unsuspecting officer. His eyes went wide, and he jumped back.

"You, by any chance, weren't involved in that ruckus at the zoo, were you?" the second cop asked, talking softly to me, like I might blow at any second.

I stared them down and answered with a simple, "Yes. That was me."

The officers stood aside, gestured to the door, and the first one said, "Please be on your way. I'll pay for your groceries."

Pleased but surprised, I replied with a prim, "Why, thank you." I gazed at the staring customers, most with phones in their hands, and my face reddened underneath the guck.

As I rushed toward the door, one officer said, "I guess she really loves Cheetos."

"Maybe they're good gorilla-fighting food?"

"I'm not asking."

"Me neither."

I hurried to the school, zipping into a "pick-up only" parking spot and flashed my parent badge at the startled security guard. I carried my prize in blue plastic bags in my hands, and I clutched those bags like winning lottery tickets as I shuffled, boot…flip flop…boot, to the kindergarten. I stopped for a moment to smooth my hair, straightened my shoulders, and rapped a polite knock on the door. It opened, and the kindergarten teacher, Mrs. Chen, said, "Oh, Mrs. Friedman…." She trailed off when she got a look at me. "What happened to you?"

"I fell."

"Into what?"

"Trash compacter. Very long story, very *Star Wars*, no time for it now. Don't the kids want snack?" I held up my blue bags.

"Well, Mrs. Friedman, we thought you forgot about snack…"

"Oh no. I would *never* forget snack," I said, brushing past the blinking woman, whose eyes were watering from the stench.

"Hi, Mommy!" Devi jumped up and waved her hands in the air. She couldn't care less what I looked or smelled like. It warmed my heart.

"Hey, Devi. I brought snack." I held up the bags.

"Cheetos!" the kids chorused, leaping to their feet, fighting to be the first at the sink to wash his or her hands and get a snack mat.

Another mother, dressed in stylish jeans, a peach cotton sweater, Gucci floral-embroidered sneakers, and a delicate gold necklace and earring set, stood there, mouth open in an "O." She held a platter of cut carrots, celery, and cucumbers, accompanied by healthful whole-grain crackers and hummus.

Mrs. Chen cleared her throat. "Since we thought you forgot, Mrs. Friedman, I asked Amanda's mom to bring in an alternative. We do prefer healthy snacks for our growing children."

I gave her a sideways glance, opened each bag of Cheetos, and placed them in the middle of the three tables where the kids bounced up and down in their chairs, waiting for their treat. "Yay!" they all yelled and dug into the bags, Cheetos flying everywhere as they smashed handfuls in their mouths, joyfully rubbing their orange-stained hands on their shirts.

I shot Mrs. Chen and Mrs. Perfect a look, tried to toss my hair, and strolled out, head held high. Ha. I win.

Later, at dinner, Devi regaled us with the story of my arrival and how her friends told her she had a cool mom since I let her eat processed orange powder inflated with air. I reveled in my hero status and got a wink from Nathaniel for a job well done.

I was content, aching a bit, but content that justice had been served. That teacher and fancy-pants mom had gotten what they deserved.

As for the were-gorilla, he'd gotten what he deserved, too, although I couldn't help but feel a little sorry for him. Being made fun of is damaging, and it sounded like his parents didn't respect him or what he wanted. Nevertheless, he paid for his mistakes with his life.

Only later, clean and snuggled in bed with Nathaniel, the kids asleep, did this thought occur to me. If Alupo bit a gorilla and he changed into a gorilla-man, what would happen to the wolves who bit into him and may have *eaten* his flesh?

*Ah, shit.*

I got out of bed and did ten pushups, followed by as many more as I could knock out, paying penance for the swearing of the day. I wasn't going to get any more sleep, so I called Liam and asked if we could chat.

"Now? Why?" he said.

"Because I'm afraid things are going to get busy."

"Will you warm up my bagged blood in the microwave and let me have whipped cream with it?"

"Whatever you want, Liam."

## CHAPTER FOURTEEN

After the Goatee/Curt fiasco, I was certain we were done with threats. Liam and I started seeing each other outside of Starbucks and became friends. He wanted it to be more, but I didn't. I didn't love him that way, and I'd met this guy named Nathaniel, yes, Jewish, and I was thinking he might be the one. Liam settled in with it.

At my urging, he got some help with his wardrobe, started working with a trainer, and before I knew it, I'd created a monster.

"That's a natty jacket, Liam."

"You like? I thought it went well with the wing-tips. Now that I've built up a little muscle, I fill it out."

"You are aware that we are going to watch a basketball game at a bar?"

"One has to look one's best, Jess. You taught me that, and it's worked out well so far. I got the job, right?"

"Yes." I smiled. "Congratulations again."

Liam had busted his butt and graduated early, applying for and winning a job in the IT department of Sherwin Williams, one of the biggest local employers, and well-known for good pay and advancing from within. This was a whole new start for him.

"I'm getting that apartment in Beachwood," he said. "Moving my mom in with me, too. I want her to be worry-free for the first time in her life. Now, I get to take care of her."

It was those statements that made me glad I'd arm-locked him months ago.

The bar was full of Cavalier fans wearing burgundy and gold, watching the TVs while they threw back drafts, or for the more finicky, a bottle of Eliot Ness, an amber lager made by the Great Lakes Brewing Company. A few folks got a little fancy with Yuengling, which made me laugh because my mom remembered when Yuengling was the draft beer she bought for a dollar.

"Can I get you a drink, Jess?" Liam asked, as he headed to the bar. Now that he was gainfully employed, he was always generous and bought the first round, especially since I was still on student status and getting worried about the future. My dad may have been a jerk at times, but he wasn't wrong about not being employable. No one cared that I could read Latin, Hebrew, Greek, and a little Arabic, or that I knew that accidental drowning was a common cause of death in Medieval England, or even that Lerna, the ancient city that was supposed to house the mythological Hydra was considered a sacred site and an entrance to the Underworld. I thought this was fascinating, but outside of trivia researcher for Jeopardy, I could think of no jobs for which I was qualified.

"I got you a Yuengling," Liam said, coming up behind me. He held a draft beer, which was already half-way gone.

"Thanks. Looks like the Cavs are on fire tonight."

"The Cavs are good for Cleveland's economy."

"Always thinking money."

"When you don't have any, money is important, Jess. You grew up comfortable, in a nice neighborhood, with both parents. I didn't."

"I know, and that is why I am so proud of you for what you've done to live your dream." We clinked, bottle to glass. He pivoted to watch the game.

I faced the TV screens, too, but froze when it started. A feeling crawled over me, a foreboding that crept like a shadow stealing across the street at that time of day when the temperature drops and the cold seeps into your bones. My skin tingled, and the hair on my arms stood up, and my first thought was, *death is near*.

Whoa. That was a strange thought, but it stayed with me through the half-time. My heartrate sped up, and I became hyper aware of everything around me. The water ring on the table. The scraping of chairs on the scarred wooden floor. The man next to me yelling, "C'mon LeBron." I could even the smell his date's perfume. I concentrated on that scent and realized I could go deeper. I could smell her sweat and sense her annoyance at her boyfriend for paying more attention to the game than her. Her antiperspirant smelled faintly of lavender.

A weight settled on my shoulders, urging me to sleep, to forget, to let my eyes close and relax. It whispered that everything was fine and that I was safe, Liam was safe, and nothing mattered except getting rest. The feeling was hypnotizing, and I almost capitulated, but one niggling thing in the back of my brain kept me from letting go. Who was Death, and why should Death care about me? I resisted the feeling, the alarm bells in my brain blaring louder until I was self-aware again.

The itchy, prickling feeling continued to travel across my body, and I knew eyes examined me, dark eyes, frightening eyes, eyes that no one should see in the dim light. I sat stock still, eyes on the round table in front of me, the din of the bar receding while my subconscious searched for what stalked me. The feeling worsened as the stalker's focus concentrated on the back of my neck, trying to wiggle not just on me, but in me, trying to get to my brain to trigger that primordial terror that assails us in the deepest night. *Death is near.*

I refused to let it in. Statue still, I fought so hard I soaked my shirt with sweat, and I gasped for breath.

"Jess, what's wrong?" Liam asked, shaking my shoulder. "You're pale and sweating. Are you getting sick?"

I shook my head but didn't say anything. I was afraid to move, like a rabbit caught in headlights, and I knew, just *knew*, that going out into the night was a mistake, that staying in the bar provided relative safety.

"Could you get me some water?" I croaked. Liam, brows furrowed in concern, elbowed his way to the bar to fulfill my request. As soon as he left, the feeling went away, but that didn't provide any relief, for I realized that the stalker's attention had moved to Liam.

The game ended, and the revelers left, some tipsy, some drunk, one throwing up, and others elated that the Cavs won in overtime. I still sat at the table, not moving.

"Jess. Jess. I'm worried. What's going on?" Liam shook my shoulder.

I jumped up, grabbed his hand, and tugged. "Let's go while the crowds are still here. We shouldn't be alone." I pulled him out of the bar and pushed my way into a larger group of people walking down the street to the CSU campus.

"Jess! Talk to me! You're acting spooky." Liam yanked his arm back, forcing me to turn to face him.

"Holy Jesus, Jess. Sorry. Holy Moses, Jess. Your skin is white. You have no color at all. I'm taking you to the emergency room."

I cast my eyes in every direction, trying to identify what scared me. "Do you feel anything out of the ordinary, Liam?"

"No, what do you mean?"

"Like someone's watching us?"

"If they're watching, it's only because they admire my jacket and are jealous they don't have one like it. Or, maybe it's the biceps and pecs in the jacket. That would be nice." He waggled his eyebrows up and down like Groucho Marx and posed like a runway model.

I didn't scream when hands grabbed my friend by both shoulders and pulled him into the alley behind us. I didn't scream, but I did dump my bag, grab my car keys, and my hatchet and run in after him. After all the buildup, a part of me was relieved the danger decided to appear. Action is better than inaction any day of the week.

I ran a few steps and then stopped, realizing that I had no idea what was happening, and moving forward at breakneck speed would only get me killed. I stepped backward and hugged the alley's brick wall, a lump in my throat, a chill consuming my body so that I trembled in the night. My unease settled in my stomach, and the churning acid gave me a metallic taste in my mouth.

One step. Listen. Another step. Listen. Breathe in, scent the air. Hair gel, aftershave…blood and panic. My breath was shallow as I focused on the Thing, for by now I knew it was a Thing, before me, holding my friend. I pressed a button on my key chain where I had a mini-flashlight, raised my hatchet, and…

Stopped dead.

The skinniest man I'd ever seen held Liam in his arms. His skin was bone white and contrasted with his black shirt, pants, and tie. He cheekbones stood out in sharp relief from the rest of his face, while his hooked nose and protruding browbone loomed large over his mouth and chin.

Liam was unconscious now, draped over the man's leg while the man…drank…from Liam's neck. Standing next to the skinny man, oh, hell, call him what he was, a vampire, were Goatee and Curt, somehow managing to look smug and revolted at the same time.

"I told you we weren't done with you," Goatee said. "You think you can embarrass me and get away with it? This dude's scarier and tougher than you and I put together, and I'm working for him." He let out a fake sigh. "Guess that makes you and Ginger here his target."

I ignored the human threat and leapt forward, slashing with my hatchet. I caught the corner of the vampire's trench coat, missing because he moved like lightning. I swung again and missed, the vampire far faster than I, leaving me with only a swish of sound to go by.

Goatee and Curt started at the vampire's speed and shuffled back. I shot them a look to tell them that I wouldn't forget this, and listened for Liam's breath, or his heartbeat, or anything to tell me he was alive.

"Hunter." The voice was skeletal, creaky, almost inaudible.

"Are you talking to me? Why do you call me that?"

The voice moved, and I slashed in the new direction, but missed again. The voice hissed. "Because it is what you are, even if you don't know it yet."

"Whatever, dude. Drop my friend and vamoose. I'm not afraid of you."

"I can tell, and you fought well in the bar. That's when I decided not to harm you, but to deprive you of your friend. You care for him."

"Yes, I do. What is it you want?"

"I want," whispered the vampire, his voice coming from everywhere at once, "for you to remember me." Then, a nauseating ripping sound tore through the air, and I cast my flashlight back and forth, looking for the creature and Liam. I didn't see them until I looked up at the fire escape. The vampire was three stories up, still holding Liam like a rag doll.

But now, he was dripping blood from his right wrist into my friend's mouth. I bounded up the fire escape while the vampire was poisoning my friend and slashed again, aiming for the vampire's right arm. I connected at the shoulder, using as much force as I could.

The vampire's arm landed on fire escape with a wet plop, and the vampire screamed and jumped, to where I could not tell, leaving my friend with vampire bites on his neck and vampire blood in his mouth. I turned him to the side to dump as much of the blood out as possible, but he gurgled, and I realized that there was already too much in his stomach and throat. If the tales of vampires were true, then my kind, gentle friend was about to become a monster.

That was the night Liam lost everything. I cried as I held him in my arms, not able to make sense of what had happened. Goatee muttered, "Holy shit," and ran off, Curt close on his heels. I sobbed.

A voice said, "Wow, you severed his arm at the shoulder? I don't think he can regenerate that. Can he, Mary?"

A female voice said, "No, I don't think so. Maybe. It would take a whopping amount of powerful blood to make that happen. I think that vamp is the unhappiest vamp we have in Ohio." She paused and then said, "hands down." Her male companion groaned.

"Hello! Who's there? My friend needs help!"

A man wearing a clerical collar with jeans, work boots, and a flannel shirt, held his hands out in a gesture of peace. The woman beside him wore a long skirt, a droopy long shirt, and a cross the size of a McDonald's hamburger.

The man spoke. "I'm afraid it is too late for your friend. He's going to rise."

"You mean, he's a vampire now? There's no such thing!"

"You don't believe that. You can't ignore what you saw."

"Well, I'm not letting you behead him, or whatever it is you want to do." I grasped Liam tight to my chest.

The priest sighed. "It would be a blessing for him, but I understand. Let me help you bring him down. We'll do what we can, but he will have to be monitored. If he breaks any rules, even once, he'll be destroyed."

"How? By whom?"

"By you. I have a proposition for you, Jess."

"How do you know my name? And what proposition?"

"First, we'll help your friend. Then, I'm going to offer you a job. My name is Father Paul."

"Nice to meet you, sort of. What kind of job? Who was that guy? Why was there a vampire, a *vampire*, by all that's holy, after me?"

Father Paul took the stairs, stopping before me with his hands still out. "I will explain everything, but suffice to say, you have some unique skills that we look for in our employees."

I looked at Sister Mary. "This seems to be a Catholic thing. You know I'm Jewish, right?"

Sister Mary shrugged. "We all bat for the same team."

## CHAPTER FIFTEEN

I often dreamt about that first experience, where Liam lost all he'd ever wanted and I found my calling. Now, as I dozed in our hammock out back, enjoying the feel of the breeze, I relived it again.

I became a monster hunter, and Liam learned the rules of living as a monitored vampire. He left for a while, heading down to southeast Ohio, where he could take night courses at Ohio University. I didn't know what he told his mother because that was the one subject he never spoke about, and any time I'd tried, he'd held out his hand in a warning, and I knew not to push.

He got a master's degree in computer science by taking night and online classes, but had no way to use them in any ordinary company. So, he was hired as my partner, and we put his computer skills to use for the good guys. He learned how to take blood in sips and how to get bagged blood on the black market. He also learned a couple of neato tricks, like changing his clothes with a little shimmy. I had the feeling he was more capable and powerful than I knew, but that was okay with me. He was still my friend.

I married Nathaniel, and we had a night wedding so Liam could attend. My old high school friends wanted to know who the super-cute guy was and if I would set them up on a date. I lied and said he didn't swing that way, which pissed him off to no end. It got a little more tangled when my friends passed that news on and a few guys asked me to introduce them to my mysterious friend. I blurted out that he was involved with someone, thinking that would stop this, but it was a total turn-on for some of the men.

I'd gone over this in my mind a hundred thousand ways, trying to figure out how I could have stopped it. I never found an answer, and eventually, I stopped trying. What was, was.

I shook myself out of my reverie and returned to the present. My neck was cold since I cut my hair.

I'd walked into the salon, and my hairdresser melted into hysterics, but after she calmed down, she figured out a solution, and I didn't think it looked bad at all. My husband preferred it long, but it's my hair, and I control my body.

Speaking of Devi, my messy-headed mini-me, she jumped so hard on the hammock that I only managed to escape flipping by sheer luck.

"Honey, what is it?"

"Can we keep him? Can we keep him?"

"What are you talking about?"

She tugged at my hand. "Come, Mommy. Look. Isn't he beautiful?"

I followed her to the far back of the yard. We owned a full acre, and the back part was wooded. I stopped in my tracks, and Devi jumped up and down in excitement. "He says we can call him Blaze, Mommy! Isn't that a great name? He says we can be friends."

Blaze, the phoenix, was wrapping twigs, branches, and something that looked like Christmas lights into a huge nest that sat on the ground underneath our largest tree, a cottonwood that I sort of hated because it turned my yard into a white, allergy-inducing mess every spring. James and Jack, over for a playdate with David, stood next to Devi, eyes wide. Even Jack recognized that this was the biggest parrot, or ostrich, or emu, he'd ever seen. No glamour would work on the two of them now. The veil was drawn.

Before I could stop him, Daniel snuck up behind me and ran past, his arms out wide to hug the big bird. Blaze wrapped him in his wings and nuzzled him on the head. I walked over.

"Staying awhile?"

*I like it here. There is good work to be done. I think I can help.*

"Your language is better. You're using sentences."

*I'm a fast learner. Are you okay with me staying?*

"I'm not going to argue. Glad to have you aboard. I'll have to introduce you to Liam, my vampire assistant."

*You work with a vampire?*

"It's a long story, but yes. He's got a great fashion sense and is good when the chips are down."

*I don't understand that phrase.*

"He's loyal."

*Ah. That I understand.*

I sensed a sadness in him that I wanted to ask him about, but it felt rude. "I'm warning you, the kids may want rides."

*Phoenixes don't do parties. We aren't ponies.* He drew up to his full height.

I laughed. I couldn't help it. Life had gotten even more absurd.

*You cut your feathers.*

It took me a second. "Oh, my hair. Yes, it needed to be done since I'd hacked at it with a piece of glass."

*Only defeated warriors cut their feathers.*

"Human hair is a little more complicated."

Devi came running, having gotten Nathaniel from the kitchen. "This is Blaze, Daddy. Isn't he awesome?"

Nathaniel was flabbergasted for a second, but he was skilled at making huge mental adjustments, and he went with it. "Hey, man. Nice nest."

Blaze settled in and preened his feathers.

"Do you need anything?" Nathaniel asked. Blaze shook his head no.

"Okay-d'okay then. I've got steaks to get on the grill. You sure you don't want one? I've got extra."

Devi spoke up. "He says that'd be great, Dad. He's never eaten cooked meat."

"Interesting. Well then, I'll cook his rare. See you back at the house."

And there we were, a half-hour later, eating steaks, baked potatoes, and green beans on the deck, just me, my kids, Angie's boys, my husband, and a phoenix. Liam was coming over for dessert. It felt normal. After dinner, I watched Blaze play with the kids. He was gentle, kept an eye on all of them, and they loved it when he wrapped them in his wings. He was also a damn good soccer player.

Maybe I didn't need to be afraid of babysitters anymore.

# RUNAWAY

# CHAPTER ONE

"Mom, I need to talk to you."
I was chopping veggies for our salad, but I set my knife down, turned, and regarded my eldest child, David, age eight. My husband, Nathaniel, placed the spice rub for the chicken to the side and turned as well. I brushed my hair out of my eyes, and Nathaniel pulled out a chair.

"Okay, lay it on me," I said. "If it is about the experiment you did in your room, that's okay since nothing died. The smell was a little obnoxious, but we like your curiosity."

"It's not about that, Mom, but thanks for the understanding."

"Okay, then what is it? Is something wrong?"

"Mom, come sit down." David pulled out another chair and patted the seat.

Nathaniel chewed his bottom lip. Devi, our five-year-old daughter, put her Legos away. Even Daniel, the three-year-old, toddled to his room to play with toys by himself. I picked my cuticles, forcing myself to take deeper breaths. I was almost hyperventilating.

What could it be? Age eight seemed young for girl stuff, or boy stuff, we didn't know who he might like yet. Sex stuff.

"Are you in some kind of trouble, honey?" I asked.

David shook his head. "No, Mom, nothing like that, but I do have a favor to ask."

"What is it? Tell me. I'm dying here."

"Would you chaperone our field trip the day after tomorrow? We're going to the Museum of Peoples and Culture. Matt's mom had to bail at the last minute because the baby is due and she's having, what do you call them? Confractions. So, we are down a chaperone, and they may not let us go if we don't have at least three parents. Plleeeeeaaasse. You've never gone on a class trip with us."

Nathaniel let out a whoosh of breath, clapped his hands, replaced the chair, and went back to the chicken. "You should think about it, honey," he said to me.

There was a reason I'd never gone on a class field trip. I love my children, but the thought of being on a bus with thirty fourth graders, and their teacher, and other moms made me break out in flop sweat. I would rather face down a troupe of goblins, or bargain with sasquatches, or even home a baby gowrow, if I had enough apples. I'd heard two babies were born recently, but I think they got a place to house them.

I was a Monster Hunter, and the mother of three children, David, Devi and Daniel, and I knew chaperoning would be like hell. Correction. In my line of work, we had to be careful of using words "like hell" because one never knew if we meant the literal Hell or were making an analogy. In this case, I wasn't sure which this would be.

"Let me think about it, David." Nathaniel shot me a look which meant, *"Really?"* I avoided his eyes. What did I have planned for the day after tomorrow? I checked my phone. Nothing. Training with Ovid, but that could be rescheduled. I stood, hip out and casual, thumbing through my phone, ostensibly looking at the calendar, but inside my mind was flailing for a way to get out of this.

"I'm going to place a call," I said. "Nathaniel, can you carry on with dinner?" My husband rolled his eyes to the heavens, but nodded.

Speaking of the heavens, I decided this crisis was worthy of spiritual advice, so I placed that call, then hopped into the minivan and drove where I always did when in a quandary.

Rabbi Stein knew about my monster hunting and that I worked for the Church as a Knight Templar of some sort, and he approved since I was ridding the world of evil and working for the big G. As he said, "We're all on the same team."

"Rabbi?" I knocked on his office door. His secretary was already gone for the day.

"Jess?"

"Yes, it's me. Do you have a few minutes?"

"Of course, for you? Always. Come in." Rabbi Stein's voice was strong despite his years. He lived with back pain and had gotten too thin. He needed to eat. Of course, Jewish mothers always say that about everyone. Our answer to any problem, big or small, was food. Someone died? Bring a lasagna to the family. Someone born? Bring a casserole. Someone was ill? Make chicken soup. Someone broke a leg? Cake.

"Next time I visit, I'm bringing some homemade schnitzel. You've lost weight."

"Will you make it the real way, with veal?" he asked.

"No. I don't eat veal on moral grounds. I'll make it from chicken breast."

He dismissed the offer with a wave of his hand. "Ach."

"I make very good chicken schnitzel, Rabbi. I promise you will like it."

He lowered himself to his chair, and I ignored the wince he made halfway down. He looked at me from half-lidded eyes and pointed to me with his wire glasses.

"You pound it nice and thin? It must be tender or it's no good."

"I pound it nice and thin."

"And not too much oil. Just enough, no more. You know how to do it just enough?"

"I do. Rabbi, I've been making schnitzel my whole life."

"You'll make it with salt? It needs salt. Don't go whining to me about watching my salt intake."

"What's schnitzel without salt?" I asked, my palms up.

He stared at me for another moment. "Okay, maybe I'll try it, if it's not too much trouble."

It may have taken twenty minutes of intense negotiation, but I had won round one. I texted Nathaniel to remind me to make the schnitzel.

Having reached détente on the great Schnitzel War, I told Rabbi Stein what David had asked.

"I fail to see why this is such a hard request, Jess. It's one field trip. I'd go with him if I could walk that much."

"It means I have to interact with people, Rabbi, and not just any people."

"What do you mean, Jess? I don't understand. Who are the people you are so scared of?"

I tucked my head, refusing to look at him. "Moms."

He leaned forward. "What? You're afraid of the other mothers?"

"I'm not *afraid*, Rabbi. I'm not afraid of anything." He made some movement with his hands to acknowledge my bravery in battle. I think he may have also rolled his eyes.

"I'm not comfortable around the other moms because they are so perfect, and poised, and always know what to say. I don't fit in."

The Rabbi gave me a hard look. "Jess, you sound like a seventh grader. Grow up and go with your kid to the museum. You'll both treasure the memory. It's a museum for goodness' sake. What could go wrong?"

In truth, it did go well for the first thirty minutes or so. The children were loud on the bus but didn't misbehave. I sat in a middle seat to "keep an eye on the kids," so that kept me from having to make conversation with the moms and the fourth-grade teacher, Mrs. Butler, and there was little traffic. I began to think this might be fun after all.

The Museum of People and Cultures was on the beautiful Wade Oval, near the Museum of Natural History and the Botanical Gardens. It was a lovely, sunny day, with blue skies and a pleasant temperature. I had a feeling it was all going to be okay.

My grandmother used to say, "Man plans, and God laughs."

He must have had a real knee-slapper of a day.

## CHAPTER TWO

We started the tour with a discussion of modern technology, and then the plan was to go way back in time to the famous Lucy exhibit, which presented information about our closest ancestor on the evolutionary tree. Donald Johanson, a paleontologist at the next-door Cleveland Museum of Natural History, was one of the team that uncovered Lucy, and her skeleton was originally studied at the museum before being shipped back to Ethiopia. Now, both museums had a model of her and an extensive exhibit to explain her importance.

We were lucky because a Japanese academic from University of Tokyo, Professor Noyoko, was giving the tour herself.

I would have been excited, but I'd already pissed off Mrs. Butler by giving some of the boys chewing gum. "We do not allow chewing gum in class, Mrs. Friedman! And we certainly don't allow it in the Museum!"

She said Museum with a capital M. I heard it. Having nowhere to dispose of the gum, I gestured for each kid to spit the gum into my hand. I only realized that I'd messed up yet *again* when Mrs. Butler's mouth curled in distaste.

"What?" I'd asked. "You said they couldn't chew it." She shook her head and strode away while I was left wondering what I should have done. I thought about it for a moment, got nowhere, and carried on. Social proprieties were sometimes a conundrum. I preferred straightforward monster hunting. At least you knew where monsters were coming from.

I held a palm full of partially chewed gum and boy spit, so I was relieved when Mrs. Butler suggested that we take a water break. The kids broke out their water bottles or proceeded to the nearby water fountain. I headed toward the ladies' room to throw away the gum and wash my hands.

I felt someone behind me and glanced in the mirror to see that Professor Noyoko had followed me to the restroom. I was going to thank her for taking the time to give a fourth-grade class a tour when a *fox tail* sprung out nowhere from under her skirt.

Actually, what there were seven tails. Seven bushy, reddish fox tails. I whirled to look at her and caught her staring at me. Her eyes were dark pin-points, and she twitched her nose the way a dog does when it smells something good to eat. She released a musky scent that reminded me of something from my back yard.

"Hey," I said, because I'm a dunce sometimes and that was all I could think of. "You're a fox person? A person fox? A werefox. No, that's not right." I smacked my palm to my forehead. "I know! You're…you're, what do they call it?"

Noyoko let out a bark, and the pieces fell into place. A Japanese fox spirit. A kitsune, and it was inhabiting Professor Noyoko's body.

I reached for the fox, but she ran out before I could get a good grip. I did manage to catch the tip of one tail with my hand before she pulled free, which meant she ran off with a huge gob of pre-chewed gum stuck in her fur. That was going to take a lot of peanut better to get out.

I exited, walking as fast as possible without going so fast as to raise suspicion. Yup, here I am, a mom on a field trip, nothing to worry about. I'm trying to find the class, not a fox spirit that is inhabiting a visiting Japanese professor. These are not the droids you're looking for.

Ironically, finding the class was how I found the kitsune, now firmly in human form. Professor Noyoko's body had fled to the Lucy exhibit and established itself in front of the children, in tour guide form, where she sent me a smile of triumph, trusting that I wasn't going to call her out in front of the kids. I hung in the back, trying to decide what to do about our crafty, four-footed spirit friend and why it had revealed itself to me.

We were halfway through the Lucy exhibit when one of the boys, a troublemaker if ever there was one, decided it would be funny to torture the tour guide in the only way he knew how. I realized what was happening too late.

"Shhhhh...watch..."

"Ronnie, you can't do that," came a stage whisper back. "You'll get suspended."

"Yeah, yeah I can. Look, she happened to get caught on a tree branch…" Ronnie, being quite clever although obnoxious, leaned against a fake tree centered in the exhibit meant to show that Australopithecus was partially-tree dwelling. He let it pop back up and with the innate precision of an eight-year-old boy making mischief, and caught Noyoko's skirt with a branch so that the skirt flicked up and everyone could see her underwear, or in this case, seven reddish-brown fox tails. The kids stared open-mouthed. One girl asked, "Hey, are you into cosplay? Is that an animé character? Which one?"

Professor Noyoko shrank to her fox form, a red fox with a white spot on its back, gave a yip, and ran off, knocking down several pieces of the exhibit as she did so, which caused alarms to blare and shocked security guards to put aside their Sudoku.

The kids hooted and hollered as if they couldn't believe how lucky they were to see what they thought was a museum exhibit come to life, but Mrs. Butler fainted, landing in a puddle leaking from the nearby fountain.

It was like living in the movie *Night at the Museum* but during the day and with less Ben Stiller, which was a shame because it would have been much more fun with Ben Stiller.

There was nothing I could do for the teacher, but I *could* chase the kitsune. I didn't know how Noyoko got a fox spirit inside of her, but I hoped the professor was still in there. I'd read about kitsune in some of my studies, but this was the first time I'd ever seen one.

I was ready to follow but realized I couldn't pursue the fox yet because Alice Pembro's delicate mother, Alicia Pembro, had screamed at the sight of the fox spirit and yanked the children to her side like she was pulling them out of the way of an oncoming bus. The kids' hooting turned into sobs as she pulled their arms out of their sockets.

"What was that thing?" she asked, her voice trembling and high-pitched. "It is scaring the children, and poor Mrs. Butler has had a case of the vapors."

I giggled. "A case of the vapors? That's funny! I haven't heard that phrase ever said out loud. Good one, Alicia."

Alicia's mouth hung wide and her cheeks flushed red, and I knew that I'd screwed up again. Alicia whispered something to Nathan's mom, a woman who looked like she hadn't eaten a good meal in her life but somehow managed to stay upright while wearing a king's ransom in gold and diamonds. Her left hand was so jewel encrusted, I was surprised she could lift it in the air to fiddle with her equally impressive earring, but she did, regularly. Nathan's mom, Collette—what a pretentious, snooty name—nodded sagely, looking at me the whole time with accusing eyes. I sighed.

David, my fourth grader and wise beyond his years when it came to monsters and spooky things, pulled me aside. "Mom, what was that?"

"A Japanese fox spirit. It's called a kitsune, kit-soon-ay."

His eyes lit up. "Cool!"

"Not cool. The fox spirit has taken over Professor Noyoko's body."

He pushed his lower lip out. "Damn. I think being possessed by a fox spirit could be amazing. I mean, imagine all the things you could do as a fox."

"First, young man, watch your language! Ten pushups when we get home. And second, I don't think Professor Noyoko is aware of what is happening, at least I hope not. What we must do now is get the rest of the kids together and pull Mrs. Butler off the floor. Can you help do that?"

David's look was sly. "Pull her?"

I crossed my arms. "You know what I mean. Be gentle."

"Oooooookay." David turned and called to a couple of his buddies, James and Jack, my best friend Angie's twins, and the three boys knelt by Mrs. Butler and talked to her in slow, low voices.

"I don't know what happened!" Mrs. Butler said. "Bless you boys for helping me up."

Collette and Alicia rushed over to help her, too, even though they were not needed, but they still managed to throw me the stink eye. I perked up though. At least the kitsune showed. A creepy cryptid had come to visit. That, I could deal with.

## CHAPTER THREE

With Mrs. Butler alive and well, I felt comfortable leaving. I ran in between glass cases filled with priceless items and prayed I wouldn't knock anything over, but I knew I had to move fast to follow the fox. I caught sight of Noyoko/kitsune, now in full fox form, scurrying into a room I wouldn't have noticed under normal circumstances. Its door was propped open, but when the fox ran through, it slammed shut. I slid to a stop and listened to the fading chuckling of the fox spirit.

I felt for the edges of the invisible door, as there was no obvious doorknob, and found a thin crack barely wide enough for my fingernails. Having no way to get enough leverage to open the door, I decided that I had to get in there the hard way.

I backed up, steadied my breath, and ran directly at the door executing a perfect front snap kick, which struck the door on an angle as the door opened from the other side. I ricocheted backward, fell on my ass, and knocked over a statue, which knocked over a vase. The statue, a happy sitting Buddha, lost an ear, and the vase tumbled, hitting an innocent bystander on the hip, until crashing to the floor, shattering into porcelain splinters. The room fell silent, that awful silence when you know everyone is looking at you and it would be best if the floor opened and swallowed you. It took no more than ten seconds.

What's more, I fell on my tailbone and that *hurt*.

The man who emerged from the door was a tall, thin, Japanese man with glasses wearing a suit, tie, and a name badge that read, "Dr. Katso Juro." His face was pale, like he'd never seen the sun, and he had a skinny little mustache that looked like a millipede had set up residence on his face. The suit fit badly, his tie was stained, and when he got near me, he smelled of stale body odor, staler coffee, and something fishy. He towered over me as I climbed to my feet.

"What's wrong with you?" he demanded, his eyes buggy and his mouth opening and closing like he was sucking on something sour. "You've destroyed a priceless vase and cracked a flower garden Buddha, worth hundreds of thousands of dollars."

"I was chasing a fox."

Dr. Juro squinted at me, moving close so he could see my eyes. "Did you hit your head?"

I pulled back to avoid the stench. "No, I don't think so."

He pursed his lips and pointed a finger at me. "Drugs? Alcohol?"

"No, I needed to get into that room, and there was no way to open it."

Dr. Juro crossed his arms. "Did it occur to you to knock?"

It honestly hadn't.

My faced flushed, so I turned toward the damage and watched as the bystanders backed away in graceful ripples, giving me a wide berth. I grimaced at the statue laying on its side and picked it up, along with the ear, and murmured an apology. The statue winked, and a voice inside my head said, *Exorcism. You must chase the spirits out.*

I peered at the statue. "Did you say that?" I asked out loud, not noticing the security guards being ushered into the room, along with an actual cop. I think the woman following them was a hostage negotiator.

The voice didn't return, but I knew it had spoken. I brought the statue closer to my face and studied it, murmuring, "I know you spoke. If you have other pieces of advice to give, now would be the best time. For example, you could explain why you said spirits, plural. There's more than one?"

Nothing. Silence.

"Fine! Be evasive. You're a Buddha, after all. Isn't that sort of your shtick?"

The hostage negotiator, or counselor, or whatever she was, spoke to me in a careful, kind voice. "Ma'am, my name is Dr. Patty Turillo. Please put the statue down and slowly step away. The officer here will help you and we'll get this all straightened out."

It finally dawned on me that I might be in a wee bit of trouble, and I could have sworn the fox cackled again. I turned to the police officer, ready to somehow, someway, talk myself out of this.

Instead, I sagged in relief, holding out my hand for a shake. "Officer Bob! How's the car? I didn't ever get inside it, so it should still be clean, right? I'm so glad you're here. You can vouch for me. How's Captain Morgan?"

Officer Bob ignored my outstretched arm and dropped his face into both of his hands and mumbled something that sounded like, "Oh God, not again." But, I could have heard wrong.

The hostage negotiator peered at Officer Bob, her face so scrunched up I was afraid someone would hit her on the back and she'd stay that way. "You *know* this woman?"

Officer Bob gave a grudging nod. "Do you remember the zoo incident a few weeks back?"

Her eyes widened. "The…the…gorilla…one?"

"Yup!" I said. "That's it. That's the one. Messy. I admit I hadn't ever seen a gorilla turn into a human before. That was a shocker. That reminds me. I have to visit and see how Rocko and the wolves are doing."

Dr. Turillo rubbed her temples and pulled Bob aside. Meanwhile, the security guards moved the other visitors out of the room. Officer Bob placed a call to someone, and the three had a convo of some kind while I waited, unconsciously rubbing the Buddha on his round belly. Juro was examining the porcelain shards, trying to put them back together. I could have told him there was no way that would work. My family has broken more water glasses than I could count. Plus, several wine glasses, beer bottles, picture frames and a pane from our front window. We are tough on glass.

A low, comforting humming sound, like a cat's purr, filled the air, and I looked around for its origin. I couldn't see anything that would cause that sound, so I closed my eyes to hone in on it. I opened my eyes in shock when I realized the humming came from the Buddha. I held it out from me, like Hamlet with Yorick's skull, and examined it from every angle. I shook it, turned it upside down, even looked for a key in the back, but even without any obvious way for it to make sound, the Buddha kept humming at a modulated pitch that I found quite soothing.

I took a few moments while the three members of the authorities had their convo to move myself to a place of acceptance. The Buddha was humming to me, enjoying the tummy rub, and had told me we needed to do an exorcism to remove the fox spirit, or spirits. I didn't quite follow that part. *Take help where you can, Jess. Take help where you can, no matter how improbable the source.* I'd recently popped the head off a zombie were-gorilla with a bat. A talking Buddha statue was nothing.

The three judges came to a decision, but I could tell by Dr. Turillo's posture that it was a two to one majority decision, not unanimous.

"We've decided we are not going to arrest you," Officer Bob announced, ignoring Dr. Turillo, whose face was a picture of disgust. "But Captain Morgan wants to know what is going on, and he said to tell the truth. He'll believe you."

"I respect that man. So, here's the situation. A lovely young woman, a professor, has been possessed by a kitsune, a Japanese fox spirit. This one has seven tails, which is good, because it means it is not at its full strength yet. If it had nine tails, that would be…"

Juro spoke up. "…bad. Very bad. Are you saying Professor Noyoko is possessed?"

I nodded.

"That's great!"

Now it was my turn to scrunch my face in confusion.

"No, I mean, it's not great that she's possessed, but she hasn't, well, you know, wanted to go out with me, and maybe this is the reason why. We need to exorcise the kitsune right away."

I pretended to think about it while Officer Bob turned sideways and whistled and the negotiator stared, slack-jawed. I thought Patty Turillo was becoming more unhinged minute-by-minute. I didn't have the heart to tell Juro that Professor Noyoko's lack of interest might not be the result of the fox spirit and could be more about his personal hygiene.

Buddha was silent on the subject.

Breaking the silence and pushing us past that odd moment, Officer Bob took a deep breath and said, "Okay, I believe you. This isn't any stranger than the were-gorilla. Is the kitsune any danger to museum visitors?"

I cocked my head. "By danger you mean, like eating them?"

"Yes, Mrs. Friedman, eating people is a good example of what I mean." Officer Bob was gritting his teeth.

"Snarky! I'm impressed." I got serious for a moment. "Kitsune are troublemakers but not killers. If we can close the Asian antiquities area and neighboring exhibits, I think we'll be fine."

"I'll let the museum officials know, and I'll stay here with you in case you need backup. Dr. Turillo, you can go now. Thanks for your help."

Patty Turillo was less than pleased at being dismissed, and it was obvious she thought we'd all lost our minds. She whispered something into Bob's ear, and he shook his head. She tried again, but he held up his hand. "You weren't there, Patty. You don't know."

Dr. Turillo threw up her hands, pivoted on one heel, and stormed out. Bob followed, holding up a finger to indicate we should wait for him.

"Officer?" I caught him before he walked out of hearing range. He turned.

"My son is here on a field trip with his school. Can you tell them that I'm sorry I can't finish the tour with them?"

"Which school district?"

"Shaker Heights."

"You got it."

That left me with Juro, which wasn't good because Juro and I immediately squared off into a spaghetti Western Mexican stand-off. "How could you not notice Professor Noyoko's tails or changes in her personality?" I asked.

"How come you know about kitsune?" he countered.

"I'm an official Monster Hunter."

"No such thing."

"Yes, such thing. We're sort of modern Templar Knights."

He snorted. "You'd think you'd be smarter."

I shot back. "You'd think you'd bathe."

Officer Bob returned, unaware of our hostilities. "So, how do we catch a fox?"

"Well," I said, "this fox spirit is quite the runaway. It might want to lead us on a chase, for the fun of it, or it may be doing it for another reason. It revealed itself to me in the ladies' room, like it was taunting me, and I have no idea why. In lieu of knowing that answer, the other big question is, what do we do when we catch it? Remember, Dr. Noyoko is still in there somewhere. We don't want to hurt her."

Juro blinked, and I thought his eyes changed from round to almond-shaped. I gave it a brief "huh," and then my brain moved on when Juro said, "I know something about the exorcism ceremony, but I can't recall all of the ingredients. I do have a text somewhere in my office that might tell us." Juro made a weird blooping sound, sort of a burp and almost a hiccup. "I know we need a Buddha statue. The Buddha oversees the exorcism."

"We already have a Buddha, so we're ahead of the game," I said, holding up the statue, who sent me a wave of emotion, telling me he was delighted to be a part of the ceremony.

"I can't believe you broke him. We'll have to reattach his ear. Hand him over, and the ear, too," said Juro.

"Or the fox gets it?" I rolled my eyes. "No. We need him, and I think he wants to be a part of the exorcism."

"You think it wants something? It's a statue; it doesn't *want* anything."

I should have left it there, but my mouth sometimes keeps going before my head can stop it. "No, this representation of Buddha is communicating with me, and he says he wants to be part of the action. Here," I said, holding up the statue, "if you listen closely, he's humming something. I think it is a mantra of some kind."

"A mantra." His voice was flat.

"Yes. Listen for yourself." I held the statue up so he could listen to it like a seashell.

Juro scoffed and released a bubble from his lips. I was about to ask if he was okay when he said, "You're infuriating."

I gave him a slow up and down of my head. "You are not the first to notice."

"Arrogant."

"Maybe. Sometimes. Not really."

"Careless."

I toggled my hand back and forth.

"Impious and sinful."

My anger was a harsh and exquisite thing, and it rose like a flame to a wick. The Buddha's spirit flinched.

I got in B.O.-coffee-fishy-smelling Dr. Juro's face, and I knew that my mouth was curled in a snarl. "That, I am not. You may accuse me of many things, and I'm human, so I'm probably guilty of all of them. But impious? Sinful? Wicked? No. That you do not get to decide."

Officer Bob got in between us and did what police officers are supposed to do, kept the peace. "Hey guys, let's tone things down here, okay? Gotta save Professor Noyoko from the nine-tailed fox, right?"

"Seven-tailed," Juro and I said simultaneously. My jaw was clenched, and my arms were crossed over my chest. I felt the tension radiate from me, and worse, I realized that the Buddha's spirit had withdrawn. I took a deep breath, counted to ten, let it out, and said a prayer for patience. I said this prayer often. I was aware of my faults, and impatience was at the top of list. I whispered another apology to the Buddha and gave his tummy a quick rub. He warmed in my hands and hummed a long ohm to help me calm down and focus.

Forgiveness is a beautiful thing.

I smiled, a genuine one because the Buddha's spirit warmed me inside as well, and said, "Let's start again. My name is Jess Friedman. I'm a Monster Hunter, which I know is unusual, but it's true. The Catholic Church established a defense force to combat the things that go bump in the night. We're an odd mix of folks, but in the end, our main goal is to rid the world of beasties before the beasties wreak havoc on the world."

Juro looked me up and down, fixating on the six-pointed star necklace I wore. "Aren't you Jewish?"

"We all bat for the same team."

The Buddha's voice was solemn. *That we do.*

Juro's eyes narrowed. "You don't carry a gun."

"I prefer hatchets and baseball bats, but I left mine at home today."

Juro said nothing, but did take a step back, glancing at Officer Bob to make sure he'd heard what I said.

I continued. "Now that we've gotten over the pleasantries, Dr. Juro, can you take us into your secret lair, or whatever lies behind that door so we can learn about what items we need for the exorcism?"

Juro led the way to the door and ushered us in. I was ready for voodoo dolls or other rare objects, so I was sadly disappointed.

It was an office. A boring office with a four-drawer steel cabinet, two wooden desks, one with paper stuck under its front-right leg, and two rolling chairs that had seen better days. One of the desks was covered in papers, pens, and books. Two half-full cups of coffee balanced on the corners, and the Dr. Juro's lunch bag was on top of the cabinet. Juro had a sweater hanging on the back of his chair. The other desk was immaculate and unused. There was a door on the other side of the room.

Juro gestured with his arm, releasing a wave of body stink. "This is the office Noyoko and I share. She doesn't like to work here, however. She prefers the museum's research room on the top floor. I don't know why. It's so hot up there."

Officer Bob coughed and stepped on my foot. I breathed through my mouth.

"It's a little close, you know?" I said. "Maybe she needs open spaces."

Juro seemed to consider that. "Good thought. I'll have to ask her." He searched in a mountain of books that were piled in a tilting tower on a stool in a corner of the office. I wasn't sure what was in those books, but I really didn't want them to hit the ground. Sometimes paranormal things get annoyed when their sacred writings aren't treated with respect.

Juro isolated one book, leaving the others in a leaning tower of tomes. He scrambled through the pages, running his fingers down each folio, speed-reading as he went. Officer Bob and I waited, Officer Bob standing still, his face serene, me tapping my foot and chewing my nails.

"Did you find..." I got no further when Juro held up his palm.

I hummed "Stop in the Name of Love," and I could tell by the shade of his ears that this annoyed him to no end. I kept it up until Bob elbowed me.

I was so frustrated that I thought I was going to bleed out my eyeballs. Juro flipped to another chapter, and I thumped my head against the door in a steady rhythm. Another eon passed, which was probably only twenty minutes, when Juro said, "Found it!"

I nearly cried with relief.

"Here are the ingredients. An egg, a Japanese cherry blossom, a piece of volcanic ash, purified water, and a slab of petrified wood. Oh, and the Buddha statue."

Officer Bob's face was screwed into a question mark. "Why those things?"

I answered, realizing what they were from other ceremonies. "An egg for rebirth; a cherry blossom for air; ash for fire; water, well that's obvious; and wood for earth. Buddha is the divine will that brings these things together and creates life."

Juro nodded, blinking furiously.

"Are you okay?" I asked.

He shook his head. "Feeling a little funny, in fact. I'm parched. I need to get some water."

"What's on the other side of the door?" Bob asked, jerking his chin to the far wall.

"A hallway. We have inner corridors and rooms that allow us to move from exhibit to exhibit without walking through the museum proper."

"Why don't we do a sweep and see if we can find the fox while you get something to drink and take some acetaminophen or something," I said. "You look a little blue around the gills."

The back alleys of the museum were bare of any decoration, which seemed strange to me given the amount of arts and crafts in the place. Plain wooden doors led to offices on either side, and the overhead lighting was gruesome. There was no possible way anyone could look good in that light, but I assumed the museum staff were above that type of thing, concentrating on the cultures and evolution of the world. Or, something like that. They may have been frugal, given they worked off grants and disappearing state and federal funds. I clucked my tongue at that, experiencing a wave of fury at the stupidity of the people in Washington who thought it was okay to cut funding to the arts and sciences. Idiots.

The Buddha sent me a quiet ohm, and I bit back my anger. *Focus, Jess. Focus.*

I smelled the fox before I saw it. It gave off a musky scent that tickled my nose.

"There, up ahead!" Officer Bob pointed. "Whiskers!"

A flash of fox fur had us running down the hallway, to the left, and down another hallway, the white underside of the fox's tails our beacon forward. That and the snicker, snicker the fox made as we chased it like the Three Stooges.

"Wait!" I said, drawing to a stop. "We're chasing it, but that's stupid because we have no way to catch it. Will a box hold a kitsune? A cage? Or could we chase it into a closet?"

Bob looked up at the ceiling as if the answer was written there.

"Okay," I said. "We don't chase the fox now. We gather our supplies for the exorcism and then figure out how to catch the damn thing. Meanwhile, we also look for clues to the bigger picture. I'm not convinced the fox is on its own."

"Why do you say that?"

"Someone had to summon it." Bob's eyebrows scrunched together while he considered that statement.

"So, we have a bigger bad guy? The fox is an underling?" he asked, tapping his index finger to his lip.

"That's my hunch."

"In real life, the underlings get it in the back, and the big boss gets away."

"Not this time, Bob."

We made our way to Juro's office to get back into the Asian artifacts room. Before we got there, Officer Bob held me back. "Are you thinking what I'm thinking?" he asked.

"Yeah," I said. "Juro isn't telling us everything."

"I really don't like that guy," Officer Bob said, putting his hand on his Taser.

I glanced at his hand. "Bob!"

"I have a sixth sense about people, Mrs. Friedman. You have to develop it when you become a police officer, and I'm telling you, something about that guy is fishy. Maybe he's the big bad guy and he's playing dumb."

I studied him with new interest. "Tell me about this sixth sense of yours, Officer."

"It's nothing. No more than other cops have. I'm a good lie detector, is all, which is why I believe you, even though what you say is unbelievable."

I continued to study him. "Verrrrrrry interesting, Officer Bob. Verrrrry interesting."

We headed back out into the exhibit area, and I placed the Buddha on a display table. "I'll be back," I promised. The Buddha let out a deep cleansing breath and sent me a mental picture of a person doing a downward dog. Great, now I had a statue suggesting yoga postures. Maybe I did have anger management issues.

## CHAPTER FOUR

Officer Bob's statement about his sixth sense reminded me of my mother. She was an excellent lie detector, which strangled my youth something fierce. My mom was no bigger than I am, but she seemed huge to my eyes, and I admired her ability to chop an onion, bone a chicken, or shred a carrot without looking at her hands. She had a talent for knives.

Only two months after Liam's turning by the skinny vampire and my introduction to the Diocese's role in monster hunting, my world exploded again. My mom was hit by a runaway truck while driving over the Williamstown Bridge from Williamstown, West Virginia, to Marietta, Ohio, approaching Ohio State Route 7. The original bridge was built in 1903, but it had been updated in the early nineties and was the twenty-eighth longest bridge in North America, at least that's what I've been told.

I still remember the knock at the door. It came in the middle of the night, and I refused to answer it because I knew, just knew, that something was terribly wrong. My father answered, heavy flashlight in his left hand.

"Who is it?"

"Mr. Friedman, my name is Trooper Finlay, from the Ohio State Troopers. I need to speak with you. I'm sorry, but there's been an accident."

Silence. I waited upstairs with my blanket to my mouth, not screaming out loud but screaming inside. I rocked back and forth. "No. No. No. No…"

My father opened the door, and the news was plain.

"Sir, your wife was driving a 1985 Chrysler LeBaron with the old-fashioned wood paneling, correct?"

My father hung his head and whispered, "Yes."

The Trooper, whose job sucked at that moment, put his hand on my father's shoulder, a genuine touch of grief to his voice. "I'm sorry sir, but your wife's car was struck by a pickup truck and went overboard…"

I tuned out the rest out because none of it mattered. We didn't go when they pulled out the wreckage, but we did briefly see my mother's mangled body. She had bounced around inside the car, even though she always wore a seatbelt, and was battered, bruised, and bloody. Her body didn't look anything like the loving mother I knew.

They never found the truck or the driver, and we buried her in a Jewish cemetery only a few blocks from our home. I could walk there whenever I wanted to talk to her, and sometimes I did, but as time passed, I realized she wasn't there. She'd gone somewhere else, and I'd have to wait to see her again.

For months, I couldn't speak without crying, so I became silent and grieved with my father, who diminished in size and personality like a balloon deflating.

"Dad, do you want dinner? I'll make you something special. Anything you want."

"No. I'm not hungry."

"You have to eat something. Maybe an egg?"

He waved his hand at me but smiled a small smile. "You sound like your mother."

"She would want you to eat."

He tilted his head. "Okay, maybe an egg."

I made him the egg, slid it in front of him, and handed him a fork. "Here, Dad, just the way you like them with a little cheese and fluffy."

"With too much salt?"

I nodded. "Of course, with too much salt."

He sighed and put the fork down. "Your mother wouldn't want me to eat too much salt. She was always bugging me to be careful."

"Right now, she would have wanted you to eat anything. Please, I'm not leaving until you get some protein in you."

"Stop pestering."

He finally ate the egg and a little bit of pineapple, but his meals were always small, and though he returned to work, there was something missing that never came back. A piece of his soul broke away the day she died and went with her.

I threw myself into my training, which is how I met Ovid, and I learned that he dished out advice and insults like a baseball pitching machine programmed to kill.

"Move your foot over to the right. You'll get more balance."

"If you only focus on your feet, how will you know what the monster is doing right in front of you?"

"Now you've lost your feet again." He'd slap his hands together in frustration.

"What do you mean, you can't concentrate on your hands *and* your feet? Don't whine. Keep practicing! This has to be natural."

"You're out of breath already? Only one mile. Guess what, slow-poke, you get to do another. When a chupacabra is chasing you, he won't slow down and say, 'Take a minute.'" He poked me in the chest. "Run like your life depends on it. Because it does."

Since I'd chosen a camping hatchet, he insisted I learn to throw it. "Camping hatchets don't have the best shape or weight distribution for throwing, but it can be done if you focus on technique. Hatchets are really much better as a hand-to-hand tool or for functional things."

"Like cutting off fingers?" I asked.

He gave me a pained look. "No, well, yes, but I meant for building fires, prying open doors, smashing crates, and breaking windows."

"Oh." I measured my steps from the target, turned, and threw again. I threw hundreds of times. I also trained with a real tomahawk, which was much easier to throw.

"You've got that down with your right hand," he noted one day. "Aren't you a switch hitter?"

"Yeeaaahhh," I replied, looking at him sideways. I didn't like where this was going.

"Time to learn with your left hand," he replied with an evil grin. I dropped my head, resigned to my fate.

That's how it went, day-after-day, until one practice, I got a "good."

I stopped chucking the 'hawk.

"What did you say?" I asked.

"I said, 'don't get cocky,' and get your head in the game."

"I thought so." I waited a beat. "When do I get to kill real monsters? When do I go after that son-of-a-bitch vampire that turned my friend?"

Ovid got right in my face. "You don't get to go after Pascal. Ever. Got it? There are other monsters to fry."

"He has a name?"

"Yes, Pascal."

"Any relation to Blaise Pascal, the mathematician?"

"You remember your history. I'm impressed. Yes, not just related, but the very same one."

"No! That's impossible."

"Yes, possible," Ovid said, shaking his head. "Pascal was always in ill health in the mid-1600s and he sought healing through prayer, but illnesses of the body do not always respond to the wishes of the spirit. After he turned thirty-nine, he'd had enough of being sickly and resolved he would either find a way to heal or die before forty."

"Who turned him?"

"When Blaise Pascal was younger, his father broke his hip, and two of the most prominent doctors of the day, Deslandes and de la Bouteillerie, attended him. The father survived and walked again, rare for the time, so Blaise sought help from both. It was Monsieur Doctor de la Bouteillerie who proved to be the man with the answer. In his study of medicine, he had looked for the secrets to life, to eternity, to avoiding frailty and death. That led him to vampires, which in turn, led Pascal to vampires. We don't know who turned Pascal because, despite de la Buteillerie's fascination, he himself never became the undead."

I considered this as I slugged down a bottle of water and wiped away the sweat from my neck. I wanted to get this Pascal, and even though I wasn't ready yet, I would be ready one day. I didn't care if Ovid or the Catholic Church gave me permission. I was going to find this guy and stake him so he couldn't move and drag him into the sun. I'd let him watch the sun rise knowing that any minute he'd burn, and I'd place him feet to the east, head to the west, so he could watch himself burn inch-by-inch.

Yeah, that sounded about right.

## CHAPTER FIVE

After he'd been turned, Liam had rented a tiny apartment in the dark side of town, where they didn't ask questions about why he wanted to sign the lease at midnight. The Diocese hadn't let him out of their sight for a full month, teaching him the rules of behavior. If they'd had a leg bracelet to put on him, they would have. Instead, they had me. His behavior was my responsibility.

He'd been working a night shift at a local bar and had hidden his current situation from the owners, but it was tough. He became my liaison to Father Paul and Sister Mary, and our computer expert. He'd become proficient in hacking, which though illegal, was helpful and necessary. Each day, I said a prayer to thank the big G for helping us fight the big bad and slipped in a request for a hall pass on our pernicious ways.

"He's really *the* Pascal?"

"That's what Ovid said," I responded, sitting way back on the blood-red suede sofa Liam bought as an ironic symbol of what he'd become. The apartment had one walk-in closet, and that's where he slept.

"Why me?" Liam asked. "Why choose me of all people?"

"I don't know, Liam. I'm sorry."

"Stop saying that. It's the millionth time, and once again, I say, it wasn't your fault. It was that rat-bastard Pascal's fault, and I mean to see him dead for it! He ruined my life!"

I was silent. It wasn't that he wasn't right. It was the growl and vehemence with which he said it. I wasn't used to that tone, that ferocity, coming from Liam's mouth. This was the gentle young man who asked me to walk him to his bus stop.

Except it wasn't. Not anymore. The person in front of me was a vampire, and without guidance and friendship, he would lose his humanity and become a killing machine like the vampire that turned him. I highly doubted that little ten-year-old Blaise Pascal had turned to his mom and dad and said, "You know what I want be when I grow up? A skinny, blood-drinking raging creature of death."

No, he did it to avoid pain and live longer without suffering, but whatever it was, the virus or chemical or magic, that turned people into vampires ate at them. As it had been explained to me, if Liam didn't have constant contact with humanity to ground him, his goodness would leak away until there was nothing.

Liam pulled a bag of donated blood from his fridge, tore the corner, and downed it. He drank at least three of these, every night. "I hate that I have to drink this, Jess, but if I don't..." He trailed off.

"What?"

"If I don't, I can't think normally. I thirst for blood like a dying man in the desert thirsts for water. It's all I can think about. I can smell it in the air, taste the particles on my tongue, and I'll do anything to get it. Anything, Jess."

"So, we'll keep you well fed."

He sat next to me on the couch, looking down at his shoes. "Jess. I've lost an essential part of who I am. I can't promise I can control this thirst. What if I'm near you when I lose control? What if I hurt you? Kill you?"

"You won't." I swallowed hard as I said it. I knew I couldn't promise that, but I wanted to.

He grabbed my arm and looked me in the eye. "Promise me you'll kill me if I show any sign of losing control. Any sign at all. Don't hesitate. Take my head with that ridiculous hatchet of yours. Carry a stake at all times."

My tears ran hot down my cheeks. "I promise."

"Okay." He stood, tugged the corners of his jacket, held out his hand to me, and said, "Let's go hunting. I don't care what the Church says or Ovid says. I want to find Pascal, and I know where to start."

I grabbed my bag, wiping my eyes. "Lead on, MacDuff." I held the door for him and gestured him through.

He paused in the entrance. "You know the real line is 'Lay on, MacDuff?' right?"

I pulled up sharp, affronted, hand to my heart. "And damn'd be him that first cries, 'Hold, enough.' Please, who do you think I am? An amateur? I was a classics major, for God's sake."

He held out his hands in mock defense. "Just making sure you haven't lost your edge."

I muttered under my breath. "I'll show you my edge, vampire."

Liam snorted. It was nice to feel normal when everything was off the rails.

We walked a few blocks and made it to the bus stop where he used to disembark for home. Now, we went the other direction.

Few people were on the bus at that time, but one college kid flinched when we boarded. I didn't understand why until I took a second look at Liam. At night, he was nothing less than terrifying, even doing absolutely nothing at all. His skin was drawn and cheekbones hollowed, but his lips were full and barely covered his fangs. As I followed him to the seat, I got a chance to look at his eyes. They glittered like diamonds set in coal, and there was no way anyone could mistake them for human. They were the eyes of monster keeping control of his humanity by a thread.

That's when it really hit me that I might have to kill him one day.

We took the bus to the Cleveland State University stop where I had waited with him many evenings, and where we had taken on two creeps who I had not-so-affectionately named Goatee and Curt, the first because he had a goatee and the second because his name was actually Curt. I'm nothing if not creative.

The thought of them made me realize what we were doing. "We're going to find Goatee and Curt, aren't we?"

Liam grinned, his incisors gleaming long, sharp, and white in the streetlight. "I thought we should see how they like me now."

"Where should we look first?"

"Let's wander a bit. I think I'll know them by their smell."

I squinted at my dentally challenged friend. "You can smell them?"

He winked at me. "Seems to be a perk."

I stepped back several feet. "What does my shampoo smell like?"

He answered promptly. "Almonds and vanilla. I think it's that one with argon oil that you like."

"Dang."

We walked away from the university, as if we were headed toward the

Flats, then turned onto East 13th Street toward St. Clair. We knew the slugs wouldn't be hanging out anywhere near ritzy Playhouse Square, so they'd be somewhere between where we were and the Lake. That was a lot of territory, but all we could do was look.

Or, maybe looking was not all we could do. Liam was up for a little intimidation.

"Hey," he called to some teens drinking on the corner of Hamilton Street. The kids shoved their bottles behind them, and several scattered, but one guy and his homies decided they'd stand up to the intruders.

"Why you down here? This is our territory, whitey," said their leader while his friends snickered in the background. This wasn't even a racist thing; the boy called it as he saw it. Liam was paper white.

Liam took a few steps closer, and the leader stepped back a few steps before realizing what he was doing. He did a little jerk with his neck and puffed up his chest and shoulders.

"You need to leave, now." Gotta give it to the little guy, he was brave.

"No. I don't. I need you to deliver a message." Fast as a snake, Liam whipped his hand out and caught the boy by his shirt. The boy's compatriots took off, running as fast as their legs could carry them. Nice friends.

Liam pulled the boy close so he could see his fangs and eyes. "A while ago, I ran into a guy with a goatee and a friend named Curt. I'm looking for them. You know where they are?"

The poor kid pissed his pants, and I felt sorry for him.

"Hey," I said to Liam, placing a hand on his shoulder "He's a teenager drinking on a corner. Gentle."

Liam let the boy go. "Pass it around. Tell them I have some information for them and they should meet be at the bus stop up by Euclid and East 22nd."

"Oooookay, man. Whatever you say," stammered the boy, backing away fast. As soon as he was twenty feet or so away from us, he threw his fist in the air. "You freak!"

"You scared the bejeezus out of him." I had my hands on my hips and was not happy.

"I didn't hurt him, and I didn't drink from him, and now we can find the creeps we want. Walking around blind wasn't going to do it."

"I'm not sure about this."

"Well, get sure, because we're going to do it again. Come on."

I followed, but I stopped after a few feet.

"What?" he asked, turning to look at me.

"No more scaring kids."

He hung his head, eyes closed, and we stood in silence for several seconds. "Right. You are right, Jess. Keep reminding me. Don't let me fall over that cliff."

"I won't. Promise. Now, who do we go rough up?"

"How about Snuggles?" His face split into a grin.

Now, that was an idea I could get behind. We crossed a couple of streets, getting a little closer to the Lake, until we saw the row house where Snuggles dealt his poison. Everyone knew about Snuggles, but no one did anything to him because he had chased out all the competition. Even the cops found it easier to deal with one thug instead of three, so they made arrests on a quarterly basis, kept an eye on the purity of the stuff he was selling, and tried to keep kids away. I wasn't blaming them. It was, honestly, a good plan.

That didn't mean I had to like him. I'd watched some friends fry their brains on his heroin and heard of too many drug deaths where the cops found the bodies in the streets. If we could ruffle him up a bit, I'd consider it a public service.

Snuggles was a large man. Jabba the Hut size large, with a penchant for beer. He never touched his own product, but he swilled beer six packs at a time. As a result, he had the unfortunate habit of belching every few seconds. I was never sure how'd he gotten the nickname Snuggles, but no one called him anything else.

"Stealthy or head on?" Liam asked me, as we watched the ebb and flow of users and pushers in and out of his house. I got my arsenal situated.

"Fuck stealthy." I strode across the street, hatchet in one hand, bat in the other, other goodies in my backpack.

Liam caught up. "With you, it's always head on."

"No need to bring my sex life into this, Liam. Now, be a good vampire and put your scary face on, would ya?" Liam grunted, and I turned to see what he'd done. His fangs were down, and he must have deliberately cut his tongue because they dripped blood down his shirt. His eyes were that unnerving black diamond glitter and, new to me, he'd grown long claw-like nails. Nice. If I didn't know he was such a pussycat, he'd scare the shit out of me.

Liam took the lead, and one look at his face made anyone standing on the steps, the porch, or sidewalk step aside. He gave one good growl, and they scattered.

A deep voice echoed from inside the house. "Who's the animal out there scaring off my customers? Is that you, Jimmy, showing off your tongue piercing again? That's unsanitary, you know. Buuuurrrrrrrrppp!"

We opened the screen door and walked right in.

Snuggles sat in a Laz-e-boy chair that must have been special ordered to hold his bulk. Dollar bills in a multitude of denominations lay in piles around him, as well as envelopes of white powder. A small rat of a man kept the inventory organized. When rat-man saw Liam, he backed into a corner, holding a bag of smack like it was magic fairy dust that could make the monster go back under the bed.

Snuggles couldn't move so he pulled the lever to sit up, and said, "What the hell? What the fuck are you? Who are you?" He guzzled the rest of a beer and belched.

That was my cue.

"Hey, Snuggie. My name's Jess, and this here is Liam. He's in a bad way. His plastic surgeon messed up, and he's pretty ticked about it."

"What the fuck is he? He want some stuff? No problem. First bag free."

I swung my hatchet in a circle like a lifeguard's whistle. "No, no drugs. We want you to do something for us."

Snuggles may have creased his eyes. It was hard to tell. "You want a favor?"

"We want you to let Pascal know we're back in town."

"Don't know a Pascal."

"Oh, don't lie to me Snuggle-buns. Everybody on the dark side of the street must know Pascal."

"Not getting involved." The rat-man in the corner tittered in agreement.

I shrugged. "Liam?"

Liam moved with a leonine grace toward Snuggles and licked his fangs. That was all he had to do.

"You're one of Pascal's, aren't you?" Snuggles asked, pushing his bulk back in the chair with his arms like he was trying to get away. "Why can't you find him yourself?"

"It's sad, but we've had a difference of opinion. A small family squabble and we misplaced his cell number."

"Fine. I'll put the word out that you're looking for him. But don't think I'm going to forget this, girlie. Don't come around here again."

"I'll come here as many times as I want." I picked up a bag from the floor, opened it, and dumped it all over the floor. Rat-man leapt forward to stop me. I sliced with my hatchet, and his pleather jacket shredded on one arm. I sliced again, and the other arm split right down the seam. I turned sideways, brought the hatchet down from his throat to his belly in lateral fashion, and every button on his shirt popped off, revealing a hairy chest that made me recoil.

"See, what we have here is a failure to communicate, Snuggley-poo. I can come here and do what I want, take what I want, and demand that you do things for me. In return, you get to keep all of your blood on the *inside* of your body."

A man with a gun popped around the corner from the kitchen. Liam heard him before I did, of course, so it was no shock that when I turned, Liam already has his fangs in the guy's throat. I took the gun, holding it by two fingers like a dead mouse. "Gosh, I hate these things."

Liam sucked enough to make the man faint from blood loss, stopped himself, wiped his fangs with the back of his clawed hand, and said, "Yuck. Users taste disgusting."

Snuggles belched loudly and downed another can of beer. Or, tried to. I tossed the hatchet and knocked it clear out of his hands. "Do we have a deal, Snuggly-dums? You understand where we are coming from?"

Snuggles nodded, murder in his eyes.

"Thanks, baby. That's all I wanted."

I retrieved my hatchet and did a little pump fake at rat-man as we left. He squealed and went back to his corner. As we left, Snuggles yelled, "You won't be so sure of yourself during the day, princess, when your pet can't keep you safe." We kept walking, but inside I acknowledged that was true.

"Anything else you want to do?" Liam asked, face back to normal.

"What about your super sense of smell? Is it telling you anything?"

He tilted his head, nose in the air. "Too many smells down here. Garbage, urine, body odor, bleach, and a soupcon of Chinese food."

"Emperor's Palace is a few blocks away."

"That must be it."

"Think we should come back tomorrow?" I asked.

"Oh, yeah."

"Let's stop to drop this gun somewhere safe." Before I drove home, I emptied the bullets and threw them in a sewer, then I stopped by the police station and handed it in, telling them I found it on the street.

## CHAPTER SIX

I was remembering Liam's crack about users tasting bad as I stared at the museum restaurant. When I went to the museum, it was hot dogs, hamburgers, and soggy fries. Boy, had the museum upgraded. One of Cleveland's most famous chefs, Simon Bruell, had opened a trendy bistro featuring seasonal ingredients and a variety of choices, including the kids' favorite, the "build your own pizza" option.

"How do we explain why we need an egg?" asked Officer Bob.

"Leave it to me."

Officer Bob seemed good with that.

I spotted someone wearing a nametag, and by that weak evidence alone, I assumed she worked at the museum. No one had ever excused me for being too smart.

"Miss? Can I speak to the kitchen manager in the back, or the chef?"

"I don't know," she said. "Can you?"

I cleared my throat. *Patience. Patience.* "May I?"

She shrugged. "No idea. I don't work here. I work nearby and was getting lunch."

I blinked. Blinked again. Officer Bob chuckled behind me.

I turned on my heel and approached another person, wearing an apron *and* a name tag. "Excuse me? Sir, we need to get an item from the kitchen. Can we talk to the manager?"

"You can get anything you want, long as you pay for it," the guy said.

"I know and I'll pay for it, but I need something specific."

"What do you need?"

"An egg."

"We cook eggs, no problem."

"I need a whole, raw one."

"Go ask Gary, the one wearing the apron with the tie. Maybe he can help you, 'cause I sure can't. Who the hell comes to a restaurant and buys a whole, raw egg?" He looked at Bob. "Are you her escort? Keeping her safe?"

Officer Bob adopted a serious face. "Yes, I am. On special duty to keep her from hurting herself. We like to let her out now and then."

I smacked Bob on the shoulder.

"Good luck," said the man to Bob, clucking his tongue. "Tough gig."

"Tell me about it," Bob replied. I hit him again.

Pretending like I couldn't hear them chatting about what a job it was to "watch" me, I left Bob and approached Gary. "Excuse me, sir? I understand you are the manager of the restaurant?"

"You have something to complain about? You didn't like your grilled cheese? Your kids hated the vegetable soup you made them get? What is it?"

"Grouchy. Yikes. No, I'm not here to complain about anything. This is a lovely restaurant."

Gary, who *also* had a nametag, said, "Sorry. What can I do for you?"

"I need an egg."

"Ask the cook to make you an egg."

"I need a raw egg, whole."

Now it was Gary's turn to blink.

"Get the hell out of my restaurant, lady. Hey, Officer." He was speaking to Bob. "This lady is making a ruckus. Can you get her out of here?"

My palms itched. I tried to ask nicely. I was polite. I reconsidered my tone. Yes, I was polite. But, now, I needed one goddamn egg. I spied the swinging doors to the back and sprinted toward them. Gary sprinted after me, managing to grab onto my knitted sweater, catching a thread on his watch, falling to his knees. I pulled forward like a bull in a china shop, towing Gary along behind me so fast that he tumbled to his stomach.

I did my best Iditarod impression and pulled my sled, I mean, Gary, through the doors into the kitchen. He screamed the whole time.

"Get her! Get her! She's crazy!" he yelled.

The cooks and dishwashers gave me a lot of room at first. "Pardon me,

I need a raw egg. Where may I procure one?" I asked. One of the guys, at the salad station, pointed to a large stainless-steel fridge. "Thank you," I said.

While I was being polite, Gary had gotten to his feet, pulled hard to disconnect his watch from my sweater, and red-faced as a beet, jumped on me and threw me to the floor. I grabbed a pot on a low shelf and swung over my head, making a weak connection with his cranium.

"Help me! Don't just stand there!" he screamed at his team, holding his hands to his head. The staff jumped into action. One grabbed at my wrist, trying to wrestle the pot from my hand. Another one grabbed my ankle and only succeeded in pulling off my sneaker. Gary pushed up to a sitting position, rubbing his noggin', and that gave me the opportunity to make a break for it. I dropped the pot, forgot my shoe, and ran toward the fridge.

"Lady, watch out there's..." yelled a guy in a traditional chef's hat.

I wiped out like a cartoon character, feet flying, and landed hard on my back.

"Oil," he finished. "It's greasy near the stove."

"Got it." Despite my bruises, I shoved myself to my feet, determined to walk the next few steps to the fridge. I was stopped by a button-popping, hyperventilating, red-faced Gary.

"You will pay for this mess! Where is that cop? I want her arrested!"

I took a deep breath. "Gary, look, I'm sorry, but I need a whole, raw egg to do an exorcism on a fox spirit who is inhabiting a small Japanese woman."

Gary stared. "You really are off your rocker."

"I get that a lot," I said. I reached around him to open the fridge door, but he moved again, blocking me.

"This is totally not necessary, Gary. Give me one egg, and I'll be on my way."

"No. That cop isn't helping so we've called the police."

"Oh, good. I love Captain Morgan."

"The rum? Is that what this is? You've been drinking? You don't smell like rum. You smell slightly fishy."

"That's Juro."

"I don't know that liquor, but it doesn't matter. Stay here and don't move."

"Can't. Sorry about this." I grabbed Gary by the arm, pulled him toward me in one fast move, and had him in a headlock before anyone else even twitched.

"Stay still or Gary sleeps with the fishes," I said in my best mafia impression. No one moved. I swiveled around, opened the fridge with my one free hand, and spied my target, a twenty-four-count carton of eggs.

"Ugh!" I let Gary go and held my head where he'd hit *me* with a jar of jam that he'd managed to retrieve from the door shelf. The jam, strawberry, must have been one of those organic, locally jarred things because the glass was quite fragile and broke on my head, pouring jam all over me, my hair, and my clothes. It was then that I noticed that Gary's watch had unraveled my sweater row-by-row and it was now a crop top.

I pushed Gary away from me, and he slipped on the jam, sliding like a runner into home with red goop all over his pants, along with slivers of glass. He smashed into a bread oven.

I shook out the glass shards from my head, finger-combed my jam-sodden hair, reached into the fridge, and removed a single egg. "Excuse me," I said, remembering to be polite, and I stalked out of the kitchen, having no idea where my sneaker was, so I left with one shoe and a jam-slathered white running sock. Given that, saying I stalked might not be accurate. I limped out of the kitchen, truth be told.

I entered the main dining area to find Officer Bob grinning from ear-to-ear. "Nice job," he said.

"Why didn't you help me?" I held my arms out in disbelief that he was enjoying this.

"You said leave it to you," he said, holding his fist to his face, as laughter tears welled in the corner of his eyes, sniffling to avoid breaking into hysterics. He half-way succeeded, biting his lip and doubling over making muffled choking noises.

I ignored him. He wasn't worth my time. I looked up and realized one thing.

I had forgotten about the people.

The dining area was a still frame, with dozens upon dozens of people, including parents and teachers standing in front of their children with their arms stretched wide in protective stances, staring at me. I reached over to a condiment stand, pinched a napkin out of the dispenser with one index finger and thumb, and wiped my hands and face. I smoothed my hair and hobbled out of the dining room, head held high. Bob shuffled behind me, taking time to stop and calm Gary, promising to write a report and send an inspector.

"How do you always manage to lose a shoe and get sticky stuff in your hair?" asked Officer Bob, once he'd gotten his chill back.

"Just a gift," I said, still miffed that he hadn't helped me. I cradled the egg so that it wouldn't break. We'd never get another one without leaving the museum, and I had a school bus to catch at three p.m. I placed the egg next to the Buddha. "Watch the egg, big guy, okay?" Buddha was in full-on Zen and didn't reply.

"What's next on the list?" he asked.

"A Japanese cherry blossom."

"Is it cherry blossom season?" he asked.

"Not even close, and I don't think they grow here. It's too cold."

"Well, maybe a twig?"

I shrugged.

Officer Bob thought for a minute. "If you can manage to stay out of trouble for a moment, I'll go over to the Botanical Gardens and see if I can find one."

"What if I come with you?"

He looked me up and down. "Dear God, no. Please don't."

"Fine," I said, giving him the cold shoulder. "I'll look for volcanic ash. They have a Pompeii exhibit somewhere, don't they?"

"Not in the Asian center."

"Obviously not. I bet I know more about Pompeii than you do."

"Big volcano erupted, covering town in ash. Everyone died."

"That sums it up, but it doesn't convey the drama of the event, and no, not everyone died. A lot of the townspeople made it to safety." I held my arms up as high as they could reach, standing on my tippy-toes. "The cloud was twelve miles high!"

"Great. You do drama. I'll get a cherry blossom." Bob headed toward the door.

"Heathen," I said to his back.

I made my way to the nearby European section and wandered into the rooms with Italian cultural knick-knacks. Visitors wove around me, shaking their heads.

The Pompeii exhibit had a model of an exploding Mount Vesuvius, with tiny toy people being buried on the ground. It was several feet long, and the height was to scale, so you had to walk around it to see the whole thing. There was a rope around it and signs that said, "Don't touch," but they didn't apply to me, so I leaned over and touched the model.

Immediately, alarms blared and the closest security guard raced into the room to tell me to get my hands off the display. I looked at him, and he stopped. That was it. Complete halt.

"Are you the one with the Buddha and the vase and the fox spirit whoojamabob thingee going on in the Asian collection?" he asked.

I nodded.

"Gotcha. People! This way, please." And just like that, another wing of the museum was off-limits to paying visitors. The alarms shut off at some point, and I was alone in the room. I touched the exhibit again and realized that the "ash" was carefully constructed plastic of some kind, not real ash, not even a little bit, and my plan to get volcanic ash from this exhibit wasn't going to work. I stared hard at the model volcano and tried to come up with plan B.

A tiny red pointy thing popped up in the opening of Mt. Vesuvius, followed by another equal and opposite red pointy thing. It was hard to see because of the fake smoke, but the pointy red things turned out to be ears as they emerged and were followed by a small, black eye, a sharp pointy nose, and the point of a devil's forked tail. The one black eye glowed with hate. The second eye was a mangled mess of burned flesh seared shut forever.

"Monster Hunter! Ha! You're nothing but a stay-at-home mom with illusions of grandeur. Can't even get the ingredients for a simple exorcism."

I couldn't believe my eyes. I knew this creature; we'd crossed paths before in a most unpleasant way. I knew he had reason to hate me, and I had clear reason to hate him, but what was he doing in the museum? I crossed my arms and glared at the imp in disbelief.

"What? Didn't expect me?" he taunted.

"Zric, you vermin! Are you involved with this?"

The imp shrugged, revealing serrated yellow teeth that clashed with his coloring. He reached to the back of his head with both hands and flicked his hinged horns back into place and cackled again, saliva dripping from a corner of his mouth.

"What? Me?" he asked with false modesty. "I know nothing about fox spirits and fish spirits and…"

"Fish spirits!" I snapped my fingers. "Juro! He's inhabited by a kappa, a fish spirit?"

"Why would you ever think *that*?" The imp held up two glowing balls, each about the size of a golf ball. One gleamed with a reddish light, the other with a blue. "Why on earth would anyone summon a kitsune and a kappa at the same time?"

"Because you're an evil son-of-a-bitch?"

"Ten push-ups for you."

"I should have killed you last time."

"But you left me alive, didn't you, after destroying my eye!" The imp leapt out of the volcano, slid down the side to stand a few feet away from me, and stomped his foot.

"You set this whole thing up?"

Zric bowed. "It did take more planning than I am traditionally known for, but, yes. I'm going to force you to shame yourself publicly. You are going to ruin the museum, let your kid down, and die. It's all in the plan," he said, index finger to his temple.

"That's not going to happen, you vile piece of crap." I jumped forward to grab the three-foot-tall red monster, but he saw me coming and did a back flip out of the way. "Good luck with the exorcism, bitch." He fled by bouncing up to an air vent, turning into smoke, and seeping through the slats.

I sat in the guard's abandoned chair to think, my mind wandering to the past, when I'd first caught sight of Zric, but hadn't understood what I was seeing. I was younger and couldn't see the long game.

Liam and I had, indeed, gone back the next day and waited at the bus stop for Goatee and Curt to appear. They showed, all right.

Goatee was a hulking monster by that time. He'd put on muscle, and I could tell it was from a combination of steroids and weight-lifting because he walked funny, like he'd blown up his leg muscles so fast that he didn't have time to learn how to use them properly. He'd also focused on his pecs and biceps, so his arms curled up and his chest pulled in. He looked like a Neanderthal.

Curt now sported a bandana around each wrist and wore a heavy chain clipped to his belt, which dragged down his pants on one side so I could see his tighty whities. I was never one to keep my mouth shut, so I mentioned his pants malfunction, in case he wasn't aware of the breeze.

"Hey, Curt, your mama buy you that underwear? You look like an arthritic plumber who can't remember where his ass crack is."

Turned out that giant chain had a purpose and Curt had been training. Second banana no longer, tougher and meaner, Curt pulled the chain from his back pants pocket, unclipped it from his belt, and swung it nunchuck style, swish, swish, swish, around, around, around. I didn't want to get hit with that thing.

My bat draped over my back in a self-made holster, like a sword. My hatchet was in a thigh holster on my right leg. I extracted the bat and swung counter to Curt's swings, trying to catch and wrap the chain around the top of the bat. He was fast though, and I couldn't get my footing. He backed me up farther and farther, until I was at the mouth of an alley I didn't want to go down.

He didn't count on my partner, however, who shifted position as fast as the wind, got behind Curt, grabbed him with both hands around his neck, and yanked backward. Curt fell and Liam rode him down to the ground, holding the front of Curt's shirt. Liam knocked the chain out of Curt's hand like it was nothing.

That left me with Goatee, who was strong but slow. He charged me like a bull, and I sidestepped like a matador, pointing my bat at him when he'd realized he'd missed. He stormed back, not changing tactics, and once again, I side-stepped. "The steroids have rotted your brain, Goatee. You used to be smarter than this."

"I'm strong and becoming stronger, you cunt, and Pascal will love it when I bring you back to him unconscious. You'll be his pet, until he decides you are no longer amusing. He might be happy enough to let me have some of his blood."

"You want some of his blood, you jackass? You'll lose your humanity." I held up a hand. "Fine, you have a point. You aren't much of a human, but you aren't a vampire." I swung the bat at his head, not truly trying to hit him, but push him farther away. Something about the way Goatee's eyes darted to the right and behind me made me stop and spare a look at Liam.

I screamed, "Liam! No!"

Liam had his fangs in Curt's neck, sucking down blood like a two-pack-a-day cancer patient sucks down smoke. Curt's head lolled back, and his face was pale.

"Liam! Stop!" I dropped the bat and pulled Liam's shoulders, but he was latched on to Curt's neck like a tick. Goatee laughed in the background. "Pascal's gonna love this!" Then, he chanted, "Kill him. Kill him. Kill him."

"You want him to kill your friend?" My mind whirled so fast I saw colors.

"Curt's expendable, but if Liam kills him, you're going to have to kill Liam yourself. Pascal is hoping for that."

I shoved Liam once again, but it was for naught. I had no choice. I picked up my bat, and without thinking more about it, afraid I'd fail, I swung the bat at Liam's right shoulder as hard as I could, twisting my body at the hips to get the full amount of torque. Liam took the blow and tumbled off Curt, flying several feet until he hit the rear brick wall. I kneeled to find out if Curt still had a pulse. I breathed a sigh of relief when a clear *lub-dub* beat under my fingers.

Goatee took this as a sign that he should attack me from behind and crashed forward to wrap me in his gargantuan arms. I'd placed the bat down on the ground when I checked Curt's pulse, not that I could have done any damage with it anyway, given that I was wrapped in a bear hug by a wannabe pro-wrestler. I did manage to pull my hatchet from my holster and flick it down toward his thigh where it sliced through the muscle and the iliotibial band on his right leg. The thing about the IT band? It helps you stand, or in this case, not stand, as Goatee fell onto his right knee and released me to grab his right thigh.

I'd, thankfully, missed the femoral artery so though he was bleeding, he wasn't bleeding out and would survive if he got to a hospital in time. He was a monstrous human, but still a human.

My chest was tight, and I gasped for air, managing to squeak out, "Like before, get to the hospital. We only want to know where Pascal is holing up."

Goatee grabbed Curt with his left arm, holding his bleeding leg with his right. "After this, Pascal will find you. You should have killed us when you had the chance."

I didn't care a whit about anything he had to say. I turned my back and sprinted to Liam's side. He was fine, but when I looked in his eyes, they held the fears of a human who has seen the darkness in his soul.

"You didn't kill him, you hear? It's okay."

Liam got to his feet with a weariness that spoke of anguish of spirit rather than body. "It's never going to be okay, Jess."

"We didn't find Pascal."

"I got his scent. I think I can find him, but Goatee is right. Pascal's going to find us."

We limped out of the alley, and I thought there was a flicker of a red, devil-shaped tail skirting the corner.

## CHAPTER SEVEN

Remembering that entire episode gave me fuel to fight. I didn't care if I had one sneaker, a jammy sock, crazy hair, and no weapons. I had a Buddha statue that talked to me, and Officer Bob. I was going to take Zric down.

Zric had given me an opening by showing me the two glowing life-force balls. Both spirits, fox and fish, were controlled by the owner of their ball. These spirits were prickly about being forced to do things they didn't want to do. If I could get the balls from Zric, I didn't have to do an exorcism. I could release the spirits within a second.

Officer Bob found me sitting in the chair, tapping my fingers together as I schemed. He had a cherry blossom branch, no blossoms, and placed it next to the egg and Buddha. "That's the best I could do," he said. "They have cherry trees, but no blossoms yet. I hope that the twig will work. If you look closely, it has a tiny bud."

"That's great, Bob, but we may have another way."

"I don't understand."

"I met an old friend a few moments ago, an imp named Zric. He's the one responsible for all this. He's summoned the spirits using their life-force, captured in two balls. If we can get those balls, we can free the spirits. They should leave on their own."

He canted his head, brows furrowed. "Why do you keep saying two spirits?"

"Right. I forgot you weren't here. Juro's infected with a kappa, a fish spirit."

Bob rubbed his eyes and shook his head in the tiniest of motions, as if a normal shake took too much energy. "At least that explains the smell."

"You're taking this awfully well."

"Mrs. Friedman, at this point, I don't think anything could surprise me."

"Challenge accepted," I said with a grin, adding, "Bob, you can call me Jess."

"I'll stick with Mrs. Friedman, if you don't mind. I'm old-fashioned that way."

"Okay," I said, crinkling my nose. I motioned with my hand for him to speak.

"What?"

"Is Bob your first name or your last name?" I prompted.

"It's just my name."

"Aren't you going to tell me your whole name?"

"No. Officer Bob works fine."

I poked him in the shoulder. "I'm going to break you." He didn't respond, but closed his eyes and whispered, "I know You are testing me."

I knew he wasn't talking to me, but to the big G, and I gave him for props for that. It didn't keep me from chuckling though. "Let's go find us an imp. Is there a snack machine around here?"

"Downstairs in the basement near the restrooms. You hungry?"

I headed for the stairs. "Yes, come to think of it, but I wasn't thinking of me. There's only one thing imps like more than sowing chaos."

"What's that?"

"Chocolate. Do you have any singles? I found some quarters in my pocket."

We loaded up on candy bars, and each of us ate one, swigged some Coke, and shared some pretzels. Feeling a lot better, we returned to the Asian room.

I held Buddha in my hand and petted him until I felt his presence. "Did you know about Zric?" I asked.

*Ummmhummm.*

"You did?"

*In the way that any of us know anything.*

"Why didn't you tell me?"

*We are what we think.*

"How does that help me? Is there any other detail you'd like to share?"
*You won't be punished for your anger. You will be punished by your anger.*
"Well, aren't you a fortune cookie of knowledge today."
He ceased his nattering.

Officer Bob and I placed the pile of chocolate in a little pyramid on the floor, except for two candy bars I kept in reserve. It looked like we were making a campfire of melty goodness.

What I needed now was a weapon. I thought I'd seen the perfect one around the corner in the Native American displays. Sure enough, there it was. It might as well have had a spotlight on it with angels singing, it was so perfect. I readied myself for a giant side kick to break the glass when Officer Bob stopped me. "If you wait a moment, I'll get a key. You don't always have to do it the hard way."

Right. Once again, hadn't occurred to me.

I waited. I waited some more.

I considered eating another candy bar but rejected the thought. Waited some more. Ate a candy bar.

Finally, Officer Bob waltzed in with an older woman wearing a thick bunch of keys around her neck on a lanyard. She was exceptionally short, only coming to my shoulder. I'm sure her hair was white, but it had taken on a blue hue.

"You want to do what?" she screeched when I showed her what I wanted. Her face was gaining color quickly, moving from flushed to fire engine red in no time.

"I need a weapon," I explained, my voice reasonable.

"This is from pre-Colonial times! It's a relic to be treasured."

"It's a tomahawk and the closest thing to a hatchet. I require it." Still reasonable.

"If you think I'm going to authorize the use of a precious display item to indulge your flights of fancy, you are gravely mistaken! It is my responsibility to protect these treasures, and I'm not going to hand them to a greasy, unkempt, con artist like you!"

I was no longer reasonable. I took several steps back and executed a well-placed side kick to the glass, which cracked, and then, after my second kick, broke into pieces. I pulled the tomahawk from the display case, turned to the apoplectic museum lady, and said, "Listen, you little Oompa-Loompa, I am not a fake. I work for the Catholic Church and have saved Cleveland's ass multiple times, not to mention the golem thing in Athens and the nastiness in Columbus, so... Get. Out. Of. My. Way." I handed her a card. "Send the bills here. Tell them I was ridding the museum of a kappa and a kitsune, and killing Zric. It'll make sense to them."

Oompa Loompa lady backed away, only stopping to turn off the sirens. For that, I was grateful.

"See, Officer Bob, sometimes you do have to do it the hard way."

His lips were pursed, and he did that thing where he talked silently while moving his lips, communing with someone other than me. He collected himself and said, "I see that now. What was the nastiness in Columbus, besides the normal political nastiness of our state's capitol?"

"Sentient black mold infestation." I shivered. "Truly revolting."

"Of course, it was," he said, and I got the feeling he was being sarcastic, but maybe not. I'm not always good at discerning such things. He exhaled. "Let's go hide and see what's happening with our candy."

We approached the Asian artifact room on tip-toe, and I knew the imp had found the chocolate by the sniffling, scratching, and rustling of candy bar wrappers.

Sniff. Sniff. Scratch. Scratch.

"Is that him?" Officer Bob asked.

"I think so."

I rounded the corner, tomahawk high, screaming at the top of my lungs, "Got you, you sneaky bastard!"

Then I yelled, "Juro! What the hell are you doing here? This candy isn't for you. Oh, wait, you're a victim. I forgot. Since when do fish like chocolate?" Juro, who had been laying on his stomach, shoving candy into his mouth, burbled, "I'm hungry."

"Mr. Kappa, sir, you are locked into a body you don't want to be in, right?" The kappa nodded. "And Juro the person is slowly receding and leaving you in charge, also right?" The kappa nodded again.

Officer Bob came up behind me "I don't understand what's happening at all."

"When we first met Juro, the human Juro was still mostly in charge, unaware of what was happening to him. Now the kappa is in charge, and doesn't want to be. The fish spirit wants to leave as much as we want it to. The fox spirit is a little different because they instinctively like to wreak havoc, but even a fox spirit hates having its life-force captured and used to control it."

"What do we do about it?"

"First, can you go down to the candy machine and get those bagged kale chips? I think the kappa will like them better. Also, bring up a couple of bottles of that artisanal, purified water. We need one for the exorcism."

"What are the others for?"

"Officer Bob, *think*. We've got a fish out of water."

He shot me a look but walked to the stairwell to get the supplies.

I got down on my hands and knees and looked in Juro's eyes. "Hey Kappa, I need Juro to tell me something. Where would I find petrified wood in this museum?" The fish spirit puckered Juro's mouth, sucking in and out, swiveling from side-to-side. Finally, it said, "Earth and Minerals," which sounded like, "Wurp and Mrinls," but luckily, I speak Toddler, which, as it turns out, is very close to Fish, so I got it.

I retrieved the tomahawk, which I had placed on the floor, and left the Kappa/Juro combination on the floor, waiting for his kale chips and water. My mind was in the past.

## CHAPTER EIGHT

Liam and I did return to the shady side of town. I was armed for bear with my hatchet in my left thigh holster, a squeeze container on the right, and my baseball bat in the sword position on my back, ready for an overhead draw. I had two thin stakes I had whittled myself out of a downed maple, both tipped with silver. I'd met a silversmith and jewelry maker at a craft fair and asked her to do the silver tips for me. She didn't ask why or even blink at the request. Maybe it was the exorbitant amount of money I paid for ten stakes. Maybe creative people had broad imaginations.

The stakes were in my inside left jacket pocket, and my right inside pocket housed a grill lighter with a long metal wand, filled to capacity with lighter fluid. The damn thing cost a couple of hundred bucks online and incurred a thirty-dollar hazard shipping fee, but I didn't feel comfortable buying one at my local Lowes, where half of my high school worked. There would be questions and gossip, which I wanted to avoid. The mean girls in high school had become mean women, and the jocks were now overweight armchair quarterbacks. Most importantly, every single one of them knew me.

Liam and I had driven this time. I was behind the wheel, and Liam hung his head out the window like a dog, searching scents for any of our bad guys. We cruised the neighborhood at five miles an hour, making sure we were seen, coiled and ready for a fight.

"Hello, Liam, Jess. Pascal sends his regards."

I jammed my foot on the brake, left the car running, and shoved myself out of the car in a few seconds. Liam was faster, and by the time I got out, he had our conversationalist in his hands.

The imp was red, with a devil's tail, two beady black eyes, and two horns that I learned later were hinged so they could flip up or down, which seemed so handy. Liam held him up by his neck.

"What, in the name of all that is holy, are you?" Liam asked.

The imp squeaked an answer, but it was impossible to understand given that Liam was crushing his neck.

"Put him down, Liam. Let's see what the midget has to say."

"I'm a full-grown imp, disgusting human. You should apologize, and don't use the word holy with me. I don't talk to that side of the metaphysical street."

"I apologize to the real little people out there for comparing them to you."

The imp's eyes slitted. "I'm going to enjoy watching Pascal torture you."

"Why is Pascal so interested in us?" I asked.

"He needed a plaything, and you remind him so much of your mother." The imp did a back handspring and fled down the alley, while I stood stock still, shocked out of my mind. Liam recovered quicker than I did and took off after the imp. I pulled a stake and scrambled after him, my mind a whirling tornado of confusion.

The alley connected to yet another alley, and as the imp ran, he'd knocked garbage cans over so that we were running through muck of every kind. We almost lost his trail when he leaped up and climbed a brick wall with his gecko-like feet.

"How do we follow him?" I screamed, pacing back and forth for a fire escape, a ladder, anything. "He's getting away!"

"I jump. You go inside and climb the stairs. He went into the fourth-floor window." Liam did a standing jump that boggled my brain, and he caught the third-floor window sill. I didn't hang around long enough to see how he did the rest. I flew into the building and with a stunning amount of stupidity and carelessness, crashed up the stairs directly to the fourth floor, running from door-to-door to find the imp.

I found him in the third door I tried. I pushed the door open, took one single furious step inside, and toppled to the ground as a hand pushed me on my mid-back. I hit nose first and got a good look at the dirty, porcelain floor with scratch marks from a hundred desks and chairs of the past.

Liam wasn't in the room, but a skinny, white-faced vampire was, and the imp danced with glee beside him, looking like a circus clown. The room was unadorned, the walls plain, but there were two hard-backed chairs, a round side table covered by a white doily, and a pair of lit candles. The candles burned bright, casting flickering shadows on the walls as the light fell on the vampire and imp.

"Pascal, I presume?" I wiped the blood from my nose with my sleeve and shifted to my knees. Inside I was shaking, but I kept my voice calm and certain.

Pascal wore a shirt that may have once been white, but now was a faded yellow, and gray suit pants that hung on his frame. One shirtsleeve hung loose, and I grinned as I remembered that I'd taken that arm the last time he and I had met.

His hair was disheveled, but his shoes were shiny black, and he wore gold cufflinks, which he fingered occasionally. The cufflinks flashed in the candlelight.

"Oh, little, little Jess. So brave. So foolish. I could have snapped your neck right now, but I didn't. I don't think I want to kill you until you are more trained. It's too easy." Pascal placed his hands on his chin and studied me. His voice was hoarse and crackly, like old newspapers being rolled for kindling. I tensed at the sound, a shiver running down my back, and pushed to my feet, my tiny, pee-wee stake in hand.

Pascal laughed a raspy belly laugh, and the imp followed with an ear-splitting cackle like Salacious Crumb. My teeth set on edge.

"Your tiny stake isn't going to be worth the effort, little Jess. Put it away."

I did. It seemed better to have my hands free. "How do you know me? How do you know my mother?"

"I knew your mother. You didn't."

"What the hell are you talking about?" I clenched my fists, holding myself from charging him.

"Oh, Jess, they kept the truth from you. Your mother was a Monster Hunter. That's why the Diocese kept an eye on you, and why she died."

"She had a car accident."

"She did."

"But you're saying it was murder?"

"I'm saying it's why she died."

I stomped my foot like a little kid, tears pooling in my eyes. "What do you mean? Answer me!"

Pascal held up his only palm like he was weighing something. "I had a love/hate relationship with your mother. I hated her, which was fair because was always trying to kill me. I'd say, 'on the other hand,' but I don't have another hand, thanks to you, so on the other side of the argument, life had gotten so boring, so droll, until she came along. She spiced it up a bit. I appreciated her attempt to blow me up on the Valley View Bridge. It made the news, you know."

"That's why it collapsed?"

"Uhmmmhummm. She'd prepared for weeks, making sure no one else would be on the bridge, planting bombs, luring me to the bridge that evening. It would have worked except for Zric here. He warned me just in time."

"Your pet rat saved your life."

"Hey!" said Zric. "I'm his assistant."

"Yes, you are. Yes, you are." Pascal petted Zric's head, and Zric cackled again, that evil sound grating my nerves.

"I've decided I'm going to let you live, little Jess, at least for a while." He took two steps toward me, and I flinched. "You need to suffer for what you've done to my arm, and toying with you will be fun." Despite his veneer of calm, his eyes were hard, vicious, and spoke of death. Losing his arm had seriously pissed him off.

"I thought big, bad vampires like you could regenerate a limb."

He opened his shirt so I could see his skinny, white, scarred chest and withdrew what remained of his limb. I had cut it at the shoulder, and I could make out a sprout, like a garden vegetable, growing from the stump.

"We can, and I will, but it will take some time. It doesn't matter. I've got all the time in the world. You, little Jess, do not, but I haven't decided how long you have, yet." He had the satisfied face of a man tasting a fine wine and became even smugger as he inhaled deeply. His face twisted with something I couldn't name, but it made my blood boil. My mind raced with ways to kill him, but just as quickly, it rejected each one. I wasn't ready.

"You have a similar scent to your mom," he said. "Liam, you can come in now."

Liam crawled through the window, breathing hard, which was unnecessary for him but was a sign of his agitation. As soon as his feet hit the ground, he launched himself at Pascal, and Zric launched himself at me.

Pascal caught Liam one-handed and threw him to the ground, but I couldn't help my friend because Zric leapt toward me, claws out, aiming for my face. I hopped backward, reaching for the squeeze container with my right hand, my lighter with my left. I kicked Zric hard in the belly, and he sailed several feet onto his back but bounced back up. He sprung forward and raked one hand down my cheek. The pain flashed hot, but I still managed to get ahold of my secret squeezy container. I jumped on him, holding him down with my weight, pointed the nozzle down, and said, "I'll do it. I promise. This is your last warning."

Zric bit me on the hand, so I pressed the nozzle and blinded him with Easy Cheez. I know he didn't see that coming.

I shoved the lighter right in his face. He managed to turn his head, and I struck his left eye only.

Turns out setting someone's eye on fire is an effective way of getting their attention, and true fact, Easy Cheez makes a great fire starter. The Boy Scouts taught me that. Goes to show how much oil has to be in the cheese-like product.

And, if I hadn't needed it, I could always eat it later when I was hungry.

Zric was occup-eyed, (sorry-not-sorry) trying to put out the flames, which burned on the Easy Cheez accelerant, so I turned my attention to Liam and Pascal. Liam bled from multiple cuts and was bruised around the neck from Pascal's ministrations. Liam dove low, trying to take out the ancient vampire at the shins, but Pascal simply jumped over him, turned mid-air, and kicked Liam in the ass. Liam flew into the back wall so hard he left a man-sized indentation right out of Scooby Doo.

"Tell me what you know about my mother!" I screamed while I jumped on Pascal's back like a monkey and stabbed him with my pencil-sized, silver-tipped stake. It sizzled, made an unusual burning smell, and was immediately expelled from his body by whatever magic kept him alive in the first place.

I slid off Pascal's back, reached for my baseball bat, and swung toward his head. Pascal ducked easily and straight-armed Liam, holding him by the neck.

"Don't swing again, Jess, or I'll snap his neck right now."

I sheathed the bat, and Pascal dropped Liam.

Liam was beaten and knew it. He dragged himself up and out of reach, blood streaming down his chin, pink tears streaming down his cheeks, and pink snot dripping from nose. Sobbing vampires give new meaning to ugly crying face.

"Why did you pick me?" he pleaded. "Tell me why. I'm not anything to you."

Pascal dusted some dirt off his shoulder and readjusted his cufflink "Au contraire, Liam. You mean a lot to me because you mean a lot to *her*." He gestured toward me. "I'm looking forward to seeing what happens to her spirit when she has to kill you."

"You mother-fuckin' son of a bitch!" My anger was a burning fire in my belly once I realized what he'd said. He was playing with me, with us, because of my mother, if what he was saying was true. Now that Liam was out of the way, I drew my bat again and unleashed a swing meant for Fenway's green monster, only I caught his left shoulder, not his head. Nonetheless, I connected hard. He grunted with the impact, his arm hanging limp, his shoulder dislocated. He skirted around me, quick as lightening, so I missed on my second swing, which was wild because I had lost control. A loud pop let me know he'd already snapped his shoulder back into the socket. He scooped up the injured Zric and poof! He disappeared.

"Where did he go, Liam?" I raced to the window and then around the room, touching each wall for a hidden entrance. I pounded the floor searching for a trap door, but I realized that was ridiculous since we were on the fourth floor. I opened the door to investigate the hallway, but saw nothing. I thought I bumped into something solid with my foot, but there was nothing there, and when I trod on the same space again, it was empty.

He'd gotten away. I collapsed to the floor, and Liam and I held each other while we each mourned. I mourned my mother, and Liam mourned his past life. We both wept for what could have been and what was taken from us.

We hung onto each other for a long time, he comforted by my human warmth, me regretting what had brought us here. As I thought about what I'd learned during the confrontation with Pascal, the more I clenched my teeth. I hit my fist into my palm and pushed away.

"Liam. We're done bemoaning our fate. We will deal with it. Blubbering about our situation isn't going to make it better."

"I know, Jess, but I'm so lost."

"You are not lost. You are with me, and though you've lost some things, you've gained awesome powers. That jump you did out there? AH-MAZE-ING. Your sense of smell? Insane. Your strength is developing, too."

"I wasn't strong enough to beat Pascal."

"He's got a couple hundred years on you, my friend. There is only one thing to do."

"What's that?"

"Train harder. This isn't over."

## CHAPTER NINE

I might have let the events of the previous night slip during my training session with Ovid. He'd changed his name from Adolf Sitler to Ovid Sitler to stop the teasing. Personally, I don't think he thought it through carefully.

"What? Why did you do that, you idiot! You could have been killed!"

"Why didn't you, or the Church, tell me about my mother in the first place? I had a right to know!"

"Your mother felt the time wasn't right." Ovid walked away from me, turning his back.

"Why would my mother not want to tell me when she essentially started my training at three years old?"

"She wanted you to be able to take care of yourself, even if you weren't a Monster Hunter. She never wanted you to feel helpless. Remember when she taught you to throw knives?"

Despite myself, I smiled. Those were good times. "Yeah, we threw at human-shaped targets, and she made me aim for the head."

"Right, because if you can hit the forehead, you can hit anywhere, and even hitting a vampire in the forehead, as long as you pierce his cranium, will take him out for a while."

"Tell me about her."

"While you train."

"Okay!" I did a fast-change into a pair of shorts and a shirt, ready to learn more about my mom.

Stupid, stupid, stupid.

We ran, and ran, and ran. We ran around the high school track, then another five miles through the local neighborhood, took those five miles back, and then, after all of that, he made me do intervals with my hands over my head. No lie. I was out of breath, sweaty, and focused on putting one foot in front of the other, not asking questions.

"Ask me what you want to know," Ovid said, breathing in and out like he hadn't run ten miles at a seven-minute mile pace. I, on the other hand, was so out of breath that I couldn't speak and held up my index finger to indicate I'd get to it in a moment. That's when he decided I needed more core work, followed by knife throwing target practice. I couldn't think at all. My feet hurt, as did my abs, my knees, and my lower back. I heaved up my lunch, which earned a pat on the back from Ovid.

"Finally! You're giving it your all. About time."

"Did my mom train like this?" I wheezed this question.

"She could run ten miles like it was nothing. Let's go, cupcake. One more round of intervals, this time juggling three tomatoes. Don't drop them."

I did drop them, and the replacement tomatoes after that, and the onions, apples, and oranges. The grapes were a complete washout.

After three days of this, I rebelled. "Ovid, tell me about my mother. I'm not moving until you do." I sat on the grass and made it clear that I wasn't going anywhere. "Did you train my mom? Wait, that can't be right. You aren't old enough."

"My father trained your mom, and then I trained with them."

"Why aren't you a Monster Hunter?"

"I get startled easy."

"Huh?"

Ovid huffed a breath and turned to me, but his eyes were down, and he hesitated for several moments. Finally, he said, "I startle super easy. If we were walking down a hallway having a normal conversation and someone came up behind us, a friend even, and tapped me on the shoulder, I'd jump so high, I'd cling to the ceiling. I don't have the personality for it."

"I didn't know this." My mind was already whirling.

He shook his finger at me. "Don't use this knowledge for evil, cupcake," he snarled. I'd never seen him this angry. "I'll crush you." He squeezed his thumb and index finger to show me how flat I'd be. "I'll annihilate you. Don't forget, I'm in charge of your training, so anything you do will come back to haunt you."

Chastised and respectful, not, I later taped an air horn to the bottom of his adjustable chair, and I planted grass seed in his spare pair of shoes. I've never, ever seen a man leap so far or heard one screech at such a decibel as when I dressed as a bear and jumped out from behind a wall, growling at the top of my lungs.

The best one was when I inserted chicken-flavored bouillon cubes into his shower head and cut off his hot water. A cold chicken soup shower is hilarious when it happens to someone else. Trust me.

"Fuuuuuuuuccccccccck! Jess, what did you do this time? What is this? Why is my water yellow and freezing cold? Why do I smell like soup?"

I laughed until I couldn't stand, but Ovid was done with me. He stomped out of the shower wrapped in two towels, dripping wet, leaving a gold puddle on the floor, which made me laugh all over again because I think pee is funny. He didn't.

"That's it. I quit!"

"What? No! You can't quit. I was playing a prank. I didn't mean anything by it." I stood in front of him, my hands together in prayer. It never occurred to me that he'd react like that. I thought it was fun and games in the middle of hard training. He did not.

He got in my face. "What I'm training you for is serious, and you're treating it like it's a game. Do you not remember Pascal and how unprepared you were? Well, that freak is coming for you, and if you don't value your life, I'm not spending any more time with you. You're disrespectful, and on top of it, you don't value Liam's life either. Pascal isn't going to stop with you."

The problem was, I was still furious that no one had told me about my mother—he still hadn't given me any real information—and playing practical jokes on Ovid was a way to get back at him for withholding information from me.

So, while he yelled, I froze in place, muscles straining to pummel him, to take him down a peg or two. I leaned in, pushing hard against him, and shouted. "I value my life and Liam's, but you obviously don't, you and your little team of church mice, because you never warned me about what my mother's real job was. You let me go out into the world in complete ignorance! Pascal was looking for me, for my vulnerabilities, and he picked a good one alright—Liam! It's Liam who has paid the price for your silence!"

Ovid yelled right back at me, not two inches from my face. "It wasn't our choice!"

I shook my head hard, not believing him. "Bullshit! If it wasn't your choice, whose was it?"

The air went out of him, and his voice lowered, his head hanging low. "It was your father's. He didn't want you to know, and we honored his wishes."

---

My father was sitting in his easy chair, mind elsewhere, staring out into space. The television was on, but he wasn't watching, and its flickering screen was the only light in the room. Seeing him like that forced me to take a few moments to calm down. I had veered into the driveway, leaving tire marks on the pavement, planning on flying up the stairs and demanding my father tell me the truth, but he was broken and I needed to respect that.

I stood in the hallway and took ten deep, cleansing breaths until my pulse slowed and my blood pressure decreased. I was still angry as hell.

"Dad?"

His face brightened. "Yes, honey?"

I had thought this through, how I was going to broach the subject with deliberate questions, taking time so as not to not hit him over the head with it. I'd first ask about how he was feeling, then ask if he could tell me more about my mother, offering him the chance to fess up. Maybe ask if she had any secrets, or if she might have left something behind for me that I didn't know of yet. Step-by-step. Careful.

Utter fail.

"Dad, was Mom a Monster Hunter? Did she work for the Catholic Diocese, and is that what got her killed?"

As fast as his faced had brightened was as fast as it crumpled, and my father, the strongest man I knew, the man who ruled the house with a tip of his reading glasses, a perfect pocket square, and a shot of bourbon, broke down into tears.

This was not what I expected, and I rushed to his side to hold his hand. "Dad, I'm sorry I'm such a klutz at these kinds of things. I was going to approach the subject in a better way, but...well, I'm sorry I've hurt you."

He took a handkerchief from his pocket. It was a soiled, crumpled ball, and my alarm rose several notches at the sight of it.

"How did you find out?" he asked, gulping down another sob.

"I had a run-in with Pascal and an imp named Zric. Ovid told me the rest."

He popped up to his feet. "Ovid! Are you training? After all I have done to keep you away from them? Those Church zealots who think they are recreating the Knights Templar? The ones who got your mother killed, and probably you almost killed?"

"Uhhmmm…"

He stormed past me and paced the kitchen.

"I tried everything. Everything! Do something else, I said. Go into law, I said. But your mother had infiltrated your thinking by having you trained in gymnastics and martial arts. I was thrilled when you played softball, only to find that you thought the bat could make a fine weapon! When you told that to your mom and she laughed, I almost had a fit right then and there. How did they get their claws into you so quickly?"

"The Church?"

"Yes."

"Uh, well, I think they've kept tabs on me for a while, and after Pascal accosted us…"

"Who's us?"

"Me and Liam."

My father whirled on me. "What did that sadistic vampire do to Liam?"

I swallowed. That's all. I couldn't bring myself to tell him the answer.

My father stepped back, hands to his mouth. "Oh no. He *turned* him? Have you killed Liam yet? That poor boy."

I blew so hard my bangs flew up. "Dad, I have not killed Liam. We are working on a way to keep him connected to his humanity."

My father let out a hollow laugh. "Just like your mother, always believing the monsters could be saved. There is no coming back from being a vampire, Jess. They're the bane of human existence and need to be exterminated one-by-one."

I clenched my fists, unclenched, clenched, struggled to find words. "Dad, I get that you are upset, but why didn't you tell me the truth? Why was this kept from me my whole life? I deserved to know!"

"No, you didn't! I wanted to keep you safe. I didn't want you to get involved, but it seems I've failed. It was all for naught." He collapsed into a kitchen chair, shoulders heaving with anger and sadness. "Once you're in, you're in, Jess. Your job will be to kill the most loathsome, beastly, depraved monsters on the planet, and that is all it will be. It won't ever be anything else, and take a lesson from what happened to you, to your mom. You can't have a family because you can't risk their lives as well as yours. Think carefully, Jess."

He leaned back in his chair, still breathing heavily but not crying. I sat at his feet, like I used to when I was a little girl, and put my head on his knee. "Tell me something about her, Dad. Please."

My dad stared into the middle distance, his eyes unfocused and wet with unshed tears. He stayed like that for several minutes, and I waited next to him, letting him get lost in his own memories. Finally, he took a deep breath and spoke. His voice was different, a little softer, a bit slower, as if he'd decided that if he was going to talk about my mom, he wanted to take his time, stroll down memory lane, not race.

"Your mom was the toughest chick I'd ever met. I fell in love with her the moment I saw her. She was in an advanced math class, one I was barely passing, and she was arguing a point with a graduate assistant. She was so persistent, the grad student gave her the points for the problem, just to get rid of her. She was so fierce, so passionate. I couldn't stay away. I asked her out, and we were dating for about a month when we encountered a spider the size of a car."

"What? Really?" I asked.

He nodded, a small smile on his face. "Yup, some kind of gigantic spider species that was supposed to stay underground, but this one surfaced and discovered it liked people for breakfast. It looked like Shelob, from Tolkien, remember? I think Shelob was based on this species. Most damnable thing you've ever seen, or at least, I'd ever seen. I hid in the car like a baby while your mom faced off with it, holding, of all things, a broom. The broom was leaning against a wall where someone had left it, and she grabbed. In her hand, it became a weapon of arachnid destruction."

Now I laughed.

"She tried to reason with it and get it to go back to its nest, but this thing was foul and had lost reason a while ago, if it ever had any. Your mom tried anyway, not wanting to kill it if she didn't have to."

He got misty-eyed, remembering the scene.

"Eventually, she knew she had to destroy it. She—I swear this is true—grabbed a rope she swiped from somewhere, lassoed the damn thing, and jumped on its back like she was riding a bucking bronco. She broke the broom into two jagged pieces and shoved both of them into the spider, right behind its eyes. That didn't kill it, but it sure as hell blinded it. Your mom pulled on the rope until she flipped the screaming, flailing, blinded spider onto its back, tore one of the broom stakes out from behind the spider's eyes, and slammed it into the creature's abdomen. That did it. She placed a phone call and someone came out to clean up the mess."

I stared at him, wishing I had heard this story before, rapt and proud of my mom.

"What happened next?" I asked.

"Well," he said, looking down at me, "the cat was out of the bag then. She explained everything to me, told me she'd understand if I chose to leave, and waited for me run for the hills."

"But you didn't."

He petted my hair. "No, sweetheart, I didn't. I couldn't. By that time, she was the center of my life. It's hard though, knowing that your spouse, your best friend, put herself in danger every single day."

"Like the police. Or firefighters."

He cocked his head at that and appeared to consider it. "I hadn't thought of it that way, but yes, the difference being that I wasn't afraid of a man with a gun, or an out-of-control fire. I was afraid of things I couldn't even imagine. Things that I never knew existed. There was no place to focus my anxiety because she fought monsters out of fairy tales."

He turned to me and placed his hand under my chin. "And, now, I have to worry about you, too."

"You don't have to worry about me, Dad. I'm careful."

"That's what your mom said, but something got her in the end. I knew that car accident was more than it seemed, but what was I going to say to the police? 'Maybe it was an enormous spider?' Not likely."

"I'm sorry, Dad."

"Me too, pumpkin. Me too."

## CHAPTER TEN

The memories of my mom made me wonder what she'd do now if she were in my position. I sure wished she could tell me, but since she wasn't, I was going to have to make do.

Whenever I heard the words "petrified wood," I tried to imagine what could possibly scare wood so much that it was petrified. Fire, I guess. Axes. Woodpeckers. Tent caterpillars. Gypsy moths. Ewww...Japanese beetles.

Of course, I know that isn't what petrified means, but my mind is an unusual place.

I weaved my way to the Gems and Minerals section, slowing down enough to admire the pretty, flashy stones as well as an actual moon rock in the middle of the exhibit. I wondered if you could even fence some of those jewels. Probably not.

The petrified wood turned out to be right next to the volcano section, where there were—*Eureka!*—volcanic rocks as well. I was in business. Add the water that Officer Bob was getting, and we had all the ingredients for the exorcism. Even if I couldn't get the life-force balls from Zric, I could at least release the kitsune, and maybe the kappa.

I was reaching for a nice solid piece of wood when a gale wind gusted through and snatched it out of my hand. I turned in time to catch sight of the fox's tails flipping around the corner. It moved roadrunner fast, char marks on the floor blistering with the friction of its speed.

"Fine, you can have that one," I called. "I know you are being ordered around by that imp and can't help but obey, but if you and Professor Noyoko join forces, we can free you both."

I reached for a second piece, snatching at it with my left hand, holding the tomahawk in my right. I was ready this time, and as the fox zoomed past, I brought the blade down, cutting off two of the fox's tails. Despite being a spirit fox, the tails were remarkably solid, a mixture of the fox spirit and the human body it inhabited. I jolted backward with the effort, recoiling with the force and speed I'd had to put into that move, and crashed into a display case of exotic diamonds and sapphires, as well as a separate display of peridot, amber, and some spectacular jade. Oops. At least the diamonds couldn't break.

I held the tails, scrambled to my feet, snatched the last piece of petrified wood, and sprinted for the Asian artifact's room. I dropped the tails next to the Buddha, the egg, and the cherry tree twig, waving to a confused Officer Bob as I did so. I ran back to the Gem and Mineral room to grab the volcanic rock...

And tripped on my way there, as the fox tackled my legs and snapped at my face while I hit the floor. I landed on my knees and heard a worrisome crack. I grabbed at the fox, trying to catch it around the waist, but was stopped by two slimy arms grabbing me from behind. Juro/Kappa had slithered his way in, by order of Zric, and the fish wrapped me with Juro's arms, which were now part fin. The fox pulled on my sock with its teeth while the fish held me fast, and I screamed bloody murder.

"Get OFFFFFFFFFFF!" I yelled. "I'm trying to help you!"

Officer Bob tobogganed into the room, arms outstretched. He grabbed Juro around the knees, but the man was so much fish by this time that Bob slid right off, cutting his hands on the top frill that had suddenly sprouted from the man's back and thighs. Juro's mustache straightened and lengthened, becoming whiskers.

"Hey!" I said. "You're a catfish. Cool!"

I was so happy to have that question answered that I almost didn't notice Zric, who appeared out of nowhere and dangled the life-force balls in my face while I struggled with the irony of being hooked by a fish. The fox, now missing two tails, glared at me from the floor where it held my big toe in its teeth. Officer Bob was nursing a bleeding hand, a black eye, and he might have been missing a tooth. I didn't have time to look for sure.

Zric eyes gleamed red, and he held the balls high, flaunting them in my face. "I have control of the spirits," he said. "They will do exactly as I say. I'm thinking of having the fox tear off your toes one-by-one while the kappa punctures your face repeatedly with its spines. Really hurt you head to toe."

"How creative." I caught the fox's eye and once again noticed the prominent white patch on the fox's red fur. "Hey, Spot, you don't look like you want to tear off my toes, and I'm certain Professor Noyoko doesn't want to taste human flesh, so what say you turn your clever mind to figuring out a way to get out of this."

Spot grimaced and glanced at the glowing balls.

"Yeah," I sighed. "I know."

A shot rang out, which made me duck. The bullet ricocheted around the room, pinging artifacts, irreplaceable relics, and almost people, i.e., me. It sounded like a pinball game but ten times louder.

"Officer Bob! Don't shoot!"

"Sorry, Mrs. Friedman, but I'm bleeding and can't see out of one eye. My patience is gone."

"Is it your gun hand that's bleeding?"

"Yeah."

"Is it your dominant eye that's swelled shut?"

"Now that you mention it…"

"Don't shoot!"

"Well, what can I do?" he asked as the catfish stuck me with a spine, and I gritted my teeth against the pain, jerking away so hard that the spine stayed in my tummy, made vulnerable by the sweater unraveling that had occurred earlier. Spot shook with the effort not to eat me, practically vibrating like a tuning fork. I appreciated the not eating me very much.

"Get the exorcism materials and place them equidistant around the room in a circle!"

Zric jerked the balls and his head at Officer Bob and both spirits let me go to attack Bob. Bob did the smart thing, given the circumstances, and ran away. The fox was swift, but the fish wasn't made for running of any kind, much less a full-on sprint from a man whose pants…were on fire?

"Bob! What the fuck?" I leapt to my feet, or, I *tried* to leap to my feet. My kneecaps were damaged, so I inched my way to my feet and chased after them, propelling myself along by holding onto display tables and walls for balance. My tomahawk was on the floor, and with alarming cracks, creaks, and an ear-splitting snap, I managed to bend and retrieve it. I owed myself a lot of pushups for swearing, but I'd have to wait until I could move again.

"Zric did some pointy thing with his gecko hands and now, I'm on fire! Ahhhh!" Officer Bob unbuckled his pants while on the run, dropped them to the floor, and pulled his feet through the legs, which only sort of worked. He got his left foot out, the shoe stayed behind, but his right shoe was stuck in the other pant leg, so he was running in circles, bleeding from one hand, blind in one eye, dragging flaming slacks behind him, which unfortunately smoked a painting and an exotic fan into ash. The fox loped behind him, unhurried, and the kappa flopped along in slow pursuit while I hobbled after them.

Zric shot flame out of his hand again, and a display curtain whooshed to light, burning bright for a moment before drifting to the floor like a blackened tissue. Bob eventually got his pants off and kept running a path through the Asian exhibits, to Gem and Minerals, past the Mount Vesuvius model, and back into the Asian collection. He was throwing something over his shoulder, which Zric tried to dodge.

"What are you throwing?" I yelled while collecting the exorcism materials.

"Rocks!"

"What kind of rocks?"

"I don't know! I scooped them up from a broken case."

I didn't have time to think about it. I didn't. Really. The Church was going to hate me for this one. In sheer destruction, this must be up there in the top five costliest missions. I estimated top five because I heard one happened at the Louvre, and another happened right outside the Vatican. Ballsy. Those had to cost more.

Every mission racked up dollars like a big-stakes poker game in Vegas. Given my track record, they'd probably taken out insurance just to rebuild everything I wrecked.

## CHAPTER ELEVEN

My first official monster hunt was to rid a bank of an infestation, and I went without Liam. Father Paul declined to tell me the nature of the infestation, only saying that I would get the details when I spoke to the bank manager. I can't say which bank, but let's say it owns the tallest building in Ohio. 'Nuff said.

The bank was closed when I arrived, since it was close to dinner time, but the manager paced at the door, waiting for me. I didn't know someone could wear a path in granite.

"Mr. Tyndall?"

"Call me Rand. Thank you for helping with this unusual problem." He led me to a chair posed randomly in the middle of the lobby, a lovely atrium with fresh flowers and ferns, and sat once I had taken my chair. We stayed in the lobby, not going back to an office or moving away from the front door more than a couple of feet. Rand wore a black suit with a pencil-thin black tie and a blue dress shirt. He might have been good-looking with the curly mop of hair and the green eyes, but it was hard to envision it with all the sweat, fear-stink, and rhythmic rocking.

"What is going on?" I asked. "You can tell me."

"We have ROUSs."

"Pardon?" I thought I had heard wrong.

"Rodents of Unusual Size. We have a nest below the bank."

"They don't exist."

He huffed and ran his hands through his hair. "I assure you, they do exist."

"*The Princess Bride* kind?"

He nodded. "Exactly like."

"How many are in the nest?"

"I have no idea. The average Norway rat mother can have up to twenty or so young."

"That's a lot of rats."

"Yes. Yes, it is." He stood, brushed off his spotless pants, and ran for the door. He managed a "Good luck!" and then he was gone.

Not knowing what I was in for, I'd brought equipment, but not rat poison. Maybe I could ask the rats to leave? Explain that living under the bank wasn't good for business? Dragging my equipment along, I went off in search of rat tunnels.

Turned out they were easy to find because there were holes in the floors and walls large enough for a St. Bernard. I pulled a flashlight out of my bag of tricks and crawled through one in the wall near the CEO's office.

"Helllllooooooo? I'm here to speak to the head rat? The king? The queen? The grand poohbah?"

Nothing. I continued and knew I was being watched by the creepy-crawlie feeling on my skin. I was still on all fours, awkwardly dragging my bag with one hand, holding the flashlight in my other. Until the floor disappeared.

I fell over the ledge before my light illuminated the drop. I tumbled head over heels, and gravity proved to be true to its word.

"AHHHHHHHHHHHH!" I yelled, dropping my flashlight and my bag, until all three things, meaning the light, the bag, and me, hit the floor at the same time. Again, science.

I landed on something much softer than I had expected, and braced as I was for hard impact and broken bones, I was happily surprised. I wasn't quite as happy when the soft spot moved and snarled at me, snapping long yellow carving teeth, with chewing molars on the bottom. The red eyes freaked me out, but I couldn't but admire the whiskers. They were several feet long. Incredible.

"Hey. Sorry about falling on you…" The rat wasn't having it. The room, for surely it was a room since I could stand in it, was under the building and in the foundations, rocky ground mixed with concrete struts and metal poles. Detritus of every flavor decorated the ground, and describing the smell was impossible. Rats are typically clean animals, at least compared to mice, but this nest smelled like a men's locker room after a championship game, complete with the celebratory spray of beer. Urine, feces, decaying food, and for an unknown reason, one men's dress shoe, lay littered on the floor. This was the nest itself. The other entrances were tunnels that led to the nest from different angles. Now that I was at the bottom, I could see the connecting tunnels above.

My landing rat was about knee high and two feet long, with brownish fur that made it hard to see him, or her, if it stood still.

"Your camouflage is amazing. How do you do that? If I could take some of your fur with me, maybe I could figure it out."

The rat bared its teeth again.

"I won't hurt you, don't worry. Oh, but you do need to move out. The bank doesn't want you here. It's time for a withdrawal. Get it? Withdrawal? Not funny?" Another rat showed up and growled at me like the first one. I had the same problem focusing on this second rat as I did with the first. If you weren't looking for them and they were still, they were practically invisible.

"Honestly, I'm here to talk, and maybe take a sample of your fur. Would you mind?"

A fat rat growled behind me.

"Okay, I guess not. Anyone capable of speech here? I know that is a weird thing to say, but I'd like to talk this one out if you are of a magical variety."

Silence. I tried again. "Anyone? Anyone at all? Bueller? Bueller?"

I had hoped we could have a conversation, and having gotten to know the more mysterious, magical realm, it was possible that the ROUSs were from Faerie, but no, these seemed to be plain rats. Large, unusually so, but rats nonetheless. A sharp bark from the other side of the nest brought two more rats to the circle surrounding me.

A rat slinked out from behind the men's shoe, and it sauntered over to join the party. I was surrounded by six ROUSs and there were no fire pits in sight. I reached into my bag, grabbing my long lighter, and flicked it to life. The flame was enough to push the rats away, and their circle widened, giving me some breathing room. I knew fire would work and briefly considered setting the gunk on the floor on fire, but rejected that plan when I realized I might be killed, too. Any plan that involved my death was not a good plan.

I had to find a way out, but the tunnels were far away, higher than my head. I realized that this didn't make sense. There had to be lower entrances somewhere. If I were a rat, where would that be?

I dashed at the rat on my right with the lighter, waving it in its face so that it backed off, but while my attention was on that rat, another one attacked me from behind, snagging its yellow, cragged teeth into my waistband, pulling me back. That was interesting. It didn't bite me; it stopped me. Maybe there was something to these rats after all.

I slipped a little more to the right, and the rats followed, but this time they crowded behind me, herding me away from…

…the shoe! I held up my hands in surrender and listened with everything I had. Only then did I hear the mewling noises coming from the shoe. There were rat pups in the shoe. These rats were protecting their babies. Well, there was no way I was going to kill them at that point. I couldn't blame any species for protecting its young, but I did need to remove them.

An even blacker spot in the already gloomy nest attracted my attention, and I inched toward it. The rats seemed okay with this, hissing and growling, but they opened a path. Sure enough, this was an entrance to a tunnel. I grabbed my bag, put away my lighter, and flicked on the flashlight. I crawled in and went back to the surface. A single rat followed me, and when I stopped for a moment, it nipped my feet, not piercing my shoe but using enough pressure that I got the message.

It took a good five minutes of crawling to exit the tunnels into the bank proper. I sat on the floor, considering my options. I needed to get the rats to leave, but there was no way I was going to systematically kill them. I thought hard about where they could relocate. Public Square was a nice area, with a large green space and lots of interesting and respectable businesses. They even had…

…the casino.

I'm not making a blanket statement about gambling. Lots of people love it and can enjoy an evening out playing cards or betting on roulette, or what have you. They have the right to do that, and I appreciate the money they bring to the downtown area. It's that I've seen a lot of bad come from gambling, including gambling addiction, drinking to excess, and losing a lot of money—like, a life saving's worth. I'd seen marriages fall apart, kids separated from their parents, and jobs lost. A great deal of damage.

Since the building was so large, there would be plenty of space beneath for the rats. They'd never have to come to the surface. I propped a door open at the bank, ambled on over to the casino, and hunted around for openings. Oh! Lookee, there. A sewer that led directly to and from the casino. Bingo.

But, how to get them out?

I could flood them out. Rats were terrific swimmers, and if I pulled a fire alarm and got the big trucks to the building, I most certainly could get enough water pressure to force them to leave.

Another thought creeped into my head. No. Was it possible? I fished out my phone, opened it, sought a streaming program, and hunted around for what I needed. I pressed play, slipped in the door I'd left open, and headed to the tunnels.

I crawled back into the same tunnel I exited and held the phone up for the rats to hear. When I got no response, I crawled forward another dozen or so feet and turned the volume to maximum.

They approached, rat-a-tat-tat, rat-a-tat-tat, swaying in time to the music, the pups hanging from the adults' mouths like kittens. The flute music was a jaunty tune, not frantic, but rhythmic, and like the Pied Piper, I led them forward, through the open door and to the sewer entrance. I threw the phone in the sewer, and they followed it, dancing their little feet into a new home.

When I told Father Paul what I'd done, he expressed some dismay.

"You led the rats to another home next door to the bank?"

"Not exactly next door, but in the same general area, yes. Look, the casino has lots of places for the rats to hide and you only promised we'd get them out of the bank, not that we'd kill them."

Father Paul rubbed his eyes. "What are we going to do when the casino wants them removed?"

"Honestly, Father Paul, I don't give a rat's ass, and I need a new phone."

## CHAPTER TWELVE

The Pied Piper experience taught me to think outside the box, and my training made me stronger. I was hunting monsters left and right, but never saw or heard about Pascal again. Didn't mean he left my memory, though. I'd have my day, and so would Liam.

One evening, Liam and I went hunting for a vampire who'd killed a family in Danville, Ohio, population, one thousand and twenty-four. He'd continue to move and killed a trucker and his wife in Brewster, Ohio, population, about two thousand. The vampire was hunting in small towns, making one kill and moving on to another. We'd tracked him to Cambridge, Ohio, a beautiful, historic town in the foothills of the Appalachian Mountains, and the birth place of John Glenn, the senator and astronaut. I'd been there once before with my family when we'd taken a long weekend at Salt Fork State Park.

Legend had it that this vampire was none other than George R. Tingle, a former resident of Cambridge from 1175-1830, known for building the town's first tavern, which also operated as the county courthouse prior to 1813. People at that time had the right priorities and settled conflicts over a beer, so why build two separate buildings when you were going to the bar after the courthouse anyway?

"Why do you think old George came back to Cambridge?" Liam asked me, as we sat on the low roof of an antique shop on Main Street, watching for our target.

"I don't know, but I think we should call him Vampire Tingle. It has a whole other ring to it, don't you think?"

"You are such a pinhead."

"Granted, but come on, that's funny."

"Nothing funny about a vampire," Liam retorted, but he was smiling.

"Is that him?" I pointed to a shadow on Wheeling Avenue, near a gift shoppe, with an "e." The olde English way.

"I think so, and if it is, he most likely knows we are here. We're downwind," Liam whispered.

"Which doofus put us downwind?"

"You did."

"Yeah, I figured. Hey, is there another vampire with him?"

"Let's go find out," said Liam, and he jumped off the roof to the sidewalk below, while I had to run down the fire escape. I didn't bother with the noise this caused; as Liam noted, we'd been made already.

I joined Liam and thought the direct approach might be the best one.

"Hey, boys? Vampire Tingle?" I gulped down a laugh and wound up snorting. Classy.

"Ma'am," replied one of the vamps. "Yes, I'm George Tingle, and I think I sense another vampire next to you. Reveal yourself! Are you here for the assembly?"

Assembly?

Liam gave me a "what the hell do I say?" face. I rolled my hand to indicate he should continue improvising.

"Yes, I'm here for the assembly." Liam announced this with all the seriousness in the world, like, where else would he be?

"Ah! Righteous brother, welcome. From whom do you descend, and why isn't your forbear here? Have we suffered another death amongst the Founders?"

"I'm a descendant of John Chapman," Liam said, using the only name we could recall from the old Founder's cemetery. "He who lost his three-year old daughter to the Indians and had to ride to get her back."

"I am sorry to hear of John's passing. How did such an old and powerful vampire die?"

"An unfortunate Cherries Jubilee incident."

"What?" said Vampire Tingle.

"He caught fire during the flambé part of the presentation," I responded, voice flat.

"How remarkable. Allow me to introduce the late, and still undead,

Reverend Rowcliffe. It is well meet to see you again, old friend," Tingle said to Rowcliffe.

Rowcliffe turned a suspicious eye to Liam. "Why do you travel with a human? Is she your pet? I do not see that she is colored."

I almost dropped him right then, but I was curious about the assembly and how many vampires from Cambridge might be here, so I had to wait. Reverend Rowcliffe, however, had put himself at the top of my "stake with extreme prejudice" list.

Tingle continued.

"Let us proceed to the assembly. Onward! We shall see our compatriots again. Stranger, you have not given your name."

"Liam."

"Well met, Liam! You must come from the Black Irish side of the clan, eh? Come. You can bring your pet along. Good to travel with self-packed food. I've been dining on the road, myself."

I grabbed Liam's sleeve to keep from jumping forward with my hatchet.

The assembly was at the Performing Arts Center across the street. We slipped in and were hailed by six other vampires.

Rowcliffe and Tingle shook hands with the other vampires, who were either original Founders of Cambridge, or children made by Founders.

Tingle kissed the hand of a female vampire, introducing Liam to her. "Liam, son of John Chapman, since removed from our presence by a freak cooking accident, please meet the Lady Marietta."

Liam kissed her hand as well. Lady Marietta may have been hundreds of years old, but she'd kept up with the times, wearing stiletto black leather boots and a dress I'd seen on the cover of a ladies' magazine with a fabulous black leather jacket. Her dark eyes were sharp and her nose was a curved beak, making her not traditionally beautiful, but dangerously attractive, like fire to a moth. She scared me more than all the other doofus vampires in the room.

Lady Marietta accepted the kiss. "Is that your meal, Liam?" she asked, pointing to me. "It is nice to have a snack ready and waiting, isn't it? You may place her in the back."

Liam gave me a cold stare and pointed to the rear. I bowed my head and scurried off, which was preferable because I could use the invisibility of meal on the hoof to develop a plan. I didn't want to burn down the place since that would impact the entire town, but I needed to destroy them all.

I watched the scene in front of me, and it was obvious that Lady Marietta had to go first. She didn't buy the descendant of Chapman story, I could tell, and she sat near Liam to best keep an eye on him.

I'd carried my bag with me the whole time and no one has asked about it, so I placed it on the seat next to me and fished around with my hand to find the stakes. I had ten in total, which should be enough for all.

I carried the bag in my left hand, keeping my shoulders drooped and my head down, and shuffled to toward the group of vampires who were raising a glass of merlot to their reunion.

Tingle held his wine, and the others joined him. "To our fallen brother, John Chapman! May he rest in peace."

"I saw John only seven years ago, Liam. I'm surprised he didn't mention you at the time?"

"He had not sired me yet, dear Lady Marietta."

Lady Marietta placed her stiletto heel on the top of Liam's foot and shot to her feet. Liam let out a gasp of surprise.

"Lady? Why do this?" Liam asked, throwing himself to the side where his pierced foot bled freely.

"Because I actually saw John three weeks ago, and you lie. He is not your sire." She walked closer to Liam, and he twisted so that her back was toward me. "But someone powerful made you. I wonder who that was?"

She never got the chance to guess because I grasped a stake and in one smooth move, staked her through her back. She fell in heap of Prada and Louboutin, but I must have missed her heart by a millimeter because she did not die, though she was immobilized.

I'd moved past after staking her and slammed a stake into the next vampire, who turned to ash. I grabbed another stake, whirled backward, and caught Tingle, staking him through the neck when he ducked to avoid my attack. It was telling that none of them said anything but fought as if this were a minor inconvenience, that is until Tingle grabbed my right arm with his, gurgling as his trachea tried to repair itself, and brought my arm to his mouth, where he bit down hard on my wrist.

Liam jumped from behind him, wrapped an arm around Tingle's chin, and unhinged the vampire's jaws. When I was free, he pulled the stake out of Tingle's neck and finished the job properly, while I moved on with my hatchet.

I swung left and right, chopping off pieces of vampire as I went, taking the head of the next two vamps with one swipe each. That left three, and two bugged out before I could get to them. This left Rowcliffe.

"You were a minister. A reverend. Trusted by the people of this town. How did you become a vampire?" I was bleeding from the wrist, and the two of us circled on another. Liam ran off to catch the two that had flown the coop.

"I was turned by a visiting English vampire, as Tingle was. We kept our identities as secret as possible, but my position called for Sunday morning services. We were forced to fake my death. Some unlucky drunk lies in my grave. Now you, Monster Hunter—yes, I recognize you for what you are—will be buried in a pauper's box."

Rowcliffe pounced, wrapping his hands around my neck to bring it to his mouth. His hands touched my Star of David necklace, and he leapt back, shocked at the sight of his smoking hands.

"No, no, no, Reverend," I said, as I advanced. "Touching a religious object on a person of faith never works out for your kind."

I slashed off his right arm and then his left at both elbows and, in an ode to my mother, grabbed two stakes and put one in each of his eyes. He fell to his knees, armless, sightless, and unforgiven. When I took his head, he was muttering, "I repent. I repent." He turned to ash anyway. Too little, too late.

Liam ambled back into the center, wiping blood from his lips, wearing a different shirt. "They were tasty," he said. "One of them must have had a good brandy before coming here."

I motioned to Lady Marietta's body, not ash but desiccated and translucent like a snake's shed skin. "Did you drink her down?" I asked him.

His lips quirked into a sharp grin. "She was also tasty, and I wanted her to experience her life seeping away. As I drank, I got a Cliff's Notes view of her life, and it was ugly and cruel. She deserved it."

He continued, his face furrowed in sadness. "Right before she died, I caught sight of her childhood. She was once a little girl, the apple of her father's eye, and wanted to be a mother herself."

"I guess we all start innocent."

"Yes, but we don't stay that way."

"No, we don't." I patted him on the back. "Where'd you get the new shirt?"

"Oh!" he said. "I seem to have picked up a new power as a result of drinking her blood. Watch." He did a shimmy shake, and the next thing I knew, he was dressed in a completely new outfit, including an Ohio University sweatshirt that said, "Muck Fiami."

"That's not fair! I want to do that." I put my hatchet back and glared at him. He whistled a cheerful tune. "Fine, but I'm taking her jacket." I seized the leather jacket from Marietta's flaking corpse and slid it on. "Score."

"Jess?"

We walked out into the evening air, leaving the mess behind. "Hold on," I said, and sent a text message to Father Paul to get a clean-up crew ASAP. I put the phone back in my pocket. "What is it, Liam?"

"We've gotten better and stronger, right?"

"Sure."

"When do we go after Pascal?"

I gave that some thought. "I do want to go after him, Liam, believe me, but I want to take him alive. He's got things to tell me about my mom. We can't kill him; we have to capture him, and that's a totally different thing. But we'll do it, Liam. We will."

## CHAPTER THIRTEEN

Reflecting on the adventures of that night and the resulting discussion with Liam got me thinking about capturing things. I needed to capture the spirits in a circle, first and foremost. Then, I could deal with the imp.

The best thing to capture a spirit being is a circle. I've heard lots of things about how the circle has to be precise, but I've found that magic has a lot of flexibility. I gathered all the exorcism ingredients and placed them at equidistant intervals around the room to make the circle, or an oval, or some roundish shape. As Bob ran through the Asian room, I chucked the fox tails and the catfish spine into the middle of the circle and it snapped to life, capturing the kappa and the fox inside. Bob managed to slip out just in time. I winked at his Spider-Man underwear, and he gave me the finger. I was too sophisticated to return the gesture.

Zric hopped into the room, trying to remove something hard, bright, and shiny from the bottom of his foot, which was dripping scalding blood everywhere. I flung the tomahawk at him, as I had been taught, without thinking, without aiming, going by instinct, willing the sharp edge to fall where it should. My muscle memory served me well, and the tomahawk flew true.

Until that sonofabitch juked to the right at the last possible second. The tomahawk took off one ear and a horn, but wasn't a lethal blow.

"Biiiiiiittchhhh!" he screamed. "Your mother was a bitch and your father was a nobody!"

"Well, your mother was a hamster and your father smelt of elderberries!" I bellowed this as I ran away, chased by a murderous, Red-Hot red, bleeding imp. I detected a note of burnt cinnamon.

"She was a minor demon, not a hamster, you Church flunkie!" That was the end of the witty repartee because he was done playing and so was I, although I will admit to being disappointed in his Monty Python movie knowledge. Wasn't *The Holy Grail* mandatory viewing in Hell?

Zric bounced from wall-to-wall, clinging like a lizard high on super glue, leaping from corner-to-corner. His razor teeth and claws were out and ready to strike, and he'd stopped paying attention to his bleeding foot. Before I noticed what he was doing, he'd whirled with such intensity that he'd created a vortex, which herded me back into the Asian artifacts room, encircling me with a spinning dervish of air, debris, and noise while the kitsune and kappa were still caught in the exorcism circle. The imp pounced, teeth bared, eyes wide, dripping blood and an acidic spit that scorched the floor. He sent sparks from his fingers, and some hit me, burning tiny, but painful, holes in my clothing and skin. Those that missed me drifted to the floor, scoring it with miniscule polka-dots burns. The floor looked like a teenager's acne-riddled face.

There was a very real moment when I thought I might get taken down by a three-foot, demon equivalent of a cockroach, but my pride stepped up to stop me from taking that hit. I pin-wheeled my arms looking for anything, anything at all, to take him down. He landed on my left forearm, tearing at a chunk of muscle, skin, and tendon before my right hand found something rock-solid. I brought it up and over my head in a powerful arc and smashed the whatever-it-was on top of Zric's head, aiming for the horn and ear that were already injured to create maximum pain.

Zric screamed and let off chewing my arm to fall on the floor, scrambling to get up on his feet. I slammed the object down again, smashing his tail, then his jaw, then his middle spine, repeatedly hitting him until I knew he'd rise no more. The life-force balls rolled away, coming to rest under a Chinese silk ottoman. Zric was a bloody puddle of red slime by the time I finished, and truth be told, I was happy about it and glad he suffered. I'm not proud of it, but there it was.

The wind died down, and I stopped to catch my breath. My chest heaved with my efforts, and the strain on my lungs had me gasping for air. I looked at the object in my hand, and despite my desperate need for air, I caught my breath.

My world spun. I had…I had…

Oh, no.

This was terrible. I couldn't believe it. Oh, the karma, the karma.

I stared down at the object and realized that I had violently, willfully, happily, smashed an imp to death with the Buddha statue. The statue was stained with imp blood so deep that it looked like the Buddha itself was bleeding.

Murdering something with a Buddha? I was in deep shit. I felt for the Buddha's spirit, finding what I expected. It was gone. The Divine had seen what I did, using a messenger for a weapon of death, and had abandoned me.

As a Jew, I didn't go to confession, but I was certain there wasn't enough confession in the world for this sin. I'd have to consult Rabbi Stein. Could I make a donation somewhere? I couldn't imagine there was a Society to Help Imps Transfer to Society. I examined that thought. The SHITS? Not family-friendly. Maybe the Foundation for the Protection of Imps, the FPI?

Why didn't I beat him to death with the Old Testament and get it over with?

I placed the Buddha back where he belonged, apologizing to it, and retrieved the balls, getting imp blood all over the ottoman, which then burned holes in the ancient silk. More destruction for the Diocese to pay for.

Officer Bob joined me, and we studied the trapped spirits. Juro was part man, part fish, and getting fishier every second. Professor Noyoko was all red fox with the big white spot, but I thought I could see an outline of her human shape if I squinted hard.

"What do we do now?" asked Officer Bob.

"I don't know. We want them to go out of the bodies, so I guess we tell them what we want them to do."

"That's a little loosey-goosey. I thought ceremonies such as this had strict procedures."

"It's a Pied Piper moment, Bob. We do the best we can with the physical ingredients and hope it all works. Cross fingers."

"I don't understand the Pied Piper thing, but let's do it on one, two, three."

"Okay. Here's the blue one. That's for the kappa. I've got the red one for the fox. Ready?" We each took a breath, opened our mouths and yelled.

"Out, out, damn Spot!" said I.

"Go, Fish!" said Bob.

Yes, we heard ourselves, and by unspoken agreement, neither of us commented. The most important point is that it worked.

The spirits disconnected, leaving the human bodies on the ground. They floated up in the air, wispy outlines of white. The fish dove into an ocean I couldn't see and surfaced right in front Bob's hand. The fox shook its tails and trotted to float before me. I tossed it the life-force ball, and Officer Bob followed suit. Both sprits swallowed the balls, and their outlines became more distinct. With a flick of a fin and five tails, they were gone.

"Wow," I said, looking at the floor. "I really did cut off two of its tails."

"You'd better keep them, Mrs. Friedman. The kitsune might want them back one day."

"Good point." I picked up the tails, draped them around my neck, and leaned down to help a groaning Professor Noyoko and equally stunned Professor Juro. Noyoko stretched her shoulders, circled her neck, and ran her fingers through her hair. Or, tried to.

"What is this gummy stuff?" she asked, her eyes crinkled in confusion, as she hit a gnarled patch of hair.

"I…don't know…" I said, checking my watch. "Oh no! Look at the time." I made a hobbling beeline for the lobby where I found my son and his friends lining up for the bus.

"David, did you have fun?" I asked, ignoring the way the other mothers stared at me. I scooped a little jam out of my ear and flung it on the floor for the effect. I had wrapped my bleeding arm in sanitizing wipes, which the museum had in dispensers at every corner. I desperately wanted to get off my feet.

"Yeah, Mom! Since we couldn't go to certain parts of the museum, we got to go to the Planetarium! It was awesome. Also, we got to eat outside on the grass. We were supposed to eat at the restaurant, but for some reason, it was trashed. I don't know why. Best field trip ever!" He and his friends pumped their fists in the air.

David turned back to me. "Hey, Mom," he whispered, nudging me in the side, pointing at the tails around my neck. "Did you get that fox spirit thing figured out?"

I rustled his hair. "Yes, David." I patted my stiff hair with one hand. "This museum is clean."

David jumped up and down, pointing at me. "I know that one, Mom! I know that one! That's from the end of *Poltergeist*."

My mouth dropped. "When did you watch *Poltergeist*?"

David clasped his hands behind his back and looked elsewhere, anywhere. "Uh…Dad let me."

I bent down and made him look at me, hand under his chin. "Were you scared?"

"Mom, I stumbled on it while channel surfing. I thought it was a reality show."

"Okay, then." I was going to have to ponder what effect I was having on my children's formative years. "Wait a sec. You want something from the gift shop? I'd like to purchase a trinket to remind me of this adventure."

David was so happy, he skipped to the store. I made my purchase, and he chose a t-shirt that said "We Love Dead People" with the name of the museum on the back. He chose a stuffed buffalo for Daniel and book about the Inuit for Devi.

Mrs. Butler approached and pulled me aside, her face grim. "Mrs. Friedman. We do not allow crop tops at school. Our belly buttons are not for public display. You cannot accompany us on trips if you can't obey the school dress code."

"You're upset that my sweater got shredded, but the burn marks on my face and my bleeding left arm don't concern you?"

She blushed and looked down at the ground. "Of course, I am bothered by your bleeding arm. Are you okay?"

I felt bad about needling her for a moment. "Yes, I'm fine, thank you for asking."

"Good. Don't bleed on the bus seats or we won't get our deposit back."

"I'll do my best to keep my blood to myself."

"That would be most appreciated." She gave me a sharp nod and strode away. I was left rubbing my temples and muttering my prayer for patience when Alicia Pembro trotted over to me, tsk-tsking.

"Is that real fox fur? You should be ashamed of wearing real fur. You know how many foxes must have died for that thing around your neck?"

"I know exactly how many. None," I replied. "But I can't help but wonder how many silkworms were involved in making your blouse, or how many South Africans died mining for that diamond on your left hand."

Alicia's hand flew to her mouth. "Well, I never!"

"I know," I replied. "You never thought about it that way before. Glad I could help you out."

Alicia prissy-walked to Collette to tell her how rude I was, but I couldn't bring myself to care. My knees ached, and I was more tired than I could say. I wondered if Zric did this on his own or if Pascal pulled the strings from behind. It was an intricate, sophisticated ambush. I couldn't image the imp planning this on his own, but maybe I'd underestimated him.

Professors Juro and Noyoko, restored to full humanity, trotted into the lobby to find me, holding hands. I sniffed Juro as he got closer, and though I still found his mustache disturbing, he smelled okay. Ish. Okay-ish.

"Mrs. Friedman, I'm told that I should thank you," Noyoko said, her voice and posture stiff.

"You're welcome."

"I don't remember much about the last several hours, but I've been told that I was possessed by a fox spirit you named Spot."

"That's correct, but we exorcised it."

Her nostrils flared. "And Juro was possessed by a fish spirit?"

"Got it in one. A catfish to be precise, which I found interesting. Why a catfish and not a koi, for example?"

Noyoko sniffed. "Mrs. Friedman, I am a woman of science. None of this is plausible. I'm going to have some blood tests and find out what really happened."

Juro sent me an apologetic look, but spoke up. "I have two questions," he said.

"What is the first one?"

"Why is the Buddha statue covered in blood? I thought it was supposed to oversee the ceremony. It should have been clean."

I squirmed in place, thinking of how to answer that question. "I used the Buddha to smash the imp."

Juro gaped like the fish he used to be.

Noyoko snorted. "You are off your rocker. There is a real, scientific, provable reason for why I can't remember this day, and I will work with real doctors to find it. Don't chatter to me about imps and fox spirits.

Juro, let's go. We have many restoration projects, thanks to this one-woman wrecking machine."

Juro stood there, blinking at me as he processed what I'd said. "I'm not sure what fate has in store for you, Mrs. Friedman."

Noyoko tugged on his sleeve. "Come on. Don't waste time with this charlatan. Oh, good, the police. Sir. Sir?" Officer Bob turned to her. "Something very strange has happened in this museum today, and I believe this woman is a part of it."

"What do you think happened, Professor Noyoko?" he asked.

"I am unsure right now, but I will gather facts and evidence. I suspect drugs and hypnotism were involved."

"I can assure you, Professor, neither of those were a part of what happened." Officer Bob had redressed, but with his black eye and missing tooth, he looked like gangbanger after a bad day.

"We'll see. And clean up, Officer. You aren't a good representative for the force."

"Yes, ma'am. You're welcome." His jaw was locked, so I had to lean in to hear him. Noyoko tried to flounce off, but Juro held her hand and had more on his mind.

"I have another question."

"What is it?" I sat in a chair and pulled another one over so I could rest my feet. My knees were throbbing.

"The egg. I was cleaning up the mess in the room a moment ago and accidentally dropped the egg. It was raw. The yolk went everywhere."

"Yeah, so? You said we needed one raw egg."

"No, I didn't. I said we needed one egg."

"You did!"

"I didn't. A hard-boiled would have been fine, and easier to procure, I would think. Who comes into a museum looking for one raw egg?"

Officer Bob gave a sharp intake of breath and sank to the floor, laughing, gasping for air. "Oh, my goodness…Oh, this is priceless. Wait until I tell Captain Morgan…Oh, oh, oh dear…"

I straightened my shoulders, sniffed, stood, and limped away. I turned before leaving. "Professor Noyoko, the sticky stuff in your hair might be chewing gum."

"Chewing gum! How'd that get there?"

"I have no idea."

## CHAPTER FOURTEEN

"We got to go to the Planetarium, Dad, even though that usually costs extra because some of the museum had to be closed due to a fox spirit," David said, bouncing up and down in his chair as he told the family about the day. It was Nathaniel, me, the three kids, and Blaze, our resident phoenix.

Being totally Nathaniel, Nathaniel replied, "Wow. That sounds great, David. I'm sure Mommy will tell me more about the fox spirit later. How was it having Mom on the field trip?"

"Awesome." David bit his lip.

"It is okay, David, you can be honest," I said.

"Well," David cast me a sorry face, "I would have liked it if she was with us more, but I understand that monster hunting comes first."

OUCH. Can we say work/life balance? I hid my face by looking down at my knees and rearranging the ice packs.

Nathaniel saw my stricken face. "David, you and this family come first, not monster hunting. But monster hunting is a way that Mom can keep all of us, and other people, safe. Like a policeman, but without a badge. Or a hat. Or an official car, a uniform, or handcuffs. Hey, this job doesn't have enough perks." He said this to me with a smile, and we played footsie under the table. Gosh, I loved him.

"I know, but I worry she'll get hurt," David said to his father.

"Your mom is good at her job, and we have to trust her to do all that she can to be as careful as possible, but we both understand your worries."

"David," I finally said. "I won't tell you that my job isn't dangerous sometimes, but lots of jobs are dangerous. Remember when we watched the construction workers high up in the air walk on the girders?"

"Sure, Mom, but they don't have monsters trying to push them off the girders."

The kid had a point.

"But, I do know what you mean." His tone of voice just about killed me.

David quirked his head, and I knew Blaze was talking to him telepathically. David's lips twitched, became a smile, and then, without anyone else knowing why, David laughed a so hard he got the hiccups.

"Anyone want to tell me what is going on?" I asked, crossing my arms over my chest, glaring at Blaze.

"Hic! Nope, Mom. Hic! We weren't making fun of you, no way." He hid his face behind his hands, but the sounds he made were one step from hysteria. Blaze ruffled his feathers and looked across the yard to avoid my eyes. Devi poked him, and Blaze must have shared the joke with her because she burst out laughing, too, which was gross because she spurted lemonade out her nose. That made Daniel giggle, and soon the whole family was laughing, half of it at my expense, but the laughter felt so good, I didn't care.

Later, when Nathaniel and I cuddled in bed, Nathaniel stroked my arm, the signal for let's make nookie or I've got to say something you won't like. I was hoping for the nookie.

"Jess."

I stiffened. "Yes."

"The kids are going to worry about you, as do I. Could you possibly give what we talked about some more thought?"

"Retire?"

"Find another way to help."

"I'll give it some thought, but it isn't that easy."

"Think about it?"

"Promise. Go to sleep."

I lay in bed staring at the ceiling while Nathaniel snored beside me. My stomach churned, and my heart beat fast as I pondered the most important question.

I hadn't made up my mind until the day before yesterday to chaperone the field trip, so how the hell did the imp know I was going to be there?

The thought made me get out of bed and wander to the living room, where I'd placed the little jade Buddha I'd bought from the museum gift shop. I fingered the tomahawk that lay next to it. I'd need to store the 'hawk somewhere safe, but I enjoyed holding it. It seemed to hum in my hand as if it had woken up and was happy to back in action. I hadn't intended to take it, but it was in my hand, and if it slipped into David's backpack? Who's to know?

I held the Buddha in my hands, sat back on my heels, and placed the Buddha to my heart chakra. I settled in and muttered the only mantra I knew, which was to Ganesh, not Buddha, but I was improvising. I intoned the four words, taking care to express each syllable.

"Ohm Gam Ganapataye Namaha." Deep breath.

"Ohm Gam Ganapataye Namaha…" I forced my mind to focus, bringing awareness to my body, how I felt physically, mentally, and the crack in my spirit that doubted, hated, angered. In my heart, I apologized to Buddha for using his representation to annihilate an imp. It was an odd prayer, but I'm nothing if not truthful, especially when speaking to the Divine, no matter the aspect.

*Do not dwell in the past, do not dream of the future, concentrate the mind on the present moment.*

Forgiveness is a beautiful thing.

I spent the next day running errands, playing with the kids, and making schnitzel. I made enough for our supper and made another couple pieces for Rabbi Stein. I drove to the synagogue in the late afternoon to find my spiritual mentor.

"Rabbi?"

"Come in, Jess."

I handed him the Tupperware containing the food, and he opened a corner to take a sniff. "That is going to be delicious, Jess. Thank you."

"You're welcome. It is my pleasure. I care for you, Rabbi."

He gestured to my normal chair and let his creaky body settle into an equally creaky chair.

"I care about you, as well, which is why I am glad you stopped by."

"I don't understand."

"How did the museum trip go?" He asked this while sitting back in his chair, eyes closed.

"It wasn't what you expected." I told him the gist of the story.

"Was it what *you* expected?"

"No. Yes. Crazy things happen all the time in my line of work." I licked my lips, unsure where this was heading.

"How's David?"

"He's good. He loved the museum."

"But you were not actually with him, right? You were ridding the world of an evil imp and rescuing two people from possession."

"Exactly."

"I think you should spend time asking why you are being presented with all of these obstacles."

"What do you mean?" I was totally confused.

"Something is coming, Jess. These events are getting you ready for what is to come."

"Oh, that doesn't sound menacing."

He smiled. "I want you to stay on top of your game, Jess. You're going to be tested."

I drove home thinking about what Rabbi Stein had said. *Tested. Tested how? What could possibly test me to my limit?*

I walked up the stairs to be greeted by three kids talking at once, each grabbing a leg or an arm, and a gorgeous man handing me a glass of white wine. This is what I fought for; these are the people who make life worth living.

The thought stopped me flat. My family. Nathaniel noticed my face and sent me a look. "You okay?" he mouthed over the kids' heads.

I swallowed hard, reclaimed my thoughts, let the anxiety go, and laughed when the kids tried to make a pyramid. Daniel, the little one, insisted on being on the bottom, and Devi was trying to reason with him, explaining why he should be on top. I could have told her that reasoning with a three-year old was useless, but I chose not to, letting her work that through herself. When Daniel stomped his tiny foot and Devi threw up her hands, I laughed hard. It felt great.

There was a thump on the front door, and I thought that Angie had stopped by. I continued giggling as I walked to the door and opened it. I fell silent, squinting at who had come to visit.

There was a wolf at my door.

# HANDLE WITH CARE

# CHAPTER ONE

I sucked in the gummy material, trying desperately to breathe. The muck ran down my face in thick clumps, clogging my nose and mouth. It was only my training that allowed me to keep calm, hold what was left of my air, and wipe the goo from my face. As soon as my nostrils and mouth were free, I inhaled a glorious breath and licked my lips.

Sweet, cloying, annoyingly toothsome, but David loved it.

Getting smashed in the face with a cake was a normal birthday tradition in the Friedman house, but why I was the one who got the face smack when it was *David's* ninth birthday, I didn't know. At least it was only one slice.

I opened one eye, blinking white frosting off my eyelashes, and stared at my son. "Are you happy now?"

David nodded in big ups and downs, hopping with excitement. "That was awesome, Mom! Gleeeeeep!"

I had grabbed a generous piece of cake and smashed it right in David's face. He shook off the frosting, his eyes shining. "Good one!" All his friends laughed, including his besties, James and Jack, Angie's older set of twins. Angie was my best friend, in fact, my only female friend, and she was there with the younger twins, Rose and April.

The wolf was there too, hiding under the deck, keeping a close eye on the kids. She'd shown up at my door a couple of days ago, told Blaze, our resident phoenix, "Danger is near," and that she came to watch the pups, meaning my children.

Not alarming at all. Nah.

The wolf came from the zoo where I'd had a wee fight with a were-gorilla turned *zombie* were-gorilla in the past. The wolves helped me kill the gorilla and had partaken of his flesh. The main effects seemed to be increased intelligence and a cat burglar's ability with locks.

I wasn't sure if the zoo officials knew she was here, but I figured what they didn't know wouldn't hurt them. If a wolf says danger is coming and she's here to protect your children, I believe you simply say, "Thank you." There's no manual for such an occurrence, much less defined etiquette, but it seemed the right course of action.

Now, I was having a birthday party with nine children, the rule being the number of guests equal the age of the birthday child, plus a few parents, my husband, a wolf, and a phoenix. I'd also placed my small Buddha statue in the window facing out. Ever since I'd bought him from a museum gift store, he'd liked to be a part of the action. Buddha had helped me exorcise a Japanese fox spirit, a kitsune, from a visiting professor at the museum and kill a pint-sized vile demon named Zric, so I brought him home in jade form.

"Mrs. Friedman?" A boy from the neighborhood stood next to me, bopping from one foot to the other.

"Hi, Brian. Bathroom is inside, down the hall."

"No, ma'am. I don't need to go."

I took a quick glance around and noticed all the boys were paying attention to our conversation. Brian had been drafted.

"What is it, Brian?"

"Can we ride your pony? We don't know anyone else who has a pony."

"Pony? We don't have a…oh, right. You know, he's more of a donkey-pony, an ass if you will, but I'll go talk to him."

Brian bit his lip in concentration, trying to make heads or tails of what I'd said, but he nodded at the end, not understanding what I'd meant, but accepting that this might be one step closer what he wanted.

I skipped down the stairs from the deck to the yard and walked over to talk to the pony.

*I am not an ass.*

My lips quirked, and I tried not to laugh, I really did, but it was impossible. I rotated away from the children so my back was to them and held onto Blaze's wing. To the kids who didn't see past the glamour, I was guiding my pony toward the back of the yard.

*I told you we don't give rides. I am not a pack animal.*

"I know you aren't, but the kids see a pony. That's all on you. You cast that glamour."

*I have to glamour myself as something close to my size. Conservation of matter, Einstein, or did you skip that class?*

"Testy. You could've been a donkey."

*You aren't helping.*

"Or a cow."

*I won't forget this.*

"You'll do it? Okay!" I turned toward the kids. "Who is first on the pony? Make a line."

Blaze did the spectacular eye roll thing that only a phoenix can do. His eyes are so large that when he rolls them, they look like moons circling the Earth.

*This is ignominious. I hope none of my brothers and sisters see this.*

"You have brothers and sisters? Where are they? How many?" I peppered him with questions because he'd never mentioned family.

*Put the first kid on.*

"Okay! Brian, you asked on behalf of everyone, so you get the first ride. This is Eeyore, yes, like the grumpy character in *Winnie the Pooh*. You sit here," I said, positioning his legs on either side of the phoenix, "and hold here." I pointed toward the space where Blaze's long neck met his body. The feathers at this part were bronze metal, so I held my breath to see what it was that Brian felt beneath his hands.

"His mane is so soft!" Brian's smile was beautiful, wide and full-on. A happy kid enjoying a pony ride at a birthday party. I whispered to Blaze, "Thank you. You have no idea how happy he is."

Blaze gave a grudging nod. *I like to make the kids happy.*

"Yeeyahhhh!" yelled Brian, and Blaze took off. He took off at a speed that felt normal to him but was way too fast for a little kid. "Eeyore! Slow down!" The other parents had jumped up, prepared to stop the pony and rescue the boy. The other children were hollering, "Go, go, go!"

Blaze slowed to a sedate pace and finished a circle around the yard. Brian slid off, his cheeks red with wind and happiness. "That was awesome! Why did you make him slow down?"

"Safety, Brian. You don't have a saddle or a helmet. It could be hard to hold on."

*If you think you are putting a saddle on me, you have another think coming...*

"Let's see, who's next?" I lifted the new boy onto Blaze's back, and Blaze harrumphed off.

"Jess?" One of the moms, also a neighbor, stood next to me with a sweet smile.

"Hi, Judy. Thanks for coming."

"Oh, Joseph wouldn't have missed this for all the world."

"I'm so glad to hear that. I like when Joseph and David play together. They're so close, it's almost like brothers. I bet they'll be friends for life." I pictured them as adults, Joseph living somewhere erudite and academic. Maybe Boston. David living somewhere close to the action, maybe the District of Columbia, or Maryland, so he could take the metro into the city. It was a lovely thought.

Judy blinked at me. "It's just that I was wondering if you knew that having a pony is against the Neighborhood Association policy. No livestock of any kind."

"He's not livestock. He's a pony, and the house across the street has chickens. Every once in a while, they get a rooster by mistake, and I have to listen to the cockle-doodle-doo at four a.m."

"We have an exception for chickens."

"Great. Let's make an exception for ponies." I wiped my hands together. "Easy peasy."

Judy blinked twice. I almost asked if she had something in her eye. "Jess, I am so sorry, but we can't do that. Eeyore has to go to a stable."

I was so glad that Blaze didn't hear that. I bit my tongue and said, "We'll see what we can do."

Judy blinked yet again, which, this time, seemed to indicate relief. "Oh, good, Jess. I'd hate to have to fine you."

"I wouldn't like it either."

## CHAPTER TWO

Oddball the Clown showed up right on time. Not expecting "pony rides," I had hired a clown to make balloon animals for the kids. I'm not crazy about clowns. In fact, I think they are creepy as hell, but Oddball was recommended by a neighbor's babysitting service, so I gave it a shot.

"Hey, hey! Kids, I'm Oddball the Clown! Come sit around me in a semi-circle, and I'll tell you a silly story."

The clown sat on an upside-down milk crate, and the kids settled around him. Some of the parents gathered around as well. Everyone had smiles on their faces and was ready to laugh. Oddball did have the funny red nose and the silly banana yellow costume, but he hadn't painted his whole face white, which I liked because it made him a touch less sinister than other clowns I'd seen. Of course, the last clown I'd seen was a lava monster in disguise, so that experience might have colored my perception.

Oddball leaned forward, and the kids leaned toward him, little knees bouncing up and down at the thought of a story.

"Once upon a time…"

Good start.

"There was a beautiful maiden who loved another maiden…"

Okay, inclusivity and tolerance. I could get into this. Parents nodded to each other. One father, who was gay and married, gave me the thumbs up. I was feeling proud of myself for hiring such a progressive clown.

"The beautiful maiden loved the other maiden, but her father told her she couldn't marry the other maiden because she wasn't beautiful."

Self-acceptance, nice.

"So, the beautiful maiden tried to change her love by dressing her in pretty dresses and high heels, but the ugly maiden didn't want to wear those things."

I was liking this story. Except the word "ugly." Not so happy with that. But, I could live with it.

"The ugly maiden looked at her beautiful girlfriend, and said, 'I'm beautiful on the inside, where it counts.' The beautiful maiden replied, 'Yeah, I get that, but you must admit, your nose looks like a giant zit.'"

*Huh?*

The kids howled because they thought it was so funny. "Giant zit, Jack! Get it?" Then my son blew up his cheeks and popped them like a giant zit exploding.

Not my favorite language, but the kids laughed. A few parents tittered.

Oddball continued. "Why would you say such terrible things to me, my love?"

*Yeah, why? That was mean.*

"Because I always tell you the truth, my love."

*Well, okay. Still, it was mean. She could have said it in a nicer way.*

"Maybe my nose does look like a giant zit, but you could have said that in a nicer way."

*Exactly.*

"The pretty maiden shrugged, and said, 'Well, why don't you tell me something honest in return?'"

"Your nose is a chicken's beak. It isn't pretty at all, but no one wants to tell you the truth because your dad is rich." Oddball waved his finger in the air as if making an important point. A ping of worry wormed its way into my brain. Several parents frowned and shifted their feet.

Oddball continued the story, taking the part of the pretty maiden. "My nose is perfect, thank you very much. But, while we are being honest, your hair is a rat's nest."

"My hair is natural, and your roots are showing!" Oddball was winding up, now standing, holding both hands in front of him as if imparting great wisdom to the children. I stepped in, my stomach sinking as the parents around me grumbled and shot me nasty looks.

"I think that is the end of the story, Oddball! Very interesting, yes, yes, but how about we move on to the balloon animals?"

Oddball shook his finger at the kids again, finishing with, "The moral of the story, children, is never tell the truth."

The children cracked up, loving the mixed-up tale with the sorry moral. Parents gritted their teeth but let the moment pass since the kids were whooping it up.

"Ah, balloon animals!" Oddball announced, once again taking his seat on the milk crate. "Let me see what we have here. You, birthday boy. What kind of animal would you like?"

I sighed with relief. Balloon animals were harmless fun.

David jumped to his feet. "A dog!" he announced. "I want a dog."

"A dog it is!" Oddball blew into a red balloon and twisted it into several different knots and shapes. He finished with a flourish. "Look! I made a mosquito!"

"Neato!" said David. "A giant mosquito is better than a dog."

I wasn't so sure.

Jack raised his hand. "Can you make me a bird?"

"Of course, young man. Let me get a yellow balloon…" Oddball hummed and hawed as he once again twisted the balloon several different ways. He added a blue balloon to it, then another, and still another. "Regard! A spider!"

Indeed, it was a spider with a complete set of legs and a giant abdomen. I scrunched my face, not certain about this approach, but Jack thought a big balloon spider was hilarious. Some of the parents backed up a few inches.

Brian couldn't stay still, waving his hand in the air. "I want a bumble bee! Can you do a bumble bee?"

"Why young man, I shall try." Oddball did his balloon magic and produced…

"A hornet! Look at that stinger!"

Brian's mouth fell open. His voice was breathy with excitement. "Whoa. A hornet."

A fly. A cobra. A beetle the size of a cat. It seemed strange, but harmless. Nevertheless, I had a rock in the pit of stomach.

Brian screamed. "The hornet stung me! Owwwww. Owwww. Moooooommmmm!"

"Ouch!" yelled Joseph, as his snapping turtle bit the tip of his finger.

David scratched at his arm, drawing blood. "Mom, the mosquito bit me!"

One-by-one, the bugs and scary creatures came to life. Parents threw themselves into the fray, fighting off a scorpion with a lawn chair, clobbering a poison dart frog with a grill plate. I squashed the fly with a spatula, hitting it several times to get it down for good. I was pissed because my spatula was ruined, covered in fly guts.

Nathaniel thanked everyone left for coming, handing out party bags as the parents and kids scattered, running for the safety of their homes. "Enjoy the handmade caramel," he said, as he thrust the bags into the hands of our departing guests, one man yelling that he was going to sue us for unlawful ownership of poisonous creatures.

Which left me with a small army of noxious critters and an evil clown.

I had help, though. Blaze killed the cobra with his clawed foot, and the wolf snapped the beetle in two, spitting it out with *whuff* of distaste. She shook her head and waggled her tongue as if she needed to gargle.

Oddball glared at me with wide, crazy eyes, and he drooled in long strands down his costume. He tore at his bag and removed two balloons, twisting them into my favorite bee of all time—not. A yellow jacket. I had nightmares about yellow jackets ever since my eighth birthday party when a small battalion flew into the grape juice jug and drowned.

The yellow jacket headed straight for me, aiming for my face and neck, so I ran as fast as my legs could carry me. I ran for our garden hose as the yellow jacket and psychopathic clown chased me. I didn't make it and got stung on the shoulder. I bellowed in pain. It felt like the largest hypodermic needle in the world had been jammed into my shoulder, bone deep, and the burning sensation made me think I was actually on fire. It took my breath away.

"Why are you doing this?" I wheezed as the jacket and clown continued to give chase. I jumped a wood fence at the back of our yard, which didn't matter to the yellow jacket but did slow down the clown because he hadn't flipped off his giant red shoes. That gave me time to circle back around, jump the fence again, and beeline for the hose. I twisted the water on full force, brought the nozzle up, and blasted the yellow jacket, which had swelled to the size of a chihuahua. The yellow jacket flew into a wall of water and fell to the ground, belly up, legs clawing at the air in a futile attempt to flip itself over, its sodden wings useless. I didn't feel the least bit sorry. My shoulder was swelling, and it stung like nothing I'd ever experienced. I didn't know if I had enough Benadryl cream to cover it.

Oddball drew himself up short and dodged the water, but a bit of the spray hit his arm, and he screamed in pain. Intrigued, I chased him with the hose and, in an exciting turn of events, he fled, running toward the back of the yard, attempting to get out of reach of the water. We'd installed an extra-long hose to reach the rose bushes, bushes that Oddball discovered all by himself. Caught in thorns and screaming un-clownlike epithets, he cringed when he saw me with the water.

"Why are you here?" I demanded.

"You have made a lot of enemies, Monster Hunter. There's a bounty on your head if we bring you down."

"Who is we?"

"Monsters, villains, devils, evildoers. Life would be better in Ohio without you, bitch."

"The Buckeye Bitch thing again." I yawned.

"If the foo shits, wear it, babe. Now, why don't you put the water down, and I'll leave, tail between my legs, okay?"

"I'm curious about this water issue. Did you almost drown as a child?" I turned the water on him, and he went berserk, flailing and screeching.

"I'm melting! I'm melting…I'm melting…woe is me…"

The clown's face dripped onto the costume in long, waxy drops. His body collapsed into a tacky puddle of goo, leaving a blue, yellow, and red stain on the grass.

Nathaniel appeared at my side. We stared at the Crayola mixture seeping into the grass. "I wonder if Frank Baum met this guy?" he said.

I recoiled the hose. "It would explain a few things, but I'm wondering what happened to the real Oddball. Or, is this the real Oddball, and he was evil the whole time? If he was the real guy, didn't he ever shower? This is a conundrum."

"I don't think any of that is your problem. Let's some ice on this sting," Nathaniel said, touching the tips of his fingers together, shuddering at the sight of the wound. "This is going to prick a bit, and we need to conjure an explanation for all of this, or the kids won't play with the neighbors ever again."

"We could tell them that Oddball placed his crate over an unknown wasp nest. That would explain the stings," I said.

"Nature science experiment out of control?" he offered.

"Maybe realistic mechanical toys under recall?"

Nathaniel snapped his fingers. "Illusionist!"

I shook my head and nodded thanks as he opened the back door for me. I collapsed into a kitchen chair while David, Devi, and Daniel fluttered around me, asking if I was okay.

"He was a magic bad guy, wasn't he, Mom?" asked the too-old-for-his-years David.

"Yeah, pumpkin. I'm sorry. I didn't know."

"It was cool, Mom! How many people get balloon spiders at their party?" He had a wide smile on his face. "Don't worry, Mom, they'll all forget the magic stuff soon. They never remember it."

Devi nodded her little head in agreement, and her hair, askew as always, bounced along. "It's true, Mom. David's right."

Daniel handed me an ice pack.

"How did the three-year old get an ice pack from the top shelf of the freezer?" I asked. "And, how did no one see him do it?"

Nathaniel shrugged, too exhausted to worry about it. "He's resourceful," he said, tugging Daniel's ear and gathering him in a hug.

## CHAPTER THREE

Liam spat a good Malbec out his nose and lay his forehead on the kitchen table, trying, and failing, to keep a straight face.
He stumbled an apology. "Oh, oh, I'm so sorry, Jess...but Blaze is a pony? And you need a permit for him? This is too funny."

"I don't *need* a permit. I can't get one at all. He's considered livestock and is outlawed by the Neighborhood Association code."

"So, what are you going to do?"

"I have no idea."

"Hey, sport!" Liam hugged David, who'd run into the kitchen to see him. "I got you a present."

"Really? What?" The kids always got the best presents from Uncle Liam.

"Guess."

David wiggled and played with his loose front tooth. "Is it bigger than a bread box?"

Liam shook his head with a sigh. "No. Sorry. Try again."

"A book?"

"Nope."

"Good. I don't want another book."

I gasped. "That. That is a knife to my heart."

Liam said, "Speaking of knives..." He handed David a small box. I threw Liam a glance. What was he up to?

"A pocketknife! Wow, Uncle Liam! This is the best present ever." David jumped up and gave Liam a huge hug, not minding that Liam's skin always ran a little cold.

I scowled at Liam. "What are you doing? He's only nine!"

Liam replied, "Nine is a perfect age for a first pocket knife. This is a Swiss Army Recruit Knife. It's good for smaller hands."

Nathaniel wandered in. "Hey, whatcha got there, David?" David held up his new red knife.

"A pocketknife? Fantastic. Thanks, Liam. Nine is a great age for a pocketknife."

Liam stuck his tongue out at me.

Nathaniel gave Liam a wink. "Come on, David. Let me show you how this works. The most important safety tip is to never, ever, carry the knife around with an open blade."

"Where's the wolf?" Liam asked, when they were out of earshot.

"She's made a den under the deck. She hunts on her own at night and our garden has never looked better."

Liam crinkled his nose in confusion.

"No rabbits, gophers, moles, voles, or other such ilk to eat my tomatoes. Even the deer stay away. Last time I counted, we had a herd of twelve running around our back yard, but no more. I've got daffodils again."

We returned to the real topic at hand. Liam peeked under the bandage on my shoulder, winced, and let it go. I hissed in pain as the fabric touched the wound.

"You're going to need an antihistamine. It's as large as a plastic food storage lid. You know, the kind you get soup in from Chinese restaurants? Several inches across? It's like yay big…"

"I know what you mean, Liam. I got it, no need for pictograms. It hurts a lot, too."

"What I want to know about is the bounty," Liam said, getting serious. He retrieved some cortisone cream from the third drawer down near the sink and gestured for me to remove the bandage.

"I wonder how much it is," I said, thumbnail in my teeth because otherwise I'd shriek as Liam spread the white cream on my skin.

Liam nodded. "And who is offering it? That's important. My bet is Pascal."

"I agree. It's the only thing that makes sense, and yet, he wants to kill me face-to-face, all personal-like. He's the only real supernatural baddie with the mojo to do this, but it doesn't feel right."

"I'll ask around."

"Don't get staked."

"Never do. Except that one time…"

"What?"

Liam grinned. "Kidding."

"Ha, so funny. Not."

Liam pushed back in his chair so only the two back legs were on the ground. I hate when my kids do that, so I threw him a glare, which he ignored. "By the way, the zoo posted an ad about a missing wolf. I'm betting it's the wolf under the deck."

I thought about this for a moment. I still wasn't sure what danger she expected, unless maybe it was Oddball? If so, she could go home. "Let's go talk to her."

We tromped outside, and I gestured for Blaze to join us. "Can you please ask our wolf friend to come out and chat?"

Blaze peeked under the deck, did that communing thing he did with other species, and the wolf came out fixing her eye on me.

*What is it, den mother?* Blaze translated.

"I'm wondering if you could be more specific about the type of danger you fear is looming. I can't prepare for battle without more details."

*I have images of a black presence searching for your pack.*

"Specifically my children, or is my husband targeted also?"

*I can't tell. Only that your pack is in danger. Your mate could be at risk, or your pups. I came to help you, but I don't have anything else.*

"Thanks for coming. What's your name?"

The wolf appeared puzzled by this question.

*I'm mate to alpha.*

"Yes, I get that, but we like to use names. It is a way of being polite."

*I fail to understand this, but you can give me a name, if you would like.*

"That's a big responsibility."

*A name is important?*

"Yes."

*Then, choose wisely. I should not like an unworthy name.*

I took this responsibility seriously. Names have power. Whatever I named her could have consequences. I left the three to chat amongst themselves while I rifled through my mental mythology rolodex for something that would suit. I mucked around in the garden, pulling weeds, letting my mind roam. When that didn't work, I went for a walk around the block. Finally, it came to me.

"Shura," I told her. "It means 'protector of humanity' in Greek and Russian. It's a royal name, but also one related to the gods, particularly Hera, the mate of the Greek pantheon's alpha, Zeus."

The wolf considered it and nodded her acceptance. "It's a strong name."

Liam had gone inside for a while but came out to join us. He made an important point. "Shura, I believe the zoo is looking for you."

The wolf opened her mouth in a wide grin, teeth on display. *I will go home to my pack when my work is done.*

"How did you get out?" Liam asked.

The wolf turned her face in an obvious expression of, *I'm telling you.*

"Do you think the zoo officials know you are here?" I asked. This is the precise moment I discovered that wolves can *shrug*. Crazy.

## CHAPTER FOUR

Shura's warning pinged and ponged around my brain until morning, when I rose at the crack of dawn, accepting that I wouldn't sleep in that Sunday. Nathaniel was dead to the world, so I tucked his blanket under his chin and snuck out of the bedroom on quiet feet. The door made the faintest click as I closed it.

I needed a workout to clear my head, so I texted Ovid, my trainer, had a cup of coffee and a slice of wheat toast with almond butter, and slipped out the door. I left a note on the kitchen table for Nathaniel and the kids.

I breathed a sigh of relief as I realized that I didn't need to deal with the Jewish Community Center's scariest villain. I was terrified of her and knew of no way to defeat her, no matter how many ancient texts I consulted. I had tried an exorcism of sorts by sneaking holy objects into the main playroom, placing them in a rough circle, and calling on the evil spirits inhabiting her body to leave.

It made no difference. Neither did the smudge stick, the so-called magic wand that I got suckered into buying at the "witches apothecary," or the spell that I got when I returned the wand.

I'd tried meditation, medication, and outright prayer, begging the Almighty to smite her, for which I did extra pushups, but it was worth the price if it worked.

Nothing. I was forced to deal with most malicious, vile, evil creature ever put in my path.

The babysitter.

That's right. The babysitter.

Regina was the director of the daycare at the JCC where folks could drop their children when they came for programs, classes, or to exercise. Daniel enjoyed the place and would happily play while I trained. He had his favorite daycare provider, Faith, and a few kids he knew. It was a great situation, and while a little pricey, worth every penny.

Except for my nemesis. Regina had a habit of lifting her nose and pursing her lips in disgust when confronted with my lax parenting skills. I flushed and became tongue-tied in the face of her disapproval. Give me a horde of zombies, a coven of witches, or a creep of trolls any day, even bog trolls, which smell putrid, but save me the scorn of a babysitter.

Happy it was so early, I tiptoed by the daycare center, relishing my reprieve.

"Oh, Mrs. Friedman!"

Mother leapin' Christmas! What was she doing here so early? My chest tightened, and my breathing went into overdrive. I bit the inside of my cheek and rotated my torso toward Regina. I'm certain I looked stupid, half twisted with my feet facing one way and my body the other, but I couldn't bring my lower half to move, frozen as I was by mortal fear.

Regina clip-clopped her way over to me, her nurse's clogs smacking the floor with every step. Her nose was raised to its normal angle, her glasses down on the tip, her hands clenched in front of her. Her lips were puckered like she'd eaten something sour, and her eyes held the false concern of a woman enjoying her power over another woman.

"Yes, Regina?" I couldn't help it if my voice trembled.

Regina gave a delicate cough into her elbow, so as not to spread germs. I believed in the philosophy of what did not kill children made them stronger. Of course, I'd been known to blow my nose on my sleeve, so possibly I wasn't the best judge.

"Will we see Daniel here today?"

"No. He's at home with his father."

"Oh, that lovely Nathaniel of yours! He's such a gem."

I clenched my teeth. "Yes, he is."

Regina cleared her throat. "Mrs. Friedman, we believe it is in Daniel's best interest to enroll in a preschool with structure and discipline. I've been meaning to talk to you about it."

"Who is the 'we' of which you speak?" My feet finally moved a quarter of the way toward her, which was good because my hips hadn't liked that position at all.

Regina blushed. "Well, there isn't a 'we' per se. Just some discussions I've had with the other staff."

"What does Faith say?"

Regina waved her hand. "I didn't consult her. I do have several recommendations for schools for a child with his, how should I say it, *imagination*. I'll put a list with Daniel's things for the next time you bring him here."

"Okay, thanks, I'll look at it." I wanted to get away so badly that the soles of my feet itched, but I had a question.

"What do you mean by imagination?"

Regina frowned, and then leaned in toward me in a conspiratorial fashion. I jerked back.

"Daniel jabbers about large birds that speak to him in his mind. He also insists he has, I know this is silly, a *vampire* for an uncle. Last time he was here, he drew a wolf that he says lives under your house. I may be misunderstanding him since his speech is so behind, but you get the idea. He's not living in reality."

"Really."

"Yes, and while I love his imagination, we should harness that energy into something positive."

"He's three."

"Exactly. What better time to help him learn how to focus?"

Was I harming my child allowing all these preternatural creatures into his life? Would he get into fights in elementary school when he brought in a talking Buddha for show and tell? My mind was reeling at the possibilities that I was screwing my baby up. Then, I realized that Regina was the one not living in reality.

My feet moved of their own free will. "I've got to go, Regina. I'll take a look at that information, though."

Regina crossed her arms and watched as I fled. That's right. The monster hunter fled across the linoleum, and the babysitter didn't follow.

Ovid met me in the sparring room with a pair of ear plugs and a blindfold. Ovid and I aren't those kind of friends, so I knew there must be some tortuous training exercise involving my senses.

"How are you doing this morning, Jess?"

"Okay, except that Shura warned me that danger is coming but can't tell me anything else. I'm living within a hazy cloud of worry with no place to focus."

"Shura is the wolf?"

I nodded.

"Okay, well, we can't do anything about that, but let's get to work, shall we? First, we spar, hand-to-hand, to warm up. I've got pads over there." He pointed to the corner where red sparring pads lay waiting for me to prove they didn't cut the force of the blow at all. They do cut down on serious injury, but make no mistake, when Ovid hits me in the chest, I go down.

We donned our gear and faced off in a boxing dance, waiting for each other to make a move. I swung a right jab, which he side-stepped, but I came in with a left hook and got him good on his ribs. He countered with a cross punch followed by an uppercut, and since I was dodging the cross punch, I'd gotten low. The uppercut got me square in the jaw, and I was certain I'd have been spitting out teeth if I hadn't had a mouth guard. We went on like this, trading punches, for about four minutes.

I was out of breath, as was Ovid.

"I forgot how hard it is to box," I said.

"That's why we are doing it," Ovid said with a smile. "We haven't done it in a long time, and I wanted to fix that."

The last time Ovid had given me a special workout, it had been with ropes, and I had to fake a broken leg. It turned out to be unknowing preparation for battling a were-gorilla, and I'd concluded that Ovid had a little precog ability. My heart sank at the thought. Who the hell would I have to box?

I dropped and did twenty push-ups.

"Swearing again?"

"Shush. Let's go."

"This time blindfolded," he said, with an evil grin. "Turn around." He tied the blindfold over my face, made sure I could still breathe, and slugged me in my right shoulder, sending me reeling.

"Hey! You didn't say it was time to start." I regained my balance.

"What? You think the bad guys are going to warn you? Blow a little whistle? Send a pretty lady in wearing nothing but a bathing suit and a smile to carry around a round one card?"

I didn't reply. I could hear his voice, and without my eyesight, I used my ears to pinpoint his location. He shifted to my right.

Took a step back.

Rhythmic feet. He was dancing side-to-side.

A deep breath. Sneaky bastard had gone low.

I took two swift steps and knocked him on his ass. He scrambled to his feet, darting around me, but by focusing on his breathing and footsteps, I was able to follow him.

"Move, Jess, move! Standing still isn't going to help you. Vampires are fast."

Did his precog tell him I was going to box a vampire? Holy moly.

I took his advice and danced around on light feet, so I could still hear him breathe. He approached me from the left, and I blocked the punch but couldn't avoid the shot to my kidneys. I reacted by kicking him in the shins and shoving my gloved hand into his belly.

"Oooooomph! That...isn't...boxing," Ovid panted.

"What? You think the bad guys are going to agree to fists only? Maybe get a girl in hooker boots to call a time out?"

"Fair point. Now, let's plug up those ears."

"Are you trying to kill me?"

"Don't be stupid," Ovid said, shaking a finger.

"Oh, so now I am deaf and blind."

He handed me the earplugs, and I stuffed them in my ears, astounded by the quiet. The earplugs were meant for plane noise, and they worked well. I held still to adjust to the lack of sound and the lack of sight. I was cocooned in a dark, muffled world, and it took exactly ten seconds for me to panic. My heart beat fast, and I snuffed in and out of my nose and mouth, making strange gagging noises as I fought the urge to spew all over the floor. I dropped to all fours and scrambled toward the corner of the room, surrendering to a primal fear that egged me on, cackling in glee when I curled up in a ball, back to the wall.

Calming hands pressed on my forehead and the back of my neck, and the touch was an island in the vast ocean of nothingness. I leaned into Ovid's touch and concentrated on steadying my breath. Once I was calm, I noticed something.

I could feel the vibrations of Ovid steps on the floor. I removed my gloves and touched the floor with my fingertips, and, wait...yes, the wood floor radiated slight tremors as Ovid shifted position. I smelled sweat and sniffed again, recognizing workout sweat mixed with a little fear as he worried that he'd pushed me too far. I crawled up the wall, keeping my back to it, and waved Ovid away.

I knew he'd backed off when his body odor dissipated, but I didn't know where he was. I bent and took off my shoes. Now barefoot, I could feel the reverberation of his steps. He wasn't coming after me; no, this was a game of hide and seek. He moved to my left, and I tracked him. He moved backward, and I stepped an equal distance forward. He moved in a diagonal, approaching my right shoulder, and I shot out my hand, fast as a whip, and grasped him by the neck.

This made me ridiculously happy. I removed the ear plugs with my other hand, and the noise of the room came whooshing back. The fan on the ceiling, Ovid's choking sounds, the creak of the floorboards. I heard anew.

I released Ovid and removed the blindfold. I blinked at the sudden brightness, stunned by the intensity of the light. I looked at Ovid, and he was smiling.

"Excellent," he said and gave me a high-five.

# CHAPTER FIVE

Exhausted and worried about what might lay ahead, I slipped into my front seat, started the car to get the air going, and checked my phone. I opened a text from a number I didn't recognize.

*Dearest Jess:*
 *I need you to do an errand for me. Since I know you would not do it out of the goodness of your heart, I have taken collateral to make sure you understand this is not a request you can ignore. I'll leave it to you to find me.*
 *P.*

He attached a photo of a beaten, battered, bloody face.
Pascal had Liam.
My blood turned ice cold. There was no time for emotion now. My biggest enemy had my closest friend. The game was on, and there would be no mercy. I texted back, *What is it you want?*
I waited. Nothing came back. It was morning, and the sun was up. It meant I had the day to find him. I drove home, and in the midst of the breakfast cacophony, I showed Nathaniel the text. His breath grew even, and he circled his neck like a wrestler getting ready to go into the ring.
Daniel tugged on my yoga pants, and I picked him up and cuddled him close, smelling the top of his head where his baby scent was still strong. Absently, I noticed that Devi flicked a spoonful of cereal and milk at her

older brother and that he responded in kind. They both looked at Nathaniel and me for our reaction, but neither of us said anything. Our brains were working on how to save their uncle.

Nathaniel recovered first and pulled out a chair for me. He made me a cup of lemon ginger tea with honey, my favorite, and handed the older children paper towels and some kind of green cleanser to clean up the cereal. Daniel drowsed in my arms, already tired from the events of the morning.

Nathaniel sat catty-corner from me, blowing across the top of his coffee mug. He drank the damn stuff black. I could never understand how he did it, but now I was thinking that if I wanted to drink coffee, that's the way I'd take it. Straight, dark, and bitter. Later, there'd be time to put whiskey in it.

"What do you want to do?" my husband asked.

"I'm wondering if Shura could track the way Liam went home."

"I doubt it, but Blaze might. Besides, I want Shura right here with me, protecting the children."

I crossed my arms and eased back in my chair, taking steady breaths into my nose and out my mouth. "Yes, I do, too. I'll ask Blaze."

First thing I did, though, was walk into the living room and retrieved the jade Buddha. It warmed in my hand.

"Buddha, danger is near. Shura feels it, and so do I. Worse, Pascal had taken Liam."

The Buddha shivered.

"Can I leave you with Nathaniel? Will you give him a warning sign if you feel something? A disturbance in the Force, or whatever it is you can do?"

The Buddha contemplated my request.

*I dare not disturb karma. Bad things are but a facet of one's destiny. But if I sense an unnatural danger, something trying to subvert karma, I will let your family know.*

In other words, if my child was about to be hit by a car driven by a drunk human, Buddha would stay silent, but if a three-headed, pustule-ridden, ten-foot tall Scoamon demon arrived with a desire to spit acid on my kids, Buddha would give fair warning. I could live with that.

"Thank you."

I held Buddha, exited the back door to the yard, and walked toward Blaze's nest, a large mess of branches and unlit Christmas tree lights, dotted with bits of feather and moss. Blaze's head was under his wing, and I was certain he was sleeping, but as I approached, he woke. He may have sensed my anger, now restrained by a mental brick wall, because his face was serious.

*What is it?*

"Pascal has Liam."

*What does he want? The only reason to do that is blackmail.*

"He wants me to do an errand for him."

*He didn't say what?*

"No."

*You need my help?*

"I won't know what he wants until sundown, and I have to locate his position by then. He neglected to tell me where the meeting spot is. It's part of his game." My voice stayed steady, but I couldn't keep the thread of anger out completely. I showed Blaze the text, assuming he could read. Turns out, he could, no problem.

The phoenix paced. *Shura's nose is better, but if he took him in a car, that won't be helpful. I will reconnaissance in the air.*

"Thank you. How will you glamour yourself? Ponies don't fly, last I heard."

*Not completely true, but no worries. I'll be a blur. No one will see me.* The phoenix didn't wait around for more chit-chat. He leapt into the air and flew off, silent as an owl, despite the fact that he had bronze feathers. I reminded myself to ask what kind of ponies fly. Unicorns?

With Blaze off, I returned to the house to find my mystified kids watching a Disney movie, wondering why they were being given this privilege. I smelled chocolate and knew Nathaniel was baking cookies. When in doubt, bake. That's been a tried and true response to stress in my family for a long time.

"Blaze is on the wing."

"How absurd. I thought the wing was on the bird." Nathaniel came back with the line despite his concerns. This's why I loved this man so much. I handed him the Buddha.

"Buddha says that if a paranormal threat comes near, he'll give you a warning. He won't if it is a natural part of destiny. He doesn't mess with karma, but if a creepy baddie from outside this world decides to drop in, he'll give you as much warning as he can."

"Thanks, Buddha," Nathaniel said, taking the Buddha in his hand. "Now, how will I hold you? You are way too big to fit into my pocket."

The Buddha rocked side-to-side and smoke came out of his ears.

Alarmed, Nathaniel put the statue on the table, and we watched, open-mouthed, as the four-inch high carving shrunk to the size of a nickel. We both blinked at it. I'm pretty sure the Buddha giggled.

"Handy," Nathaniel said, continuing his practice of just rolling with it. He snatched the Buddha off the table and dropped him into the front chest pocket of his blue golf shirt. "What now?" he asked.

"I'm going hunting." I grabbed my bag to pack some stuff, but Nathaniel stopped me. He looked me in the eyes. "Be careful. Promise me you will be careful. I care about Liam, too, but if it comes down to you or him? I need you." He pulled me in for a kiss that made me wish we weren't in the middle of this crisis and had a lot more time. "Cancun soon? No kids."

I stared at him. "No kids? How is that ever going to happen?"

Nathaniel held onto both of my arms. "Babe, we have a phoenix and a wolf living with us. It shouldn't be too hard to get a babysitter."

"Don't say that word. Yeesh. It's scary."

Nathaniel laughed. "I'll work on the babysitter. Oh, stop your shuddering. Okay, I'll work on finding someone to stay with the kids while we are away."

"In other words, a babysitter."

"A loving, kind maternal and paternal substitute so we can go have wild, kinky sex without three kids threatening to knock on the door."

"I might be able to get behind that."

I gave him one more peck and readied my bag. My tomahawk was vibrating, it was so excited to go on a true hunt. It must have heard what was happening. Yes, I know I'm talking about an inanimate object, but this tomahawk was special and particularly reliable. I packed my usual grill lighter, baseball bat, a few empty small Tupperware containers, like you'd pack raisins or nuts in…or at least, like *other moms* would pack raisins and nuts in. I wore a leather jacket and stuffed every pocket with weapons. My pack was ready to go, and my harness for my bat was in the car. First, one stop.

I screeched into the synagogue parking lot and jumped out. Now that I was moving, I felt better, but my stomach was still in knots, and my mind raced with the possibilities of what Liam might be going through. I stopped at the water fountain for a quick slurp and headed for Rabbi Stein's office.

"He's in with a congregant!" said his assistant, who I ignored. I knocked and entered the Rabbi's office. "Rabbi. I need your help."

Rabbi Stein looked at me over his glasses, and the woman sitting in his guest chair gazed at me, face scrunched up in confusion. It was then that I noticed that she had tears in her eyes and tear stains down her cheeks. My face flamed hot.

"Uh. Sorry. I'll wait out here." I retreated a few inches but then stuck my head back in. "It is sort of an emergency though."

"I understand, Jess. Please wait for a moment."

I sat in a chair while his assistant glared at me and harrumphed with righteousness. My knees knocked up and down with my anxiety. The rabbi opened the door, and the woman exited, saying, "Thank you, Rabbi. I appreciate your listening to me."

"Loss and grief are not something you go through alone," the rabbi replied. "That is why we have a community to support one another. Let those people in."

"I will, Rabbi. Thanks again."

I stood and held out my hand. "I just wanted to apologize for barging in like that. It was thoughtless of me. I hope things get better for you soon."

She shook my hand. "Your emergency must involve someone you care about very much."

"It does."

"Then, I hope things get better for you, too."

# CHAPTER SIX

"Please, sit down, Jess."

"I can't. I need a favor."

"Sit down. Jess."

I sat.

I wanted to apologize. "I'm sorry for what I did. It was callous of me, and I am truly sorry. What happened to her? Who died?"

"If you came to services, you might know that she lost her husband in a car accident. The synagogue has created a fund for her and her children."

The worm of guilt squirmed through my gut, while a drumbeat of shame banged in my head. "Here's twenty for the fund, Rabbi," I said, pulling out a bill, "but please email me her name and phone number so I can reach out later."

"I will. Thank you. She could probably use a shoulder now. What is it that has you all aflutter?"

"Pascal kidnapped Liam, and now I have to rescue him. I don't know where he is, but Blaze is in the air. Shura is helping Nathaniel watch the kids. Could you bless this water?"

Rabbi Stein licked his lips, sat back in his chair, and looked at me. I was on the edge of my seat, tapping my foot.

"Let me see if I have this right. The bad vampire kidnapped the good vampire."

I nodded.

"The phoenix, who you originally killed and locked in a lorikeet cage, is now flying around in the air trying to find Liam's location."

I tapped my nose.

"So, who is Shura?"

"A wolf."

"The one that escaped from the zoo? It's been all over the news."

"Yeah, she'll go back when she feels her duty is done. She senses danger to my pack, so she came to help and is living under our deck. My garden has never looked better, but my bird population has taken a hit."

It was a credit to Rabbi Stein that all he did he was steeple his hands.

"You want me to bless the water?"

"Exactly. A good weapon against a vampire."

"We don't really do that in our religion, you know."

I was bouncing with impatience. "I know, but I need every angle I can get."

"Go dump the water. I have a better idea."

I grabbed my bag and did as he asked, returning with three Tupperware Mini-n-Midgets squares, still damp on the inside but otherwise empty.

"What are you going to do, Rabbi?"

The man turned, holding a clunky bottle. "We don't normally bless water, but..." The rabbi held up one finger. "We do bless Manischevitz every Friday."

Despite my tension, I laughed. The rabbi filled each square with kosher wine and said a blessing. I capped them and put them away.

"You think it will work?"

"It would take a miracle."

Point one, Rabbi Stein.

With my holy wine hand grenades and the rest of my weapons ready, I headed downtown blaring AC/DC's "Dirty Deals Done Dirt Cheap."

Getting downtown took no more than fifteen minutes. I parked in a lot near Cleveland State University and walked toward the outer part of the city, like I was heading to Lake Erie, but I angled to my left, deep into druggie territory. There was only one dealer in this neck of the woods, and he didn't like me at all. In fact, he'd threatened me the last time we met, reminding me that I wasn't as scary without Liam, but if I needed to find Pascal, I was using every resource possible.

I'd donned a hockey neck guard, a fast-pitch batting helmet with a faceguard, and shoulder pads. The helmet restricted my peripheral vision, but I felt better having my head and face protected. It wouldn't stop a bullet, but it could protect me if I fell or took a punch. I wore steel-toed shitkickers in black that I had heeled with a layer of silver. The silver wouldn't last long, but it might help today. I had my various doo-dads on my back, in my pack, or in my pockets. Armed for bear, and really, with the size of Snuggles, I was armed for elephant.

Lots of nasty men stood on the steps of Snuggles' dilapidated house, several with big guns at their sides. If you didn't have money, you weren't getting in. I could have fought my way through, but money was simpler. Two guards approached me.

"What the fooock we got here?" a pock-faced man said. His hair was stringy, and his pants were soiled, but the high caliber rifle in his hand and the machete at his waist made me take pause.

"What the fuck you wearing, bitch?" said another guy. He appeared unarmed until I saw his fists, which were adorned by brass knuckles. That was a good idea. *Note to self, brass knuckles.*

"I have a form of Ebola, and I don't want to spit or bleed on you," I replied, as if this was normal. I held up a fifty-dollar bill to each of the guards. "All I want is a conversation with Snuggles."

"You mother fuckin' have Ebola? Why'd you get so close to me?" yipped one guy, dropping back. He grabbed Mr. Grant though.

The other guy ignored the money and drew a pistol from his back. It probably had been tucked into his pants. What a douche.

"You go away before I make you bleed in the street," he said, sounding convincing. His eyes were hard, and though his stance was all ways of wrong, I knew he would pull the trigger, and if he did, none of that would matter. A three-foot shot would kill me sure as anything, and you didn't have to be a marksman to make that work.

"You don't want me bleeding in the street, tough guy," I responded. "I told you. I'm sick, and if you get any blood spatter on you, you're going to be sick, too."

"What you think I am? A fool?" he said. "Get your ass off our steps."

"These are Snuggles' steps, as you well know. Why don't you ask him? Tell him Jess wants to talk to him and that she's here to buy information with cash."

The lanky haired guy shot the one holding the pistol a look, and pistol guy jerked his neck toward the door. Lanky Hair went inside, and I could hear him from where I stood.

"Boss, there's a woman out there dressed like Casey from the Ninja Turtles, says her name is Jess, and she's here to buy some info."

There was a massive belch from the back, and an angry voice bellowed, "Shoot her! That bitch doesn't get in here, even with money!"

I whipped out my 'hawk and sliced in a counter-clockwise circle, sending pistol guy to his knees with a slice across his hamstring, then cutting two others on their arms and chest. I leaned forward and spit into the bleeding leg of my pistol-wielding friend. I didn't want to hit the gun, just in case it fired, so I held the blade to my friend's other leg and picked up the pistol between two fingers. "These things are gross." I dropped it, gently, on the grass next to the steps, right into a pile of dog shit.

Pistol guy was frantically wiping the blood from his bleeding leg with his sleeve. "Why'd you go and spit in it? Now, I'm gonna die of Ebola or something. Help me, please!" He looked around for anyone who would help, but they'd backed off, and the two other bleeders staggered away before I spit at them, too.

I marched up the steps and right into Lanky Hair's chest. We were too close for his rifle but not too close for the 'hawk, which hummed with happiness. Using a short grip, I sheered down his arm, shoulder to hand, taking off skin, muscle and tendon, and almost hit bone. The man fell, screaming, and I spit in his wound, too. I didn't know a man could make those sounds. So high-pitched, like the Vienna Boys' Choir.

I left the bleeding dudes where they lay, holstered the 'hawk, and drew my bat, clomping into the house with my silver-heeled boots.

"Hey, Snuggie."

The Jabba the Hut wannabee shifted in his specially-made Laz-E-Boy. "What the hell you doing here? You freak! Boys, I said kill her!" No answer came except moans and shrieks as the men tried to get their arms and legs to reconnect to their bodies. Snuggie's beer empties were piled around him, and I wondered if he bothered to get up to piss or if had a few bottles hidden around his chair. I couldn't tell, given his sheer bulk, and his accurate aim as he threw cans at me.

"What did you do, you nutcase?" Snuggles roared, throwing a few more at my head. I batted them away.

"What do you want?" Snuggles was huffing and puffing with the exertion. A noise from behind me made me whirl, and I swung the bat with enough torque that when I hit the man sneaking up on my six, his shoulder popped, and he fell down the inside steps to the cellar, screaming the whole way.

I leaned on my bat. "I wanted to buy some information."

"What kind of information?"

"Where's Pascal?"

"I don't know where that perversion of nature hangs out. Why would you think I know that?"

"Because you know everything that goes on down here, you worm, and I don't have a lot of time. So, give me a direction."

"I don't know."

I held a hundred-dollar bill in his face and wished I hadn't gotten so close. He smelled something awful, like a soiled diaper combined with sweat, nacho cheese, and beer. With a top note of Dr. Pepper.

"A hundred ain't enough for me to tell you anything. Pascal's bad ass, and I don't want to get on his bad side."

"He doesn't have any good sides."

Snuggles squirmed a little. "That's true, gotta give you that, but even more reason to not rat him out."

I swung the bat as hard as possible on the table next to Snuggles, sending white powder, money, a spoon, and lighter in the air. I held my breath and stepped back.

"Whatcha do that for!" Snuggles yelled again, holding his hand over his nose and mouth. He didn't partake of his own product.

"You can recover the money, big boy, but if I swing again, it is going to be your knee, so choose."

"Fuck me." Snuggles wiped the sweat from his brow with his other hand. "Fine," he said. "But I need more money."

I handed him four hundred dollars. "That's all I have, Snuggles, so take it or leave it. After all, knees *are* optional."

Snuggles downed a Pabst. "He's near Little Italy. I don't know where, but that should give you a place to start."

It did. Little Italy was basically a small, rhombus-shaped area in the corner created by Mayfield Road and Euclid Avenue. This helped, assuming Snuggley-poo wasn't lying.

"Why do you want to find him in the first place? He's bad news." Snuggles popped another can.

"He's holding a friend of mine hostage."

"That other vampire who came with you last time you beat up my people?"

"Yeah."

"You shouldn't go. Free advice. If Pascal has him, he's dead or being tortured until he's dead. You can't save him."

"We'll see. I think your guys are bleeding out. You should call an ambulance."

"Screw them. They couldn't do their jobs."

I stomped out, grabbed two bandanas from inside my pack, and tied the one man's arm up as best as I could. The bleeding leg on the other guy had slowed. I pulled out a burner phone and called 911, putting it down next to the ashen, suffering men. I felt guilty hurting them so badly, but it was only a tiny bit of guilt because they were bad people, and bad people need to be put in their place. In fact, as I considered it, I might not feel any guilt at all.

I headed for my car. Time to drive east to University Circle and Little Italy. I spied a blur of activity above me, keeping pace with my car. Blaze was headed in the same direction.

# CHAPTER SEVEN

I managed to find a lot and paid for parking. Most of the parking was for residents only, which is why if you went to Little Italy for dinner, you used the valet service that worked for all the restaurants.

I walked up to Murray Hill Road and stood in front of La Dolce Vita, whose buffalo caprese salad with prosciutto was to die for. I'm not much one for eating pork, being Jewish and all, but I did allow myself that specific treat now and then. If the Eternal didn't want us to eat pork or shellfish, it would have been nice if He hadn't made them taste so good.

On the other hand, that was the whole point. It's easy not eating disgusting stuff.

A whoosh of air told me Blaze had arrived. He was still glamoured, so if anyone was looking, it would appear that I was talking to a hazy bunch of air, which made me look crazy but at least hid the reality of a huge, emu-like bird with feathers of bronze and large, grapefruit-sized eyes.

Blaze spoke in my head, as usual.

*He's somewhere here.*

"How did you know that?"

*I found Liam's car. It was halfway to his apartment but abandoned on the side of the road. I did concentric circles until I caught his scent. Was this confirmed by your Snuggle-bunny?*

"It was, which gives me high confidence that we are in the right place. Now, we have to find him somewhere here."

*If I had known you were going to shake that guy down for the info, I wouldn't have wasted my time flying around the city like a chicken with my head cut off. Never mind, scratch that. Wipe that shit-eating grin off your face.*

"It's a funny mental image, that's all, and now you must do ten push-ups."

*I do not have to do push-ups. That's your thing, not mine.*

"House rule."

*I'm a bird. How would I do push-ups?*

"We'll figure out something. Do you have an idea about where to start searching for Liam?"

*My nose tells me Tony Brush Park, at the end of this road, was visited by a vampire recently. It smells of death and decay.*

"As good a place to start as any."

By this time, diners were staring, some whispering to each other. One pudgy man approached me with his hands spread wide. I could practically hear him thinking, *Don't upset the lady talking to herself.*

"Are you okay, miss? Do I need to call someone for you?"

I gave him a wide smile. "No, sir, I'm fine. I'm in a play at the community center, and sometimes I have a habit of rehearsing my lines to myself. I apologize if I worried you."

"Ah! A thespian! I, myself, sought a life in the theater. Alas, it was not to be." He wiped his brow with the back of his chef's jacket sleeve. "Do you do Shakespeare? *The Merchant of Venice* is a personal favorite."

I gave him a cold stare. "It isn't mine."

He didn't understand my reaction but did perceive my ire, so he backed away and whispered to a beefy doorman at Mi Bella, across the street, who gave me a concerned look. Mi Bella makes excellent eggplant parmesan, and I briefly wondered if I could order some to go.

The big Mi Bella doorman looked like he was heading in our direction, so it seemed a good time to move. Blaze and I walked to the park and found suitable observations posts. I hid in a tree at the edge of the park, where I had a good view of the playground equipment and the church beyond. The truth is Pascal could most likely smell us, so he'd know we were here, but I was glad to be in the park when it was still light so I could get the lay of the land.

I couldn't imagine what Pascal wanted, but whatever it was, I'd find it. Liam's life was on the line. My stomach flipped, and tears gathered in the corners of my eyes, but I shoved that away to focus on the task at hand. It worked for a few minutes.

Dusk settled, and as it did, my sense of dread sunk to new depths. It was joined by its best friend, guilt, and my nerves were on fire. Finally, a text came.

*I see you found the park. I'm about to walk in now. Don't do anything stupid or Liam is dead.*

*Got it,* I texted back.

The skinny vampire ambled into the park, dragging a sack along behind him. At least, that is what I thought it was, until I realized it was Liam, so black, blue, and bloody I couldn't see his features. Pascal pulled him by the leg, and Liam's arms dragged above his head.

I jumped out of my hiding spot, holding only one weapon in each hand. "What did you do to him? Why isn't he moving?"

"He's passed out, not dead. I beat him, drank from him to weaken him, and he fought back. I'm afraid the time passed slowly for him."

"You son of a bitch. Let him go. I'll do whatever you want, find whatever this is, but he's innocent."

"Yes, he is innocent, isn't he? He's never supped from a human except that one drug dealer, which doesn't count, and he's never killed. This is a puzzlement to me, and something I plan to rectify. He's a vampire, and he should act like one. I plan on guiding him in his journey to the shadowy side of the street." He hoisted Liam up and held him by his neck. I noticed Pascal's arm had grown back. Pity.

"Forcing Liam to kill is the same thing as killing him outright. You promised you wouldn't kill him!" My nerves morphed to rage. "Why are you doing this to me? To us? What is your interest?" I was bristling with fury but didn't dare make an offensive move.

"I have my reasons. Let's get to it. I need you to find a crystal ball."

"I don't understand."

"How do you think Zric knew you would be at the museum that day? He'd gotten his hands on a magic crystal ball, which looks exactly as you would think, by the way. All crystal-y and round, or so I've been told. I've only seen a picture, and I don't know where he got it, which I find vexing." The vampire ground his teeth, and his nostrils flared. "If he wasn't already dead, I'd kill him myself."

Liam struggled against Pascal's hold. "Am okay. Old man thinks he's a big deal." Liam's voice was weak, and his words were slurred. "Jess, don't…danger…"

"You are not okay, Liam, but I will find this ball and get you back, I promise."

"Don't…"

Pascal shook him quiet, Liam's teeth rattling like old bones.

"Do you have a starting place where it might be?" I asked Pascal, my knuckles white on my weapon. I considered methods of attack one after the other, dismissing them as fast as they came. There was no way to get to Pascal without endangering Liam. I wished another Monster Hunter was with me. Maybe Mason Dixon. He would have loved the footage. More importantly, another Hunter could attack from Pascal's rear.

Pascal snapped his fingers. "Jess? You with me? Do I have to do something awful to get your attention?" He smiled a sinister grin, and I wanted to smack that ghoulish look right off his face.

"I'm listening, Pascal."

"The ball is in the Beachwood Mall."

I must have heard wrong. "The mall?"

Pascal sniffed, pursing his lips. "Yes, the little twit hid it from me in a place I couldn't easily go."

"Why didn't you break in at night and look yourself?"

Pascal dropped Liam, who fell in a heap, and held his hands wide. "I considered it, but I thought this would be more fun. Also, I get caught up in window shopping and get things I don't need."

"Funny."

"No, I mean it. I pick up extras, like patrolling security officers, employees who leave late, and cleaning crews. So many cleaning crews to mop all that crappy fake wood laminate. Believe me, Jess. You want me to stay away. It's like a smorgasbord."

"Macabre. Evil. Disturbing."

Pascal fluttered a hand. "Awww, such a flatterer."

Blaze took the chit-chat as his opening and flew fast toward Pascal and Liam. He managed to slap at them with one of his powerful wings, and Pascal fell to the ground with a growl of fury. I rushed to Liam's side, grabbed his shoulders, and tried to pull him away, but Pascal was too fast, seizing Liam's ankle.

I was afraid we'd tear Liam in two, so I used my thumb to flip open my Tupperware mini-square and hurled the blessed Manischevitz in Pascal's face, hoping it might sting a bit, or at least tingle aggressively.

I didn't expect his face to liquefy where the wine hit it or the piercing shrieks to match. Pascal's face melted like a wax candle, skin and tissue sliding down his skull. One gushy drop plopped at his feet.

I swung my tomahawk, letting it loose for the first time. It hit Pascal in the chest, and though it wasn't a killing blow, it is fair to say that Pascal found his disintegrating face coupled with a bleeding chest wound a little too much to handle. He cupped one hand to his chin to catch his face, and with his spare arm, seized Liam and evaporated. I looked to my left and right, ran forward and backward, hunting for them, cursing Pascal for his disappearing act. He'd done this to me once before, and it was maddening. I clenched my hands into fists and screamed to the sky.

My 'hawk lay on the ground. I picked it up and reminded myself to get more wine; it was surprisingly effective. The tomahawk groaned in satisfaction, happy to be blooded, and as I watched, it absorbed the blood like a sponge, giving a little shudder of satisfaction.

No, that wasn't disturbing. Not at all.

## CHAPTER EIGHT

The next morning, I slept in, something I never do, but I needed the rest. When I finally woke, I scuffled out to the kitchen, yawning a loud "good morning." My voice echoed back. The kitchen was empty but for a note on the table. Nathaniel was worried and had taken the kids to his mother's while I figured this out. He was sorry to leave without talking to me, but he needed to think about things. He'd call me later.

I sunk into my chair, heaving stuttering breaths, tears cascading down my face. I gazed around my kitchen, and no one was eating, or arguing, or painting with ketchup. No one was overcooking toast or pouring gallons of syrup on their pancakes. Nathaniel wasn't touching my shoulders each time he walked by my chair. No sticky hugs, and the fire alarm wasn't going off because of the toast. I was abandoned.

I stayed like that for a good couple of minutes until there was a peck at the door, followed by a sharp bark. Blaze and Shura stared at me from the other side of the sliding door, and from the way their heads were tilted, I could tell they were worried about me. I wiped my eyes with my bathrobe sleeve and sat up straight. Time fix this mess and get Liam back. And my family.

I signaled to my outdoor friends that I'd be there in a minute. I changed into black clothes, leggings, a cotton t-shirt, and black Converse. My bra and panties were black, too, but only I knew that.

I spent the rest of the day discussing strategy with Blaze and Shura, and packing my gear, taking things out and putting new things in until I settled on my tools. I made a quick stop to talk to Rabbi Stein about what happened and the plan I'd concocted. He agreed that I should find the crystal ball to keep it out of enemy hands.

"Rabbi, I don't know if I can keep it out of Pascal's hands. He has Liam."

Shadows crossed the Rabbi's face as he struggled, again, with the idea that I could care for a vampire.

"I don't understand your relationship with Liam, Jess."

"All of God's creatures, Rabbi."

"A vampire is a perversion of the Eternal's purpose. Ashes to ashes, dust to dust. We die and move on. Our bodies disintegrate. It's the natural way of things. Dead bodies aren't meant to walk and talk."

"Look, I understand. We eat the antelope. We die, and our bodies become the grass. The antelopes eat the grass. The circle of life."

The Rabbi looked a little lost.

"Rabbi, all I know is that Liam is a good person and he loves me and my family."

"You would trust Liam with your children's lives?"

"Absolutely."

"You care for him very much."

"I love him as a dear friend, Rabbi, as a brother, and I am responsible for what happened to him. If it hadn't been for me, Pascal would have left Liam alone."

Rabbi Stein was silent for a moment but then gave me a sharp nod as he came to a conclusion.

"Love is love is love. I can't guess the Eternal's plan, or why He allowed this to happen to Liam, but he who saves a life, saves the world. You are right. You must help your friend."

I let out a breath I hadn't known I was holding. "Thanks, Rabbi. Maybe I'll figure out a way to keep the ball, too." I wiggled to the front of the chair, excited. "It'll be cool, don't you think, Rabbi? To know the future. We can make it a weapon for the good guys."

Rabbi clucked like an old hen, shaking his head back and forth in the manner of one explaining things to a small child.

"The ball could only show one possible future. Humans are not supposed to know the future. That's what makes free will matter."

"Ah," I said, making subtle sounds of agreement as if I understood the wisdom he was imparting. I tapped my finger on my chin. "Yes, Rabbi, I see what you mean." His face brightened. Anything to make him happy.

I left still thinking it would awesome to know the future but was hell-bent on saving Liam.

This time, Shura came with me instead of Blaze, and off we went to the unhappiest place on Earth—the mall. The mall, *any* mall, was the unhappiest place on Earth because it was filled with things you didn't know you wanted and couldn't afford to buy. Malls create gluttony and greed, envy and despair. It had four of the seven deadly sins in its pocket.

Even I fell prey to the pull. I once stood in wonder in front of a mallet, a beautiful mallet. It was light but strong, and the advertising promised it could pound meat thin. I was going to use it to pound meat, too, not the type the manufacturers were thinking about, but close enough that I was salivating. I pictured myself wielding it, imagined the fear I'd instill in monsters of all shapes and sizes, and realized I had no place to put it. My pockets were taken, and I didn't want to add any more weight to my pack. Besides, I told myself, it was a little too Thor.

I'd borrowed a leash off my neighbor and pulled out a doggie jacket I'd once swiped at an airport that said, "Dog on duty." I didn't know why I wanted it, but it seemed like a great idea at the time and was coming in handy now. Shura was…displeased.

"Shura, we have to pretend you're a dog, or we'll never get in there."

Shura turned her head. I resorted to flattery.

"Shura, you are a beautiful wolf. You are so regal and powerful that people are drawn to you." I hung my head and sighed. "That's the problem. Without this little disguise, there is no way we could hide what you are."

Shura winked to tell me she knew what I was doing, but she allowed the jacket and leash. That didn't mean she enjoyed it, and she let me know with an undercurrent of growl bitching, pun intended, as we entered the mall.

The mall was a half-hour to closing, which is what we wanted. Shura got some glances, but we ignored them. We did a sweep of the top floor of the mall, including the food court, the sports memorabilia store, the massage station, and a store where all the mannequins wore ripped clothing. Why do people pay money for tattered jeans? You're paying *more* money for *less* fabric.

We descended the winding staircase, Shura's claws making a tappity-tap sound on the faux marble. She didn't like the open steps at all and went down at breakneck speed. This landed us in front of Hillard's, one of the anchor department stores. She stopped in front of the entrance and gave a tug at her leash.

"Is the ball here?"

Shura did that wolf shrug thing that freaked me out.

"You smell something off?"

"More than the perfume?"

She nodded.

"Something with a magical energy?"

She smiled, lolling out her tongue, which had the unfortunate side effect of showing her canines.

"Mommy! Look at that wolf!"

Shura and I looked away, and I rocked on my toes a bit, whistling.

"That's not a wolf, son. That's a very big dog."

"But look what big teeth she has."

I could see out of the corner of my eye and noticed that the mother gave a closer look. Her eyes grew wide, and she stepped back and pulled her son along with her. "Hush, child. Let's get to the car."

I breathed a sigh of relief until I heard, "Jess! I never see you in the mall! Wow. Did you get a dog?"

Oh. Dear. God.

Joseph whined. "How come David gets a dog and a pony? I never get anything. He's got all the cool stuff."

"Uh, hi Judy. How are you?" Shura gave another smile, and my knees almost buckled. I stepped in front of her, gesturing behind my back for her to shut it. There was no way this was going to work. Any minute now…any minute… I waited for the alarms and police.

Judy pulled on my sleeve to drag me closer and whispered in a hiss. "What does this dog do? Sniff for bombs? For narcotics? And why in the world are you working with him?"

I cast about for an answer. "Her. Shura is a female and is a multi-talented dog. She finds guns and bombs. Sometimes narcotics. You know, whatever needs smelling." I almost smacked my forehead with my own palm, I was so lame.

"But why are *you* handling her?"

I didn't mean to. I never lie, so I said the first thing that came to me, which wasn't technically untrue. "Judy, I'm undercover."

Judy's eyes grew wide, and she rubbed her hands together, so excited by this news. "I knew it!" she said. Then, looking back and forth, she stage-whispered, "I always knew you had a secret job."

"Yeeessss, Judy." I took the lifeline. "Exactly. A secret job. A secret mission. Right now, I need to get to it. Nice seeing you, but remember, mum's the word." I drew my fingers across my lips like a zipper.

"Oh, I'd never tell!" She looked at me sideways. "Is this why you need a pony?"

This was my chance. "Yes, Judy. The pony finds lost children."

She drew a breath. "Ahhhh. I wish you had told me that in the first place." She gave me a knowing look. "I'll see what I can do with the Neighborhood Association for you. I feel safer knowing there's a search and rescue team right on our street."

"Thank you, Judy, that would be appreciated. I knew I could share my secret with you."

She crossed her heart. "I've got your back." She sidled away, Joseph in tow.

I sighed. God bless stupid people. I amended that as soon as I thought it. Judy wasn't stupid. She was gullible, innocent, and blind to the dangers around her, which is why I had a job.

Although how she could believe in a Cleveland search-and-rescue pony was beyond me.

Shura tugged at the leash, so I got going. We entered the department store like we should be there, all boss and confident. Shura's nose was to the ground, and I said idiotic things like, "Sniff. Find. Search."

"Can I help you in some way?" asked one of those perfume sample people, bearing two bottles.

"No," I said, my voice stern. "Just let us do our jobs, ma'am, and please try not to spray that perfume near my dog. It makes her nose blind."

The last part was true, and to prove it, Shura sneezed.

"Oh, yes, of course. I'll tell the other sales representatives as well." Her eyes got wide and her voice low. "Is it terrorism? Are we in danger? Do we need to evacuate?" Instead of looking scared, she appeared excited by the possibility of a threat, biting her lip in anticipation of the story she could tell later.

I leaned in close. "Nothing imminent, but we train all the time."

Her face dropped. "Oh, okay. Well, I guess it is good there is nothing..." She trailed off. "Nothing *serious*." She perked up. "But there could be, any day. We have to be diligent."

I nodded, my face stern. "Exactly. Thank you for your help."

She gave me a conspiratorial wink and ran off to tell the other women in the department. I rubbed my eyes, gave myself a mental shake, and put my game face on.

Our main goal was to find a place to hide. We explored quickly, as the loudspeakers were blaring that the mall would close in fifteen minutes. When the coast was clear, Shura and I squeezed under a sample bed decorated with a bedspread and a bed skirt in bright fuchsia. I felt like Claudia and Jamie from one of my favorite childhood books. Those children hid in the Metropolitan Museum of Art and retrieved change from a fountain for spending money. I laughed at the thought, and poor Shura, who was squished and unhappy, gave me a small growl. I took the hint and swallowed my giggles.

The managers did their last sweeps, and the cleaning crews came through to tidy up, making me think of Pascal's threat. Shura and I were almost caught by a vacuum.

Finally, the store was quiet, the front rolling shutters locked and the lights off, except for dim blue lights that cast an eerie glow. We squiggled out from under the bed, both of us relieved to be out of that small space and not inhaling cotton fibers.

"Okay, Shura. Let's start at the top and go down. We'll move counterclockwise from the children's clothes through petites. Make sense?" It must have because Shura led the way to escalator, turned off for the night, and we climbed the metal stairs to the top.

The store was quiet, but not silent. There were mummers and mutterings, squeaks and groans from all corners. The air was thick, and the blue lights twisted every object into a chilling silhouette that made my skin crawl. I have never wanted out of some place so much in my life. Shura felt the same things, and her agitation made her rush.

I stopped and bent to hold Shura's head in my hands. "Brave den mother," I said. "Mate of alpha male. There is nothing that the two of us together cannot face. Show no fear." The wolf closed her eyes, gave herself a good shake, and we proceeded, Shura now carefully sniffing, and me peering at every item to make sure we didn't miss the crystal ball.

We proceeded through fancy brand-name sections, a display of bathing suits, petite "working woman" clothes, and finally uncomfortable-looking dressy outfits I wouldn't be caught dead in. *Oh dear, note to self, if I die, tell Nathaniel to bury me in jeans.*

I got a lump in my throat at that thought. He'd left and taken the kids, to protect them. From *me*. From my world. I took a moment to offer a quick prayer.

*Please, watch over them.*

The next floor was full of handbags and a large accessory area, perfume and makeup. We worked methodically, widdershins, step-by-step. We could hear our breathing, the scrape of my feet on the carpet, and the click of Shura's nails where there was linoleum. That's when I noticed the tapping coming from behind us. Tap-tap. Tap-tap. Double tap-tap. Two of them. Triple. More? Whatever made the tapping sounds followed our path and walked when we did; stopped when we stopped.

Shura and I shifted our eyes to take sideways glances at each other, and we exchanged a tense nod. Lockstep, we took three big, bunny hops and twisted to hide behind an enormous display of scarves. We peered around the display, hearts beating bird-like pitter-pats. I never, ever, expected what we saw.

Mannequins. Naked, eyeless, mouthless, mannequins, a horde of them, huddled next to each other as if for warmth, angled forward at the waists, studying us with non-existent eyes.

True fact. Wolves can scream louder than humans. Ask me how I know.

## CHAPTER NINE

Shura yelped loud enough to make me think she'd been physically injured, so my first response was to do a once-over of her body to make sure she hadn't been shot by an unseen enemy. I patted her down, looking for blood, but she pulled on the leash and yipped.

We fled for the hills, or more accurately, the escalators. They weren't moving but we figured mannequins couldn't do stairs without ankles. Surprise! The laws of biology and physics don't apply with magic. Those naked mole-rats followed us right down to the bottom floor.

We continued to charge ahead, paying no attention to what we ran over, bumped into, or knocked down, but the mannequins kept pace, and, even with the tapping, it was difficult to estimate how far behind or close to us they were. My skin crawled, and my anxiety rose to the point that my lips were numb and my fingers tingled. Shura was so strong that she pulled away from me, so the leash was dragging on the ground.

Around and around we went, men's clothing, big and tall, belts, shoes, more shoes, tuxes and ties, women's undergarments, baby clothing, and home goods. We zigged and zagged, moving in sharp angles to avoid their outstretched arms. I spared a look over my shoulder and noticed two of them were child mannequins, which made me squawk and pick up speed.

We split up, and the mannequins paused, tilted their heads to the side, one even put its hand on its chin, and then split into two groups and followed us both. I needed to take these creepy Chuckies out, and I only had one idea. I rushed through home goods and slid full speed into tools and hardware, looking for what I needed. When I saw it, I grabbed it and pushed it in front of me. I was distracted by the terrifying Barbie and Ken dolls, so I ignored the new shiver of magic that ran up my spine.

The mannequins backed up, but two left the group to encircle me I didn't even look. I just flung my tomahawk at the one on the right, and mannequin number one took it right in the face, going down like C-3P0 in the Genonosian execution arena. The second almost made it to me, but I executed a back kick, and he fell as well, losing a leg. He got up, but hopping wasn't his strong suit, and he tumbled back over.

I turned my weapon on. It was a floor model industrial space heater, designed for warehouses and other spacious areas. It was meant to be plugged into an electric outlet, but it did have an enormous battery that would last a few hours in case of power outage. The battery made the thing super heavy, so I pushed it on the ground.

I hadn't been certain that heat would bother them, but they were made of plastic, so it stood to reason that it might make them uncomfortable. Again, they split off, this time directly in two groups, one to my right and one to my left. It was a great tactic because I couldn't heat both directions, which made me wonder who had made them. I rushed the ones to my right, pushing the mighty heater like a battering ram, and as they back peddled, they hit a pottery shelf and went down in a heap of clay shards. That was enough to slow them down, so, making sure the heat was still as high as it could go, I whirled to face the other crew, prepared to do as much damage as possible.

Except they weren't attacking but rotating in a slow half circle to face the entranceway.

A deep red light gleamed in the darkness, dissipating into orange and yellow rings as the light came through the door. There was only one thing that made that kind of entrance, and I closed my eyes in disbelief.

The mannequins knew what the light meant as well, or at least the person controlling them did. Deciding not to kill me, they cleared the way, happy for me to go first. I turned off the space heater and tiptoed to the entrance. I was worried about Shura, and my mind cast about for a way to get out of this.

I spied Shura sneaking toward me, keeping to the shadows, and noticed that the wolf had disabled some of the mannequins with her teeth and claws. They lay discarded on the hard floor, flopping like fish in a bucket. Shura gagged and spit, wrinkling her nose at the taste. I almost smiled. I would have smiled if the red, orange, and yellow glow coming from the other side of the escalators didn't mean what I thought.

I rubbed my hands over my face. First the mannequins, now a demon. Was there no one who didn't know about this damn crystal ball? Was everyone in the paranormal community after it?

The answer was yes, because a smaller red portal opened in the floor, revealing long red fingers grasping the rim. Two beings hoisted themselves out of the portal, reminding me of five-year-olds exiting the deep end of the pool. They were imps, and they could have been doubles for Zric—same red skin, short stature, and hinged horns. Shura flopped to the ground and covered her eyes with her paws, no longer in fear, but in disbelief.

What happens when zombie mannequins, a demon, two imps, a monster hunter, and a wolf walk into a department store?

We were about to find out.

The imps scrambled to their feet and stared wide-eyed at the glowing flames coming from the other side of the escalator.

"Why is heeeeee here?" asked one, hitting the second on the shoulder so hard the imp fell backward and tumbled ass over teakettle.

The second imp rose to his feet and hit the first one upside the head with a vicious slap. "Why should I know, brother?" The second used the first's name. It started with a "T" sound, but that was all I got.

"Because you were supposed to keep the information secret, knucklehead, and obviously you didn't." The first one elbowed the second. Again, something like a "T" name. I angled my head to listen more closely, but the "T" sound coupled with the "Z" sounds, along with the addition of a rolling "R," made no sense to my ear. I decided to call them Tic and Tac.

Tac shoved his brother and hissed, "I kept the secret! You must have spilled it to that female you met at the lava pool, you cretin."

"I didn't."

"You did!"

The brothers pushed and shoved each other, back-and-forth, until they were wrestling on the ground flapping their hands and legs, kicking and screeching. Tic pulled Tac's horns while Tac yanked Tic's tail. Tic screamed, and their tussle drew the attention of the demon we had yet to see. Shura and I ducked into the shadows and covered ourselves with coats.

"Who disturbs my trip to the surface world?" The demon's voice thundered through the air, and the display jewelry tinkled, sounding like a flock of terrified birds. Tic and Tac jumped to their feet but couldn't help elbowing each other. They smoothed their horns and slipped on masks of respect.

"Kokochar! Are you here? Wow, what a coincidence," stammered Tic. "It's good to see you, my lord." Tac stepped on Tic's toe, and Tic squeaked, jumping back several inches to rub his foot. Tic jammed his elbow into Tac's back, and Tac backhanded Tic, who flew into a display of women's underthings. He sat, stunned, with a bra on his head.

"Lord Kokochar, Purple One of Mucous and Terror, as you may know, our brother, Zric, was destroyed by the Monster Hunter in these parts, and his crystal ball has never been recovered. It is our intent to retrieve our bother's property and bring it to Hell, where it can be used in service of our prince." Tac bowed so low that his horns scraped the floor.

Koko laughed, a breathless hiss that rose to an ear-piercing screech and settled into a subsonic chuckle. "Puny, weak imps, my teensy-tiny little pets, you will not retrieve the crystal ball. I will, and I will bring it to Lucifer myself, but it is amusing that you think you can fetch it." Four of his arms wrapped around his bulbous body as he shook with laughter. The other two wiped his lower eyes. The upper eyes bore into the imps and displayed no humor.

Tic took a delicate step over the slime left in Koko's wake as Koko's massive purple snail body slithered across the floor. Koko's antennae twitched in annoyance. I didn't like the cagey look in Tic's eyes.

"Oh, Great One, we will retrieve it for you and share the glory. We can move with ease in this world, while, you, I mean, you..." Tic trailed off when Koko leaned close. Tic swallowed and regained his courage.

"While, you, in your magnificence, might find these small human spaces to be insufficient for your comfort."

Koko put all his hands on his...hips...and squeezed out an appendage that he tapped like a foot. I shuddered and wished I had closed my eyes. I would never un-see that. I used to think snails were amazing.

Koko touched his black tongue to the tip of his smaller nose as he considered what Tic had said. "You have a point, you overgrown rat. Perhaps I shall wait for you to find it, but if you don't bring it to me, I will punish you until the end of time. Deal?"

Tic and Tac exchanged a quick glance and said, "Deal." Both had their fingers crossed behind their backs.

## CHAPTER TEN

The imps' small hands hugged their bodies, but it turned out that putting their fingers behind their backs may not have been the best move, as the mannequins I'd been battling had joined their mutilated brethren on the floor, silent and sneaky as snakes in the grass, and slithered on their bellies toward the imps. They rose like cobras, striking fast and quick, and somehow, from somewhere, maws opened from their blank faces and bit the imps' fingers. Both imps lost several digits. Their blood flowed to the floor, creating red lakes. Tic wobbled at the sight, and Tac had to hold him up. They were both hyperventilating in pain.

I shuddered as the demon howled with hysterical laughter but smiled in satisfaction as his good humor withered when the mannequins eased toward him, their gaping, impossible mouths chomping the air in futile, persistent bites.

Koko snarled, roaring his anger to the skylights, but backed off several mucus-y steps as he tried to figure out what to do with these maniacal, overgrown dolls.

"Are these my sister's toys?" he bellowed. "Kikichar, do you seek the crystal ball as well as I? Forget it, you witch-demon! You always win, but not this time."

A disembodied, tinny voice, like the speaker was far away, echoed in the room. "Sorry, my brother, but that crystal ball is mine. Do you like my friends?" The mannequins moved closer.

"Get up here and find it yourself, you cheater!" Koko yelled, slapping at the mannequins with big bulbous hands that manifested from his torso's bulk.

"I don't think so, Kokochar, my brother. I'm sorry, but you lose again."

Koko kept slapping down plastic people like a pissed off mafioso, but his voice was whiney. "Just because you are a witch *and* a demon, you always got the nicer things. It's my turn!" He stamped a slippery appendage of some kind. The imps tried to sneak behind him, but one of his arms grew two hands and caught them both by the throats.

"Stop being a big baby and get out of the way!" The voice was louder, and I became afraid the other demon might show up in person. We needed to get to that ball fast.

I elbowed Shura, and she got the hint. We scuttled backward to get out of the way and found ourselves in a dressing room. The dressing room had a door at the far right, which turned out to be a storage closet that shared another door with the home decor area of the store. We closed the door behind us, taking care to be quiet, but any sounds we made were drowned out by the fight between the three bad-guys factions.

I closed my eyes and took a calming breath, and then another, focusing on the tingle of magic I'd felt before.

"There it is, Shura. That way." She followed my finger, and we walked toward the decorations area, full of dainty rugs, lamps, coasters, vases, and other delicate things that would never find their way to my house. I closed my eyes again and refocused. Anyone could sense magic, if they were trained to do so. You know that feeling when you have an itch on your back that is just out of reach? It feels like that.

I moved forward two more steps but lost the magic when I stepped behind the throw rugs and pillows. I reversed course until I felt it again and moved to the left, toward the holiday section, which was seasonal and had items marked "Clearance." I tilted my head and felt for the magic again.

"There, Shura. It's stronger over there."

Her fur bristled, and she nodded, letting me know she felt it too. I held out my right hand, searching, searching, and boom! Got it.

The snow globes. Leftover Christmas snow globes sat on a sale rack, forlorn and lonely, and while most snow globes were only a few inches in diameter, in the back corner was a milky white globe the size of a bowling ball. Shura's tongue lolled out of her mouth in a wolf smile, complete with teeth. It was meant to be pleasant. Really.

I reached out, my fingers slow and steady, and moved the snow globes standing in my way. Little alpine scenes tilted this way and that as I cleared the shelf of everything but the crystal ball. Ever so gingerly, I touched the ball with both hands, lifted it, and held it in between my palms. The world fell away, my vision a roiling blackness until an image emerged. It was my house, late afternoon, my kids playing tag with some friends in the back yard. Despite the happy scene, I had a sense of foreboding as I watched Nathaniel cross the deck to the grill, marinating chicken in a Tupperware container in his hand.

My mind searched the scene for the danger, my vision scurrying this way and that, trying to figure out what was happening and why I was being given this vision. All three of my kids were there. Nathaniel whistled to himself as he lit the grill. The other children laughed and screamed in glee as they got tagged, were freed, and then tagged again. One, two, three kids. One husband. Other children but no one I wouldn't expect. What was wrong?

A new scene, Blaze and I out at night, staring at our roof. I held my tomahawk and Blaze's wings were raised, poised for flight. A lump formed in the pit of my stomach.

My vision tunneled back, moving at whiplash speed, over houses, roads, golf courses, and shopping malls, until we raced past the suburbs and arrived downtown. A dark building, one in which I'd met Pascal before, came into view, and the vision slowed to show me that was our destination. The vision swooped in a window, and there was Pascal, staring into the crystal ball, using it to spy on my family.

I cried out and almost dropped the ball, but Shura leaned against my leg, giving me support and I recovered, gasping for breath, my heart pounding with fear.

"We have to destroy this ball, Shura. It isn't safe to take it with us. Somehow, Pascal will get it, and he'll use it to target my family. I think this is the danger you have been sensing."

I crouched so Shura could put her nose to the ball. Her body tensed and quivered until she tore her face away. Her yellow eyes darkened, and she snarled under her breath. Yes, she saw what I saw. I had thought to use the ball for good, but it was too dangerous to hold onto it. It had to be destroyed. I briefly considered shattering it on the ground, but that didn't feel like enough. It needed to be obliterated.

Before I could figure out my next steps, I felt heat at my back and heard a high-pitched chittering, coupled with uneven scraping sounds that made the back of my neck crawl. Shura and I turned to find Koko, the imps, and mannequins in various configurations of arms, legs, and missing limbs, staring at us. The scraping sounds came from one standing mannequin, who'd somehow replaced a missing foot with a Nike sneaker.

My brain, which doesn't always know when to speak up and when to shut up, opened my mouth, and I said, "Hey, that's my gig. I'm always the one who winds up with one shoe on and one shoe off."

They charged, and home decor would never be the same. I slashed with my tomahawk, cutting, slicing, and dicing, fueled by my need to get home and make sure everyone was safe. Shura grew two sizes larger, or at least it seemed that way, and she bit, clawed, and harried the mannequins until I could chop most of them to pieces. Koko reared back and, with a retching sound, hocked a giant loogie on the ground in front of me. I threw my body to the side to avoid it, but the gooey mucus was too much. I slipped and fell on my butt, hard. The jolt knocked the crystal ball lose, and it rolled across the floor and under the bed Shura and I had hidden under earlier.

I scrambled to get to the ball, but Tic and Tac jumped me from behind, and I lost my 'hawk. I didn't worry too much about that because it always seemed to find me, but I was down to fists without it. My bag was where I'd left it, by the snow globes.

The imps scrambled over me like monkeys in a tree. I swatted at them, smacking their faces while they pulled my hair and ripped my shirt. Shura leapt on one of the boys and dragged him away while I reached wildly for anything I could find. My hand grabbed a pillow, and I squeezed it between me and the remaining imp and smashed it to his face, suffocating him until he reared off me, gnashing his teeth in anger. I flipped to my side, clambered to my feet, and dove for my bag.

Koko, Tic and Tac, and all the Barbies and Kens stood in a circle, pointing at the crystal ball on the floor, which somebody had retrieved and planted in the middle of their tête-à-tête. The demon and the imps yelled at each other, the imps standing their ground to the more powerful demon while the mannequins pointed and stomped their ludicrous feet. Kiki's thin voice melded into the larger mêlée.

Koko growled, "This belongs to me! Tiny imps, bow down to me, and you, you carnivorous, disgusting, stick figures, you don't count. Kiki, bite me!"

Tic and Tac objected. "We are the owners as it belonged to our brother, Zric. Even elderly demons..."

Koko growled again.

"Ah, we mean, *elder* demons can't fight inheritance rules. The Great Lord wouldn't allow it."

"I will not be denied!" roared Koko. "This was promised to me by the Great Lord, and I will have it. Hey! Back off, stick people! Kiki! Call your pets!" The only response from the great hellacious beyond was a snarl. The imps jumped on Koko, slipping and sliding, but getting enough purchase to scramble at most of Koko's eyes.

The mannequins made a play to get the ball by sending in one of the kid-sized models to slip into the middle on a stealth mission, hoping the demon and imps were too distracted by their rumble to notice. Koko, having eyes on the back and sides of his head that the imps couldn't reach, wasn't fooled, and he swiped out a glutinous foot and encircled the ball, pulling it toward him, coating the crystal in a layer of slime.

The imps jumped on the ball like it was a hand grenade, and suddenly all three parties were in a scrambling pile as if a football was loose. This was my chance.

I opened my bag and pulled out a full bottle of Manischevitz wine, which I'd had Rabbi Stein bless. I opened the bottle, took a few slugs, missing my mouth so some dribbled on my ruined shirt. I finally drank about half, grimacing at the cloying sweetness but figuring ingesting holy wine might be good for me, like vitamins. You don't know if they really help, but you take them on faith.

I removed some cotton from my bag and retrieved a small bottle of gasoline I'd collected from the emergency five-gallon canister we kept in the garage. I soaked the cotton in the gas, shoved it into the wine bottle, and lit the whole thing on fire.

I said a little prayer and lobbed the Mazel Tov cocktail over my head. It crashed onto the floor, right in the middle of the monsters' mash.

The explosion threw bits and pieces of mannequin, imp and demon, as well as crystal, in every direction. The fire caught the nearby bedding, and before anyone could say boo, the area was in flames.

Koko emerged missing arms and other chunks of his body, braying a scream of frustration. He opened his portal and returned to Hell, screaming his sister's name.

The imps and mannequins didn't make it. The mannequins charred in the direct flame. The imps were on fire and were missing golf ball-sized pieces from their torsos and legs, all the time still arguing about whose fault this disaster was.

"Why did you get me involved in this?" yelled Tic, running in circles.

"Because the ball is our property!" hollered Tac, patting out flames.

"Not anymore, and now you get to be Koko's pet!" taunted Tic.

"What did you call me?" Tac pulled on Tic's horns.

"You mean *who* did I call you? Koko's pet! Koko's pet!" Tic punched his brother in the stomach.

"I don't know about that!" Tac punched back.

"Maybe Kiki's pet!" sneered Tic.

"If I'm that, who do you think you're going to belong to? Humm? The Dark Prince might take special interest you, you utter failure!" Tac slammed his fist into his brother's nose, connecting hard.

"What? I can't hear you!" Tic stuffed his stubby knuckles in his ears, ignoring the gushing blood.

The two collapsed into their portal, which had opened again. The last words I heard were, "Big sisters aren't going to like this."

# CHAPTER ELEVEN

We'd destroyed the ball but trapped ourselves in a burning building, and I swear, it wasn't my fault.
Okay, it might have been a little my fault, even all my fault, but I'd have to live with it.

Now that the ball was destroyed, we had to get out. Flames flickered around us, but it was the smoke that concerned me. Going low, we scrambled to the entrance, which was farther from the flames. I didn't make it. I slipped on some Koko slime, fell, and slid across the linoleum, right into a smoldering lump of plastic mannequins. My pant leg caught on fire as the flame found fresh purchase on the fabric. I had nowhere to roll on either side, so I screamed and flapped my leg in the air, panicking as the heat singed my leg. Shura jumped into action, holding my leg down with one enormous paw while she squatted on my leg and peed.

Just then, the sprinklers came on, which meant there had been *no need to urinate on me*, but Shura hadn't known that, so as disgusting as it was, I couldn't complain. Expecting fresh water, I held my sooty face up to the ceiling and my charred leg in the air, only to be hit with smelly, brown liquid from the rusty sprinkler system.

We heard the sirens and knew help was on the way, but I was scrambling to figure out how to exit without the firefighters and police finding us.

"Okay, Shura, we've got to play this one stealthy. Let's stand with our backs to the wall at the entrance. The main flames are straight ahead; that's where they'll head first. Maybe we can sneak by."

The security roll-down reversed course and rolled up, and the cavalry dove in. Shura and I waited until the first wave passed and then scooted around the corner straight into a familiar face.

"Captain Morgan! How nice to see you." I sounded foolish even to myself, and Captain Morgan rubbed his eyes and sighed. The cop behind him clapped both hands together in prayer position and started mumbling.

"Officer Bob! Wow. Both…of…you." I scraped my toe across the linoleum. "What a coincidence to see you here."

Captain Morgan spoke, and his tone was wry. "Let me guess. Were-gorilla?"

"No."

Officer Bob tried. "Imps?"

I nodded and touched my nose. "Two imps, plus a demon named Koko-something, and a horde of animated mannequins enchanted by Koko's sister. It's complicated."

The police officers stared at me, open-mouthed.

"Hey, I wouldn't hang like that too long, gentlemen. A lot of smoke here. Anyway, good to see you. I need to jet."

Captain Morgan placed a hand on my arm, took a sniff, and backed away. I couldn't blame him. I was covered in wine, wolf urine, and foul sprinkler water, and on top of that, my pants were charred and smoky, as was my face. There was no way I was nothing less than rancid.

"Yeah, sorry about that. I know I smell bad." Captain Morgan shot me a look. "Okay, I smell well and truly awful, but if a wolf had peed on you, I don't think you'd be fresh either." I placed both of my hands on my hips and winced as I heard a firefighter go down hard, yelling, "What is this slippery stuff on the floor?"

Captain Morgan ignored everything I said and gave me a stern look. "You can't leave, Mrs. Friedman. You are our only witness to what happened here. You will need to make a statement. A complete statement. Don't leave anything out."

"As much as I'd love to, I need to get back home, get cleaned up, and hunt down a vampire to free a friend, all the while tricking said vampire into believing I still have a crystal ball that I do not have. It's a full to-do list, and I'm running out of time. I'll make a statement later."

"Oh no, you don't." Captain Morgan braved my arm again. "Officer

Bob, please take Mrs. Friedman's statement now." He jutted his chin at me. "Then, you can go take care of that to-do list."

"Fine. Officer Bob, here is my statement. I was searching for a crystal ball, one which can tell the future. It was hidden here by Zric, the imp you met, remember? Pascal, the vampire, kidnapped my friend Liam, who is also a vampire, but a good one, and is holding Liam ransom until I get the ball. I snuck into the store with Shura." I gestured toward the wolf.

"Then we hunted for the ball, which we found, but not before we were attacked by mannequins, two imps, and a demon. The demon's sister is a demon-witch, and she hocus-pocused the mannequins but was work-from-home, so she wasn't here in person. Meanwhile, the ball showed me a glimpse of the future in which Pascal uses the ball to watch my children and husband, very stalker-y, so I knew it was too dangerous to keep. As the ground crew from Hell argued over the ball, I threw a Mazel Tov cocktail and destroyed it. Now, I have to go save Liam without the ball, which will be tricky."

To Officer Bob's credit, he wrote all of this down without a word, only asking me to repeat a few things here and there. He'd been with me in the museum when we fought Zric and freed two people of Japanese spirit animals, so his brain had expanded. Not to mention the were-gorilla. That was a show-stopper if ever there was one.

Officer Bob chewed the end of his pen. "I only have one question."

"Yes?"

"What is a Mazel Tov cocktail?"

"A Molotov cocktail made with a bottle of Manischevitz wine and gasoline."

"I should have guessed. You are free to go."

"Great, thanks. I'll just retrieve one thing…" I ran into the store and came back, shoving my find into my bag.

Shura and I fast-timed it to the trusty minivan, which sat complacently where we'd left it, although two patrol cars were parked right next to it, which explained why Morgan and Bob barely twitched an eyelash when they saw me. Sighing and praying at the sight of me was a mild reaction, given our history.

The night was clear, and the stars twinkled against the dark background of the universe. The broad expanse of unfathomable space reminded me how small and insignificant I was and how I couldn't know the Eternal's plan. I could, however, do my part by taking care of my own backyard. That included keeping my family safe and getting Liam back in one piece.

## CHAPTER TWELVE

Our house was dark and empty, and though I knew everyone was gone, it startled me just the same. Blaze tore around the house to greet us in the front.
*Did you get it? Are you okay?*
"We're fine. Just a little banged up."
Blaze wrinkled his beak, which baffled me. *You smell horrible.*
"Shura peed on me."
Blaze looked a Shura, and they did a mind meld.
*You were on fire?*
"Just a little. Now isn't the time to review the specifics."
*How is it that you always come home like this?*
"Talent. God-given talent, and at least I do come home. Which I need to remind Nathaniel about so he doesn't leave again."

I took a quick shower to get the nastiness off me and gulped two cups of coffee to get the energy I needed for what I was about to do. The fact that I burnt my tongue didn't surprise me.

I went into the garage where we kept the tools, did a little improvising, and then grabbed my tomahawk, magically back with me—handy that—and my phone, which I put in my pants' pocket. I wanted to be light and quick, so I used a drawstring backpack to hold a few other things, only one of them heavy, and readied to take off.

Blaze stopped me by putting his enormous wing on my shoulder.

*You need backup.*

"I need my family back."

*You can't do this alone.*

"Maybe not, but Shura is in no shape to tag along, and I don't know how a bird your size could manage the inside of this building."

Shura padded up to us both and gazed at Blaze.

*Shura is offended that you say she is in no shape to help, and I will stick to the air. Between the two of us, you won't be alone.*

Allies. Unusual ones, given, but allies nonetheless.

"Thank you."

Blazed pursed his beak. Again, I was perplexed by this.

*I have become oddly attached to the young ones.* Shura body-checked Blaze and gave him a look that said it all. *Pups. Who doesn't like pups, you moron?*

I laughed, and it felt good.

Our trio flew or drove downtown on empty streets so still that traffic lights were unnecessary, though they blinked on and off just the same. The city held its breath as its people slept, restored, and prepared for the coming day. A few windows were bright in the inky landscape, startling in their luminance, sharp-edged against the night. I took a deep breath and smelled the water, a sign of how close we were to the lake. This part of the city was practically lakefront, but it had yet to see its value realized. One day, the city would hire developers to turn this area into an outside entertainment strip like Baltimore Harbor, and everyone who lived here would have to go somewhere else.

That, however, was not happening now. Now, we headed to a vile, degenerate part of town.

The brick building had five floors, but the last time I'd been here, Pascal was on the fourth. I didn't know if this was his daytime lair or just a building he haunted, but either way, there wasn't another living creature in or near it. Even the rats stayed away.

I parked my minivan at the curb hoping it wouldn't be stripped by the time I came back. That silver Toyota Sienna had proven remarkably resistant to theft, body damage, and breakdown. Steady was my steed, and suburban mom enough to repel vandals and troublemakers. If they wanted it, they'd have to take it as is, with its potato chip crumbs, empty juice boxes, and changes of clothes for every size child. They might be surprised by the batting helmet, Easy Cheese, and multiple shoes, none of which had a mate.

But, the real reason I didn't worry was simple. I had a guard wolf.

Blaze circled the building and gave a quiet hoot to tell me the coast was clear. Shura sniffed at the base of the building, looking for ways in and signs of other beings besides Pascal. I didn't expect a trap on entering because Pascal wanted me here, but leaving carrying Liam, who was most likely injured, would be precarious. I didn't want any surprises.

Shura sneezed as if she'd smelled something unsavory, but her look told me she didn't suspect anyone else was inside, and I let out a relieved breath. I'd been worried about collateral damage, but it seemed it wasn't a problem. I didn't know whether to knock and enter, or try an alternate, stealthy way, but I figured Pascal sensed me by now, so I opened the front door and crossed the threshold. A small overhead lamp struggled to provide illumination, but it was faint and wan, the light losing ground to the encroaching darkness. This was Pascal's version of a welcome mat.

"Honey, I'm home!"

There was a whisper of movement, like a snake's belly over leaves. "Pascal? It's me. I've come to trade the ball for Liam. Don't make we wait in the entrance like I need a hall pass to continue."

"Do you have the ball?" Pascal's voice came from everywhere.

"Yes, it is in my bag. Where's Liam?"

"Up top. He only has a few hours before sunrise."

"So, let's make this quick. The ball for Liam."

A snicker, followed by Pascal's voice, slithered in the murk, "Come find me, then."

"Why the subterfuge? This is a simple exchange."

"Nothing is simple, Jess. You should know that." His voice rasped like sandpaper.

I shook my head. "Forget it. I'm getting Liam. I'll leave the ball on the front stoop once he's safe. I'm not playing games, Pascal. I don't have time or the energy for that."

"I'm not playing games either." His voice grew faint.

Shura stayed at the entrance to guard our escape route, and I followed Pascal's voice and headed up the stairs. Every step I took led me into deeper and deeper blackness. It was if all the light had folded up on itself and slipped away, not able to bear the weight of the evil in its presence. I remembered my training session with Ovid and, once again, thanked his precognition.

I closed my eyes to help me concentrate on my hearing and took a final step up the first flight of stairs. The stairs from ground floor to first floor were concrete, but as I felt for the next step, I realized it was wood.

My hand held the banister, and I placed my foot on the step, pressing on my foot with even force, avoiding a creak. I did the same with the next step.

And, the next. And the next.

I stopped at the top of the second set of stairs, cocked my head to the right, and listened. It was an eerie quiet without the usual background noise caused by mice, electricity, and people. No birds nested inside. Not even a cockroach touched my feet. This was no-man's land.

I took in a sharp breath and drew icy air into my lungs; even the warmth of the evening was forbidden in this place. The hair on my arms stood on end, and if I could have, I would have run. This was no place for mortals.

I had no choice, however, as Liam's life depended on me overcoming my fear. I squared my shoulders and listened harder, bringing all my attention to what my ears could tell me.

There. Not the third floor, but the fourth, where he was last time. Keeping my eyes shut, I took the third flight on swift feet, barely touching each step. I sniffed and smelled burning candles, the old kind with yellow beeswax. I inhaled again and caught another smell, dry and fetid, coming from behind me. I whirled with 'hawk, swiping in a long arc, but met nothing but air. Pascal emitted a sound that wasn't quite a laugh and wasn't quite a wheeze, more of a phlegmy rattle, and the oddness of it jangled my nerves. I realized that he was clacking his teeth together like a dangling skeleton in biology class. Metal hit metal, and my head rang with the sound, leaving me with a buzzing noise that blocked out any other sound.

I shook my head to clear my ears, which was a futile and stupid thing to do because it meant I stood in place instead of moving. Pascal hit me hard in my chest and swept his leg so I lost my footing. I doubled over and smashed my forehead on the steps, my feet flipping out from under me, and slid on my stomach to the last step. Something in my knee popped. The pain came a moment later, and I sucked in a breath as it lanced though my calf and the arch of my foot.

My ears rang, my right leg was almost useless, and it was so dark that I couldn't see an inch in front of my face. I threw myself against the wall and removed my shoes, putting most of my weight on my left foot. I sheathed my tomahawk and lowered to all fours, saving my own life when Pascal whipped something heavy and metal in a horizontal sweep that crashed into the wall.

I felt the vibrations in the wooden floor and knew he was coming at me again.

I scuttled back to the top step of the second set of stairs and placed my hands on the landing. He was on the fifth step.

The fourth.

The third.

His wet, stinking breath grew closer.

The second step.

I crouched low, leaning on my left leg, and kept my fingertips light on the wood, concentrating on the vibrations, waiting until…

…he hit the landing.

My arms shot out, and I grabbed both of his calves just at the knee, shoving up and over, and threw the bastard down the second set of stairs, where my bare feet told me he landed heavy and hard.

I bit my lip as pain shot through my injured leg but forced myself to scramble on all fours up the next flight of stairs. I could feel Pascal drawing to his feet and knew I had to get to Liam now or we'd both be dead. Out of breath and out of time, I forced myself to climb the last flight of stairs. My chest was tight, banded close by a corset of fear, and my mind shorted out, static replacing thought.

A light broke through the ceiling, and in the opening, Blaze stomped with his giant-ass, crazy Tweety-bird feet until he had created a sizeable hole. I lifted my arms, and the damn bird reached down and grasped me in his beak by the back of my shirt, pulling at me as I hoisted my body up and through the hole.

I almost made it, but Pascal caught up and pulled on my bad leg. I fell back to the floor.

"Is Liam up there, Blaze? Get him to safety!" I yelled this as I pulled out my grill lighter and flicked it on, shoving it into Pascal's face. We froze, his face only a few inches from mine.

His chest wound was oozing a thin, bloody mucous, and his face still looked like Dali's melting clocks. One eye was glued shut, and the other blinked in a continuous quick rhythm, like it was trying to clear a persistent eyelash.

He hissed at me. "I know you don't have the ball. I heard about the fire."

"You're wrong." My voice was strangled as I battled fatigue, pain, and stress. He pinned me down on my bad leg, and every tiny movement of his body caused a fresh wave of agony. I panted so hard that I was afraid I'd pass out.

"Get up," I said. "I do have it."

"Liar!"

"There's only one way to know," I choked out. I could feel the tears flowing down my face onto the floor. I wouldn't stay conscious much longer.

Curiosity won out, and Pascal lifted his weight from me. I gasped at the lack of pressure, and though my leg hurt, I could think again. I inched backward until my back was close to the wall, removed my string bag, which had remarkably stayed on during my tumble down the stairs, and pulled out a six-inch square of Styrofoam. I twisted the top section off, revealing the outer curve of a small crystal ball.

"I thought it would be bigger," Pascal said, crouching to take it from me.

"I'm sure you've heard that a lot, Pascal, but this isn't about you."

"Give it to me."

"Blaze, is Liam safe?" I shouted this to the sky, through the hole in the ceiling.

*Yes.*

Relieved, I heaved myself to my feet and gingerly backed out the door using one hand to hold the ball, still nestled in its protective foam bed, out in front of me. "Stay at the top of the stairs, Pascal. I'll drop it if you don't."

He stayed, and I backed up to the last flight of stairs, where I placed the ball on the landing. As I did so, I used my other hand to gently shake my bag, letting the rest of the contents fall to the floor with little clinks. I talked to cover the sound.

"Why do you want this ball so much, Pascal? What is it you're trying to see?"

"None of your business, little girl." His chest wound made a sucking sound.

"All these years. All this experience. All the power, and here you are, your face a watercolor in the rain, your chest a cratered moon rock, and you're following a human down the steps panting at the bit to get to this tiny crystal ball. How sad. How pathetic."

It was dark as we descended, having left the light of the fifth floor behind, so I couldn't see what his face looked like, but I could hear him growling.

I kept up the prattle, covering the tinkle as the vials of Manischevitz hit the floor, little land-wines covering the first set of stairs and the entranceway, where they cracked open and leaked their contents on the ground.

I hobbled out the door, and Shura met me, supporting my right side. I hopped out the door to the minivan. Liam lay in the back, beaten, cut and bruised. I flung my body into the car, threw my injured right leg over the passenger seat, and started the car with my left, just in time to see Pascal at the front door, holding a useless snow globe, his shoes and pants legs wet, his feet and legs glowing like hot coals beneath them.

I hit the gas and tore through the streets, knocking over a few overflowing garbage cans as I went. I caught a face at a window, but it quickly withdrew. Liam was silent in the back, which scared me more than anything. I was reminded of a pediatric emergency room doctor who once told me it wasn't the crying children who scared him, it was the silent ones. It's true. I'd rather he was screaming and cursing, but no, he stayed mute. I wasn't even sure if he was awake.

## CHAPTER THIRTEEN

We rushed Liam to his apartment, grateful that his key was still in his pocket, even after what he'd been through. His wounds were hideous, big bruises that would turn all sorts of colors, dried rivulets of blood caused by something sharp, and a bite mark at his neck where Pascal had drained him. He seemed in a twilight, not awake but not fully unconscious.

I gathered all the blood Liam had in his fridge and fed him one-by-one. He sucked them down by instinct, now aware of his surroundings, but the speed with which he consumed the blood convinced me we didn't have enough. I grabbed my phone and punched in some numbers.

"Father Paul?"

"Jess?"

"Liam needs more blood than we have in his apartment. We need an immediate delivery. Can you help?" My voice was strained and unusually high-pitched.

"What happened to him?"

"Pascal."

"Pascal attacked him again?"

"No. Pascal kidnapped Liam to get me to do something for him. I don't have any more time to explain this, Father. Please come over with more blood."

I hung up, done with that conversation. He'd either show or he wouldn't, but I believed he would.

We had two more pints of blood left, and I considered what I could do after they ran out. Donating my blood would be fine, but we didn't have any way to get it except Liam's teeth, and with the way he was, that wasn't a good option. He might not let go.

I wondered if I could bleed into a cup so Liam could sip it and was ready to give it a go when the doorbell rang.

"Jess. It's me, Father Paul."

Blaze flicked a wing and unlocked the door, then glamoured himself so he blended in with the heavy drapes. If he didn't move, you couldn't see him. Interesting.

Father Paul entered, stooped, dragging a blue and white picnic cooler behind him. He opened the latch, pulled out a pint, and slapped it in my waiting palm so I could shove it at Liam.

"What happened, Jess?" Father Paul wasn't wearing priestly garb and looked like your everyday grandpa in jeans and a Cleveland Indians t-shirt. His voice was low and modulated, but I braced myself anyway, guessing what was coming.

"Pascal kidnapped him."

"And…?"

"He used him to blackmail me into finding an object he wanted."

"Which was…?"

I didn't look at him. "A crystal ball. It was hidden in a shopping mall."

"The Beachwood fire?"

I pointed to my nose and then to him.

"What did he want that ball for? What made it so important that he threatened your friend's life to get it?"

I shrugged and stuffed another blood bag from the cooler in Liam's hand. "It gives glimpses of the future, or futures, possible scenarios, so Rabbi Stein says."

Father Paul paced a few steps to the right, almost walking into Blaze, but he turned in time and re-tracked to his left, continuing to wear a spot in the carpet as he considered the situation. Meanwhile, I fed Liam. He depleted more than a dozen bags of blood, but, thankfully, he was slowing down.

Father Paul spoke. "He's trying to see the future, maybe get ahead of us and the Church."

"Possibly, Father, but I get the sense this is personal. I'm not sure that

Pascal gives the new Knights Templar any thought, other than his singular focus on me."

Father Paul stared at me, then looked at his shoes, seeming to make up his mind about something. "You know he had a, ahem, what's the word I'm looking for? A relationship of a kind with your mother."

I whirled on him, suddenly reminded that he was one of the people keeping important information from me. "Yes, I do know that, not because you or anyone else in the Church saw fit to enlighten me!" My anger, pushed aside by recent events, returned in full force. I'd already had it out with my dad, and Ovid, but I'd forgotten about Father Paul's role until he reminded me of it.

Father Paul held his hands together in supplication. "Jess, your father didn't want you involved in monster hunting. We promised we'd keep you out of it."

"Fat lot of good that did, and yet, still no one told me, even when Pascal attacked Liam." I gripped the bag of blood in my hand so hard it almost burst. I handed it to Liam and put my hands behind my back to keep from socking the priest in the mouth. That wouldn't be good karma under any belief system.

Liam lay on the couch, eyes open, staring at nothing, but he didn't drink anymore. I didn't know if this was good, bad, or indifferent, and I took my frustration out on Father Paul.

"Anything else you are keeping from me, Father? Any other information slipped your mind that you might need to impart? Does *Father* really know best? Do you know who killed my mother?"

My knee took that moment to collapse out from under me, and I hit the ground with a moan. Father Paul approached me with caution, not sure how I would react to him touching me, but I let him examine my knee. Silently, he pulled out a small first-aid kit from a backpack I hadn't noticed he'd been wearing and handed me four ibuprofens. I popped them dry. He wrapped my knee and gave me an ice pack.

He left without looking at me, worry in the creases of his face. I didn't have the energy to care.

Liam blinked, and I breathed a sigh of relief, until he focused on my face and leapt from the couch, screaming, "Get out! Get out! It's not safe here!"

I hopped up on my good leg, reaching out to touch him, but he jerked back. "Liam, you're back in your apartment. We got you away from Pascal, and you're safe now."

Liam's eyes glittered diamond black as he held onto the back of an armchair, his fingers pressing into the fabric, his knuckles white. He was holding on by a thread.

"By all that is holy, Jess, get out! It's not me I'm worried about. It's you. It's not safe here." He gasped, a sudden intake of breath, and his whole body twitched. He managed to choke out, "Run!" before his fangs dropped.

Blaze, Shura, and I moved, me and the wolf to my minivan and Blaze to the sky. I was as weirded out as I wanted to be that night, and my knee pulsed in pain. I had no idea what had happened to my friend, but that was going to have to be a worry for tomorrow. We went home, and I was beyond thankful to see Nathaniel's car in the driveway. He greeted me at the door with arms open wide. I hugged him for dear life, crying tears of pain, anger, sadness, and frustration.

Nathaniel stroked my hair. "I'm sorry I left so abruptly," he whispered into my ear. "But, I'm scared, honey. The universe sent us a guard wolf, a guard *wolf*. What does that mean?"

"It means we are being taken care of," I replied, but I screwed up my face to mirror his, both of us concerned about our children. I told him what happened to Liam. Without a word, early in the morning, Nathaniel, my rock, my calm in the storm, turned, walked into the kitchen, and pulled a bottle of vodka out of the freezer. I didn't even know we had it. I didn't keep alcohol in the house. Recovery is always, and I never wanted to make it more difficult on him.

Nathaniel held it, staring at the cold, clear liquid while I waited with bated breath. I hadn't seen this side of him since we'd been married, and I held my hand out, grasping his arm, clinging to him, begging him with my eyes to come back to me.

He did. Nathaniel shook his head and returned the bottle without taking a sip. I gripped his hand and led him to a chair, turning back to make him a cup of tea.

He jumped up. "You're hurt!"

"My knee is messed up."

"Who wrapped it?"

"Father Paul, but he's on my doody list right now, so don't talk to me about him. He mentioned that my mother had a 'relationship' with Pascal, and I lost it."

"You mean, he knew, too, and didn't tell you either?"

"Just so."

"Bastard."

"Easy there, big guy. He's a man of the cloth."

"Who kept information from you that you needed. I don't think that gives him a pass; in fact, it makes it worse, in my book." He guided me by the arms to the couch so I could sit and turn long ways to prop up my knee. "*I'll* make *you* tea."

He busied himself with the kettle. Our kitchen and family room were all one large space, so we could still talk to one another.

"Let me tell you about Pascal, Nathaniel. It may give you more peace. He's badly hurt, and it's going to take time for him to be at full strength. We've got time to plan."

"You know, he's a mathematician by training, a follower of logic. It feels weird that he wants a crystal ball."

"A lot of time has passed since the 1600s. Who knows what he believes now? He's still crafty and intelligent, and he obviously knows magic is real."

Nathaniel gestured toward our overflowing bookshelves. "I read about him recently. He had some kind of mystical, religious experience on November 23-24, 1654. Do you think that's when he was turned? He continued to work but disappeared from society after that."

"Possible, but I'm not sure where that leaves us."

"Just data. I'll keep digging into his past."

"Mommy! You're home!" Devi ran in and jumped up on the couch to snuggle beside me. I couldn't help the smile on my face. We were together again, and together, we could face anything.

Normal mayhem took control, much to my relief.

"Dad, can I have eggs for breakfast?"

"Okay, David, what kind of eggs?"

"Scrambled, please!"

Daniel tugged at my shirt and pointed at his mouth.

"You want eggs, too, Daniel?"

"Yeggs!" I started to correct him but realized that "yeggs" was a brilliant combination of "yes," and "eggs."

Devi decided on cereal but wasn't happy with the options. Nathaniel began the negotiation while I limped into the kitchen and slipped some raspberries and juice in front of her to get her to eating before she had a total meltdown. David brought a toy car to the table and raced it across the butcher block to his sister, veering close to knocking over her glass. Devi batted it out of the way, and it flew to the floor where

Daniel picked it up and placed it in his mouth. David yelled at his brother.

Ah. Home.

The day went on, and I pushed my worry about Liam to the back of my mind, hoping that a day's rest plus the blood would return him to normal, or as close to normal as a trauma victim could be. I knew it was going to take time for him to heal mentally.

I was in the middle of washing dishes, enjoy the satisfaction of a mundane job well done, when Nathaniel hurried into the kitchen, holding the Buddha, who was now full-sized and whistling like a train. I barely had a second to register this warning when someone screamed my name. I dropped the sponge and detergent and dashed to the front door, which was almost buckling from the pounding it was taking.

"What? Who is it?" I yelled, as I unlocked the door.

"Jess, it is me, Judy. Joseph is missing!"

I finally got the locks undone and opened the door to find a red-faced, crying Judy in front of me. She was wringing her hands and speaking so fast I had trouble understanding.

"Jess, we need your rescue pony! Please! Joseph is missing. I can't find him anywhere!"

I grasped her hand. "When did you last see him?"

"Last night. I tucked him in, and he rolled over onto his right side, as he always does, and I closed the door, since he likes it dark in his room. But he didn't come down this morning for breakfast. I thought he must be tired and sleeping late, so I didn't go up for a while."

"How long until you looked for him?"

"Maybe an hour? I got worried, thinking maybe he was sick, so I knocked on his door, to no answer. I peeked in, and he was gone. The window was open, but no Joseph. I can't find him anywhere!"

"Can you bring me his pillow, please? I'd like to have something with his scent."

Judy wiped snot from her face with the back of her hand and nodded, turning to run to her house to do as I asked. Blaze and Shura crept out of their sleeping places and stood with me on the front lawn, one disguised as a pony, the other not bothering to disguise herself at all. I threw her "Dog at Work" vest on her and figured that would have to be enough.

"Nathaniel, can you please bring me Buddha?"

Nathaniel appeared, mouth tight, and held out the jade statue. I took it and held it in my hands.

"I'm assuming by this warning that the kidnapping is real and not by a human entity?"

The Buddha warmed slightly, but there was no reply.

"I was kinda hoping for a little more notice."

The Buddha closed its jade eyes, and that's when I realized I'd gotten all the information I was going to get. I went back in the house and slipped on a knee brace, took two Tylenols, and went back outside, motioning to Blaze to follow. At least I knew it was something unnatural. That eliminated the need to call the police.

I turned as two wailing police cars hurtled down the street and stopped in front of Judy's house. Officer Bob and Captain Morgan exited their vehicles and gave me sharp nods as I approached. Captain Morgan started right off.

"Mrs. Friedman, tell me the truth, is this a human problem or your kind of problem?"

My mouth was dry. "It's my kind of problem."

Captain Morgan replied, "Well, then. You take point. I want this child found, and I want him found fast. Tell us what you need." Officer Bob already had a pencil.

I walked around the house to the back where Joseph's window remained open. I searched around the area with my eyes, noticing that there were no ladder marks or footsteps on the ground. The grass, which had not been mowed in a while, was untouched. I called out to Blaze and asked him to come with Shura and give a look.

"I could use a ladder, a baggie, and a knife. I don't see any signs of feet, hooves, or paws. It makes me think whatever it was can fly, and that narrows things down a bit."

Officer Bob didn't even ask me why I needed those things. He just hurried down to his car and got on the radio.

"Captain Morgan, do you agree with my assessment?"

He nodded. "I do, and if it was human, there would be ladder impressions. When you get up there, you can double-check to see if there are any signs of a ladder being leaned on the sill, but no, there really isn't anything here to indicate how the person, thing, whatever, got up there."

Blaze flew in, and Shura loped up the driveway to the back. Captain Morgan jumped back in shock, his eyes wide, with a hand on his gun. "What the hell bird is that?"

"Stand down, Captain! These are my colleagues."

Captain Morgan had proven himself resilient before, and I was hoping he would be again. I was surprised that he could see Blaze through the pony glamour.

"Blaze is a phoenix, Captain," I said, in hushed tones. "You are seeing him in his true form, but everyone else sees a rescue pony."

"Who's ever heard of a rescue pony in Northeast Ohio?" he asked.

"No one, ever, but that's the story, and we're sticking to it."

"Is that the wolf from the zoo? I didn't get a good look in the mall, but I knew there was no way that animal was a dog." Captain Morgan turned to me, an accusing look on his face.

"Yes." I held up my hands to stop his next comment. "I did not steal her. She came here on her own to protect my pack—my family. She sensed danger to us."

"So, the phoenix is a rescue pony, and the wolf is a scent dog?"

I patted him on the back. "Now you get the picture."

Officer Bob hurried with the things I needed and also handed me a windbreaker that said "Consultant" on it. "Wear it," he said. "We'll figure out how to rationalize this later." He quickly turned and left, a dedicated man doing his job.

A fire truck roared down the street and stopped in front of the house. By this time, families had gathered on the sidewalk. Officer Bob and another cop were keeping the neighbors busy by interviewing each of them, one-by-one. I watched as David slipped by all of them, in a sneaky way that made me proud. I bent to hug him.

"David, I will get your friend back."

His little face was pinched and worried, and it just about killed me. "I know, Mom. I've told everyone that you will find him and that it will all be okay."

My heart broke a little.

He held out his new pocketknife. "The police officer said you needed a knife. Here's mine. If it can help you find Joseph, I'd like you to use it."

I took the knife with both of my hands and looked my son in the eye. "Thank you, Daniel. This is just what I needed." I gave him a kiss on his forehead and whispered, "I love you. Go be with Daddy so I can find Joseph, okay?"

He nodded, his face a little less stressed now that he'd done something to help.

The firefighters humped up the driveway with a ladder.

"Captain, where do you need this?" asked the hunk of a fireman who led the way. I forced myself not to stare, but those green eyes were just too much.

I smacked my head.

Green eyes. Dammit. I thought of who it might be. I hated those things. I made a "hold on" motion with my finger and sprinted, or, more accurately, hobbled in a speedy manner, to my house to get an ultraviolet light I kept in my supplies.

Hunky fireman held the ladder while I climbed up. We'd had a brief exchange where he wanted to be the one to ascend the ladder, but Captain Morgan pointed at my windbreaker and explained that I had a particular expertise.

The fireman shrugged, which was okay with me because it emphasized his pecs. "Okay, Captain. I believe you seeing as she's got a search dog and a rescue pony. Never heard of a rescue horse outside of Colorado, but it's a good idea with all the nature trails we have here. Have to think about that more. Any way to train the mounted police?"

Captain Morgan made a noncommittal sound, and I turned my back and climbed the ladder. The top seemed untouched except for one thing. It was cold. The window sill itself was cold to the touch, despite the heat of the sun. The damn thing had been touched by Darkness. Biting my lip and hoping against hope, I held the UV light out to the sill.

Pointy fingerprints popped into view, almost as if the fingers were triangles at the tip, rather than ovals, which would be accurate because the thing that had taken Joseph had just that type of hand shape. I used the knife to scrape a few slivers of the windowsill wood into the baggie.

Blaze hung around the bottom of the ladder. *What is it?*

"Black elf."

*Nasty buggers. Handle with care. Shadow Court.*

"You're familiar with them?"

*Unfortunately. This one flew to get the child.*

"Right. Meaning it's female."

*The females are larger.*

I sighed. "I know."

*And they spit poison.*

I sighed again, my mouth grim. "I know that too."

*And you must watch for the...*

"...tail. I know."

Shura padded over to us and said something to Blaze.

"What did she ask?"

*If it would succumb to killing teeth.*

"What did you tell her?"

*Yes, but it might not taste good. She said mannequins taste bad too.*

I wiped my hands on my shorts. The only reason a black elf would take this child was to sell him to the fae, or to draw me out. I was betting on the latter, given that the fae usually liked their children younger, and there was a bounty on my head.

Captain Morgan walked over, popping antacids. "So, what did you learn?"

"Good news, I know what it is. Also, good news, it's not after Joseph but me, so it wants me to hunt it."

"What's the bad news?"

"Black elves are vile creatures. This is a female, which means she's about the size of Blaze, can fly, and spits poison. Oh, and her tail is as sharp as any sword."

Morgan didn't seem too fazed by all of that. He must have figured, rightly, that those things were my problem.

"Why didn't it come after you directly?"

"Not their way. A black elf would think this a laugh riot. All the pain, tears, and fear. Like chocolate to them."

"I hate them already," Morgan replied, jabbing another antacid in his mouth. "How do we find it?"

"*We* don't. Blaze, Shura and I will hunt her. She wants to capture me or kill me, so she shouldn't be too hard to find."

"You don't get to lock me out of hunting a child kidnapper."

"If it was a normal piece of human garbage, I'd stand back and let you take the lead, but this isn't the case."

He paced in a circle muttering to himself for about ten seconds. "Why does it want to capture or kill you?"

"She, not it. I was told by an evil clown that there's a bounty on my head, right after I got stung by a chihuahua-sized hornet he'd created out of balloons."

Morgan stared at me. "You mean that literally."

I thought for a moment. "Yeah, I do. Every word."

He blinked a few times but acclimated quickly. "What do you need from me?"

"Get everyone out of here. Take them all to the police station or something. Gather them at a neighbor's house and keep them inside. Whatever.

I'm going to start the hunt now, in daytime. At night, she'll be a shadow and able to hide anywhere."

Captain Morgan gave me a little salute, pivoted on his heel, and headed down the driveway to do cop things and make it sound like everything was in hand.

## CHAPTER FOURTEEN

I gave Shura the windowsill shards to smell, and the second she did so, she sneezed violently, followed by a serious shake of her head.
*She says that stinks of evil.*
"She's right on that score. I need one more thing from the house and then I'm ready."
*Where do we start?*
"There's only one place a dark elf would hide during the day —the woods."
Blaze gazed in the direction of the walking park where lovely, kind people walked their lovely, friendly dogs and enjoyed tai chi, roller blading, and biking. *Oh, dear.*
"Yup."
On the way to my house, I asked Captain Morgan if he could get the Beachwood police to evacuate the walking park and immediate area. The captain gritted his teeth but said he'd try. "I'm a little out of my jurisdiction, you know, but I heard the call and recognized the neighborhood as yours, so Bob and I drove to the scene. Shaker police are caught up in a fire and were grateful for the help. I'll see what Beachwood says. Gary's a good guy. He'll assist, but he'll want in."
"I'm sure you'll think of something."
I gave all the kids quick hugs and smiles, promising them everything would be okay. Nathaniel handed me the Buddha, who'd shrunk again. I

placed him in an old fanny pack from the 1980s, grabbed two bottles from the laundry room, tucked them into the fanny pack belt, and headed out. The only other thing I had was David's knife. I hopped back to Joseph's house, jerked my head at Blaze and Shura, and hoofed it to the park. I looked like some crazed weird western character with spray bottles instead of guns.

Captain Gary and his men were there when we arrived.

"Ma'am, Captain Morgan told me you have special skills and that's why you're taking point on this. It is against every tenet of police procedure, but I trust Morgan."

"Thanks, Captain, I appreciate…"

He held up a hand. "But, you will be accompanied by two of my officers and our bloodhound." He gestured toward two officers who came forward, pulling along a bloodhound with the longest ears I'd ever seen. I bent to pet the dog, who gave me a sniff. I opened the bag for him to get the scent.

The dog fainted.

Ever see a bloodhound faint? Me neither, but it wasn't the sight of the dog fainting that did me in. It was the sound. The poor thing hit the ground with a thwack. I mean, bloodhounds are big, and gravity isn't kind.

Shura came forward as the officer, K9 Officer Alison MacKenzie, knelt in panic to help the dog, whose name was Loki.

"I think I'll use my dog," I said, as Captain Gary and Officer MacKenzie gave Loki some water. The dog opened his eyes, took one look at Shura, and closed them again. The Captain and Officer MacKenzie looked lost.

We left them where they were and Shura, Blaze, and I headed off. We walked the paved path of the near side, once around, and got nothing. We crossed Richmond to the far side and followed the loop. Blaze took to the air, becoming a blur, and Shura and I moved on. We didn't hide; it made no sense to, but we were silent as we kept our eyes and ears sharp.

We were at the farthest end of the park, near the overpass, when we heard it. A sibilant, liquid vibration, like a snake through a mossy bank.

"Youssss found me."

"Give it up with the Sméagol imitation and give me the child. He's nothing to you. You want my head."

"I could have both," came the whisper. The sound came from the center section, which was wooded, and seemed to be moving, the trees shifting as we walked. I signaled Shura to enter, while Blaze circled with me. Shura lowered her head and padded in on soft paws, eyes fierce, claws ready, a mother searching for a pup.

"I've enjoyed this game, Monster Hunter. The parents' panic wassss…delicioussss."

"You are contemptible."

A wheezy laugh wafted by.

"I am Black to White. I am Darknesssss to Light. You can no more do without me than you can do without Goodness. My despicable existence is the only thing that keepsss people like you alive. That'ssss the sssecret no one tellsss you in monster training ssschool, you miserable, pathetic, feeble disgraccce for a Hunter."

Blaze snapped at the air next to him, and I rotated in time to see a faint gray wisp of smoke breeze by, but this was like no smoke I'd ever seen. It left a gash in Blaze's bronze armor that sizzled like oil on a hotplate.

The smoke appeared again, this time whistling by me. I was ready for such an attack and grabbed one of the spray bottles I'd latched to my fanny pack, twisting the top to open and spraying the air.

I was too slow, and the droplets fell harmlessly to the ground.

"The child is ssssleeping. Your wolf has found him, but she can't wake him up. I'm the only one that can."

I doubted that. Blaze could do amazing things, and I held onto that hope. Raising my spray bottles in the air, I said, "How do you want to handle this?"

"Come into the woodsss, into the shadow of the trees. Once I have you, I'll wake the child."

I pretended to consider this. "First of all, no. Second of all, no. You think I'm stupid enough to give myself to you before the child is safe? By the way, how much is that bounty?"

"Two million, three hundred thousand, forty-two dollarssss and seventy-six cccents."

"Wait a minute." I moved my spray bottles to my hips, like six-shooters in a duel. "What? That's an odd number. Although it's more than I thought. I'm flattered."

Without an ounce of snark, the voice said, "You sssshould be. It'sss the highest bounty in a while."

"But why the bizarre number?"

"It'ssss not in casssh. It'sss the estimated worth of a ruby."

"A ruby."

Blaze circled his wing in a way that indicated that I should keep the elf talking. He looped around to the back.

"Yessss…a ruby that used to be in the crown of the King of Franccce, Louissss fourteen."

"It's pronounced Louie; the 's' is silent. Didn't you learn anything in history class?"

My attempt at a distracting monologue was a failure. The asshole Shadow Court fae didn't respond to my remark, and the air grew tight around me.

Clouds drifted in, shadowing the blue sky and the ground. I huffed as the oxygen grew faint, as if I was climbing a mountain, and I grew dizzy, gasping for air.

A creature leapt out of the trees, more solid than the wisp version from earlier. This elf was taller and skinnier than some I'd seen, with midnight black skin, green eyes, and a tail as long and lethal as a whip. She flicked her tail, and I crouched, duck-walking backward, tossing off the blanket of lethargy and heaving it aside. I sprayed my laundry spot remover with my right hand and a bottle of mold-and-mildew cleanser with my left.

The chemicals, particularly the bleach cleanser, crackled as they hit the elf's skin, leaving tiny dots of white on the elf's torso. This elf's ponderous breasts got the bulk of it, and she screamed at me, opening her jaws and spitting venom while her long dark hair levitated, creating a creepy, static shock halo around her.

I backed up, step-by-step, aiming for her eyes, but losing ground because her venom strikes were scary as hell, and she spit with pinpoint accuracy, so my back-peddling was pulling me farther away and my aim was off.

Blaze spoke in my head. *We have the child.*

"Can you wake him?"

"I can, but I won't until I have you tied up safe and sound," said the elf, tail whipping over her head, claws out.

"Not you, moron."

*I think so.*

"Great. Get him out of here and let me take care of this speck, this blemish, this blotch on the paranormal community." I was taunting the elf to keep her focus on me so Shura and Blaze could rescue Joseph. My words must have hit a nerve because the elf's eyes opened wide with anger. She rolled her neck and raised her wings in a good imitation of a pissed off dragon.

Blaze had a question. *Is that why you're using laundry stain remover?*

"You have to believe."

*I don't understand how magic works.*

"Which is weird because you are magic. Now, scat."

*Scatting.*

Blaze had Joseph draped over his back and ran as fast as the wind. As he skedaddled, I threw my fist in the air and let out a loud, "Meep, meep!"

It was a moment of triumph and levity, but that was all it was—a moment. It was past noon, and with each passing minute, the elf would get stronger and I more tired. Now that Joseph was safe, I had to act fast.

I turned tail and fled. No shame in running., or given my knee, doing a speedy, step, hop, skip, wince pattern that still got me out of there as fast as I could.

The elf pursued, taking to the air. She dove in a spiral and got me with one clawed hand, lashing my back, causing ripples of agony to flow through my body. I zig-zagged along the path, aiming in the direction of the police, hoping they were still there and someone had a rifle. And handguns. Maybe a grenade or a bazooka. The zig-zagging tweaked my injured knee, and my leg collapsed out from under me. I crawled into the woods, just missing what would have been a killing blow from her tail.

The woods were as dark as night because of the elf's presence. She was Darkness, darkness at its most evil and cold, and I had walked into her territory with two almost empty spray bottles and a pocketknife.

Was I stupid or what?

I belly-slid my way into the shadows, hearing her cackle behind me as her victory drew near. She could taste it. I was hers, and she knew it. Fate was with her on this day.

Until it wasn't.

A huge gray wolf jumped on the elf's back, grasping the elf's neck between her jaws, bringing the ferocious beast down. Shura continued to shake the elf by its nape, handling her like an unruly kitten. I scrambled to my feet with a gargled cheer, which was all I could manage as pain coursed through my body from my injuries.

Just as suddenly, my delight stopped short, and I gasped in horror as the elf's tail arched and plummeted for Shura's body.

"Shura! The tail!"

I twisted off both bottles' tops and dodged in, making it in the nick of time as Shura was forced to let go and the tail slammed into the earth where her midsection had been. I poured the rest of the bottles' contents on the elf's head, and her skull fizzed and sputtered, emitting a musty barbeque odor.

The elf tried to scream, but her face was in the dirt, and all we got was a muffled snort that sounded as if she was asking us to stop, but Shura gave no quarter. The wolf had taken the initiative and snapped her teeth on the elf's tail just below the point, grinding the appendage into tiny bits and pieces while I watched it separate. The tip fell to the earth, and deep green blood gushed out. Shura shuddered and staggered toward the path, coughing and spitting as she rid herself of the elf's gore.

The elf turned its eyes toward me, beaten and dying. "Let me go," she said, her voice quavering.

Maybe if she got home in time, she could be saved, and the thought almost stayed my hand, but then I remembered she *stole a child out of his bed*, and I dithered no longer. I extracted David's knife and plunged it into the back of her neck, at the spine, twisting it until she no longer moved. Her body collapsed like a balloon, and as I stumbled back, it turned into an oily black slick that oozed into the ground. The grass died wherever the oil touched. I studied the widening grease stain and looked at the small knife in my hand. It shouldn't have been able to do that much damage.

Yet…a child's weapon to find a child. An innocent's gift to find an innocent stolen. Magic comes in many forms.

## CHAPTER FIFTEEN

Shura and I meandered through the park toward home. I couldn't move fast, given the pain in my knee and the burning claw marks on my back, and I needed some quiet time to soak in the last few hours' events.

Someone was offering an enormous ruby from a French king's crown as a bounty for my head, or body I suppose, as long as the head wasn't with it. The ultimate goal was my death. I couldn't imagine who I'd killed that would inspire such retribution, and I had no idea who would have access to such a prize.

*There's a wheel that lasts generations, longer than your life span. What goes around, comes around.*

"What?" I looked around for Blaze and realized he wasn't anywhere nearby. I slipped the tiny Buddha out of my fanny pack.

"Are you talking to me?"

Shura's eyebrows rose to her ears.

The Buddha's jade tummy expanded as he took a long inhale and then let it out. *Meditate on this. What if it wasn't you who did anything? What if this is karma circling around after a long, slow stroll through time. Karma doesn't measure time like you do.*

"I'm paying for someone else's crime? Why?"

Buddha's eyes were closed, and he was silent.

"Oh, no, you don't! You have to give me more than that."

*You may pay for a crime you didn't commit, if you benefited from it.*

Buddha fell silent, and I knew that was all I was going to get. I told Shura what he'd said, and she huffed in disgust. She didn't understand either.

Confused, hurt, and thoroughly pissed off, I limped the rest of the way home, Shura patient by my side. Despite my foul mood, I smiled when David ran toward me, arms out for a hug.

"I knew you'd do it! I told everyone that my mom always kills the monsters!" He wrapped his arms around my thighs, and I bent to kiss his head. I held myself still for a moment, enjoying his scent, that special scent that was only his, and I prayed that nothing I ever did would circle back to him.

Which gave me a thought, a thought so heavy that when it crashed down on my shoulders, I staggered from the sheer weight. I didn't have time to examine it, so, with an effort of will, I pushed it aside, gathered it in a ball, and stuffed it into my hindbrain to examine later.

Nathaniel ran to greet me, Devi and Daniel at his heels. He scooped me up like a baby and carried me the rest of the way to Judy and Joseph's house, where he placed me on the lawn.

"That was very Richard Gere of you."

The corner of his eye twitched. "You weigh more than Debra Winger."

"How do you know? When was the last time you carried Debra Winger?" I punched him on the shoulder. "I'm a Monster Hunter. I have muscles. They weigh more."

"You keep telling yourself that," Nathaniel responded with a wink. An ambulance medic arrived holding a much-needed ice pack and moved everyone except Nathaniel aside so she could look at my back. Her name tag said Amy Beth Walker Nolan.

"These are claw marks!" Amy Beth said, staring into my eyes. "Now, don't lie. I can't treat you if you don't tell me what this is."

I sighed and went for broke. "A black elf." I waited for the obvious reaction, but I didn't get it. Instead, she nodded. "Haven't seen one of them since Afghanistan. You need an antibiotic and a tetanus shot."

She spoke in a quiet voice that only I could hear. "I'm authorized by DEMON to give you both. If you see the edges getting black, call me immediately. Here's my card. You understand?"

I startled. "DEMON? I've heard of them but have stayed out of their sights. I don't need the bureaucracy. You work for them?"

"You got it. The Department of ExtraDimensional, Mystical, and Occult Nuisances."

"Sounds like someone really wanted the acronym to spell DEMON."

She laughed. "It does, doesn't it? I worked with Agent Amy Hall. Do you know her?"

"I don't know her personally but heard a little bit. A real spitfire, right? Sorta Bubba's girlfriend?"

"More than sorta."

"There's something I can't quite picture about that..." I scratched my head and gave her a sideways glance. I leaned in close and looked both ways to make sure no one was listening. "I mean, how can that *work*...he's so big and she's so..."

"Normal sized? Slim? Yes, true, but so is anyone compared to Bubba."

"Yeah, but..." I cocked my head. "You think she's always on top?"

Medic Amy Beth Walker Nolan held out both hands. "Oh, no! I'm not going there. You can't make me." She wrinkled her nose. "Crap. Now, I'm going to be thinking about that. Gross. Just for that, I'm going to make your tetanus shot hurt."

"They hurt anyway."

"True 'nuff. Wait here."

## CHAPTER SIXTEEN

Three shots later, my family lay around the front yard on lounge chairs watching bonfire sparks fly into the inky night sky. Devi was on her fifth roasted marshmallow and David his seventh s'more. Daniel was still working on his first, but that was because most of the marshmallow was stuck to his cheeks, lips, and nose. He'd resorted to eating the chocolate and graham crackers straight.

The entire community was out, mingling, hugging, and comforting one another, relieved they survived the unthinkable. Every parent stayed close to their kids, grateful that it wasn't their kid gone missing. I could guarantee that windows were locked that night.

Judy approached me, hands clenched, thumbs rubbing over one another in an endless loop. "Jess, thank you for saving Joseph." She gestured to her husband who was clutching a beer and watching his son's every move. "We owe you a debt we can never repay."

I held up a hand. "Stop saying that. You don't owe me anything. This is my job, remember? That's why I have Blaze and Shura to help me." I placed a hand on Judy's arm. Her tear-stained face brimmed with a mixture of sorrow, fear, and anger, and she kept rubbing her eyes as if trying to erase the memory of the last several hours from her mind. It wouldn't work, something I could have told her, but imparting that information wouldn't have helped her deal with the trauma of the day. Only talking about it would do that. Talking about it, as many times as needed, made the fear familiar and forced it to recede. You beat fear into submission; you didn't avoid it, or it would gain power, growing larger, darker, and more paralyzing.

"That's something I wanted to discuss with you. I know your job is secret, but the other families deserved to know why you were the one to search for Joseph, and the cops acknowledged you as a consultant, so I figured it was okay. Anyways, I told them that Blaze is a rescue pony and Shura is a search dog, and they were relieved to have someone like you right here in our neighborhood. I mean, look what happened today! We need you here." She drew a breath. "So, we had an emergency huddle a few moments ago, meaning me and the vice-presidents, and we unanimously decided that Blaze is an honorary member of the Neighborhood Association and that he and Shura are elite exceptions to our codicil."

She gripped my shoulders; her whole body was shaking like a tuning fork. "Jess, I have no words for what happened today. It was my worst nightmare come true, but you saved him." She hugged me tight, her body vibrating so hard I thought it would snap. She let the tears go, and I held her as they slid down my back, seeping into my bandages, which stung, but I didn't let go. I cradled her for as long as she needed to be there.

It was the least I could do, given that I burned with shame and hypocrisy. I didn't save Joseph. I got him kidnapped in the first place. I'm the reason he was snatched from his bed at night. Me. No one else. My dangerous life put other people in danger. First Liam, and now an innocent child, and Nathaniel was rightly worried about our own children. I swallowed the self-loathing that came with these thoughts.

I needed to focus. Danger circled ever closer; vultures spiraling in silent concentric circles earthward, pinning me in place like a butterfly to a board. I gave Judy one more embrace and stepped away from the fire and people to be alone with my thoughts.

Buddha, who was back on his shelf, told me that I could pay for someone else's transgression if I had benefitted from it. I assumed that an infraction serious enough to instigate a call for my death would have to be a heinous crime, and there was only one person who could have accomplished this stunning feat in the paranormal community.

I knew her well, and yet, I didn't know her at all.

My mother.

Now, the question was, who did she hurt, and what did she do?

I lived with her and studied her every move for most of my life, but she had secrets, some she shared with my father, but others…I doubted she shared everything. Unearthing the past could be dangerous, leading me to knowledge that I might not like, or that could hurt my dad, but I didn't have any choice.

I did have a choice to be as good a person as I could be, and there was one thing I knew I could do, so I headed inside and opened my laptop. Rabbi Stein's email sat unopened. I clicked on it and read the information. It was late, and I hesitated to call, but then I thought about what I would be doing if Nathaniel was taken from me, and I knew it wouldn't be sleeping.

"Hello?" The woman's voice was quiet, but not sleepy. I was right, she was awake.

"I know it is late to call, but this is Jess Friedman. Rabbi Stein gave me your name and number. He thought you and I might help each other. How have you been?"

That small amount of prodding and I got the whole story. Her husband died in a car accident caused by a combination of lake effect rain and a sharp curve. It wasn't anyone's fault, and there was no one to blame, so she railed against the Almighty. At the same time, she turned to the synagogue and its community for comfort and support. Her emotions were on overload.

I shared a little bit about me, about how my mom had died suddenly in a car accident, too. I only did this to empathize, and I made sure to listen more than talk. We conversed for an hour. I asked if she needed any food, and she gave a weak laugh.

"To be honest," she said, "I'm overloaded with lasagna and brownies."

"Bereavement leads to comfort food. Tell you what, come over for Friday night dinner, and I promise we won't have lasagna and brownies."

"It's a deal."

I thought about her situation the rest of the night, tossing and turning, considering what life would be like for Nathaniel and the kids if I were killed. Perhaps Nathaniel was right and I needed to retire.

I couldn't take myself off the front lines, yet. The bounty was still on my head, and the trouble and danger were there, like it or not. The fight had come home to me, and it was time I went on the offensive. Tomorrow would be a strategy and training day. Plus, I needed to check on Liam. I hoped he was better.

I drifted off…

A voice woke me, adrenaline rushing through my veins at the clanging alarm from my subconscious. Forcing myself to move with care, I huddled next to the bedroom door, grabbing my bat, which I had propped in the corner.

Something. Something on the edge of my hearing, a trace of sound. I closed my eyes and listened harder. It was outside, not in the house, coming from the front. I slipped into the shadows of the hallway and tiptoed to the living room, where my tomahawk practically leaped into my hand. Armed with a bat in my left fist and my 'hawk in my right, I pressed my back against the front door.

A stench drifted in through the cracks of the doorframe, something rotting, like food left out in the sun. It smelled burnt, no, that wasn't right. It smelled like heated, softening plastic.

The scent moved, shifting from the front. I moved to the back of the house, opened the sliding door as quietly as possible and found Blaze staring at the roof, wings at the ready, head and neck stiff as he, too, sought the cause of our disturbance.

A shadow moved high up on the roof, and I flung my tomahawk, aiming slightly to the left, following the shadow's directional shift, trying to get in front of it. The 'hawk returned to my hand unbloodied, begging me to try again.

Blaze took off, charging at the solid black blot on the sky, but tumbled as he was hit by a long, bone-white hand.

"Pascal!" My voice was a hushed, airy scream, as I realized who it was.

The dark smudge turned, and Pascal removed his hood, part of a long, black cloak that covered his entire body.

I gasped at the sight. His face was still dripping like a melted crayon, the holy wine denying him the ability to heal.

"Why are you here?" I demanded. "Do you want to fight right now? Because I'm ready anytime! Do you want to tell me the truth about my mother and who placed a bounty on my head?" Pascal averted his gaze, which infuriated me.

"Face me!" I chucked the 'hawk again, but Pascal, even injured as he was, ducked, and the weapon only shaved a few strands of hair.

Pascal's voice wheezed in the night air. "I'm not here to fight you, granddaughter."

Blaze raced in, launching himself at Pascal, but the vampire was already gone.

Pascal's voice came on the wind. "I'm protecting you."
Granddaughter? Protecting?
Blaze and I looked at each other, both paralyzed by those words.
What. The. Hell?

# END OF THE LINE

## CHAPTER ONE

The monster with the wild hair stomped her foot and gnashed her terrible teeth, then, rethinking the approach, gave me weepy, doe-eyed stare, and said, in a sweet voice, "A mock sleepover, then? Four girls and they leave at midnight? That's almost as good as a real sleepover."

Devi, my daughter, wanted a sleepover, and my five-year-old mini-me was a good negotiator. She also had her father in her hip pocket, not that he would admit it, and I perceived he was about to give. I jumped in to bolster his resolve.

"Devi, you are too young for any kind of sleepover. Maybe next year."

The insidious little minx turned to her father. "Daddy, can't you think about it?"

The kiss of death. He never said no to her.

"Honey, Mommy and I will talk about it tonight, okay?" He dropped a kiss on the crown of her head.

"Thanks, Daddy!" Off she went, knowing full well that she'd all but won, the schemer.

Nathaniel turned to me, using the same eyes that his daughter applied so successfully. "What do you think, Jess? How could it hurt? She's so excited."

"Nathaniel, how could it hurt? It will hurt a lot when a monster attacks the house because of the bounty on my head and I have to worry about four more little girls in the crosshairs."

"Didn't you get that witch to cast a protective spell? What's her name again?"

"Lila Hanft."

"So, what did she do? A protective spell, right?"

"Yes, she did, but it's specific to us. I'll have to get her to widen it to include anyone in the house or in the yard. It will be pricey. She's gotten pretty uppity since that cranky wizard, Donald Kirby, retired to Florida. She knows she has us by the short and tinies."

"Ick. That's a terrible turn of phrase. Please don't use that again. What about that Vodun priest? Can he help strengthen the protective spells? Jim something-or-other?"

"Jim McDonald? Are you kidding me? He's so pasty white I don't think he's even been to the southern United States, much less Africa. Trust me, he doesn't have a drop of African or Vodun blood in him. He's Scottish, for goodness' sake. He wore a kilt when he thought I wasn't looking, and I'm pretty certain he wore it true. He's a complete fraud. I already turned him into the police once for selling fake fetish necklaces."

Nathaniel sighed. "If you get Lila to extend the protection spells, and Blaze is on guard, maybe we can handle having four little girls for a few hours. Bounty or no, you are always in danger. It's something we've had to learn to live with. We can't let your job stop us from doing fun things. We'd never do anything."

"I'll call her," I grumbled. "But if she wants a blood donation, it's off."

One hundred and fifty bucks later, plus the liver, heart and kidneys of a chicken I was cleaning, Lila agreed to expand the protection spell to include anyone in the house or yard. She started in our kitchen, where she lit a sandalwood-scented candle, sat in a chair, closed her eyes and took a deep cleansing breath. She motioned me to her.

"Can I please have a bowl of water, olive oil, and salt, please?" she asked.

"Any specific amount of olive oil? Does it matter if it's iodized salt, rock salt, or kosher salt? Do we need filtered water or will tap water do?" I was more of a smash and grab kind of girl; this subtle stuff wasn't in my wheelhouse.

Lila focused on the candle, and without looking, replied, "Filtered water would be great. Any olive oil will do as long as it's extra-virgin, and of course, it has to be kosher salt. You're Jewish."

"Sorry. Amateur here with the wiccan stuff."

Lila snorted. "That's obvious."

Placing a bowl, oil, and salt in front of her, I said, "Anything else you require, madam?" I ground my teeth and managed to keep the snark out of my voice. I believed in what she was doing. Lila was a powerful witch, but she only did magic with a high dose of condescension. She was somewhere around one hundred and five years old, with hanging jowls and flapping dragon wings of skin under her triceps. I'm not too ashamed to admit that this made me feel a bit superior. I flexed my arm, showing off my biceps. She didn't even notice.

"Spray paint."

"You need spray paint? For what?"

"Go on, stop asking questions, girl, and find some spray paint. Any color will do. Someone has a can sitting around their garage." She waved her left hand at me in a shooing motion.

I trudged to our garage and rifled through the odds and ends. I found a paint roller, spider webs, multiple cords of different sizes and shapes, duct tape, two sets of roller blades, plastic sheeting, and a bike helmet. I yelled up the stairs, "Nathaniel! Kids! We have to clean out the garage!"

I've said the same thing a dozen times, and we've still never cleaned out anything. We pile and hoard.

My neighbor, Judy, might have a can of spray paint. A black elf recently kidnapped her son, Joseph, in order to flush me out and kill me for reward money. The bounty wasn't a standard number, like one million. Instead, it was the auction bidding price of a ruby that used to be in the crown of King Louis XIV. I had no idea who had that jewel or why they'd offered such a valuable item for my head. I suspected it was something my mother had done while she was a monster hunter that I didn't know about. My Buddha said I could suffer for someone else's crime if I had benefitted from it.

Judy did, in fact, have spray paint and gave it to me happily, eager to help in any way since Blaze, my resident phoenix, Shura, a genius wolf, and I had rescued her son. The irony was that her son wouldn't have been kidnapped if it wasn't for me, so I carried guilt in a metaphysical backpack wherever I went.

Lila waited for me on the porch, gripping a dripping candle. "Took you long enough. Any longer and I'd have to start over. You'd owe me an arm and a leg."

I studied her to make sure she was kidding and was pretty sure she was. Maybe.

We marked out the four corners of the property with the white spray paint, and Lila dripped candle wax at each corner, walking the entire perimeter. I had a very large yard with woods in the back and a little stream that ran through. It took some time, but she didn't complain. I think that when it came to the actual magic/potion/spelling part, she was deadly serious. When she was done, she placed the candle on my porch and told me let it burn out naturally.

"What if it rains?" I asked.

She raised an eyebrow. "Stand in front of it and keep it from getting wet. Listen, I threw in a little extra mojo, even though you didn't specify it. The person or creature entering your property needs to have evil intent. That way you don't accidentally zap the mailman."

"Well, thanks, but I had to specify that? You don't normally protect innocents?"

Lila shrugged. "I trained with the Fae. You need to be precise, but in this case, I figured you're too stupid to know that and I threw it in for free. Besides, there are children involved. I'm not completely heartless."

"Good to know." Internally, I was thinking, *Get off my lawn, you psychopath.*

The crazy witch left on her broom—okay, it was a Ford Fiesta, but it wouldn't have surprised me to see a broom. I scooted the candle back another foot closer to the house with my toe and placed metal deck chairs around it, hoping they would protect it if my luck continued and it thunder stormed. I almost tripped over Devi when I entered the house because the little minx was waiting for me. She clapped her hands, squirming like she had ants in her pants.

"Now can I have a sleepover?"

"Not so fast, sneaky Pete. You agreed to a mock sleepover with the girls leaving at nine."

Devi gave me a hard stare. "Mom, we said midnight. How about eleven?"

"Ten."

She jumped up and down. "Perfect! Thanks, Mom!"

She'd played me like a fiddle.

The next evening, Devi laid out her list of desires, needs, and wants for her party. The girls were easy to choose, since she had four close friends. Debby, Abby, Sammy, and Dany, the "Y" team, would join us at 7:00 and leave at 10:00. Each needed a costume, a sleeping bag—although they weren't actually sleeping at our house—and I promised gluten-free snacks since Dany had celiac. When I asked if her highness had any other wishes, she gave me a breezy "no," not recognizing my sarcasm, and scampered off to her room. On second thought, she may have noticed it, but ignored it, which is what her father usually did.

I'd spoken to Blaze about the mock sleepover, and he was nonchalant.

*Between the protection spells, me, and you, the girls will be fine.*

"I'm not sure my carpet will survive."

*That sounds like a "you" problem.*

A yip caught my attention, and I looked to my left to see Shura strolling in. Shura, a wolf from the zoo who'd eaten a bit of were-gorilla flesh and gotten smarter because of it, liked to visit. She was also a fearsome fighter and a treasured ally. Still, her appearance meant danger was on the horizon.

"You left the zoo *again*?"

Shura lolled out her tongue, and Blaze translated her thoughts.

*My pups are all grown, and it's boring at the zoo. You're always good for some mayhem.*

"The zoo will be looking for you, and what about your mate?"

*Men! He made his den and now he can lie in it. I'm taking a break.*

"Ahhhhh, okay. Good adaptation of the idiom by the way."

*Did I get it right? I practiced on the way here. Oh, I brought a friend.*

"Who?"

I heard a "hoo-hoo" from the side yard and I scooted to investigate. Rocko jumped out from behind a bush hooting a gorilla version of "surprise!" He wrapped his massive arms around me and hugged me so hard I thought my teeth would fall out.

"Rocko! You came to visit. It's so good to see you. How's Lulu? Are you getting a better selection of fruit? I told them no bananas."

Rocko squeezed me harder.

"Big guy, put me down, please?"

He dropped me and patted me on the head with one dinner plate-sized hand.

Suddenly, I realized that I had a gorilla in my yard. This gorilla was special, having been turned into a human for a short while when the aforementioned were-gorilla turned nature all topsy-turvy. It was a long story, but it also left Rocko more intelligent than your average gorilla, and he'd been plenty smart to begin with. This is how I met Blaze as well, my phoenix friend. Blaze looked like a cross between a parrot and an emu, if emus wore bronze armor and communicated telepathically. He lived in a nest at the back of our property that he'd made out of Christmas lights, sticks, and recently, copper electric wire that he'd stolen from somewhere. I didn't ask.

Despite my pleasure at seeing Rocko, I had a sudden moment of clarity and realized something important. "The zoo is going to notice the absence of their favorite gorilla, don't you think? I mean, Shura missing is bad enough, but what are we going to tell people you are, Rocko? We can convince people Shura is a dog, and Blaze is a pony, but a gorilla defies explanation."

Rocko's face dropped, and he stuck out his lower lip, making sad snuffling sounds. I stroked his arm and lifted his chin with my other hand. I hated to see him sad.

"It's not that I'm not happy to see you, my big muscled friend, but I don't know how to keep you a secret."

Rocko's face brightened. He jumped to his feet and hid behind the bush again. It covered his bottom half, and he looked so silly standing still like a rabbit, lips pressed together, eyes squeezed shut, hoping no one would notice that he was a three-hundred pound silverback. I relented. Maybe if you weren't looking for a gorilla, you wouldn't see one? I crossed my fingers.

"Okay, Rocko. You can stay, and Shura," I said, pointing at the wolf, "you are responsible for him. How did you sneak a gorilla out, anyway?"

Shura gave me a baleful stare, turned in three circles, settled in a sunny spot, and went to sleep. Blaze covered his face with his wing.

"Are you laughing?"

*No. No. Not at all. There's nothing funny at all about a mock sleepover with five girls, a phoenix, a wolf, and a gorilla. I mean, what could go wrong?*

"Arrrghhhh! Fine. Rocko, please see if you can find another hiding spot, and Blaze, don't hurt yourself laughing at my expense, you backstabbing bird." Blaze collapsed to the ground, both wings covering his head, his body shaking with amusement, which made his bronze feathers tinkle like wind chimes.

I huffed at him and traipsed into the house to tell Nathaniel we needed more food, including meat for the wolf and fruit for the gorilla. Nathaniel's face remained blank when I told him the new situation. He simply raised his eyebrows, grabbed his keys, and told David to come with him to the grocery store.

"Stop at the farmers' market, too. They have lots of greens that gorillas may like." Nathaniel gave me a thumbs up before he drove off.

I cupped my jade Buddha in my palms, translating the events of the last hour to him, and his tummy bobbled up and down with glee at my karma. I'd gotten him at a local museum after a small snafu with an imp, a Japanese spirit fox called a kitsune, and the entire Asian collection. It had the upside of being memorable.

Four girls giggled in my entryway, their parents standing at the door smiling at the sudden freedom to have an adult dinner. Well, Dany and Sammy's parents were excited. Abby's mother, Lisa, recently divorced, had bags under her eyes and sighed a lot, giving me a fierce hug that I returned with a silent prayer for strength and healing. I hung on an extra second when my gorilla friend army-crawled across the front yard, unobtrusive as a purple cow among a herd of white sheep.

Debby's father, Josh, looked like he hadn't smiled in the entire three years since his wife's death. He was too skinny, his eyes drooped with grief, and his shoes were worn thin. I hugged him too, and Nathaniel pulled him aside with a handshake, speaking softly. Nathaniel maneuvered Josh so he didn't see our stealthy friend either.

The girls headed to the backyard to play while it was still light out, and I followed to make sure Blaze was on the case. The phoenix, disguised as a search-and-rescue pony, watched from the corner of the yard. Of course, little girls couldn't ignore a pony, and they ran toward Blaze, squealing at the top of their lungs, begging to pet the small horse.

Blaze allowed the petting, and when he thought I wasn't looking, nudged their hands to continue. Blaze had bronze feathers, hard and sharp as a chef's knife, but they touched him without a problem. In fact, they commented on how soft he was.

*Magic is a crazy-ass thing.*

I decided I didn't have to do ten pushups for the curse word since I didn't say it out loud. Don't judge me.

I expected it to happen, but I thought we'd have more time. A car pulled into our driveway, blue and white, siren silent, thank goodness, and out stepped a friend, or at least, someone I considered a friend. How he felt about me was iffy.

The policeman who stepped out of the car had fresh scars on his face and hands, plus a new set of veneers, due to the incident involving the imp at a museum, who, it turned out, threw flames from his hands. I was almost certain that Bob's injuries weren't my fault.

Mostly. Generally. Sort of?

"Officer Bob! How good to see you. How are you feeling? Did you see the ball game last night? Glad the Indians won? Couldn't believe that they rallied after being four down…"

Bob held up a hand to stop my chatter.

I slumped, waiting.

"Mrs. Friedman."

"Yes," I responded, my eyes darting right and left.

"Do you happen, by any chance, to know where a certain gorilla is?"

"A certain gorilla? Why, I have no idea. Which gorilla are we discussing?" I swallowed and shifted to my left so Bob wouldn't see Rocko trying to squeeze under the police car. I flicked my hand in a shooing motion, hoping Rocko would get the hint. If he did, he ignored me, laying on his back, squirming to make his way between the tires.

Officer Bob rubbed his cheek and quietly counted to ten.

"Mrs. Friedman, there is only one gorilla, which you well know. Rocko has escaped the zoo."

I held my hand to my heart. "Goodness! That's terrible. How did they miss a silverback gorilla waltzing out the door?"

"Is that what he did, Mrs. Friedman? Waltz out the door? Because zoo officials are quite concerned and cannot figure out how he left."

"I really have no idea." There. That was the truth. I don't lie well.

"Do you have any idea where he is?"

Rocko had abandoned the car, and I didn't see where he went, so I could honestly reply, "I do not."

Bob rubbed the top of his head and sighed.

"Mrs. Friedman."

"Yes?"

"Do you have knowledge of any type that might help me find the gorilla?"

That was a tougher one to answer without fibbing. I hesitated, then I said, "Most times a gorilla will find a forest, or at least a copse of trees. That is their preferred habitat."

Bob covered his face with both hands. Uh oh, we were already at face-covering.

"Jess, do you know where the damn gorilla is? And by the way, the wolf is missing too. Did you take them?"

He'd never, ever called me by my first name before.

"I did not take them. As for where they are, I'm not certain, but I will say that both of them are likely to return."

"Exactly how can you say that?"

I reached for anything, anything at all. "Uh, that's where their food is? I mean, don't wolves return to their dens, and male gorillas need to eat a lot?" I inwardly grimaced as I thought about how much plant material we'd have to supply Rocko.

Shura decided that was the moment to sneak around the corner of the house and make silly wolf faces at the annoyed policeman behind his back. I'm afraid my mouth smirked, all of its own.

"It's not funny, Mrs. Friedman! I've been through a lot with you, and I trust you, but these animals keep disappearing, and you're the only link."

I looked away from the wolf, schooled my face, and answered with sincerity. "I know, Officer Bob. Truly, I know. But, if we are being honest with each other, the animals do what *they* want to do. These aren't normal animals any more. They were affected by their interaction with the were-gorilla and became smarter as a result. I'm not stealing them. If they get out, it's on their own."

"Fine. I'll inform Captain Morgan." Officer Bob raised his voice. "And, if any animals would like to return where they belong, that would be deeply appreciated. The zoo is offering fresh termites for the gorilla, and they would like the wolf to know that one of the pack's females is pregnant for the first time and will need her guidance."

"Oh, that's nice! More wolf pups."

"Yes, and the first-time mother needs her alpha female."

"Shura," I said, wincing as soon as the name came out of my mouth.

Bob peered at me. "What. Did. You. Say?"

I flapped my hands in the air. "Nothing. I heard somewhere that the alpha female's name was Shura. Thought you would like to know."

Bob moved another step toward me. We were nose-to-nose. "Right. Mrs. Friedman, if you happen to see these missing creatures, would you kindly call the zoo, or me?"

I rocked on my heels and cleared my throat. "I'll tell them to go home."

"Close enough. Thank you." Officer Bob turned to leave but stopped to give me a look. "Are you okay, Mrs. Friedman?"

I escalated to a full Kermit flail. "My daughter is having a mock sleepover. She's five and has four friends. There is a bounty on my head that already resulted in the kidnapping of that little boy, and I'm still a little freaked out about the moving mannequins, not to mention a mucous demon. K?"

"There's a bounty on your head?" Officer Bob's face turned red. "Why didn't you tell me?"

This time I could be completely honest. "Because I don't want you or anyone else getting hurt. This is my fight, and I'll fight it."

Officer Bob softened. "Mrs. Friedman, if you need help, say the word. You know we'll be there for you."

I patted his hand. "I know, but you have enough to deal with responding to normal bad guys. You don't need paranormal ones too."

"I dealt with them before, or do you have short- and long-term memory loss?" The small smile on his face told me he was teasing.

"I'll call you if you can help. Promise."

"See that you do. Especially if this bounty is what caused that child kidnapping. I can't keep you safe, Mrs. Friedman, but we do have a duty to protect the general public. If your troubles become everyone's troubles, we are going to have a problem." Officer Bob gave me one last look before he returned to his car. I was grateful the gorilla wasn't under it and thrilled that the witch had made sure that the protective spell didn't blow up a friendly. That was a good call on her part. Didn't make me like her any more, but still, a good call.

## CHAPTER TWO

When the girls finished petting the pony and the "dog's" belly, they skittered inside like excited mice and made a beeline for the basement. Stage two of mock sleepover was a dress-up party, and each girl brought a costume, as I learned when I unabashedly eavesdropped.

One high-pitched giggle. "What costume did you bring, Sammy?"

Another high-pitched voice answered, assumedly Sammy. "I brought my Cinderella dress! My mom added extra sequins! It sparkles!"

I shivered in horror as the girls squealed and ooohed and ahhhed over the disco dress.

Dany's voice sailed up the stairs and pierced my ears, causing a headache similar to brain freeze.

"I have a new costume! Can you guess which one it is? I'll hold it up."

A collective gasp and then Abby joined in. "Moana! That's awesome, Dany! We can braid your hair. Do you like ribbons? We can put ribbons it in and pretend to sail the sea by the stars."

"And glitter!" said another voice. *Debby*, I thought. Debby added, "Who doesn't love glitter?"

*Me*, I thought. *Definitely, me.*

By this time, I was sitting at my kitchen table with a heating pad on the back of my neck, an ice pack on the crown of my head, and a bottle of migraine formula pain reliever in my hand.

"What do you have, Abby?" asked one of the girls. I gave up distinguishing one from the other.

Peals of laughter drifted upward, followed mummers of appreciation as Abby pulled out her costume. One voice sounded confused.

"I don't know who you are, Abby. What's that funny hat?"

"I'm Princess Kate from England! I'm a real princess!" Abby replied.

"Oh, I love her!"

"My mom says she reminds her of Princess Diana."

"Well, my mom said she wouldn't want Princess Kate's job for all the tea in China."

"How much tea is in China?"

"I think it's a lot."

"Does that mean she wants all the tea?"

"No, I think it means she doesn't want the tea and doesn't want to be Princess Kate."

"Who wouldn't want to be a princess?"

"I don't." My daughter had spoken, and I cheered inside my head. Nathaniel grinned too.

Devi continued. "I have a different costume. See if you can guess."

I perked up my ears at this part because I had no idea what costume she'd put together. We had a collection of old Halloween costumes in a trunk in the guest room. Most I'd bought because I couldn't sew. I couldn't even iron, but Angie, my best friend, had made a few of them by hand. We had a huge collection of stuff.

Curious, I dumped my heating pad, ice pack, and the rest and snuck down the stairs to get a look.

Devi was green. Completely green. Head to toe. Green tights, a long green shirt, and a green felt hat she'd gotten from somewhere. She had a leather belt around her waist and a toy quiver with nerf arrows. No bow, but I knew who she was, and it made me grin.

"You're wearing a dress, but I don't know which princess you are," Debby said.

"I told you. I'm not a princess," responded Devi. "This is a tunic."

"What's a tunic?"

"You make it into sandwiches, dummy." This, from Sammy.

Devi sighed in a way that sounded familiar, and I grinned as I realized I'd heard it coming from my own lips. "That's *tuna*, a fish. This is a *tunic*, a type of shirt."

"It looks like a dress."

"It's a little long. It's my dad's. Look! I have arrows. Does that help?"

"Where is your bow?"

"I don't have one."

"You need a bow."

"I'll search around some more, but now do you know who I am?"

Abby jumped up. "You're Robert Hood!"

Devi hopped from foot-to-foot in excitement. "It's Robin Hood, but, yes!"

"What does Robert Hood do?"

"*Robin* Hood. He's a hero. He steals from the rich to give to the poor in jolly old England. That's what the book says."

"Isn't Robin a girl's name?" said Debby.

"There's a girl named Robin in first grade," replied Abby.

Sammy lifted a finger in the air. "A robin is a bird! Not a person!"

The three girls squabbled while Devi stared at the ground, crestfallen that her friends didn't know who she was. I was about to interfere, but Dany, who'd been pretty quiet, came to the rescue.

"Ooooh! Ooooh! I know. I know. He's a fox."

Devi gave her a hug. "That's it. In the Disney movie, Robin is a fox."

Abby's face screwed up. "You mean, he's handsome?"

Dany bumped Abby with her hip. "No, silly. It's a cartoon. He's a fox."

"I'm confused," said Abby. "My older sister says this boy she likes is a fox, but he looks like a normal person to me."

Devi decided to solve this conundrum wrapped in a riddle. "Mom!" she hollered. "Can we watch *Robin Hood* where Robin is a fox? Not that goofy one with the men dancing in tights. I didn't like that one."

I'd pulled myself out of visual range, so I waited a moment, as if I were coming from the kitchen, and leaned over the bannister. "Sure, honey. Wow! You look great. You're Robin Hood. Is that why you want to watch the movie?"

"Yes. I want to show my friends that Robin Hood is a fox."

Abby's hands were on her hips. "I still don't get it. My sister said that saying someone is a fox means they're sexy."

"What does sexy mean?" asked Dany.

This was where I jumped in, although I heard Nathaniel snuffling in the kitchen as he tried to control his laughter.

"I'll get the movie, honey. What Devi means is that the movie is a cartoon, and Robin Hood is an animal."

Blank stares.

"I'll be right back."

Nathaniel had the Coke bottle to his forehead and was wiping tears from his eyes.

"Thanks for helping," I grumbled as I walked to the DVD collection.

"You…you…you've got it under…control…" Nathaniel snuckled. It's not a word, I know, but it should be. His response was a mixture of a snort and a chuckle, thus, a snuckle.

The girls were excited to watch a movie, and I promised popcorn. I popped the DVD in, grateful we still had a DVD player, and let them sit back to watch the talking foxes, badger, wolf, and bear.

I microwaved two bags of popcorn, not certain how much five little girls could eat, but assuming more was better. Looking at all the kernels, I wondered if I could teach Devi how to use a vacuum. Nathaniel finished his Coke and got another one, and I gestured for him to get me one too.

"Here you go, girls. Buttered popcorn, my personal favorite."

"Thanks, Mrs. Friedman." The response was monotone and perfunctory as the girls were glued to the screen. The only problem was, there were only four girls.

"Where's Devi?"

"She says she's seen this before. She's off looking for something."

"Oh, okay." I had no idea what Devi could be looking for, but whatever it was, I was sure it wasn't dangerous.

## CHAPTER THREE

The popcorn disappeared fast, and although the girls' stomachs stuck out like starving UNICEF kids, they wanted more. Being a responsible mother, I gave them a large bag of Hershey's Milk Chocolate kisses and told them to go to town.

Devi was still rummaging around for whatever it was she thought she needed, so the four girls shoved kisses in their mouths and played a game of Twister. They called to Devi to come play.

"Devi, let's play! Come on, play with us."

Devi emerged from the guest room covered in dust bunnies, her hat askew, and she'd ripped her tights. She sure took after her mother.

"Alright." Devi wasn't happy about something, but I didn't get to ask because the girls became excited, fluttering around like manic butterflies. I'm sure the chocolate had something to do with that, but they weren't sleeping at my house, so I didn't care.

"Hide and seek! Hide and seek!" Abby did a cartwheel, nailing the landing.

"That's a great idea!" Dany exclaimed, and not to be out done, did a handstand and walked on her hands for about three feet. *Good form*, I thought. *Strong abs*. Handstands come from the core, not the arms.

Sammy did a pirouette and nodded her agreement, while Debby jumped up and down, up and down, finally stabilizing in a crouch, and leapt like a frog.

Man, were their parents going to hate me. I briefly considered giving them whiskey to counter the sugar. I probably took longer than was needed to determine that this was a bad idea.

The only thing they could do was play an Olympic game of hide-and-seek and work it off.

"Go ahead, girls. Hide-and-seek sounds great." I threw in a bonus, gestured to Devi, who came closer, and whispered, "You can even use the crawlspace."

Devi's eyes got wide, and she rubbed her hands together in glee. "They'll never find me," she whispered back.

I winked. "A sure win."

"Okay! Let's play!" My daughter announced her decision with a new gleam in her eye.

"Okay, let's set some rules. Do not try to squeeze into a space you know is too small for you." I ticked off a finger and held up another. "If I call for you, or Mr. Friedman does, you have to come right away."

Lots of solemn nodding.

"Last, if you are still playing when your parents come, you have to stop and go home without a fuss."

More vigorous nodding.

"Then, if we are all agreed, play ball!" I announced, which made the girls squinch their eyes at me. Four of them let it go, but Dany said, "We're playing hide-and-seek, Mrs. Friedman, not ball." She patted my arm, her shoulders set in a way that conveyed sympathy because, obviously, I was quite dim.

I let them play their game and wandering up the stairs to the kitchen where Nathaniel had upped the ante to chocolate chunk ice cream.

## CHAPTER FOUR

The kids did an eeney-meeney to determine who was "It" and split in different directions, scurrying around to find the best hiding places. Our house had a lot of crevices and boxes to hide behind and in, so a game of hide-and-seek in our house had the potential to be epic. I left them to it and tramped outside to have a chat with Blaze.

Blaze was preening, sitting on the deck like a giant duck, poking and prodding at his wings with his beak. Shura was next to him, eating… something…she'd caught, and Rocko was huddled nearby behind a rolled garden hose pretending to be an extra-large gnome. I felt bad that I hadn't spent any time with him, so I gave Blaze a "one moment" sign, returned to the house, piled fruit into a laundry basket, and joined my massive cuddlekin.

"Hey, big guy, how you doing?" I asked this as I handed him the laundry basket. He didn't answer because he dove headlong into the basket like he was dunking for apples, rear-end to the sky, arms holding his weight on either side of the basket. He snarfed down half the contents, making adorable little lip-smacking sounds of delight.

I waited for Rocko to come up for air, and when he did, he had grape skins stuck to his chin, an apple core in his fur, and whatever leaves Nathaniel had gotten were now macerated green stringy goop in his teeth. I gestured to his chin with a little wiping motion, and he turned away from me and picked out the debris. I handed him a twig, and he used it to scrape his teeth. When he was presentable, he turned back around and gathered me in his arms for another giant hug. This time I stayed there, enjoy the feeling of a good friend giving me a hug, hairy or no.

"I've missed you, big guy." Rocko nuzzled the top of my head.

"It's been a bit strange lately, since I last saw you." Rocko made a "go on" gesture. Huh. That was new.

"There's this vampire, Pascal."

Rocko showed his impressive teeth.

"Yeah, I know. Vampires suck." Rocko didn't get the pun, and I was a little relieved by that, frankly.

"So, here's what happened…"

Rocko proved to be a great listener, making hooting noises at the right moments, widening his eyes in shock when I told him about the black-elf, and even rubbing his chin when I explained that Pascal hadn't healed, which confounded me too. After I finished, Rocko stood on all fours and paced, like he was thinking it through.

Finally, he stopped the pacing, reared up on his legs, and pounded his chest, thumping his fists on his pecs, which made a popping noise like just-released fireworks. At the same time, he made a rhythmic barking sound and bared his teeth.

"Hey, hey. It'll be okay, Rocko. You don't have to protect me. I was talking it out with you to get your perspective. I'll be fine."

Rocko moved in front of me, guarding me with his body, his eyes scanning back and forth for danger. Silverbacks are big, scary animals whose job is to protect the troupe. I was suddenly glad he was there.

Blaze tiptoed over, which was amusing because of his big Tweety-bird feet, but he also was smart and wanted to approach quietly, head down. Even a phoenix doesn't want to piss off an angry gorilla. He'd be born again—no, not that way—but I didn't think it was a pleasant experience and would most certainly involve fire.

*What's got Rocko on edge?*

"I told him about Pascal, the bounty, and the black elf, and he seems to have taken it as a threat to the troupe."

*That's what gorillas do, protect their family.*

"I love that he considers us family, but I don't want him to get hurt. He's been through enough. Maybe we should convince him, and Shura, to go home until this thing with the bounty is finished."

*You tell him to leave. Go ahead. I'd like to see you make him.*

"He's a little riled up."

The riled-up gorilla turned to his left and charged the woods, making that barking noise and growling. Shura rushed from the deck, and Blaze and I followed, instantly alert. I grabbed the laundry basket on the way. It wasn't a great weapon, but it was something.

Rocko cried out in pain and anger, and we worked our way through dense trees and overgrowth to find him, my heart racing with fear.

Shura got to him first, then Blaze. They stopped like they'd hit a force field.

My mighty gorilla was waving his arms back-and-forth, swatting at a dozen or so dragonflies, which were poking him with tiny swords and drawing blood with stunning accuracy.

In actuality, the dragonflies were piskies, mischievous little warriors, and I had no idea why they were here.

"Stop!"

A piskie got one good swipe in on Rocko's nose, but then the entire chorus of piskies pulled away from the gorilla, blood dripping from their swords, wings fluttering to keep themselves stationary. They looked like bloodthirsty hummingbirds.

Rocko moved away with one last swat and sat next to me. Shura cuddled up to lick his wounds.

I glared at the piskies. "This gorilla is my friend. Do not attack him, me, mine, when you are on my grounds."

A blue piskie flew within a foot of me, but no closer. In fact, she *couldn't* come in.

"I see you cannot enter. That means you arrived with bad intentions. Would you like to tell me why a piskie chorus came to my home, armed, and attacked my friend?"

*What's a piskie chorus?* Blaze asked.

"A herd of sheep, a flock of birds, a creep of trolls, a chorus of piskies."

*One day you are going to tell me about the trolls.*

"Sure, but another time."

The blue piskie scrunched up her tiny face. "Who are you talking to?"

"Blaze." I motioned to the immense bird. "And with whom am I speaking?"

"I'm Elowen, leader of this chorus."

"Elowen. Please answer my question."

"We don't have bad intent, honest. Piskies are always a little playful."

"That still doesn't tell me why you're here."

"We came to help!"

Shura did her wolf shrug, and Blaze shook his head.

"Help with what?"

"The big showdown! The finale! The battle to end all battles!"

"You need to back up and explain." Nevertheless, if I thought my heart was beating fast before, it tap danced now.

"We piskies can tell when something big is coming, and we sense it will be here." Elowen fluttered so fast that I couldn't track her.

"The bounty? Someone is coming?"

"Or something."

I turned to Blaze. "This is maddening."

A red piskie joined the blue. "I'm second to Elowen."

"You're Red Leader." I have a movie for every occasion.

The piskie floated for a moment. "I wear red, and I'm a leader, so I guess so?"

"Never mind." I waved my hand. "Can you explain what Elowen means?"

"Elowen means elm tree."

I pinched the bridge of my nose. I had girls to get back to. "No, can you explain what Elowen is trying to tell me?"

Red Leader bobbed up and down. "Pixies are the barometers of Faerie. We can't tell you what is coming, or when, only that it's soon."

I rubbed my face. "See, I knew all that. Can't you be more specific? Anything? Any tiny detail?"

Red Leader shook her head, a tiny tear in her tiny eye. "No, but we're here to help, and from what we can sense, our presence is something the big bad isn't expecting. We'll throw everything off kilter. That's what piskies do bestest!" She announced this last part with pride, raising her sword in the air. The rest of the piskies raised their swords in the air and yelled, "Huzzah!"

"Why are you here to help?"

Elowen spoke up. "We live at the zoo, near Waterfowl Lake. When you stopped the were-gorilla, you saved our home."

"If you live at the zoo, why did you attack Rocko?"

Their wings moved even faster, creating a buzz like a cloud of locusts. Elowen flew as close as possible to Rocko's face, completely undisturbed by Rocko's growl.

"Rocko? Is that you?" she exclaimed. "We didn't recognize you. Sorry, dude."

Rocko swiveled to show his back, and Shura looked away to hide her smirk. The piskies didn't seem sorry, not one tiny bit.

I held up my hands in a stop motion. "How many gorillas do you think there are in Cleveland?"

Red Leader shrugged. "We don't know. Why would we know that? But we do know that you have precisely seventy-three irises around your house, and they are overcrowded and need to be split into new beds."

"Fine, but you owe Rocko a serious apology, more than a lame, 'sorry, dude.'"

The piskies buzzed their wings again, and Elowen nodded.

I turned to my enormous emu-like friend. "Blaze, what should I do here?"

*Ask them to take a drop of blood from your hand and swear allegiance. They might be useful.*

"Good idea. Okay, Elowen, we would love your help, but since you've been stopped by the barrier, I need your promise."

I pricked my finger on the tip of Blaze's wing and pushed it through the barrier, which responded reluctantly, like sticky glue. One-by-one, each piskie drank a drop of my blood and swore allegiance to me and mine. As soon as they did so, the barrier dropped, and they flew into our property. It snapped back into place with an audible click.

Elowen spoke. "We're a little tired. May we ride along?"

"The basket?" I asked. Elowen nodded.

"Sure." The entire chorus of pixies, several dozen once I got a clear view, settled in my laundry basket. Red Leader sat on my shoulder.

"Do you have a name?" I asked. Funny as it was, I couldn't call her Red Leader forever.

"Lowena," she replied. "It means joyful."

"Well, Lowena, let's rock and roll."

"I don't rock or roll. I fly."

Another piskie appeared out of nowhere, zipping to the laundry basket to salute Elowen. She flew to my shoulder to acknowledge Lowena as well, and I did a double-take. This piskie wore black leather pants, a black shirt with a deep V-neck, a matching leather jacket, combat boots, black lipstick, and heavy, dark eyeliner.

I stared at her. "Goth piskie? Gothskie?"

The piskie floated in the air, tapping her foot. "Yeah, and what's wrong with that? You think every piskie has to wear bright colors and sparkle?"

She got right in my face, holding her sword so close I was cross-eyed. I noticed she wore leather cuffs with spikes.

"General! Stand down!" Red Leader flew between me and Gothskie.

"It's just this ignorant human here…"

"Saved our home. We have all sworn allegiance. Where were you?"

"Guarding our six. Someone has to think tactically."

I couldn't help it. I had to touch her boots. I reached out with a finger. She smacked my hand. "Hey! Gigantor! Cosplay is not consent. Got it?"

"Oh! You watched *Night at the Museum*? We love that movie." Really, my life is one interrelated movie script.

Gothskie sniffed. "Of course, many of us were extras. Better to hire us than pay animators." She scooted down to my finger, which still had a drop of blood on it, and swore her loyalty. It sounded exactly like David saying he'd clean his room.

Lowena settled back on my shoulder. "Can we get something to eat? Piskies need to feed frequently."

"Fruit juice? Honey?" They all perked up their ears at the word honey, so I walked to the house, trailed by a phoenix, a gorilla, and a wolf, while schlepping a laundry basket of piskies.

## CHAPTER FIVE

Nathaniel is one of the most easy-going people I'd ever met, and he didn't bat an eye when I told him Rocko came to visit, but a basket of busty, svelte, glittery piskies made even Nathaniel stop and stare. The piskies flew out, buzzing around, touching his hair, crooning sweet nothings in his ear. One alighted on his finger, and he stared in wonder at the perfectly proportioned, voluptuous piskie, who leaned forward to make sure he got an eyeful, almost literally, she was so close. I kicked him on the shin.

"Piskies. Friends. Allies. Need honey." I was nothing if not eloquent.

Nathaniel shook his head, shooed the little minx off his finger, and dove for the pantry before he got in any more trouble. He came back with both honey and pancake syrup, poured them into Pyrex custard cups and let the girls go wild. They were a maelstrom of sticky piskie, and more than once, I had to duck a dollop of honey as they rolled in it, throwing it in the air with abandon. I caught Nathaniel staring and gave him a look.

The insanity was interrupted by David, [MMG6] who crashed through the kitchen, not even noticing the pesky, overgrown fruit flies bathing in syrup on the kitchen table. He tore past us, knocking over a chair, screaming, "She's after me! She's after me!" He was followed by Abby, who, for some reason, was on the main floor and chasing David with her arms out, yelling, "One kiss!"

Abby was, in turn, followed by the other girls, Devi bringing up the rear. She held an item I didn't recognize and was notching nerf arrows in it and letting them fly.

"Devi Julia Friedman!"

Devi stopped mid-step at the use of her middle name. *Ah, Mommy-voice, how much I love thee.*

"May I please see that bow?" I gestured for her to show it to me. In the background, the older boy and kindergarten girls ran around the dining room like NASCAR drivers, Abby begging David to stop so he could hold her hand.

Devi handed the bow to me. It was beautiful, like nothing I'd ever seen. The upper and lower rim joined in a beautiful curve, the handle risers, elegantly meeting in a gracious notch. The string was remarkably strong for so something so delicate.

"Where did you find this, Devi?" I asked. Nathaniel heard screams from the dining room and left to investigate. The piskies were drunk and lay on the table like side-walk sketched Barbie dolls, legs askew. I righted a few skirts to protect their modesty, and to keep male eyes from lingering too long. It sounded weird to say piskies have long legs, but there it was. Amazing, and not fair.

"I found it in the crawlspace, Mommy," Devi said. She wiggled with worry, afraid she was in trouble. "You said I could go in there."

"Yes, I did. You're not in trouble. I've never seen this before."

"It's really cool, Mom. Look!" She notched a nerf arrow and let it fly. It landed smack on Gothskie's back, and she was the only one not inebriated. She'd been guarding her chorus, tapping her foot in disgust at their hedonism. "What is wrong with them?" Nathaniel exclaimed, as he reentered the kitchen holding David like a baby. "Abby is saying she's in love with David. She almost ripped his shirt."

Gothskie turned at the sound of his voice, staring at him with…lust? She flew to Nathaniel's shoulder and rubbed her body into his neck, behind his ear, like a cat. "Oh, my, such a maaaaaan!" she said. "Tell me what you desire, and it shall be yours, my love."

"What?" Nathaniel and I exclaimed at the same time. Gothskie dove into Nathaniel's shirt and did something with his…

"Hey!" I yelled, jumping to Nathaniel, shoving my hand down his shirt. "He's mine!" The piskie escaped my grasp and dove toward the floor, flipped up Nathaniel's pants leg and made a bee-line straight up. Nathaniel shook his leg violently, trying to get Gothskie out of there, all the time holding David, whose eyes were scrunched up in fear.

I grabbed David, placed him on the ground and blocked for him as he fled to his room, where he locked the door. Abby followed and sat in front of it, crying for him to come back, professing her everlasting love. The other girls watched in confusion. Devi left the kitchen to join them, leaving me, Nathaniel, that bitch Gothskie, and the other piskies who were coming around.

Nathaniel stood stock still, a glazed look on his face, holding onto the back of a chair to stay upright. He panted in a way I did not like and let out a groan. "I'm sorry..." he gasped, looking at me with a face somewhere between ecstasy and horror.

I did the only thing I could do. I smacked the front of his pants with an open palm, and Goth Tinkerbell, that hussy, slid down his leg and out the bottom, where she hit her head and lay stunned on the floor. Nathaniel's face was red, and he curled up in a fetal position.

"I'm sorry, honey. I'm so sorry!" I plucked Gothskie off the floor and placed her in a large mason jar. I stabbed holes in the top with a screwdriver and put her on a shelf with my plants. I handed Nathaniel an ice pack, apologizing again.

I studied the bow. The exquisite curve I noted previously was indeed remarkable. In fact, it reminded me of a lipstick commercial where the model's lips were lined into a...perfect Cupid's bow. I smacked my hand to my head.

How in the name of all that was holy had a Cupid's bow gotten into my crawlspace? I was certain I'd never seen it before. There wasn't one Cupid's bow; there were dozens. The original Cupid's bow, the one the god Cupid used, was hidden by the Greek government in an unmarked building, in an unmarked crate mixed in with other unmarked crates. That's where Spielberg got the idea.

I cleared my throat, picked up the bow, and marched downstairs to the back bedroom, where the crawlspace was located. I was trailed by piskies of every color, except the Goth one dressed in black, because, even though it was unreasonable, I was still mad as hell at that chick and had left her locked in the jar.

I hadn't been in the crawlspace for years, and it was dusty and full of cobwebs, as you'd expect. Devi had pulled out the old boxes of china, kids' clothing, and parts of a crib that we'd never use again, and behind all of that, she'd found a trunk that I'd forgotten about. It was a trunk of my mother's that I'd shoved in there one day and not looked at again, angry that she'd lied to me about her life.

"Devi, was the bow in the box?"

"No. It was scrunched behind it."

That was so odd. I knew I'd never seen the bow. You'd think I would remember it. I opened the trunk now, wiping away years of dust, revealing a pile of old photographs, hand-written notes, and some clothes.

I lifted a onesie from the pile and realized the clothes were all baby sized. My mom must have saved some of them for some sentimental reason. I didn't recall my mom being a sentimental person, but the presence of the baby clothes gave me pause. In addition to the onesie were some booties, a tiny dress I must have worn in my first two weeks of life, it was so small, and a baby blanket that I think was knitted by my nana.

Underneath this top layer was a scarf used to divide the baby clothes from the bottom layer. I lifted it and was struck by a faint scent of my mother's perfume. It stunned me and threw me into a memory.

She rarely wore perfume, probably for the same reason I didn't wear it: it made you more vulnerable to monsters, who had notoriously good noses. That evening, however, she wore a fancy black dress with a rhinestone choker and the scarf I now held in my hands draped over her shoulders. She'd sprayed a touch of the perfume on the scarf and in her hair, a trick she taught me later, so the scent would linger. I remember that she wore heels, small ones to be sure, but it was so unusual that I recalled them perfectly. Small, black kitten heels with a rhinestone clip on each toe. She wore little makeup but with mascara and red lipstick, she looked like a queen to me.

My dad was equally dressed up, wearing a tux and smooth, leather shoes. I watched while he whispered something to her and she laughed, a private moment. Then, he took her clutch and removed the switchblade she'd inserted, putting it in a drawer out of my reach. He gazed at me and shook his finger, warning me not to try to touch it.

He didn't know, but when he had turned his back, she snuck it into her bag again. I don't remember anything unusual about that night other than seeing my parents dressed up, for a wedding, I believe, so she most likely didn't use the blade, but she made sure she had it, just in case. I'd forgotten that little tidbit or hadn't given it any thought at the time. My mom always had something sharp with her. Now, I saw it in a different light.

Next was a pile of photographs. I flipped over the top layer and smiled. The photo was me and my dad, taken by my mother when I was about eight. He looked so young and happy. Piskies buzzed around my head, chittering.

"Who is that?" asked a light-green one.

"I'm the little girl, and that is my father," I replied, pointing.

"No," said the piskie, who was wearing a yellow dress. "This one."

Elowen had turned over another photo. It was an evening setting, a woman and a man sitting at a table. The woman's back was straight, and she'd scooted her chair back as far as it could go. She wore sensible black pants, low-heeled boots, and a sleek black jacket. The man wore a suit, leaned forward, and looked like he was saying something urgent.

The woman was my mother. The man, or vampire in this case, was Pascal.

*What in God's name was my mother doing with Pascal?*

I studied the shot more closely. They seemed to be out at a restaurant, on an outside dining patio. My mother had a wine glass on the table in front of her, and Pascal had something that looked like oysters. The obligatory bread and butter sat in the middle of the table. All of it was untouched. The person taking the photo was outside of the restaurant and not particularly close. He or she had used a zoom lens to catch the detail. My mom's face was steely, her arms crossed, and I could almost see her shaking her head. Pascal had one hand forward, reaching toward her, and seemed to be pleading with her.

I'd memorized every one of my mother's expressions, and that look meant, "No. Not on your life."

Whatever Pascal wanted, it wasn't happening, but I still couldn't figure out why they were together. She hated him, hunted him, even planned the demolition of a bridge to kill him, and here they were sharing appetizers?

I was about to bring the photo upstairs to show to Nathaniel when the screams rang out.

## CHAPTER SIX

I grabbed the bow, snagged a nerf arrow, and shot Abby with it, betting it would reverse the effect. Only a moment after the arrow hit her in the back, she reached around, jerked it off, and said, "Hey, what's the big idea shooting me with arrows?"

Debby responded, "Devi's mom did it," and all the girls turned to me with one shared accusing look, except for Devi, who studied the floor like it had suddenly sprouted fascinating ancient text only she could decipher.

Dany poked Abby on the shoulder. "Do you still love David, Abby? I thought you wanted to kisssssss him." Dany made kissy noises, and the other girls jumped in to join the fun.

Abby poked Dany back, "What are you talking about? Boys are gross. David especially. Let's go back downstairs. Why are we sitting here in the hallway?"

"Because you wanted to hug David, that's why," said Sammy. "You've been chasing him around the house saying you wanted to marry him."

"Have not!" Abby's hands were on her hips.

"Did too!"

"Nuh uh!"

"You like boys! You like boys!"

"Do not!"

I gave Devi a look, and she felt my gaze because she ripped her eyes away from the riveting floorboards and pulled her friends downstairs. I hid the bow in a hallway closet and meandered into the living room, managing a calm, outward exterior. Daniel obviously woke up at some point with all the noise and hubbub and cuddled in Nathaniel's arms, head on his shoulder. I wasn't fooled though. His eyes were wide and watching everything.

I motioned to Nathaniel to hand Daniel to me, and my sweet little boy gave me a kiss on the cheek as I gathered him in my arms. I rocked my youngest for a few minutes, then placed him in his crib. "Go to sleep, Daniel. You've slept through worse. I know you want to be a part of the action, but if you don't sleep, you'll be super crabby tomorrow." I sang him a goodnight song and snuck out, closing the door almost all the way.

The piskies! I checked the kitchen, and they were gone. I hustled downstairs, flashing a "wait a minute" finger at Nathaniel who shot me a look that meant, "Get back here!" I nearly flipped at the sight before me. The piskies were doing the girls' hair. The girls had pooled their bows, barrettes, bobby pins, and assorted hair what-nots, and the piskies were oohing and ahhing over each girl's hair, doing complex braids and up-dos. The girls clapped their hands and stared at the piskies in utter adoration. All of them except Devi, who looked annoyed that her sleepover had been hijacked by tiny warrior dragonflies.

I pointed to Sammy and the piskie doing her hair. "That up-do is entirely too sophisticated for a five-year-old."

One of the piskies flew back to take a look from a distance. "You think so? It is gorgeous, but, maybe. Petal," she said, talking the other piskie in a palest shade of peach, "we should try something a little more textured and not so severe." She turned to me. "Do you have mousse?"

Before I could ask what mousse was, Abby held up a squeeze bottle. "I have some!" she said. "I also have hairspray, gel, and leave-in conditioner." She flipped one bottle after another out of her bag. I couldn't believe she brought so many products to a mock sleepover.

"Why does she have all of that stuff?" I asked Devi.

Devi pursed her lips. "She always has that stuff. Those are her travel-size bottles. You should see what she keeps in her locker."

"She's five."

"She has an older sister, and her mom can't be with them all the time. She works, you know." The last comment was a little too pointed for my taste.

"I work."

"Yes, but Abby's mom works at a normal job. She's an electrician."

"An electrician! Really? That's awesome. What a useful skill."

"There's no magic in it though."

"I don't know. Electricity seems magic to me. Besides, I thought you admired her 'normal' job."

Devi considered my words. "Now that I think of it, normal is boring. I told my friends that you had magic and made the fairies appear. Is that okay?"

"It's fine, baby. We'll figure that out later. But you should know," I corrected, catching Elowen's look from the corner of my eye, "that these are piskies, not fairies. They don't like to be confused."

"We are totally different!" said Elowen, who flew over to sit on Devi's shoulder. Despite her herself, Devi was enchanted and held out her hand so the piskie could step onto her palm.

"What's the difference?" asked my daughter politely. "I wouldn't want to make that mistake again." I was proud of her. She knew to be diplomatic when dealing with tiny little beings with swords. Wise, my child. Wise.

"Well, it's obvious!" stated Elowen, tapping her foot, which must have tickled because Devi giggled. "We have elongated wings. Fairies, disgusting creatures, have rounded wings."

Devi gave a solemn nod. "Thank you for explaining."

Elowen continued. "We nourish the land and flowers and all blooming things. Fairies only cause mischief. They have no purpose at all."

"I thought fairies protected children and aided lost travelers," I said, not nearly as diplomatic as my five-year-old daughter. "And delivered messages." My daughter elbowed me.

"Yeah, they're a regular courier service," spat Elowen. "And they're as likely to trick a traveler as help one. It is true they shelter and defend children," she admitted. "We all do. It's only the big Fae that aren't nice to kids." This last part she muttered under her breath. A good decision. You never knew when the big Fae were listening.

"Thank you for the clarification, Elowen," I said, following Devi's lead before she stepped on my foot as well. My tactful response earned a "go-girl" nod from my mini-me.

"Now," said Elowen, letting out a piercing whistle that drew Lowena to her side. "What are we to do with this hair?" She circled Devi's head. "It's a rat's nest!" She sent me an accusing look. "Don't you take care of your children?"

I stammered. "I do, but Devi doesn't like to brush her hair."

"And you let her get away with that?" demanded Lowena. "Stupid humans. Come, Devi, let's get you sorted."

"But I don't like brushing my…" She was cut off with a quick tsk-tsk from Lowena. "That's because when humans do it, they pull, and it hurts, right?" Devi nodded. "Well, when we do it, it doesn't hurt at all. Promise. We would never harm a child."

Devi's eyebrows met at the center of her forehead, but she trudged along after the two piskies and plopped on the ground, arms crossed. The piskies sang to her as they worked with their tiny little hands to undo the knots. I bit my lip waiting for the temper tantrum, but none came. The piskies whispered to Devi, and whatever they said must have been funny because Devi giggled and didn't flinch as their dainty, dexterous fingers untangled her mane.

I wondered if I could keep these ladies on retainer.

The doorbell rang as the girls' parents arrived to take them home. We'd done it! We made it through our first mock sleepover. I pumped my fist in the air.

## CHAPTER SEVEN

"No, Daniel! No! Jess! Jess!"
Nathaniel's panic made my feet move as fast as they ever had, and I arrived at the top of the stairs like a momma bear hit by lightning. Wired, aggressive, and ready for anything.

Or so I thought.

Daniel, my lovely Daniel, had slipped out of his crib again, shoved some kind of cookie in his mouth by the look of it, and...

...had opened the closet with the bow inside, which he had notched with nerf arrows, shooting Abby's mom, Lisa, and Debby's father, Josh. Those two were now making dreamy eyes at each other, and Daniel was giggling, while dribbling cookie onto the floor.

"How did you get that?" I exclaimed, reaching for him, but before I could stop him, he shot an arrow right past me and hit Dany's mom, who was standing next to Sammy's dad. He notched another and hit Sammy's dad, and then...then...he got a twofer and hit Sammy's mom and Dany's dad with one arrow.

The couples fell all over each other while Nathaniel closed the door to the basement so the girls wouldn't hear, and I ran outside to get Blaze. Blaze rushed in at my call, took one look around, and collapsed into hysterics on my family room floor.

"Thanks a lot, you rotten bird!" I said, turning my attention to Daniel, who was still holding the bow, smiling a sophisticated smile not like him at all.

"Come here and let me look at you, Daniel," I said, eyes squinted because I had a suspicion that my young son wasn't alone in his cute little body.

Daniel shuffled aside, which confirmed my concerns.

"Cupid. I know a cupid is in there. Get out of my son, right now."

The cherub cupid responded through Daniel's mouth. "I felt the call of the bow. I had to come." He giggled like the little maniac he was. These cherubs are agitating little hellions, the punks of the mythological world.

"Why are you in Daniel? I don't like you using him as a host, you little twit."

Daniel's body pulled up in offense. "Watch who you are calling names, Monster Hunter. I'm in Daniel because I have to take over a baby's body. He's still young enough. Don't worry, Daniel is sleeping soundly. I'd never hurt a child."

I'd heard that from the piskies and knew it to be true of cupids as well. Cupids were mischievous, rabble-rousing bastards, but they wouldn't injure a kid. It wasn't in their natures.

Still…

I made a grab for the cupid, but he dashed away. "Get back here, you little weasel! I want you out of my son, and you need to reverse all of this," I yelled, pointing to the couples on the floor. "These people are innocent. You're meddling with their lives!"

I chased the cupid around the dining room table, down the hall to the bedrooms, and reeled as my son's body flew over my head, cackling madly. I ran after him, quick enough to see him settle on top of a tall bookshelf, holding the bow at the ready.

"Fix this!" I demanded.

"No."

Asshole. My poor husband was trying to unwind the mixed-up couples, but they were focused on their actions, so I tried to help, pulling on Sammy's dad, who was passionately kissing Dany's mom, which made me completely ill. Instead of separating, the two love-birds jumped to their feet and ran out the open back door, ignoring the laughing phoenix on the floor.

The second couple also ran out the door, still mostly dressed, and I ran out after them, Nathaniel on my heels. I kicked Blaze on the way, and he wiped his eyes and came out to assist. I heard a yelp as one couple tried to find privacy behind a tree and ran into a gorilla. They dodged the gorilla, held hands, and dashed across the lawn only to encounter a wolf. Nothing deterred them. They rushed in another direction, and Blaze had to intervene.

We'd cornered the loving pair who gave up on privacy and necked right there in the middle of a circle made of an emu-sized bird, a wolf, and a gorilla. You had to admire their perseverance.

I sprinted back in the house to corral the cupid and persuade him to reshoot them with arrows and reverse the spell. I got three steps into the house when Buddha shouted in my mind.

*Danger! Danger! Danger!*

I skittered to a sharp stop. "Where?"

*Nearby, not here yet.*

"What kind? Who's coming?"

*Vampire.*

Holy crap on a cracker. Pascal was attacking now? Now? I had to think and prioritize. I needed all my troops. I opened the door to the downstairs. "Piskies! Assemble!"

Lowena and Elowen arrived first. "What's going on?" they asked.

I explained as best as possible.

"We need our General," Lowena said.

I snapped my fingers. "Cupid! My family is in danger. I'm releasing a piskie from a jar. You must hit her with an arrow to undo her love for my husband. We don't have time to argue."

Cupid hung in the air, pouting. "Why should I? I'm having fun."

"Because if you don't, I'm calling your mother, and she'll spank you so darn fast, you'll be scorch mark on the road to Olympus. *Capiche?*"

I had no idea if Venus would answer my call since I didn't worship the Greek pantheon, but it was a good bluff. The cupid turned slightly green and stammered, "Ah. Okay. Okay. No need to go with the rough stuff."

I grabbed Gothskie off the plant shelf and took a good look at her. The piskie was plastered against the jar, waving a fist at me. "I need your help, Gothskie, and Cupid here is going to undo this nasty spell so you don't make a play for my husband again, you tiny little jezebel." I unscrewed the cap, Gothskie shot out, and Cupid's arrow hit her straight in the chest.

The piskie shook herself, a whole-body shake, like a dog coming out of a lake, pointed at me, and said, "This stays between us, Gigantor."

I crossed my heart.

"Situation," Gothskie demanded.

I gave a quick rundown and was relieved when she didn't blink at the word vampire.

"Troops!" she yelled. "Elowen, my liege, can you please lull the girls to sleep downstairs?" I breathed a sigh of relief. *Good idea, Gothskie.*

After that, General Gothskie issued orders faster than I could comprehend them, but I did ask that a few piskies be sent outside the protective circle to reconnoiter.

"Done," snapped Gothskie. "What do you think I am, an amateur? Our queen follows my orders in battle because I've earned it. Now, get out of my way." The piskie pushed me aside with one itsy sweep of her arm, and I decided to let her be. Not that I could have stopped her, but that also would remain between us.

Nathaniel rushed back into the house, out of breath, hair wild, and he had scratches on his face and arms. He put his hands on his knees to catch his breath. "Let's review the situation, Jess."

I squirmed knowing this wasn't going to be easy. I ticked off the summary statements on my fingers.

"Our son has a cupid in his body. The cupid has willfully and deliberately created mixed up lovers out of our guests' parents. We have a gorilla, a wolf, and a phoenix in our yard, corralling one set of said lovers. The other set is nowhere to be seen. We have a divorced woman and widowed man in our living room doing God-Knows-What, but I don't feel as bad about that one. It's probably good for them. They need to blow off steam."

I took a deep breath. "Buddha says danger is coming in the form of a vampire, so I've enlisted the piskies to patrol the perimeter and scout our surroundings. The piskies did the girls' hair and lulled the girls' to sleep so they don't witness any of this."

Nathaniel nodded along with my analysis and asked the most important question. "Did the piskies do Devi's hair, too?"

"They did! Isn't that amazing?"

"Incredible. Maybe we can get them to come before school?"

"I mean to ask them when this is over."

"Good. Oh, one other detail, David is asleep. I think the romance exhausted him."

"So, that only leaves us with one possessed child," I said.

"That's about it."

"We can deal."

Nathaniel and I high-fived each other and waded out into the morass of our lives.

## CHAPTER EIGHT

I hadn't told Nathaniel about the photo of my mother with Pascal, not because I was holding anything back, but because the new developments distracted me. I knew I needed to tell him, but he was in the backyard spraying cold water onto the mom with the wrong dad.

A yell turned my attention to the right where the second pair of unsuitable lovers ran out from behind a tree screaming, "Gorilla! Gorilla!" Rocko pounded out after them, Shura nipping at their heels, Blaze sauntering along enjoying the show.

"Can't you stop them?" I asked, miffed at my bird-brain friend for not taking this more seriously.

*No, we can't. We've tried. We need to let the spell run its course.*

"Or, you could go inside and get that damn cupid to reverse the spell and get the hell out of my kid." I didn't think push-ups would be required for the swearing in this particular case.

*I'll see what I can do*, Blaze said, pivoting on his huge Tweety-bird feet. He stopped short and turned his grapefruit-sized eyes to me, suddenly serious. *Anything from the border patrol?*

"Not yet. I'm going to weapon up. You deal with the cupid."

*Roger dodger.* I kept many weapons in my garage and elsewhere throughout the house. There was always something within reach, but this time, I wanted my favorites. I hooked up my baseball bat for an overhead draw, shoved my grill lighter in my pocket, a smallish jar of blessed Manischewitz wine in my other pocket, and holstered a magical tomahawk to my right hip. It was an ancient tool I'd procured during the recent museum trip, and no matter how or where I threw it, it would come back to me. Handy.

I'd recently practiced with another weapon, and I coiled it now, connecting it to my belt with a carabiner. I'd rigged the carabiner so that I could pull the coil out with one tug. Not recommended for rock climbing, but perfect when one wants to whip the hell out of someone with a wooden-handled jump rope.

---

The jump rope was Ovid's idea. Ovid Sitler, originally named Adolf Sitler until he changed it for the Roman poet, was my trainer, and had a bit of precognition to him, so when he brought out a new weapon, or pushed me hard in my training, I paid attention. Once he'd put me through my paces, insisting I pretend to have a broken leg. Another time, he insisted I learn to fight without my vision. Those exercises both proved to be prophetic, so when he pulled out a boxing jump rope, I simply tied on my shoes and got to practicing. I could jump fairly well, crisscrossing in front of my body, doing double jumps, you name it. I'd boxed for a long time.

So you can imagine my surprise when he grabbed it out of my hands and told me I was using it wrong.

I'd arrived at the gym that day frazzled, as always, because I'd had to deal with my nemesis, Regina, the senior employee at the facility's day care. I always dropped Daniel off so I could train, but facing down Regina gave me the hives.

That morning, the conversation had gone as well as could be expected, which is to say, not well at all.

"Mrs. Friedman. Have you given any thought to placing Daniel in a full-time nursery school where he will receive the discipline he requires? I left a list of such entities in his cubby." Regina wore a long skirt, sensible shoes, and long-sleeved top in taupe.

"Yes, I saw that Regina. Thank you, and no, I haven't given it much thought. I have to go now. I'm sure we can talk about this another time."

Regina clucked her tongue at me, and my heart sped up and my palms perspired. "Mrs. Friedman, as you know, Daniel's imagination is superlative, but he needs structure to understand what is fancy and what is fact. Three-year-olds are capable of telling the difference, and he is quite intelligent, even if his language skills are behind. It is important that we get him to understand fibbing is not allowed."

"I'm aware of your opinion, Regina." I turned to go, but she placed a hand on my arm. She was lucky I didn't break that hand. My natural instinct was to grab it, twist it at the wrist, and give it a hard thrust upward, breaking it at the large knuckles. I was proud of myself for holding back.

I did notice that her nails were filed to perfect ovals and she wore clear nail polish.

"Mrs. Friedman." I hated how she always used my name as a statement dripping with derision. I bit my cheek and nodded for her to continue.

"Mrs. Friedman, Daniel grabbed a plastic gorilla from the animal bin the other day and named him Rocko."

"So?"

"He said his mommy, meaning you, Mrs. Friedman, had a gorilla as a friend."

Sweat trickled down my back. "Rocko is the name of the gorilla at the zoo."

"He also claimed that a shadow stole a boy out of his bedroom."

I hesitated. This was true, actually. A black-elf had stolen a boy, Joseph, out of his bedroom. I decided silence was the better source of valor and simply raised an eyebrow.

"Mrs. Friedman."

I almost lost it right there.

"Mrs. Friedman. What I'm trying to communicate to you is that Daniel is mixed up, confused, and doesn't understand reality, or, if he does, is an incorrigible liar. There. Now, I've said it plain." She rushed the last part out in a stream of words but held her head high and her shoulders stiff as if she were taking a principled stand in the face of great evil.

Suddenly, I stopped being nervous and was pissed off. I used her last name.

"Mrs. Flint. My child is three years old with a wonderful imagination. He is not confused, nor is he a liar, and I resent the way you speak about him. You, obviously, are unable to deal with a creative mind such as Daniel's."

Regina Flint lifted her nose. "I only want what's best for the child."

"You're a judgmental old prune." I called to the younger babysitter. "Faith, will you look after Daniel, please?" I gave Regina a stare. "Only Faith."

"Sure, Mrs. Friedman. Come here, Daniel. Let's play with dolls." Daniel toddled over, picked up a female doll, and used the doll to punch a stuffed *Where the Wild Things Are* Gruffalo in the face. "Mommy kills you!" he yelled, making the female doll strike the monster around the head and shoulders. He followed up with a hearty, "Die, motherfucker!" and immediately dropped to his tummy, which I realized was him doing push-ups. Even Faith looked alarmed. Regina looked on in horror.

I fled.

When I'd arrived at the gym, I was already covered in flop sweat and wishing I could go back to bed. Ovid handed me the jump rope, and I got my rhythm on until he took it from my hands and whipped me hard with it, the wooden handle smacking into the back of my thighs.

"Hey! What the hell?" I ran from the wild man while he swung the jump rope around his head and lashed out at me, cracking the handle into my shoulder.

"Run, Jess! Don't sit there! Run and disarm me!" Ovid was in full fighting mood and put on the speed. I raced ahead, fetched a baseball from a bin near the supply closet, and chucked it at him. I hit him smack on his right hand, and he dropped the rope. Softball had been my game, and I had awesome aim.

"Son of a bitch!" he yelled, holding his injured hand with the other. I cleared my throat, gave him a thumbs up, and waltzed into the trainer's office, grabbing an ice pack for him.

"A jump rope is not the greatest offensive weapon," I said. He shook his head.

"I disagree. The wooden handle is quite painful when it hits you, and it makes a garrote if you use it right. I want you to practice with it."

I acquiesced and spent the next thirty minutes figuring out how to use the jump rope as a type of bullwhip without the loud snapping sound. It worked better at close range to simply beat on someone, but as Ovid said, it was a handy garrote if you had the upper body strength and some leverage.

A flurry of piskies surrounded my head, chattering over top one another until Lowena let out a sharp whistle any referee would envy.

"What has your team learned?" I asked Lowena.

"Enemies on the hill," Lowena replied. "Coming in fast."

"Who are they?"

"Vampires, but that's all our scouts could tell."

"Well, isn't that precious."

Lowena screwed up her tiny face. "No, it's not precious at all. Vampires are dangerous."

"How many of them?"

"Two that we could see, but there was a shadow in the woods that tracked their path. It smelled bad."

"Can't you provide any details? Be more specific? Anything else you can tell me?"

"There are also two demonettes."

I stopped cold. "Demonettes?"

"Little female imps, red, with horns. They held hands and skipped along. They looked happy."

I was impatient. "Lowena, is there anything else you need to tell me? Where's Gothskie?

"Who?"

"The General?"

"Oh, she stayed outside of the border."

"Why on earth did she do that?"

Lowena shrugged. "That's her way."

"Would you please go see what you can do to help Rocko and Shura?"

"Sure!"

I wasn't too worried about the vampires, bad-smelling thing, or demonettes getting into the house because we had the magical barrier up, and if they meant us harm, which was a safe assumption, they wouldn't be able to get through. I did a thorough sweep of the insides of the house, making sure windows and doors were locked, kids asleep, and Buddha on alert. I checked that my Last Will and Testament was where I'd placed it, in our locked safe, and stepped outdoors. Whatever was going to happen would happen outside.

I stopped to pray a moment, not asking for success or victory, but praying for strength to protect my family, the other children, and the innocents who had gotten in the way. Whatever caused this bounty to be on my head, it was none of their doing, and they shouldn't have to pay for it.

I was surprisingly calm now that a fight was on the way. I hoped this I'd meet the originator of the bounty, not another flunky, because I was sick of this and wanted it over. Despite the chaos usually surrounding me, current conditions as a prime example, I was a Monster Hunter, and I meant to kill some monsters this night.

The *thunk* on the roof of the house next to us caught my attention, and I peered into the darkness to see what was up there, hoping they didn't wake the neighbors. Gothskie flew past me yelling, "Incoming!" and before I knew it, I was hit by a red cannonball. The red cannonball sprung to her feet and shook her little fingers at me. I stared open-mouthed and got sideswiped by another red cannonball, who also jumped to her feet and wiped her hands on her cheerleader skirt.

"Who the hell are you?" I asked, looking down. They were about three-feet tall and looked familiar. They looked like Tic and Tac, imps, minor demons, who I had met in a flurry of activity in a department store while I was trying to find a crystal ball and battle mannequin zombies. It was a long day, but didn't I remember Tic and Tac mentioning something about sisters?

"You're Tic and Tac's sisters, aren't you, which means you are also Zric's sisters. How many of you are there?"

"One hundred and fifty-three," replied Demonette Number One, jumping up in the air to land in a perfect split on the ground, she too wearing a cheerleader skirt.

"But we are closest in age to Tic and Tac." Demonette Number Two twirled in a perfect pirouette.

I inhaled a deep breath and exhaled long and slow. "Why…why…why are you here?" I asked.

"Oh, said Demonette Number One. "We're here to cheer for the home team." From out of nowhere, both demonettes produced pom-poms in each hand.

*"You can do it, yes you can.*
*You can kill the Monster Man.*
*We believe you'll carry through,*
*And chop and chip her into two!*

*Yay!"*

"That's the dumbest cheer I have ever heard. I'm not a man, and I'm not a monster. I'm a monster hunter, and I'm a woman."

"Yeah, but we had trouble with the rhyme. We'll work on another one and see if we can do better. You deserve a good cheer for your death. Maybe something in iambic pentameter." The two demonettes ran off, shaking their pom-poms in the air.

I yelled after them. "You've got it backward! This is my home field. The bad guys are the visiting team."

Gothskie was pinching the bridge of her nose.

"Are all of your enemies this entertaining?" she asked.

"No," I replied. "But those two aren't important. What's important is understanding how they catapulted in here, and who exactly is on the visiting team?"

That's when a black elf, one of the ugliest I had ever seen, charged me from my neighbor's yard, throwing her full body into it, running for the end zone in a championship game. Until she splattered on an invisible wall and slid down like a Rocky and Bullwinkle cartoon.

I couldn't help it. I laughed. Black elves are awful things, this one smaller than the last but equally smelly. Her tail lay limp on the ground, and one of her sharp teeth lay on the grass in a pool of her green, sizzling blood.

"Blaze!" I yelled, and the bird galloped up from wherever he'd been. I heard crashing along the perimeter of the house and another yell of, "Gorillas! They're everywhere! This place is infested with them."

"Blaze, can you get me that gallon of bleach I brought home the other day?"

Blaze studied the downed black elf and then gave me a salute. "Right-o."

I couldn't go outside of the spell wall because I'd be vulnerable, and I suspected that would bring the wall down.

"General!"

Gothskie stood at attention.

"Do you think, if all the piskies worked together, that you could hold something heavy?"

"Of course, human. We move boulders."

Blaze returned with the bleach.

"I'd like you to pour this all over the big, bad black elf out there. It will put a crimp in her style. If you can call the rest of the chorus…"

Gothskie hoisted the gallon bottle of bleach in one hand and flew through the spell wall. She twisted the cap with the other hand, dropped the cap on the grass, and tilted the bottle, aiming for the black elf's head.

That's when a clawed hand rose and snatched her out of the air, the bottle of bleach plunging to the ground, spilling harmlessly on the lawn.

## CHAPTER NINE

The black elf cracked her neck, rolled her shoulders, and stood, holding Gothskie in her hand so that I could just see Gothskie's head. Gothskie struggled against the black elf's grip, but it was useless. Even a mighty mite like Gothskie couldn't wrestle out of the grasp of an enemy as large as the elf.

"Let her go," I said, dead calm, dead quiet.

"No," rasped the injured elf, sounding convincingly scary. Her tooth was gone, just gone, and the bruising made her look like a boxer after a welter weight title match.

"You killed my sister." There, she said it plainly, laid it on the table. I killed one of hers and now she wanted to kill me and take out a few allies in the meantime. It was obviously sibling night.

"I killed an elf that stole a child out of his bed in the middle of the night."

The black elf seemed perplexed, using her other clawed hand to scratch at her chin as she asked, "Why? What's wrong with that?"

I shook my head in disbelief. "Are you kidding me, Darth Elf on the Shelf? You think snatching kids out of their homes at night is acceptable?"

The big, ugly shoulders shrugged. "I don't know. I know a lot of my kind do that kind of thing. Is it wrong?"

"It's not okay. Where are your parents?"

"They aren't around much. It was my sister and me, surviving in dark elf land together, which is why I'm going to kill the mosquito here and then you."

Darth Elf held Gothskie high in the air, dangling her by one leg, and opened her giant maw. Gothskie struggled against her grip. My heart leaped into my throat. This tiny creature shouldn't suffer for what I had done.

I reached out one hand, crying, "No!"

Darth Elf stopped, still holding Gothskie like a gummy worm she'd wanted to swallow whole.

"Stop. Let her go, and I'll come out."

"No. I'll hold her here until you come out, then I'll eat her anyway and kill you."

"I don't think you get how this works. Why would I come out there if I knew you are going to kill her anyway?"

Once again, Darth Elf used a claw to scratch her chin. Not the sharpest knife in the drawer, this one, or maybe she was simply young.

She nodded. "Oh, I see. That makes sense. You come out only if I let her go?"

I ground my teeth. "Yes, that's called negotiation."

Darth Elf shrugged again. "I skipped that class, hated school. We were always bullied."

"Oh, I'm sorry to hear that."

Still holding Gothskie by the leg, Darth Elf said, "It was a difficult time for us, me and my sister. Demons are hell."

"You went to school with demons?"

"Exchange program. My parents thought it would be good for us."

"That sounds hard." I couldn't believe I felt sorry for this monster.

"It was. It was my sister who kept me sane." Her eyes popped open wide, as if she just remembered why she was there. "That's why I'm going to kill the insect and then you!"

"You've already forgotten what we talked about. If you kill her, I'm not coming out there."

"Oh, right. Negotiation. Got it. Okay, you come out, and I'll let her go."

"Now you've gotten the idea. Good work!"

"I did get it, didn't I? See, that was the thing in school, I always doubted myself. My teachers said I needed to work harder."

"I'm sure you worked as hard as you could," I responded, noticing a cloud of sparkling dots approaching from behind. "You seem very smart."

"You have no idea how much that means to me, to hear you say that," gibbered the elf. "No one encouraged me." She leaned in close. "I can't even read."

"That's not fair. All children learn in their own ways. They should have accommodated you."

Darth Elf wiped away a green tear. "The only person who understood was my sister."

A stone dropped to the pit of my stomach. I had had no choice but to kill that other elf, but I sorta felt guilty now.

"Tell you what, if you want to come by some evening, I'll teach you to read, English, not Demon."

"Really? You would? That would help a lot with road signs. I'm constantly getting lost." It was interesting how Darth Elf didn't seem so evil when she was smiling, even though the pointy, serrated extra rows of teeth were a little off-putting.

"You'll have to swear not to hurt me or my friends."

"Yes, no problem. You can teach me at night? Are you sure? Humans tend to sleep as soon as the sun goes down."

I thought about it for a minute. "Yes, I can, but I may have another person that can help." I considered my idea silently, musing over it in my mind. It might work. I tossed the idea into the "think about this later" bin and paid attention to the situation at hand.

The black elf, who I now realized was no more than an adolescent, hopped up and down, shifting from foot to foot in excitement. "That's super-dooper! Totally rad! Completely awesome!"

At that precise moment, the buzzing miasma of sparkly piskies arrived, swords drawn, vibrating with anger. Before I could stop them, they surrounded Darth Elf's head, ready to prick, slice, and dice. One piskie had her sword to the elf's neck.

"Stop!" commanded Gothskie. "Hey, elf, could you let me go, please?"

"Oh, yeah, sorry." Darth Elf released Gothskie, who flew in front of the elf's face. "If you swear not to harm me or mine, blood oath, we'll teach you about gardening. It's quite relaxing. It might release some of your tension."

The other piskies stopped buzzing their wings and floated in the air, not understanding what Gothskie was saying.

"I'd like that," said Darth Elf. "But I can't garden during the day. I have sensitive skin."

"Don't worry. Plants need attention at night, too."

Darth Elf clapped her hands. "That's amazing! Cool! Thanks, piskies! Thanks, Mrs. Friedman. Can I come back tomorrow night?"

"Sure, Darth. Look both ways before you cross the street."

"Will do! See ya!" The dark elf bounded across the street, not looking both ways, with a spring in her step.

We all stood stock still, each in our own way trying to absorb what had happened.

I was wrapping my head around it when I was thrown to the ground by a gorilla.

## CHAPTER TEN

I hit the ground with an "oomph."

"Rocko! What are you…?"

Peals of laughter hit my ears, and the pressure on my body increased as one mixed-up couple danced over Rocko's body, using his bulk as a launching pad for a complicated lift and twirl that would have won the mirror ball trophy. I watched this upside down from my prone position under Rocko's body. Rocko, luckily, was supporting himself on his elbows or I would have been squashed to death.

Nathaniel leaped over us like a running back on a mission, holding a nerf arrow in his hand like a track baton, trying to hit them with the arrow without using the bow. I tried to tell him that wouldn't work, but he was gone before I could get a word out.

I poked Rocko to indicate he should get off me, and he complied. While sitting up, I got a good look at him, which caused me to clap a hand to my mouth.

"Lowena? Elowen?" I ventured.

Rocko was decked out in bows from head to toe, with multi-colored ribbons woven into his fur in an intricate pattern. Rocko pranced in a little cat-walk shimmy to show off his new look. Truly, his fur never looked so luxurious.

"You look magnificent," I said, whacking my gorilla friend on the shoulder. "Unbelievable."

Rocko grunted in agreement and pounded his chest. "Yes," I nodded. "Quite manly."

Then I hit the ground, again. Not voluntarily, again.

The suffocating weight of another person on me was a shock, so it took me a moment to react. Reacting mostly consisted of screaming for help since my arms and legs were pinned. Rocko grabbed at the figure on top of me and hauled the creature to its feet. I rolled to a stand, tomahawk out and ready.

Shura appeared, silent as a shadow, poised behind my attacker and let out a warning growl. I was glad to see her but wisely did not comment on the garland adorning her head or the streamers flowing from her tail. Those piskies had done a heck of a job.

My assailant was a woman, about five feet tall, with shorn hair and old-fashioned, lace-up boots.

Wearing a nun's habit.

Screaming obscenities in French.

She was also a vampire.

And butt ugly.

She attacked again, scraping at me with fingernails sharpened to points. I splashed my little Tupperware of Manischewitz at her and caught her arm. The habit's fabric protected her from the holy wine's worst effects, but she hissed all the same. I threw my 'hawk straight at her, and my aim was true, but Shura dove in at the same time and knocked Frenchie down. My 'hawk flew harmlessly by, burying itself in a tree, but it didn't matter because Shura had the French nun vampire pinned to the ground.

Which is when Rocko realized what was going on and roared a challenge, startling Shura, as well as everyone within hearing distance. Shura lost her balance, and the nun used the moment to scramble to her feet, snap something at me in French, and back way, disappearing in the darkness.

"Who the hell is she? Where'd she go?" I exclaimed, hands on my hips. This was ridiculous.

Nathaniel circled up on us again, out of breath and beaten. "I'm done," he said. "They can do whatever they want. I can't undo this. We need that jerk cupid to pull his weight."

"Do you know anything about a French vampire nun?" I asked him, letting his statement float on by. Fornicating couples were the last of my worries.

"Actually, I do."

We all—piskies, gorilla, wolf and I—rotated to stare at my husband.

Nathaniel plopped to the ground. "I told you. I did some research into Pascal and his past. There's this mysterious blip in his history where he visits his sister, Jacqueline, in her monastery. Supposedly, right after this, he had a religious epiphany. While he continued to go out in public, he did so only at night, and society folks got sick of him spouting nonsense about Hell and demons, so he eventually retreated, claiming he wanted privacy."

Nathaniel stood and dusted off his pants. "I believe his sister was a vampire who turned him. They had been remarkably close in life, and he was disappointed when she became a nun. My guess is she brought him over to her side of the street, and he had trouble dealing with it."

"Very astute of you." The voice came from above us, high at the top of a tree in our neighbor's yard.

Pascal balanced on a large oak branch. His face wasn't sloughing off anymore, but it still looked like a candle put to flame. One side of his mouth drooped, and the skin under his eye was a red slash that hurt me to look at. He looked like a stroke victim who'd been caught in a fire after being bitten by a paralyzing spider. At least, that's how it appeared to me. I've never seen that exact combination of calamities in real life, thank goodness.

"That monster is your sister?" I demanded. "She means me great ill. Would you like to tell me why?"

"And how did she get in here?" asked Nathaniel. I tapped my nose in agreement. Good question.

Pascal sat on the branch, swinging his legs back and forth.

"She's a bit angry with you."

"Why? I've never done anything to her. Not that I won't now," I added, a faint growl in my voice. I was tired, and my patience was thin.

"You are the recipient of downstream fury," Pascal said. "She was originally upset with your mother. Since your mother is gone, she's directed that anger at you."

"Whatever for?"

"It's a long story, granddaughter."

"Why do you call me that? I'm no relation to you."

"I beg to differ..."

"Pascal, no more vague statements and nebulous warnings. I need to know the truth."

"It's a little hard to explain, but it has to do with your mother…"

Pascal's voice cut off as a giant black bat attacked him, wings spread, talons outstretched. There was a muffled, "Jacqueline!" and then the siblings crashed to the ground. Jacqueline let out a high-pitched scream that caused Shura to whine in pain. The two vampires grappled on the ground like wrestlers in the lightweight division.

Pascal was slow to react, perhaps because he was surprised she was there, or because she was his maker. It was difficult to analyze the situation because all I could see was a hazy, amorphous mass of swirling darkness.

"Jacqueline! You must stop," Pascal cried out. "This isn't achieving anything."

"You belong to me, brother, and it is time you remembered it. You have no allegiance to that whore."

"Don't call my granddaughter a whore!"

"She's not your family. I am!"

The two separated enough that I could make out their individual bodies, and we witnessed Jacqueline's full display of power. Physically, she'd gotten the upper hand, being the master vampire, and now held Pascal by the neck like a kitten.

She stared into his eyes and muttered to him, her voice hard to hear, but it reeked of ghastly things, violence and pain. My gut tore when he lost control. The Pascal who had been about to explain what was going on, who sounded almost reasonable, sunk deep within as his maker whispered words of hate.

"Piskies! Retreat!" I yelled at the top of my lungs. I needed those tiny warriors inside the barrier, and I needed to figure out how Jacqueline got inside to begin with. The piskies flew inside, an entire chorus of flittering, spitting-mad dragonflies screaming insults to the vampires on the neighbor's lawn in a variety of languages. Jacqueline continued to whisper in Pascal's ear, and his face went from animated and angry to slack. His eyes glazed over, and with every new word, Jacqueline let go of Pascal's neck a little more, relaxing her physical grip as her mental one took control.

Jacqueline sunk deeper and deeper into Pascal's psyche, until he became a puppet to her will, worshiping her with his eyes and nodding at her every instruction. My gorge rose in my throat.

"As hard as this is to believe, I want the old Pascal back," I said, as my troupe of allies watched Pascal fall. "This is obscene."

Gothskie had worked up a head of steam about it herself, literally as her head gave off a boiling hot vapor as she witnessed the mind control sink in. "I loathe vampires," she said. "But mind control is the ultimate crime, even beyond murder, because you kill someone's spirit while you keep their body alive. I have to believe there is some small part of Pascal who knows this is happening and is screaming inside."

"I agree, but let's not wait here for her next move." I tore myself from appalling scene. "We've got some planning to do. Gothskie, can you do that whistle thing? It's time for some battle plans."

Gothskie's piercing whistle drew everyone to the center of my yard. The exhausted but fulfilled lovers lay in each other's arms, magicked to sleep by the bow. Blaze emerged from the house with Cupid, still in my son's body, but the phoenix's beak was pursed in a way that let me know he was nonplussed.

Blaze tapped his Tweety-bird feet and said, pointing a wing at the cherub, "He won't help. He's an obnoxious tyrant in a child's body who doesn't care who he hurts."

"I'm not hurting anybody," said an affronted cupid, zipping around our heads. "I'm a giver of loooooovvvvvveee."

"You're a pervert," Blaze retorted.

"That too," Cupid acknowledged. "But my lack of morals doesn't seem to be what is creating this pow-wow." He fell silent and pulled up his wings, running fingers through his curly, blond locks. Daniel had good hair to begin with and the cupid had thickened it. Vanity.

"Who. Are. They?" he asked, making a kissy-pout with his lips. He zoomed down to waist height, and I turned to see who he was talking about.

The demonettes came at the whistle, shaking their booties and their pom-poms. They had changed into red sequined dance tops with black sparkly cheerleader skirts, and the tops showed a lot of cleavage. I didn't know women that short and busty could balance like that.

I rolled my eyes. "Demonettes, meet Cupid. Cupid, the demonettes. They're here to cheer on my death." The demonettes did back flips, landed on their feet, then bent to one knee, jiggling their…pom-poms…. Cupid stared, slack jawed.

"Well, helllloooo ladies," he said.

I had to get serious. "Troops! Demonettes excepted, I suppose. We have a new problem." I examined my army.

A chorus of piskies.

A gorilla, dolled up with ribbons and bows.

A wolf, equally bedazzled.

An emu that occasionally set himself on fire.

My exhausted husband.

And…a cherubic cupid about to make a very stupid mistake because of cleavage. Well, he wouldn't be the first guy.

That's when it hit me that he was still in my son's body. I sent him a warning glance, but Nathaniel was done and plucked the flying baby by the diaper and placed him into the house, closing the door and locking it. Cupid pressed his nose to the glass like a lonely dog.

I knew he heard me through the glass. "Get out of my son's body, and we'll talk."

"I have no other place to go." He shed a tear, and I guffawed.

"Then, too bad. My three-year-old isn't getting it on with two bodacious bosomed female imps. Period."

The cherub made a face that was all him and not a bit Daniel. "After some time with me, they won't get their periods."

I pointed at him with fire and brimstone in my eyes. "I'm going to forget you said that, you disgusting, debauched young godling. Do whatever you want, but not on my son's time." I yelled to the sky. "Venus! Get your child under control!"

I thought I saw a flash of lightning, but I couldn't be sure.

"Folks, Pascal, a deranged vampire, and his sister Jacqueline, an even more deranged vampire, if you can believe that, are here. Somehow Jacqueline got inside the perimeter."

Rocko poked me on the shoulder and pointed up.

"I don't understand. Blaze, can you interpret?"

Blaze stared in Rocko's eyes. "He's trying to say that the witch protected around the property, but not the sky. She didn't create a dome, so Jaqueline didn't cross a border. She flew high enough to avoid the border and dropped in vertically, like a helicopter."

"Kill the witch," muttered Nathaniel.

"Burn her, burn her," chorused the piskies.

I gave them a grim smile. Taking care of that witch was number one on my bucket list. First, however, I'd have to live, and so would my friends and family.

The demonettes pivoted so their backs faced us and twerked like Beyoncé. They cheered, "When we say Vampires! You say Go! Ready…? Vampires!"

Rocko pointed and uttered a sound that I knew meant "Go!"

I smacked him on the arm. "No, Rocko. No." The gorilla's face fell. "I mean, good following directions, but the vampires are the bad guys." Rocko furrowed his brow and nodded.

I pointed to the naked bodies on the ground, deep asleep. "Blaze, can you and Rocko move these poor people into the house? They could get hurt out here." Blaze gave me a salute.

"Piskies, set up a perimeter. Nathaniel, call Officer Bob and ask if they have a cannon. Shura, with me."

It was to Nathaniel's credit that he simply pulled out his cell phone

## CHAPTER ELEVEN

I remembered two things about my mom that, to me, personified who she was. She was a miracle worker with knives or blades of any kind, which I didn't know wasn't normal. I had a friend whose mother's sister married her father's brother, and the kids shared grandparents on both sides. When I expressed amazement, she stared at me in complete confusion. It had never occurred to her that siblings marrying siblings was unusual. That's how my mom's ability with sharp, pointy things was for me. It wasn't weird. It was just my mom.

The second thing was her sense of humor. No matter what, she taught me to laugh at most situations and find the fun in everything. I remembered one afternoon in particular.

We were baking, something my mother and I liked to do together. It was almost Purim, a holiday in which it is traditional to eat cookies shaped like triangles, which represented a hat worn by the main bad guy in the biblical tale of Esther.

The Hamentashen, as the cookies are called, didn't hold together. We'd followed the directions to the letter, but our triangles separated at the corners, and we had flat circles with burnt jam on our cookie sheets. Worse, the jam had also dripped onto the bottom of our oven and the sugary stuff was smoking.

Which made the fire alarms go off, shrill and loud.

Which scared the neighbors.

Who called the fire department.

Who arrived with three trucks, two ambulances, and the fire chief himself.

All because of burnt cookies.

I was mortified, a teenager certain her social life was over, and I was convinced they were going to yell at us. I hid in the house, waiting to be expelled from school, arrested, ostracized, and humiliated. It was all coming, there was no doubt. My friends on the block peeked out the windows, and I knew my life was over. We were going to have to move. I was already ticking off states far away and cities where we had no friends. Houston, I decided. Or, maybe, San Antonio. I didn't think we knew anyone in Texas.

The firefighters arrived with bells clanging, and I cringed even more. The fire chief's red car had a swirling red and white light on the top in case the other sirens weren't enough to cause attention.

Then Channel 5 showed up, and the local paper. I prayed the floor would swallow me up whole.

My mom, on the other hand, greeted the firefighters and worried neighbors with big smiles, held out the cookie sheets and asked if anyone wanted the burnt bits. She answered questions for the newsies, and the paper photographer took a photo of my mother beaming with the firefighters. The television station quoted her as she thanked them for the fast response. "In this case, it wasn't an emergency," she'd said, "but if it had been one, these amazing men and women were here in seconds. I am proud of our town's heroes, and I sincerely thank them for their service."

The fire chief picked up a blackened cookie, took a bite, and said, "My wife did the same thing once. We scraped them into a tin and ate them with milk."

An ambulance driver joined in. "I did it with almonds that I drizzled with oil. They didn't merely smoke; they actually caught on fire! Imagine how embarrassed I was when my co-workers showed up!" She, too, took a crusty bit from the cookie sheet and munched it.

A neighbor snuck a hand in and swiped a fairly unburnt cookie. "I discovered the hard way that eggplant can make a real mess. Smoke everywhere. I had to leave the windows open for three days."

One of the firefighters went into our house, disconnected and reset the fire alarms, and came out to scrape some cookie crumbs together for himself. My mom brought out some drinks, water, pop, that kind of thing, and we all sat on and around the stoop eating burnt cookies and swapping baking disaster tales. Eventually, the firefighters had to go, shook my mom's hand, saying they were glad everyone was okay, and took off. My mom slipped the good vodka out to the porch, and the block party continued.

I observed all of this from my bedroom window, stunned by what I'd witnessed. It was then that I learned that bad things happen, but how you deal with the situation is as important as the situation itself. You could greet people with honesty and a smile, or you could hide your head, ashamed of every little mistake.

It was a lesson I took with me for the rest of my life.

So, here I was, facing a true showdown of massive proportions, and that was the lesson that came to me. I didn't know how we'd gotten to such a state, but it didn't matter. What mattered is how I dealt with the situation.

"Shura, we need a plan."

Shura didn't bother to respond.

"Let's go drag out the wine box."

Shura gave me a sideways glance.

"Not the boxed wine. I'm not drinking. The wine box I ordered so that I had Manischewitz in bulk. I have ten bottles, all blessed by Rabbi Stein."

Shura helped me open the box with her claws and teeth. I poured two of them into a bucket and removed my 'hawk, jump rope, and bat. I dipped all of them into the wine, being careful to only dip the wooden handles of the rope and reassembled myself. Shura snorted in satisfaction.

"Yeah, bet they're not expecting that."

Shura shot a look at the door to the basement and licked her chops.

"Hungry? Me, too. Let's not fight on an empty stomach."

We tip-toed into the house, taking care not to wake the sleeping children, and I grabbed the cookie jar, some deli meat, a couple of apples, and a jug of filtered water. A few paper cups and Shura and I moved outside.

My friends gathered around, calm as can be, and had a snack. Shura loved the deli meat, and Blaze tried a cookie. His gargantuan eyes opened even wider in surprise when he discovered the buttery taste of a good homemade snickerdoodle. Rocko ate two apples, and the piskies shared the third.

The quiet before the storm, and as I looked at our ragtag band, I realized I loved this family I'd cobbled together and vowed I'd do anything to protect them.

High-pitched alarms rang out from every corner of the yard, and we all moved fast, splitting off in different directions to respond to the piskie guard calls.

My vision dimmed, and I looked up to see a solid blot in the sky blocking all moonlight as it plummeted down like a pillar of darkness into the yard.

I whipped my jump rope at the encroaching inky splotch in the sky and managed a hit against one of the vampire's legs, as evidenced by the whiff of smoke. It didn't do any real damage though because both vampires were covered in head-to-toe in black, flexible armor. They landed on the ground feet first and lashed out with claws extended.

Pascal rushed me, his destroyed face mostly hidden, but I could still see a string of saliva drooling down his chin.

I chopped at him with my tomahawk, and every hit landed, but the effect was minimal. Pascal advanced, pushing me back, while the piskies and Shura harried Jaqueline.

"Pascal! What has she done to you?" I hacked and hacked, but he still advanced. I ducked as he swung a clawed hand over my head and struck at his knees, only to hear a clang as my 'hawk met metal. The blow reverberated up my arm, and it went numb from the shoulder down. My 'hawk dropped to the ground as my hand lost its grip, useless.

I'd seen Pascal, bite, claw, swing, and punch. I'd seen him disappear and move like smoke. I've seen him lift things ten times his weight and shove Nathaniel aside with one arm like he was swatting a gnat.

What I'd never, ever seen was Pascal pulling a sword.

It was an Epée, a fencing sword, thin and flexible, with a bell at the bottom to guard his hand. Pascal placed one arm behind his back as he prepared for an assault, lunged, and brought the sword in for a touch at my chest.

He didn't have the power to go through my chest, but the point went through my thin shirt and drew blood. It was a message, a warning, and one I took seriously. I jerked inside and to the left, to be on the outside of his blade, and swung a back fist directly at his nose. I hit it dead center and even the vampire had to shake his head to clear the blood from his face.

He struck again with the sword, this time snapping it in a blur across my face, slashing my face with a blade so sharp it took a split second for my brain to realize I'd been cut. He slashed it again, and I lurched to the side in time. The air hissed as the blade missed my face by millimeters.

I dropped and whisked my leg in a sweep, catching him at the ankle, and though he stumbled a bit, he didn't fall. I lay on my back and reversed my sweep, lifting my leg higher to take him out at the knees. It worked, and he tumbled, but his quick reflexes got him back up and moving. I sprung from my back to my feet, pulled my bat, and swung. I went for his head and neck, and it was a good swing, but he moved faster than I'd seen him move before and was around me, fangs to my neck, in a blur of motion.

Rocko and Blaze rushed to help me, but with Pascal at my throat, they held off, not wanting to risk any sudden movements.

"Pascal," I whispered. "What is happening?"

"My sister turned me when I visited her at the monastery, bringing me to the night and the torture of blood thirst. She deprived me of my friends, the rest of our family, but most of all, she deprived me of my work. My mind, once a vault of ideas that could see the world's geometry, its natural beauty, and yearned to explain it, was blank. I questioned my faith and begged God not to abandon me, but what else could explain my new cravings for human blood? I was being tested, and failing. I was a monster, and yet..." He twisted my neck to look me in the eye.

"I loved your mother," he hissed. "My sister, my master, was ashamed of me and my feelings."

"Did my mom love you?"

"No. No. I tried to convince her that my feelings were real, but of course, I didn't stand a chance."

"Please step away from me, Pascal. We can talk about this."

"No. Jacqueline wants you to die, and she's made me see the truth. I'm a devil, an enemy, and you shall die by my hand, even if you do share my blood."

I cried, trying to control my tears and my breath, but I couldn't help it from becoming ragged and raw. I hoped I didn't make things worse, but I had to know.

"How do I share your blood?"

Pascal drew back a tiny bit, enough that I didn't feel his breath on my flesh. "Your mother was injured. She'd battled something, I never found out what, and she was bleeding out. My life would have been so boring without her. She made me feel alive. She made me feel something, after decades of ennui. Even when she hunted me, hated me, at least she was there, a part of my life."

"And?"

"I fed her my blood. It wasn't her choice. I forced it down her throat, making her swallow. I didn't turn her, but it healed her. I'd hoped that she'd understand my gift." The last dripped with regret, tinged with real anger.

"I'm guessing she didn't."

"No. She was furious, but my blood coursed through her veins anyway, and thus through yours. It's why you're fast. It's why you're strong. You have a touch of me within you, and it gives you an edge."

Tears streamed down my face as I realized what he was saying.

The time I caught that softball that no one should have been able to catch.

The time I balanced on the thinnest wire, running across like a gecko on a pond, noticing my feet were steady, even though it should have been impossible.

The time I heard a ghost, something beyond human abilities.

Memories flooded through me. My coach saying my base steal was unbelievable. Ovid staring at me open-mouthed when I flipped a knife over my shoulder and hit the target dead center.

These abilities weren't the result of training at all. I cheated, unknowingly, but true nevertheless, and now I had to question everything I was and everything I'd done. Was I truly a heavenly soldier on Earth? Or one of the bad guys who ate her own?

Screams of pain echoed across the yard, piercing my psyche. Blaze gasped as something hit him hard. A piskie dropped to the ground like a stone, and my blood curdled as the demonettes cheered the visiting team on, shouting encouragement. Shura bled from a wound in her side, and Rocko took a talon to his face, red blood spraying into the air.

We were getting our asses kicked. Jacqueline was too strong.

My friends were fighting my fights and dying for it.

It was all my fault.

I was a fraud. A fake. A phony. My pride had done this.

My mind cracked in two when Nathaniel, husband, the father of my children, dropped to the ground. I cried out, screaming his name. Blaze pulled Nathaniel away from the fight, and I fell to my knees, engulfed by doubt, my mind and body paralyzed. I was at the most vulnerable I'd ever been.

"Pascal, if I die, will your sister let my friends and family alone?" I whispered this so no one could hear.

"She only wants your head, my dear Jess."

"Then take it." My voice rang out across the battlefield. "Take my head and leave everyone else alone."

## CHAPTER TWELVE

My allies stared in horror, not sure what to do or how to help. Blaze lowered his head, made a keening noise I had never heard, and readied to throw his body across mine. I knew he was betting his bronze feathers could stop the coming blow. His feet pawed the earth like a bull ready to charge.

He pulled up fast as a hand pulled me to my feet and tossed me out of the way, and a familiar voice said, "Get away from her, you son-of-a-bitch." I flew in an arc, landing hard on my side as my college friend took center stage.

I hadn't seen Liam since Blaze and I left him at his apartment, at his urging, as he struggled to keep his inner vampiric instincts in check. He'd twitched with the effort, literally holding the back of his couch to keep from attacking us as bloodlust overwhelmed his humanity. This was a side effect the constant starvation Pascal made him endure, even though we'd fed him pints and pints of blood. He held on by the skin of teeth as Blaze and I ran for our lives. I hadn't heard from him since.

Liam dove at Pascal, a whir of movement so fast that it defied explanation. Pascal leapt out of the way, but Liam was quick and had anticipated Pascal's move. Again, and again, the two vampires, creator and created, swiped at each other, Liam even punching Pascal full-on in the face and his already broken, bleeding nose.

It didn't matter. They were evenly matched. A part of my brain told me to get in there, help Liam. But a new voice said, *No, you're tainted. You can't help.*

Blaze shot forward and enveloped me in his wing, nudging me back, away from the dueling vampires. I held on, almost unable to stand on my own. Rocko hooted at me, a gentle reminder that he was there, a friend, someone else who knew what it was like to change who you are, deep inside. He petted my face and combed his fingers through my hair, a gorilla grooming motion meant to soothe me.

Pascal and Liam flew up into the trees, something I hadn't known Liam could do. I realized I'd spent so much time worrying about Liam, feeling responsible for what happened, that I'd ignored who he had become. I'd spent too much time wishing he could go back to who he was.

That wasn't possible for either of us.

Nathaniel came out the back door with an ice pack to his head, stopping short when he saw the pitched battle going on and me sitting helplessly on the stairs.

"Jess! Jess! What is going on? What's wrong? Are you hurt?" Nathaniel patted my body to find wounds. He ran inside to fetch some disinfectant and wiped at the cuts on my face.

"Anything else? Anything serious?"

"No."

"Why are you sitting here?"

"I'm no help to them."

"What the hell are you talking about?"

I told him what Pascal had told me. He dropped to the step next to me.

"You're part vampire?"

I nodded.

He was silent too.

*Ahem.* The Buddha looked at me from the window. The battle receded from my mind, the sound muffled and far away.

*Buddha?*

*Close enough. Partly.*

The voice was Buddha's, but it was more. It was a voice within a voice within a voice. It was a deep resonant tone and a high lilt. It was male. It was female. It rang in my head with the power of a thousand cymbals, a roaring ocean, an exploding volcano. It was as gentle as a mother's hand and sweet as the slip of silk. It caught me unaware, but it was familiar. It was all of these things and none of them. I spoke to the voice.

"Here I am."

Nathaniel, confused, looked around, his head swiveling to find out to whom I spoke.

*You are the sum of your actions.*

"I contain evil."

*You are the product of your intent.*

"I'm not who I thought I was."

*Your fate is always your own.*

The voice withdrew, and I was empty, deflated. Alone.

Until Nathaniel took my hand.

My blessings streamed back to me. My loving husband. My children. My ability to help others. My sense of humor. The love of my mother and my father. Ovid's devotion. Rocko, Blaze, and Shura. The piskies who even now fought for us.

Liam's friendship and how he labored to be a force for good even as a vampire. Darth Elf, born of a race I thought incapable of good, who only wanted to learn to read and was lonely, struggling to find her place in the world.

My allies, who were right now fighting for their lives without me. The 'hawk was in my hand at that thought. I leaned over and kissed Nathaniel's worried face.

"I'm going in."

"About damn time. Kick some ass."

## CHAPTER THIRTEEN

I strode forward, held up a hand, and commanded, "Stop!" I was shocked when everyone did, but I didn't question it, just rolled along.

"General Gothskie?"

"Ma'am?"

"Gather the wounded. Shura, Rocko, Blaze, back away."

They did as I bade them, every one of them hobbling, bleeding, and bruised.

Jacqueline didn't look like she'd done anything more than drink a cup of tea.

"Bitch! You and your mother stole my brother from me. You made him weak."

"We did nothing of the kind."

"You ruined him."

"I'm thinking we might have saved him."

She hissed. "I'm going to kill you like I killed your mother."

I wasn't even surprised. It all clicked into place. Didn't mean I wasn't mighty pissed off, though.

I threw Blaze, Shura, and Rocko a look, flicking my eyes to the garage. They trotted off, knowing what I needed.

"You caused my mother's car crash?"

Jacqueline sneered, showing me her fangs. "Of course, stupid child.

My brother had given her his blood, and that ungrateful wretch spurned him. It was enough that he loved her, but to then throw that love back in his face? She was an arrogant piece of crap, and you take after her."

I went to work with my bat in one hand and my tomahawk in the other.

*Slash! Slash!*

I dodged an attack to my right by juking to my left. I dodged the follow-up attack by rolling to my right. I sunk into the fight, not thinking, not planning, and moving only on instinct.

The demonettes, cheering from the sideline, started something new.

"Jacqueline has the spirit! So, let's hear it! Goooooooooo, Jacqueline!"

My enemy disappeared, flickering in and out of existence like a star, one minute there, one minute gone. I spun in circles, trying to find her. I'd seen her brother disappear before, and I'd never figured out if he was really gone, or just invisible. Wait. Vampires couldn't be invisible. They just seemed that way because they moved fast. Gotcha, bitch.

I holstered the bat, withdrawing the jump rope, moving as swiftly as possible. I turned in a reverse circle, using the jump rope as a whip, snapping it at every angle. I could hear something move as I swiveled, one step ahead of me at every snap.

I whirled faster, reversing direction again, changing my velocity and range, moving a couple of steps in and a few steps back. I took the rope high and low. I oscillated the rope like a live wire, pulling on the vampiric speed I knew I had to pirouette and gyrate the rope at the same time.

Eventually, I hit pay dirt, and the most beautiful screech hit my ears. Breath caressed my face and I leapt back, snapping the rope once again, gaining another yelp. Forgetting about what I could see and concentrating on only what I could hear, smell, and feel, I harried her with the wine-soaked jump rope, wearing her out, frustrating her, hoping she'd make a mistake.

She did. She lost control of her speed and fluttered into my line of sight several yards to my right. I noticed her from the corner of my eye and chucked the tomahawk right at her.

My 'hawk caught a ridge in her armor at the elbow, and the blade buried itself deep within her arm. Her intake of breath told me it hit true, and after a split second, her blood flowed in long, thick drops, staining the grass. She jerked back, but the tomahawk stayed with her, and as I observed, it wiggled itself in deeper, working its way through the joint. She screamed and screamed, tearing at the tomahawk, but it had her and wasn't letting go. I stared in horror and fascination as the blade worked its way through, until her forearm fell to the earth, amputated at the elbow. The tomahawk fell to the earth, too, but I knew it would be back in my hands as soon as I needed it.

Jacqueline stared at her left arm and let out a roar of defiance. "Pascal! I need you! Hear me and obey, my brother!"

"He's having trouble hearing you, Auntie." Liam's voice came closer as he walked from the back of the yard, up the small incline to where we stood. He dragged Pascal's body behind him, and I thought Pascal was dead at first, but the twitching in his legs told me he was still alive.

His face was a mess, and Liam looked worse for wear as well. Pascal's ears were mostly torn off, and I was certain Liam had a broken cheekbone. The two of them had really gone at it, fighting tooth and nail, and it appeared that Liam had come out on top, barely.

I hated Pascal. I hated him for what he'd done to my mother, for what he'd done to Liam, and all the people he'd killed and sucked dry.

I felt a little sorry for him as well. He was a vampire who felt something he called love. Who was I to judge whether what he'd felt for my mother was love as I knew it, or as one would love a possession, or how one worshipped an unattainable goal? He was a vampire who'd felt something passionately. I was certain that was not an easy road to travel.

Pascal crawled to his sister, who looked at him with contempt, but helped him to his feet.

"Pascal." I called to him.

He looked at me through swollen, tired eyes.

"You still have choice."

"I have nothing."

"Not true. Don't listen to her. She made you a vampire, but she can't change who you are inside. You've done wrong, but you have eternity to make up for it."

Pascal shook his head.

A stab of disappointment lanced my body. In the end, like all of us, Pascal was the sum of his deeds, the product of his intent, and his fate was his own. Liam must have come to the same conclusion because he charged Pascal, fangs outstretched, grasped his maker by the throat, and bit down with enough force to break Pascal's neck. Still connected, it lolled to the side with an audible crack. He didn't die, but a vertebra or two weren't in the best of shape.

Pascal scratched at the air, his wide eyes begging his sister to help him.

Liam had Pascal locked in an embrace poisoned by hate, anger, and months and months of resentment. Pascal had almost convinced Liam that he had no path to follow but one of degradation, and now Liam delivered payback. Jacqueline could no more rescue her brother than step into the mid-day sun. Liam had surpassed his master.

After sucking Pascal down, Liam dropped him to the ground, where Pascal lay limp, but not dead. I was proud of my friend for stopping short of killing Pascal. It was yet another choice that informed his future and his fate, and it was a good one.

We are a sum of our actions, the product of our intent, and our fate is our own.

Liam swayed on his feet, and I was surprised to see him so spent after having consumed Pascal's blood. It should have strengthened him, but however much energy he'd used to fight Pascal was barely replaced by his maker's blood. It made me realize how little Liam must have been eating and how vulnerable he was when he'd attacked Pascal. It was a wonder he had won.

Jacqueline stared at her brother's form, shocked. The demonettes quieted.

Big sister screeched in fury and leaped toward Liam, who tottered back to avoid the new onslaught. He swung a clawed hand in her direction but didn't find purchase, and he stumbled. She stalked him, one foot, then the other, as he scrambled backward.

I jumped on her from the rear, yanking her away from my friend, but I was unbalanced and fell on my butt, my arms around her in a wrestling hold. We grappled on the ground, me thrashing around trying to flip her on her back. She was too strong, however, and more trained than I thought. She placed precise pressure on the joints in my wrist, an Aikido move that I recognized but couldn't counter. I released her, and she overturned, grabbing at my torso to keep me down. My baseball bat pushed into my spine, and while holding Jacqueline off with my right hand, I tore the bat from my holster and shoved it in her mouth, pushing her from me with as much strength as I could muster. Blaze scooted in and pulled my jump rope, throwing it to Rocko, who wrapped it around Jacqueline's neck and pulled.

The vampire did not need to breathe, but she could feel pain, and having your trachea crushed makes it hard to concentrate. She lunged in reverse, head-butting the gorilla, who lost his grip and fell, letting out a roar of pure silverback rage. He leapt in the air and caught one of her legs.

Blaze caught the other, and I grabbed her remaining arm. We strained with all our might, holding her aloft by three limbs, stretching her as if she were on a rack.

She gasped in pain but wouldn't give up, using what was left of her strength, which was still considerable, to fight us.

"I thought I'd get rid of you easily, Monster Hunter. But, no one could kill you, not the black elf and not the clown."

"It's hard to get good help these days," I grunted, still pulling with all my weight, but it wasn't enough, and I slipped. She got her one foot on the ground, executed a roll, hard to do in mid-air, and wrenched herself free. The force of her movement caused the three of us to fall on our rumps. It was hard to get back up, and I was so spent that I saw stars. I could tell the others felt the same.

The demonettes, on the other hand, had energy to spare. They did straddle jumps and urged Jacqueline on. "Fight! Fight! Go on, Jackie! Give it to them!"

Suddenly, a flying baby zoomed over our heads and shot both imps with nerf arrows. "Shut up! Zeus, you are annoying. And to think I was attracted to you."

The demonettes' eyes glazed over, and they blinked, blinked, and blinked again. When they cleared, both pairs of eyes settled on Rocko.

"Run! Rocko, run!" Rocko took one look at the demonettes, now cooing at the "big, handsome gorilla," and raced off like a shot. The demonettes chased after him, shaking their stuff—all of it—promising a "hell of a good time," because "once you've been with an imp, you'll never go limp."

Even Jacqueline gave a shudder at that, and I think she was secretly glad they were gone after they'd called her "Jackie."

There wasn't a soul on the battlefield that wasn't injured, including me, bleeding from talon scrapes and battered all over. We couldn't stop, though, because this had to end now. I readied my bat, flipped my palm, and said, "Bring it."

She charged, head first, like a bull.

I swung, high and tight, aiming for the change-up, knowing she'd be sneaky about her approach. It was done. It was all but done. I could feel it.

I whirled around, off kilter, carried by my own momentum as my bat swished air. I couldn't figure out what had happened. I was sure my aim was true. I stumbled and caught myself, a bronze wing stabilizing me.

Jacqueline was covered head-to-toe in Manischewitz wine. The piskies had snuck up behind her and sloshed the entire bucket on her, which they'd retrieved from the garage, and with her bleeding stump and the cracks in her armor, the wine sunk in.

"I'm melting! I'm melting!" she screamed, ripping off her armor, revealing her skin, which drippled like candle wax down her face and body.

"It was the same with the clown," whispered Nathaniel, who'd snuck up behind me and wrapped me in his arms. I choked back a tired laugh, remember the evil clown from the birthday party.

The French vampire nun liquefied a drop at a time. She used her remaining hand to catch her nose as it sloughed off, her cheeks sliding down her neck in molten rivers of tissue.

It was easily one of the grossest things I'd ever witnessed, and Gothskie, who'd come to sit on my shoulder, covered her eyes.

Suddenly, Pascal scrambled up, his neck still askew but healed enough that he could stand, grabbed his sister's arm, and leapt for the sky, using the last dregs of his strength to fly his sister to safety. I lunged for him but missed. "No! No! They're getting away! Blaze!"

Before Blaze could take off, two voices ordered, "Incoming! Get down!" We all dropped, even Cupid, as a fireball split the sky, enveloped the airborne vampires, and seared the night with a dazzling flash of white. There was no time for the vampires to course correct, and they sizzled like firecrackers.

A blinding light exploded above us with a crack of sound that reverberated, pummeling our ears. I actually bent over and threw up, such was the force of the sound wave. Nathaniel had done the same. The thunderous sound dissipated on a wave, up and down, fading slowly, and as our vision returned, the evening was suddenly silent.

Something hit my eyelashes, and I blinked, as ash fluttered from the sky and landed on our faces. The distinct smell of charcoal tinged the air. That's all that was left of the two vampires.

I turned my head, and there was a grinning Officer Bob and Captain Morgan, the two of them working together to hold a rocket launcher, both with headphones on to muffle the sonic boom. Bob gave me a wink and removed his headphones.

"When Nathaniel called asking if we had a cannon, I contacted the captain." I squinted at him and pointed to my ears.

Captain Morgan placed his end of the rocket launcher on the ground and helped Officer Bob do the same. They walked closer to me, so I had a chance of hearing. Morgan smacked his hands together in satisfaction.

"Always wanted to use one of those," he said. I read his lips.

"How?" I asked, hoping I wasn't yelling. I couldn't hear myself. I motioned for him to hold on. I shook my head, pinched my nose and blew. All of a sudden, my hearing popped back. It was like a bridge had given way and the sound crashed in.

The others followed my example.

"I can hear you now, Captain." My voice was weak and my throat sore.

Morgan smiled, and his eyes sparkled. "Called in a favor from the National Guard. We don't have a cannon, but I thought this might do."

"It did great, Captain. It was exactly what we needed, and in the nick of time. Thank you. I'm shocked they let you have it."

"They said they owed us for handling the were-gorilla alone. Most of the Guard heard about the whole zoo debacle on TV and guessed that there was more to the story. I got a lot of free beer that night."

I gave them both big hugs, which I had to release as a silverback gorilla tore through the yard, two red naked imps chasing after him, screeching like teens at a boy band concert. "Come on, Rocko! We want to monkey around!"

I stomped my foot. "He's an ape! Not a monkey!"

Officer Bob cocked his head, one hand on his chin. "Female imps?"

I nodded. "Zric's sisters."

"Don't see that every day."

"True fact."

"Why are they chasing Rocko?"

I gestured to the cherub, whose back was to us, thankfully, so Officer Bob couldn't see that it was a cherub in a Daniel exterior. All he could see were the wings. "Cupid got sick of them and hit them with nerf arrows. Rocko was the first creature they saw."

He considered that for a moment. "Why is Rocko wearing ribbons?"

"The piskies did it to say they were sorry for attacking him with their tiny swords."

"Interesting. His fur has never looked so luxurious."

"That's what I said!" We fist-bumped.

Captain Morgan studied us with deep concern. "Well, Mrs. Friedman, if you could do us the favor of returning Rocko to the zoo, that would be appreciated."

I pointed at the wolf and said, "Shura will get him back." Shura lifted her snout and gave a tired howl of agreement.

"Most excellent. We'll take our leave now. Is it fair, Mrs. Friedman, to suppose that with the death of both vampires, everything will go back to normal?"

I looked him right in the eye. "Of course, Captain. I expect things to go back to normal."

"Good." He patted me on the shoulder, and he and Officer Bob hoisted the rocket launcher, heading back to a monster truck they'd used to transport it. They covered the weapon with a blue tarp so they wouldn't cause panic on the road.

Officer Bob mouthed to me as we left, "Whatever normal means."

I tapped my nose and pointed at him.

There was only one hanging chad, and that was what to do about the imps. I called out to Rocko to run our way. The poor gorilla was beat after running all that time and loped in on all fours, beads and bows astray, looking as bedraggled as a kitten in the rain. The imps still chased after him, but they also looked a little worse for wear.

I tossed one end of my jump rope to Blaze, and we held it low on the ground so Rocko ran right over it. We lifted it to knee height and caught the imps around the neck. We lowered it a tiny bit, not wanting to choke the living daylights out of them, and wrapped them up. I held both ends in my hands and couldn't help myself.

"You will tell me the truth," I said, tossing my imaginary black mane of hair.

*Sorry, you look nothing like Wonder Woman.*

"Not nice, Blaze! I can dream, can't I?"

*Oh, certainly. Dream. Fantasize. Visualize the impossible.*

"Ouch. Well, you look nothing like Fawkes in Harry Potter, either."

Blaze waved his wing back and forth. *Tiny bird, tiny...*

"Wings? Feet?"

Blaze winked at me.

"Ick."

The demonettes were quiet, no cheering, or jumping, or pom-poms. They leaned against each other, back-to-back, holding one another up, they were so tired. Still naked, still bountiful, still red all over, but exhausted as well.

"Will you two go back to Hell and leave us alone?"

"Yes," they intoned.

"Excellent." I unwrapped the rope. "Cupid, will you please?"

Cupid didn't even look. He shot two arrows over his shoulder, each with suction cup tips. I have no idea where they came from, and I'm *not* going to mention where they landed.

Blaze grunted. *Priceless shot.*

I clapped my hand to my forehead, Shura's tongue lolled out, and Nathaniel smothered a laugh. Rocko collapsed to the ground and curled up in the grass.

The demonettes each pulled an arrow off their chests with an audible *pop* and sighed.

"Let's go," said one to the other, and they turned to walk into the woods to go back however they came. Their receding backs sagged in failure. But, before hitting the trees, one of them whirled around, a gleam in her eye. "We'll be back."

The other whirled too. "Soon, you'll see."

Demonette Number One added, "You'll remember your life belongs to me."

"To us," said Number Two.

"To us," said Number One, who then used a finger to draw a circle of burning flame in the air, and they both hopped through.

## CHAPTER FOURTEEN

Gothskie organized a triage and attended the injured. She knelt by one particular piskie and let out a cry. The piskies gathered around, their wings drooping, tears the size of grapes falling to the kitchen table.

"What happened?" I asked, fearing the worst.

Gothskie choked out one sentence. "Our leader has fallen. Elowen is dead."

"I'm...I'm...so sorry." Guilt washed through me.

Gothskie shook her head. "It is not your fault."

I couldn't speak, I was so choked up.

"If it is okay with you, we'd like to bury her with your irises."

"I'd be honored." Nathaniel nodded as well, his face wan, tired, and sad. "She lived her life with purpose. She fell as a warrior."

We made a processional to the front yard, including piskies that had to be hand-carried due to injuries. Elowen was laid to rest in the middle of my iris bed, and it was then that I learned why a group of piskies was called a chorus.

Their voices rose through the early morning light as dawn was approaching. It was a sound unlike any I had ever heard, a heavenly sound, a song of love and loss, of respect, and sadness. It was haunting, and beautiful, and I'd never forget it.

Afterward, the piskies informed me that they would be back in the future to tend to the iris beds, but now, they wanted to go home.

Lowena and Gothskie hovered in front of me, and I inclined my head to them both, and then to the whole group. "Thank you, my friends. You are small but fierce fighters with big hearts. We would have lost this night without you."

They acknowledged my statement and departed, some supporting the casualties, others silently weeping, all sad beyond reason. There was a heaviness in our hearts and we ached for them, and no one knew what to do next.

Nathaniel got us moving, focusing on the most important thing.

"Cupid, shoot those people now, and get the hell out of my son's body."

Cupid nodded, his wings drooping after the funeral. "Death and love go together, sometimes," he commented. "But I prefer life." I gave his hand a squeeze, and we all went inside.

I was so glad the Parent Teacher Association photographer wasn't there, or anyone with a camera, in fact. The six adults lay in a naked puppy pile in the middle of our living room, a mess of tangled arms, legs, and other body parts that shall go nameless. I will say that Dany's mother was a very lucky lady under normal circumstances.

"Do we know where their clothes are?" I asked.

Blaze hopped up, rounded the couch, and kicked out a pile of clothes with his giant Tweety feet.

"Let's get them dressed before Cupid wakes them," I said, so we all grabbed limbs and clothes, trying to match sizes in a way that worked. Dressing magically sleeping grown-ups isn't easy. It's like dressing a five-foot tall or six-foot tall rag doll. Floppy in all the wrong places, and I do mean, floppy.

I dressed Josh, Debby's father, the widower who had spent his night making nookie with Abby's mom, Lisa, the divorcée. I shoved his underwear under the couch, because really, I wasn't dealing with that, and pulled on a pair of jeans, making Nathaniel do the button-fly. I got a shirt on him, found two socks, they didn't match, but I couldn't care, and heaved him onto the long couch.

Next, I dressed Lisa, grabbing a bra that looked appropriately sized, shrugged when it was too small, and shimmied her ample bottom into a pair of sweats that I thought had to be hers. The underwear that I thought went with them was shredded, so I pushed them under the couch as well.

Eventually, all concerned were wearing clothes and positioned in comfortably distant positions throughout the room. I pointed at Cupid, and he notched his bow.

The first one flew, then the second, and he continued firing in rapid succession until all the parents woke, stretching and yawing.

"What happened?" asked Lisa, looking down at her décolletage, more bountiful than usual because I'd given her the wrong bra.

"Everyone! What a great time we had last night, didn't we?" I announced, clapping my hands. "Coffee? Orange juice? Vodka martini, Josh?" I winked at the baffled man.

"I...I...don't usually drink," he stammered.

I gave him a clap on the back. "You wouldn't have known it from last night." I jolted to the kitchen. "Be right back with that coffee."

By the time I made it back, Sammy's mom was awake, wiggling her butt as she realized she wasn't wearing any panties. "What happened to my..." She trailed off, not wanting to say it aloud. "I could have sworn I wore..." She gave up.

Dany's dad, who'd done the tango with her all night, extended his arms way above his head. "I feel so relaxed," he commented. "Nathaniel, what did you give us last night?"

Nathaniel stammered something unintelligible, exhaling with relief when Dany's dad said, "Never mind. Whatever it was, it was good stuff." He rolled onto the floor, snoring.

Sammy's dad stared at Dany's mom with a strange look on his face, his eyes scrunched together. Dany's mom rolled her shoulders like she had a kink in her neck to avoid looking at him, confused and disoriented. She ventured to her feet, looked at her chest, and did a little jump of surprise, quickly turning to fix her blouse.

Rocko wasn't so great with buttons. I should have double-checked.

Sammy's dad pushed himself out of the rocking chair and held out his hand to his wife. "Dear, how about we get some of that coffee Jess is offering." Still patting at her butt, mystified by the missing underwear, she gave a short little jerk of her chin and took his hand. I offered both coffee and pointed to the creamer and sugar.

Lisa accepted a cup, motioned for another, added a teaspoon of sugar, no creamer, and handed it to Josh, who sipped it without a thought. "Perfect. Just the way I like it. Thanks, hon." They froze for a moment, both wondering how that had happened, but before they asked questions, the pitter-patter of many feet bounded up the stairs.

Five girls, hair askew with ribbons and bows hanging from every end, tumbled up the stairs and blew through the door.

"Wow! We had a real sleep-over!" said Dany, running to give her mom a hug. "Thanks for letting us stay all night."

"No problem, sweetheart. Glad you had a good time." Dany's mom did an excellent job of covering her confusion with the situation, and I could see the other parents buying in.

Sammy's dad hoisted his happy daughter into his lap. "You seem well-rested. I'm shocked you girls got so much sleep."

"I feel great!" Sammy announced, and then scrunched her nose at her dad. "You smell funny. That's not Mommy's perfume."

"Girls! Breakfast!" Nathaniel to the rescue. Meanwhile, I flicked my eyes around to see where everyone else was. Cupid sat on top of the tallest bookshelf, and since no one looked up, they missed him. Blaze had left the house and reassumed his pony disguise. Shura curled up in a sunbeam, appearing for all the world like a dog taking a snooze, as long as you didn't notice her teeth.

Rocko hid behind the tall, skinny floor lamp, eyes squeezed shut, shoulders hunched up around his neck, legs pressed together. His ribbons and bows were still hanging from him in drips and drabs. I tugged at my earlobe, mentally selecting and discarding reasons for having a bedazzled gorilla in my living room.

"What an interesting gorilla lamp!" commented Dany's dad, who'd woken up and was laying on the carpet. "You really shouldn't have let the artist put bows in the gorilla's fur. It is totally unrealistic."

Dany's mom, completely recovered, added, "I don't know. There is something wonderfully reductive about it. I think it is a clever commentary on modern society's conquest of the primitive world."

Lisa also chimed in. "I see it as an observation of the essential, undeveloped primeval universe in which we still live, despite all our advances, and how we struggle to move through it, hiding our basic selves under fripperies."

Josh studied his shoes.

Dany's dad climbed to his feet. "Now, as I study it, I'm amazed by the detail on the fur, and the face. Fascinatingly derivative."

I had no idea what any of that meant, so I said what every mom says in such a situation. "Let's get something to eat! Bagels and cream cheese in the kitchen."

"Lox?" asked Josh hopefully.

"Nova, my friend. The good stuff," I replied. We all piled into the kitchen where the girls were already eating Cheetos.

"Cheetos?" I murmured to Nathaniel.

"If Cheetos are good enough for kindergarten snack, they're good enough for sleepover breakfast. Don't judge me. I'm tired."

I hugged him, equally as fatigued. "I think Cheetos are wonderful for sleepover breakfast," I said, watching Josh slip a Cheeto into his mouth. "They have all the food groups." I counted on my fingers. "Preservatives, orange dye number five, salt, and powdered cheese food."

"The best," Nathaniel replied, popping one into his mouth.

Cupid snuck up behind me and pulled on my sleeve. He pointed to the door, and I followed him out to the back and sat in a chair on the deck. Cupid sat on my lap, and I petted his wings.

"What now, Cupid?" I asked.

"I need to go. I hate to leave because it's so much fun here, but…" He cringed.

"What?"

"Oh, Zeus, she's using all three of my names. Gotta jet."

Daniel's body collapsed onto mine, and I cuddled my peaceful, sleeping child to my chest.

"Who's calling you?" I yelled to the air.

"My mom," came Cupid's voice from the distance. "I'll likely be doing chores for the millennia."

Couldn't say I disagreed with Venus's disciplinary policy, and you had to wonder what a cupid's middle name was, or his last name for that matter. I put that in the back of my mind for another day.

Daniel rubbed his eyes and smiled up at me. He pointed to his mouth.

"Hungry, kiddo? I know just the thing. Let's go inside."

He placed his tiny hand in mind, and we entered through the sliding glass door. Daniel saw his daddy, shuffled over in excitement, but before he allowed himself to be lifted into Nathaniel's arms, he drew back his right arm, holding out his left, and shot a pretend arrow at his father.

"Gotcha, Daddy!" he crowed.

"You sure did," his father agreed. I ignored the look Nathaniel sent me. I was certain there were no aftereffects to Cupid possession. Positive. One hundred percent.

My tomahawk returned to my shelf, of its own accord, and when I approached it, it honestly felt like it was snoring. I left it alone. It had done well. I mentally thanked the warrior who had made it.

Buddha reacted to that with a little satisfied hum. I held him in my hands, eye level.

"Buddha. Did I? Did I talk to God?"

*One aspect. An angel. Your mind could endure the voice of divinity itself.*

"Which angel?"

Buddha's jade arms moved to his hips, his eyes laughing, his belly bouncing. *Does that matter? Are you really going to question the identity of a messenger of the Most Holy?*

"Uh. No." I bit my lip. "Absolutely not."

*Put me back in the window, please. I need to meditate.*

"Okay. Here you go." I settled him in, and as his jade body resumed its natural serenity and stillness, I thought how I needed to do the same. I could use some yoga, a nap, time to reconnect with my soul and find my center, and I would do those things.

Right after I called that witch.

## CHAPTER FIFTEEN

"You wanted a dome? You should have specified a dome." The witch smacked her lips as she snarfed down a raspberry cheese pastry she'd snagged off my table without invitation.

"Wasn't it obvious that I wanted protection on all sides? You couldn't figure that out on your own?'

Lila shrugged. "You should have stated dome creation as part of the contract. I'm completely in the clear here."

"My family and friends almost died because of you."

The witch twirled her fingers around. "La dee dah. Like I care. Besides, a dome costs a lot more."

"What's a lot more?"

She looked back and forth, then leaned over and whispered in my ear. I blanched.

"You're kidding."

She brushed crumbs off her skirt, dusting her hands with swift back-and-forth motions. "I never kid when it comes to price. Next time, you'll know, and you'll have time to get the components together."

"You're really creepy, you know that?"

She brightened. "Really? Thanks! I can't wait to share that with the girls."

"What girls?"

"My squad. My posse."

"Who are you, Taylor Swift?"

"My coven, you moron."

"We have enough witches in town to have a coven?"

Lila sneered at me. "It's shocking you're still alive, you're so stupid. We have three covens in greater Cleveland, Monster Hunter. You really are an idiot, aren't you?"

"Well, I'm idiot enough to know that if there are three covens, there are other witches I can ask to do my protection spells, and I'm sure they'd do it for less."

Lila considered this. She rocked back and forth, lips tight, hand to her chin. "I may be willing to negotiate." She spit this out with the most grudging of tones.

"That's what I thought."

"Bitch." Lila threw out that last word, but I knew I'd won. That made me cheerful, and I hummed, "It's a bitch girl, and it's gone too far..." as she walked away, loud enough for her to hear.

Nathaniel overheard me and added, "...say money, but it won't get you too far, get you too far."

Then, "Why are were quoting 1977 Hall and Oates?"

"Seemed to fit the occasion."

I wandered off to see the piskies, who were diving in and out of my iris beds, with a side group trimming my roses.

"Gothskie, how are things?"

"We're glad to be back. Good morning!" The General wiped dirt from her brow, and I peered at her. Underneath the dark lipstick and eyeliner, she was smiling.

I eyed her with suspicion. "Why are you happy?"

"I like playing with dirt." Her natural scowl fell back into place. "This better?"

"Much."

Lowena flew to my shoulder. "Your irises are way too close together, so we are separating the bulbs, except for where Elowen rests. We've planted something special there."

"What is it?"

She smiled, and there was something about that smile that bothered me. Maybe it was the pointy teeth on such a delicate figure. "You'll see," she said.

That sounded a bit foreboding, but it was a plant, so how bad could that be?

"Hey, I want to hire one of you, whoever is best with hair."

"We're all good with hair."

"Do you think one of you could come over before school each day and brush and style Devi's hair?"

Before Lowena could answer, my daughter's head popped up from behind the deck, where she'd been helping the piskies trim the plants.

"Oh, no. Not having my hair done every day. Don't even think about it, Mom."

"When the piskies do it, it doesn't hurt."

"Hurts my pride, Mom. Hurts my pride." She fell to her knees to keep trimming.

Lowena shrugged at me. "Can't do without consent."

"She's five! I'm her mother."

"Sorry. Five is an adult in piskie years. If she changes her mind, we'll work something out." Lowena flew off to join the rest of the piskies.

"Lowena!" I called after her. She turned, foot tapping the air.

"What?"

"Where are the male piskies?"

The hum of piskie wings stopped, and the air was eerily quiet. Every piskie face turned to me, glaring.

I gulped. "Did I say something wrong?"

Lowena's face was a bright red. "How rude!"

The piskies abandoned their tasks, dropped whatever they were holding, and without a single word, paraded off, backs stiff. My gardeners left, and I wasn't sure why.

"I wanted to know…I mean, where do baby piskies come from?"

Lowena zoomed back to me, so angry her wings buzzed louder than ever before. "We will come back because we don't like to leave a job undone. But do not make the mistake of ever asking that again."

"I'm sorry. I didn't mean to offend."

Barely mollified, she turned her back. "Let everyone cool off, and we'll see you soon. When I talk to them about this, I will account for the fact that you are a human, and thus, too dense to understand. We sometimes forget how unsophisticated you are."

That was the second time in one day I'd been called stupid. I was getting kinda tired of it.

That evening, I sat on the back porch, relaxing, happy to have lived through the last twenty-four hours, when a *swish, swish* came from the trees bordering my neighbor to my right. It was on the edge of my hearing, so I concentrated, listing again.

*Swish, swish, scrape.*

I didn't have any weapons with me, and Nathaniel, Liam, and the children were inside watching a movie, lights off, so it was full dark. I stood, an inch at a time so I wouldn't make noise, took two steps to the back glass door. I slid it open an inch, inserted a hand, and held up a finger to Nathaniel in warning. He leapt to his feet as I removed my hand and locked the door after me, pulling the curtains closed. I closed my hand on a sharp shard of kindling that remained on the deck from the winter, but that was all I had. My muscles tensed, and I breathed in and out to calm my beating heart so could hear clearly.

A footstep. Two. I raised my arm, intending to stab with the strip of wood. It wouldn't kill most things, but it might slow it down.

A heavy breath, followed by a nervous clearing of the throat.

"Mrs. Friedman?"

"Darth?"

The black elf moved closer, and I could just see her shadow against the black of the night. It's what black elves did best, hide in the shadows. Darth stared downward and moved the grass around with her toe.

"I was wondering if that invitation was still open?"

"To teach you to read?"

"Yeah," she said, still not looking in my eyes.

"It is, Darth. Come sit."

I knocked on the glass sliding door and indicated all was clear to a wary Nathaniel, whose nerves had been tested to their limits. I gave him a thumbs up and shot downstairs to the reading shelves, picking out an *I Spy Letters* book.

Darth was still standing when I returned to the deck, and I realized there was no chair that would fit her. She was all elbows and knees and tail. I pulled a bean bag chair from out of one of the kids' rooms and sat down to read.

Nathaniel came out to see what was going on. He tapped me on the shoulder and gestured for me to follow him.

"Wait a moment, Darth."

I entered the kitchen where Nathaniel waited.

"Jess."

"Yes."

"That's a dark elf."

"I know. Her name is Darth. Remember the dark elf who kidnapped Joseph? That was her older sister, who I killed, of course, so Darth is lonely. Her parents are absentee and sent her on an exchange program to Hell to get her out of their hair, or scales, or whatever it is they have. It didn't work out, and now the poor kid can't read. She's having trouble with street signs. Stupid parents."

Nathaniel's head practically swiveled like an owl's. I thought I may have broken him.

"Nathaniel. You okay?"

"You're teaching a dark elf to read."

"Exactly."

"All righty then. It's good. It's insane, but it's good. What the smell?"

"Oh, that's her. Dark elves are naturally putrid."

"You'll need a scented candle, then." Nathaniel reached into a cabinet and handed me a lilac scented candle and a book of matches. "Carry on."

Happy to have a child to help, even if she was a dark elf, I skipped out to the deck and worked on the alphabet with Darth, reading by candlelight. I had a sudden brainstorm and called Liam to join us outside.

Darth shuffled back when she saw the vampire, but Liam asked Darth some questions about her home and her family, putting her at ease.

"You said your parents aren't home much?"

"They love their work."

"What do they do?"

"Hunt helpless, furry animals to make clothes and furniture for our species. They're good at it, I guess, because they keep getting commissions. Jess slaughtered my sister."

I balked. "Only because she stole a kid out of bed and tried to kill me."

"Well, it's always good to understand both sides of the story," Liam said, gesturing over Darth's head for me to go back inside.

The two sat together and continued the reading lesson. I could tell they both enjoyed it, and Darth was catching on fast. At one point, Liam clapped his hands together and patted her on the back. Darth wiggled with happiness.

It made me feel smart, and I made a mental note to explore *Hooked on Phonics*.

## CHAPTER SIXTEEN

Rocko and Shura indicated they would meet me at the zoo. I still had no idea how they got in and out, but it was for darn sure that I wasn't bringing a three-hundred-pound silverback in my car, or a wolf for that matter. I didn't think I could fit them, and even if I could, the Toyota Sienna wouldn't move with all that weight.

I sat behind the steering wheel for a moment, enjoying the quiet. It had been an odd couple of days, but we were mostly back in the routine, and it should be a lovely afternoon with the kids. I grabbed my water out of the middle cup holder, brought it to my lips, and swigged the oldest apple juice I'd ever tasted. It resembled cider, it had been fermenting in the hot car so long. I dumped the rest of it out the window and made sure to look this time. My water was cold and lovely and didn't taste like ass.

*Sigh. Ten pushups.* While I was waiting for the others, I hopped out of the car, dropped, and did ten. Then, for insurance, I did another twenty. I'm sure I owed the Almighty a few extra, and it didn't hurt to be an overachiever in this category.

The peace and quiet broke in an explosion of kid craziness. These children, all three of mine, plus James and Jack, Daniel's best friends, were spider monkey/pony hybrids, all growing legs with arms that swung every which way in a never-ending blur of motion, not to mention the chatter.

I popped two ibuprofen and handed another two, with my water, to Angie, my best friend and James's and Jack's mom.

"No girls today," she said, tossing her head back to swallow the pills. They're at a babysitter's house."

I shivered at the word "babysitter."

"Friedman bus on the move!" I announced, and off we went. It would be a swift twenty-minute ride.

It was indeed twenty minutes, but it felt like an hour.

"Mom! James hit me!" bellowed Jack.

"No, I didn't!" James yelled back.

"Stop bumping into me!" David complained, punching his buddy on the arm.

"Mrs. Friedman! David punched me!"

"Mom! The boys are kicking the back of my chair," Devi screamed. "Make them stop."

Daniel cooed peacefully, drinking a sippy cup of orange juice. My angel.

"Mom! I'm hungry. Do we have any snacks?"

"We just left the house, Devi, how could you already be hungry?"

I saw Devi shrug in the rear-view mirror. "I dunno."

"Snacks are in the bag."

I heard the zipper open, and she grabbed a bag of something and munched away. The boys kicked her chair until she passed the bag to them and they stuffed their mouths with whatever they found there. I had slipped in a few things, apple slices with cinnamon, for example. Cherry tomatoes, string cheese, healthy stuff I thought they might eat. I was turning a new nutritional leaf after Cheetos sleepover breakfast. I got a quick look at Daniel making a grabby-grab motion with his hand.

"Give your brother something, Devi."

"Ooohwight." Her mouth was full of whatever she'd gotten. I imagined it was the tomatoes. I mean, what else could fill your mouth so fully? I was proud of myself for the healthful direction our life was taking.

Angie had added some items for her kids, but I didn't know what. I turned to ask her and saw that she was fast asleep, head lolling to the side.

Moms. We can sleep anywhere.

We finally got the zoo parking lot, and I nudged Angie awake. "Rise and shine. We're here."

"What! What I'd miss? Is everything okay?"

"Shh. Relax. We're fine, at the zoo, is all."

She rubbed her eyes and nodded at me.

I undid my seatbelt and pulled the side door open. Daniel reached out to me, and I undid his harness, grabbed him around the waist, and only then…only then did I notice the chocolate.

His face and hands were covered in it, and by then he'd rubbed his hands on my light pink t-shirt. Confused, I put him on the ground behind me.

Devi and the three boys were equally chocolified, and Devi had some in her hair.

"Where did this chocolate come from?" I asked. "I packed healthy snacks."

"Yeah, they were gross," replied James.

"You mean these, Mommy?" David asked, picking up a smashed bag of cherry tomatoes from the floor. The plastic bag had split open, and there was smashed tomato on the floor of the car.

Angie spoke up from the front seat, still a little sleepy. "Oh, yeah, I packed Hershey kisses. Hope you don't mind."

"They were awesome, Mom," said Jack. "Thanks for bringing them. They were nice and melty from the heat and…"

He didn't get another word out because Angie popped fully awake, jumped out of the car, and opened the other door.

"Oh, for Pete's sake!"

Luckily, always prepared, we had wet naps. We did the best we could on the faces, hands, arms, and legs, leaving the clothes for the washing machine. Daniel leaned against my legs the whole time, so I had to brace myself against the car.

We finally filed out and headed to the entrance. I took the lead, Daniel's hand in mine.

*Snicker. Snicker.*

"What?" I asked.

*Titter. Titter.* Then, an enormous shout of laughter.

"What?"

Angie was bent over holding her sides. "I'm sorry, Jess, but Daniel must have wiped his hands on your jean shorts…"

"It looks like you pooped your pants, Mom," explained David, studying a dandelion like he'd never seen one before.

There was nothing for it but to soldier on. I didn't have a spare set of shorts.

"No one will notice," Angie assured me, patting me on the shoulder. "It's the zoo. Everyone gets dirty."

We pushed through the stiles, moving fast to avoid the gift shop, as always. A security guard stopped me.

"Ma'am," she whispered. "One woman to another, you might want to check your pants. I'm sorry, I don't mean to embarrass you, but if I'd had an accident like that, I'd want someone to tell me."

I swallowed hard and said, "Thank you, but it's chocolate." I gestured to my son, with his now clean hands and face.

"Yeah, okay. Have a great day." The guard slowly backed away, and when she got to the guard house, she picked up the phone, gesturing toward me in a frantic motion as she talked.

We went to the elephant enclosure, one of my favorites. I loved everything about elephants, particularly how delicate their feet were. They were giant animals with dainty toes.

Someone tapped me on the shoulder.

"Mrs. Friedman! How lovely to see you again."

Elisabeth, the zoo's public relations director, stood next to me, holding a sweatshirt that said, "Friend of the Zoo."

"Hello, Elisabeth. How have things been?"

"Oh, much better since you got rid of our…" She lowered her voice. "Little problem. No more odd activity, except that our gorilla and female alpha wolf disappear on a regular basis, and we have no idea how or why." She lowered her glasses on her nose. "Would you have any idea how this happens?"

"I honestly don't know, Elisabeth. What are you telling the public?"

"That they've been taken for some checkups and vaccinations. If our alpha mate disappears one more time, though, I think our alpha male might lose his mind. He keeps pawing at the fence, a sign of anxiety."

"Men," I said.

"What?"

"Nothing. Don't worry about it."

She held out the sweatshirt and cleared her throat. "Mrs. Friedman, as a zoo benefactor, we'd like to present you with this sweatshirt."

"Oh! How nice."

"And we'd like to request that you tie it around your waist so people don't have to see your little issue."

"It's chocolate."

"Good idea. I'll write that one down in case anyone asks. In the meantime, we all understand what happens to middle-aged ladies as they get older. Kegel exercises, I hear, will help the back end too. You should try them."

I gave up, snatched the sweatshirt from her hands, and tied it around my waist. "How are the wolf snacks? Getting those treats on a regular basis?"

"Oh, yes! We've let them try several different types of cheese, but did you know wolves like eggs?" Her eyes squinted a little as she told me this.

"I didn't know, but now that you mention it, it seems reasonable. Eggs are nutritious and full of protein."

She pointed her finger right at my face. "Yes, they are! And since you gave them treats, they've expanded their diet to include our swan eggs."

"I'm confused. How do they get to the swan eggs?"

Her face scrunched up with annoyance. "We don't know. All we know is we find the egg shells in their enclosure, along with the duck eggs as well. This is all your fault, Mrs. Friedman."

"I fail to see how this could be my fault."

"You introduced them to the finer things in life, and now they've gotten uppity."

I nodded at her in a slow up and down motion, filtering that statement through my mind. No, still didn't think this was my fault.

"Elisabeth, my conscious is clear on this. Now if you'll excuse me, we have exhibits to see."

Angie and the kids were already running off to the lion exhibit. I turned on my heel to follow when an elephant did a little back kick and some poo shot out of the exhibit right in front of my foot. With the grace of a gazelle, I danced around it and turned my head to give Elisabeth a self-satisfied smile, missing the poo missile that landed on my chest and slid down my shirt in a long brown streak.

Elisabeth put her hand to her mouth, sidled back to the guard house, and came back with a zoo t-shirt. She pointed to the nearest ladies' room, and without giving her another glance, I held my head high and marched to the restroom, stroller and Daniel in tow, when it occurred to me that the elephant's aim was remarkably true. I glanced over my shoulder at the female elephant and froze when the elephant, long eyelashes and all, clearly, deliberately, winked at me.

THE END...for now...

# ABOUT THE AUTHOR

J.D. Blackrose loves all things storytelling and celebrates great writing by posting about it on her website, www.slipperywords.com. She has published The Soul Wars series and the Monster Hunter Mom series, both through Falstaff Books, as well as numerous short stories. Follow her on Facebook and Twitter.

When not writing, Blackrose lives with three children, her husband and a full-time job in Corporate Communications. She's fearful that so-called normal people will discover exactly how often she thinks about wicked fairies, nasty wizards, homicidal elevators, and the odd murder, even when she is supposed to be having coffee with a friend or paying something called "bills." As a survival tactic, she has mastered the art of looking interested. She credits her parents for teaching her to ask questions, and in lieu of facts, how to make up answers.

# ACKNOWLEDGMENTS

Thank you to my friends at Falstaff Book for their support and encouragement, and to my family, who don't think it's weird when I stare into space, yell "Ah-ha!" and run for the computer.

# ALSO BY J.D. BLACKROSE

**The Soul Wars Series**
Souls Collide
Souls Fall
Souls Rise
Souls Unite
The Soul Wars - Collected Edition

# FALSTAFF BOOKS

Want to know what's new
And coming soon from
Falstaff Books?

Try This Free Ebook Sampler

https://www.instafreebie.com/free/bsZnl

Follow the link.
Download the file.
Transfer to your e-reader, phone, tablet, watch, computer, whatever.
Enjoy.

CPSIA information can be obtained
at www.ICGtesting.com
Printed in the USA
LVHW030628081218
599684LV00003B/186/P